Born For Lace

A Dark Love Story

Nicci Harris

Inki Publishing

born for lace

Also by Nicci Harris

The Kids of The District

Our Thing

Cosa Nostra

Her Way

His Pretty Little Burden

His Pretty Little Queen

Their Broken Legend

His Perfect Little Heirs

Her Pretty Little Revenge

Cradled Common

Born For Silk

Born For Lace

Born For Marble

Black Label Nicci Harris

CurVy 13

CurVy Forever

CurVy Baby

ISBN ebook: 978-1-922492-44-9

ISBN print: 978-1-922492-48-7

ISBN alternative print: 978-1-922492-45-6

Edited by Margot Swan

Proofreading by Wayward Quills: Proofreading by Hope Herrington, Wayward.Quills.Proofreading@gmail.com

Internal graphics by Nicci Harris

Cover design by Nicci Harris

Map Design by Ed Napoleao

Dedication

For my mum.
I don't thank you enough for everything you do for me.

Thank you.

Now you have an immortalised thank you.

Here is to MAX BUTCHER 2.0...
If he were a genetically engineered seven-foot-one half-beast half-man.

born for lace

Foreword

A thousand years of climate change, genetic engineering, and war destroyed civilisation as it was.

From the remains came the age of The Trade and The Crown. In return for resources, security, and a Meaningful Purpose, citizens accepted a life of service to the new world.

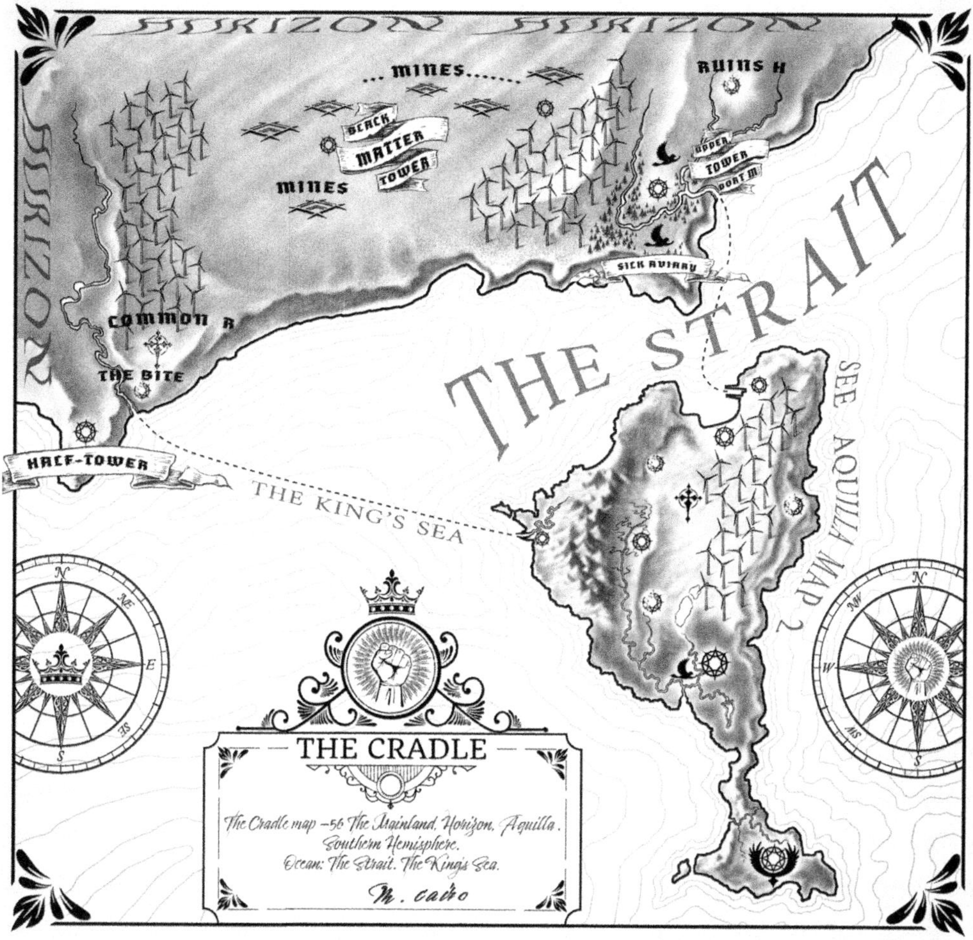
HORIZON HORIZON
HORIZON
... MINES ....
BLACK MATTER TOWER
MINES
RUINS H
UPPER TOWER
PORT M
SICK AVIARY
COMMON R
THE BITE
HALF-TOWER
THE STRAIT
THE KING'S SEA
SEE AQUILLA MAP 2
THE CRADLE
The Cradle map –56 The Mainland, Horizon, Aquilla.
Southern Hemisphere.
Ocean: The Strait. The King's Sea.
M. cairo

Glossary

If you do not like glossaries, feel free to skip it, and refer to it should you need further definitions.

The Cradle: A dystopian land governed by a socialist-inspired regime called The Trade. It comprises three separate land masses, Horizon, The Mainland, and Aquilla.

Horizon: The desert to the North and West of The Mainland Cradle. The Horizon has no mapped landscape. It is thought to be completely uninhabitable.

The Mainland: The largest land mass of The Cradle.

Aquilla: The island south of The Mainland Cradle.

The Strait: A hectic stretch of ocean between The Mainland Cradle and the island Aquilla.

Redwind: A thick, fierce, sand-laden gale that blasts The Cradle in its entirety. The desert soil is red in The Cradle; hence, the colour of the wind turns the atmosphere to a haze of crimson — a red wind.

The Trade: A socialist-type government that appoints Trades to citizens at birth. These Trades are, typically but not exclusively, inherited from a birth person.

Trade Man/Woman: A citizen of The Cradle who accepts a life of service to The Trade and The Cradle.

Meaningful Purpose: A spiritual state of enlightenment achieved by a Trade man or woman when they accomplish an act of service predetermined by The Trade.

Tower: A city governed by The Trade.

The Half-tower: A tower on The Mainland that provides The Cradle with ocean food. It transports products from The Mainland to the Half-tower Port on the island of Aquilla. It is known for being corrupt and poorly managed.

The Bite: A secret underground cave town located across the river from the Half-tower. It is a place for runaways. It operates outside of The Trade and is home to Common, Xin De, and Endigo.

Upper-tower port M (Mainland): A small port tower that transports products, typically from the mines, from The Mainland to the Upper-tower Port on the island of Aquilla.

The Compound: A massive secret compound hidden in the mountains that houses, develops, and raises the Shadows and other highly classified species of Xin De. Unmarked on any map.

Ruins E, S, N: Derelict cities/towers.

Gene Age: A historical period characterised by the mass-genetic engineering of humankind. During this time, there was a rapid shift from a natural human conception to an engineered one. In the early years, it was to better improve physical attractiveness or dissolve undesirable traits before birth. Hundreds of years later, technology was used to progress human evolution by engineering animal traits into the human genus that would aid in surviving harsh environmental changes. From this age of engineering came two different classes of humankind—Xin De and Common.

Xin De: The genetically engineered human.

Common: A human without any obvious Xin De genus.

Gene War: The civil war between the two species of human,

Xin De and Common, that eventually destroyed the old-world and civilisation as it was.

Nictitating Membrane: A third eyelid not found in Common humans. An engineered design in the Xin De genus. It is a thin membrane at the inner angle or beneath the lower lid of the eye. It can extend across the eyeball. The membrane's purpose is to clean dust and debris and is organically found in many beasts, including but not limited to, felines and birds.

Xin De Maternal Death: A death during pregnancy or birth due to the Xin De gene producing an oversized baby or incompatible DNA strain with the mother.

The King: A man born the heir to The Cradle. His duty is to support The Trade and give the citizens a figurehead leader and enforcer.

The Trade Master: A man who matches the power and influence of the king, however, he is appointed by the reigning monarch and the lords of The Cradle to uphold The Trade's Law and Traditions. He is given the key to all Trade secrets and power over the Shadows (secret agents). Once appointed, his title cannot be taken away, even as new monarchs rise.

Shadows: A Trade. A secret, elite group of individuals who are nameless and faceless assassins for The Trade. They are to kill, remove, and dissolve a target or targets.

Lords: Men who govern or manage a catchment of The Cradle within The Trade regime.

Lace Girl: A Trade. The Trade's first mental health initiative. A girl who is to accompany, relieve, and soothe a Trade man in his time of despair. It is a privilege to be given a Lace Girl. She is given to a Trade man for life and will accept The Deep Sleep (see below) beside him when he pleases. She is to remain wholesome and be shielded from depravities and the ways of men.

The Deep Sleep: A state of heavy unconsciousness associated with a Lace Girl.

Companion Nights: A ritualistic event. A Lace Girl will drink her Lace Girl Tea and fall into The Deep Sleep. Her Ward will undress her with kindness and consideration and use her body for comfort. Whether to relieve his male urges or soothe his heart. He has full access to her body under the condition she is left without physical or emotional trauma. She is to be dressed again before she wakes up to avoid any feelings of discomfort or fragility. Her pure mind and gentle heart are to be protected so she can better bring him joy and tenderness. If she reports any issues of mistreatment to The Trade, she will be taken from her Ward and given to another.

Lace Girl Tea: A mixture of herbs and sedatives, La Mu and Opi Latex, used by a Lace Girl to prevent pregnancy and sedate her for The Deep Sleep. If the Lace Girl's Ward has the means to provide more, sugar or honey or other spices can be added purely for her enjoyment.

La Mu: A genetically engineered plant that has varying medicinal purposes. The leaf: a sedative and muscle relaxant. The seeds: a powerful contraceptive. The root: in small doses, acts as an anti-inflammatory, but in larger doses is highly lethal.

Common Communit(y(ies): Minor cities for Common who do not serve The Trade and live with their own free will. With this comes minimal support or protection from The Trade, often resulting in a poor quality of life.

Community Protectors: A small Common defence force in the mountains that surround the Common Community in the North most part of The Mainland Cradle. Unmarked on any map.

Endigo: A cannibalistic human-type being. Their modifications are not part of the engineered Xin De genus, but undesirable and unplanned mutations. A byproduct of hundreds of years of corrupted human genetics.

Old-world (colloquial term): The world before The Cradle and The Trade.

First-light: An estimated period of time in the morning—the sun first lightens the hazy sky.

Crown-light: An estimated period of time at the middle of the day—the sun has the least amount of Redwind to penetrate, and its heat can be felt on the top of your head.

Last-light: An estimated period of time in the evening—the sun disappears for the night.

Time-Lamp/ Time-lights/ Time-fireplace: The Cradle uses colours to distinguish the time when clocks are not available. First-light is orange. Crown-light is yellow. Last-light is red. Variations of these colours indicate the time between each major position. Aka, dark red is night.

Missing Moon: The moon has not been seen in hundreds of years, though citizens are taught of its power and influence over the land and sea.

The Crust: Literally: the soil/dirt. Spiritually: a kind of afterlife/paradise/nirvana.

Collective: A group of individuals that work as one unit for a Trade.

Sired Mother: A Trade. Women who protect and raise The Cradle's babies. In other terms, a child-care Trade. They are retired Silk Girls who have achieved Meaningful Purpose.

Aquilla Cats: A previously extinct, large cat that now runs rampant through The Cradle. It can be identified from other cats by its larger size and stripes along its back.

Marshal Blue: A Trade. A public law enforcer.

Guard: A Trade. Military-trained personnel who guard, defend, and fight for The Trade.

House Girl: A Trade. A woman/girl used for entertainment and/or acts of a sexual nature.

Windmill Farms: Windmill farms cover over 30% of the inhabitable parts of The Cradle. They are the land's primary source of energy.

Windmill Forest (colloquial term): The stretches of Windmill Farms that feel never-ending, stretching for hundreds of miles.

Opi (colloquial term) Opi Lava: can be applied topically or taken orally. A genetically modified version of the old-world opioid—morphine—used for extreme pain and as a mild sedative.

Modistes Girl: A Trade. A girl responsible for designing, creating, and fitting apparel.

Silk Girl: A Trade. A breeding girl. A girl born of a Silk Girl with no previous miscarriages. She is protected and raised in peace and tranquillity. She is to have no negative experiences in her life in order to prevent the spread of epigenetics—generational trauma.

Part One
Welcome to The Cradle

Chapter One

Dahlia

There is so much blood.

"Take him," Maple murmurs, her voice a broken whisper, barely loud enough to pierce the cloud of terror enveloping us.

Her hazel eyes lift to me, once vibrant now dull under the shadow of death. "Please. They can't find him. They can't have him."

Fear coils in my stomach.

"No, no, no. You're going to be fine. You have to be." I shake my head, panic rising. "I can't—" I can't take him… Questions canter through my mind, each one more frightening than the last. Take him where? How do I feed him?

What will I do without you?

"What will I do without you?" I blurt out helplessly. "I've been…" My voice falters, trembling to a heavy pause. "I've been following you *forever.*"

"You don't need to follow me anymore." Maple tries to smile for me. While her blood seeps into rumpled sheets around her weak body, she tries to soothe me!

My heart shatters.

"You're unique, Dahlia," she says. "You're resilient. Clever. Loyal. You're not just a… a pet for a man."

Pet.

The cruel term hangs in the air. That is how Maple refers to us—Lace Girls. She calls us pets. A term that feels derogatory and unfairly simplified.

Suddenly, gunfire and booming voices erupt from outside the abandoned tower. Danger prowls at our doorstep in the form of a Marshal takeover.

"I am not like you, Maple," I cry. "I don't want more. I'm content. Don't leave me. Don't go—"

"*Please,* Dahlia. They *mustn't* find him." Maple lifts her newborn toward me, laboured gasps escaping her, as if each inhale and exhale is a battle fought and lost.

"There is a boat waiting for me." She wheezes, and her eyes glaze over. Fading. "*Please,* take him."

"You were going to leave?"

I can't bear to look at the mewling infant, but scoop it from Maple's arms, its weight seeming too much for her.

"I don't understand," I sob. "You have a boat? To where? Why?" *This doesn't make sense.* "The Trade will take care of him, Maple. I can't."

She surrenders to the grappling pull of exhaustion, slumping to her back. Her eyes fall to me, grip me… Then close.

No. Swallowing to temper my thickening throat, I drag my gaze across her bloodied dress to the crimson pool between her legs. My teary eyes widen on what I dreaded, what I knew— What I don't need to see. The baby nearly split Maple in two. It killed my closest friend. My favourite from my Collective.

Extraordinary Maple.

I look back at her ashen face. "Maple?" I reach out and grip her shoulder, shaking lightly. "Maple. *Please,* why can't The Trade find him? Where is the boat going?"

Her mouth opens and moves, but no words pass between us.

What?

I lean over her with the infant heavy in my arms, fussing at my chest. "What?"

Her lips touch my ear. "Tomar... Find Tomar. At the docks. *Please*. Be brave." A heavy breath escapes her, soft and *final.*

The sudden crash of a door being kicked in jolts me upright, my gaze snapping toward the exit. But I can't go yet— I haven't had time to think this through. Not properly.

"Maple." Through terror-filled eyes, I stare back at my dying friend, needing her help, *needing her.*

Don't leave me alone!

I step backward.

But I am not alone. Shaky and in shock, my eyes drift to the thing in my arms. "What... What do I call it?"

"Spero."

The floor seems to tilt when I hear the single word escape her on a long gasp, and I shuffle to keep my footing.

Spero... Spero means hope, and I only know such things because Maple can read in five old-world languages.

My friend dies with hope.

For what?

For what!

We are Lace Girls—we have no identity without a Trade man. Our Purpose revolves entirely around making them happy. To accompany, relieve, and soothe them. We are the first mental health initiative of The Trade, imperative to The Cradle. Our Trade has halved the accounts of depression, and suicides are almost non-existent.

But Maple... She is—was—different. She had ideas of individuality and self-discovery. Spoke about conspiracies that travel the deserts. Communities filled with Common where people exist without Meaningful Purpose... I can barely think the words, they sound so strange and unsafe.

She had a wild imagination, and she shared it with us—her Collective—when we gathered for sewing and conversation. The other Lace Girls and I enjoyed her fantastical mind like children might fairytales. We enjoyed them knowing we were safe, secure, and all meant for Meaningful Purpose.

We are no longer safe. Now, the tower is breaking in two. The Xin De—the genetically engineered humans—are turning on us. And Common humans are poisoning their kind in retaliation. The Marshals are breaking down our doors to end the chaos and make arrests, and— They will seize the infant.

Run.

Swallowing tears, I force myself away from her bedside and rush to my large *beibao* bag. Can't dwell. Can't pause. I grit my teeth and ram my grief down. Can't allow myself to feel.

With one frantic hand, I cram the bag with random items, clothes, Trade stamps, a toothbrush, ingredients for my tea, and a small saw Maple uses to prune leaves.

The thing in my arms mewls, spurring me on—I need to hide it. Quick.

I wrap him in a small shirt and zip my jacket over him, the hazy sun is hot through the window to my side, the infant—Spero—might get too warm in my jacket, but the wind outside is a far worse fate, so I keep moving.

I sling the *beibao* bag onto my back and feel the weight of my decision to run from all that I know as a physical thing.

If I don't do this… What happens to me if I stay? What happens to *him*? I regard the pink-faced thing in my jacket. I don't want this, but I don't have time to consider it. My Ward is dead, our home ransacked by men in black shrouds. *Run.*

A gun rattles from somewhere close by, echoing like a knell through the corridors and halls.

I bolt, taking the hundreds of steps down the deserted building, grabbing the Redwind-mask from its hook by the exit and pushing through the steel, air-lock door into the wind.

The sand slashes at me as I slide the mask on. The salty air whirls my red hair around my shoulders and face, making it hard to see, but I know how to get to the docks. I lower my head and walk, urgency propelling me toward the tower square.

The streets are eerie. Empty. Quiet but for the rattle of the occasional gun and the growl of a tank somewhere in the near distance.

As I cross the road, the wind circles me like a spoon around a porcelain cup. The sound is too familiar. Too sad. It's the sound of a Lace Girl going to sleep at night after a cup of Lace Girl Tea. Safe.

Hiding against a wall, I head toward the sound, toward the docks, shadowed by looming buildings. They are overgrown, reaching into the sky, way beyond the haze, blocking the wind as they were designed to do hundreds of years ago.

Sweat gathers on my neck.

I'm searching for a cut between buildings, a way outside the tower fort to the water when I see a pink mist ahead.

Right, that must be it.

The dockyards. It's not forbidden for a Lace Girl to visit the docks. It's just not done, because on the other side of these buildings is a gale, thick with sand and stone and salt that will carve my skin to ribbons. Common humans can't withstand the pummelling air like the Xin De can. But I have my mask, my boots, and my jacket, and the baby is covered.

Maple insulated my clothes, and I often wondered why. I've never been anywhere, and unlike her, I have no desire to. So, when she illegally traded *La Mu Root* to our Modistes Girl, Isle, to have my leather jacket and boots treated with armour, it seemed strange.

Was she planning on escaping, even back then? And taking me with her?

The day after I received my new coat, a Xin De man who often harassed Isle was found poisoned, and I knew what had happened to him. It was horrific. Isle appeared to be the model of her Trade. Loyal and committed to her Meaningful Purpose. When beneath the surface, she was different. She took a life with the *La Mu* that gained me these protective clothes.

It makes me wonder how many people are unhappy. Or are so many wearing veils of perceived obedience, waiting for a moment or reason to tear the fabric down the centre.

The Half-tower rumbles around me with unrest. Without further thinking, I cross into the light and head down the crumbling passage.

I can see the air at the end; a whirlpool of pink and grey— the Redwind, collecting desert sand and debris. Once, I thought it beautiful, a dark pink hue like the salt lakes I've seen in picture books.

Today... Today the colour resembles white sheets stained with my favourite person's blood.

As I approach the predatory Redwind, its roar intensifies, but it is the voice that cuts through the noise that sends a wave of fear through my body.

"She's a Lace Girl."

I freeze.

"She'll have Opi."

The deep voice grabs my spine while the word, Opi, twists it into a tightrope.

Slowly, I inch around to see two Xin De men approaching. They are dressed in the ominous thick navy Marshal Blue armour, clutching rifles. *Officers.* They followed me down the passage.

The baby... *Oh.*

Please be quiet.

Please be quiet.

My heart gallops as they advance, and I press my back to the building, uncertain what to say or do.

Run.

They share a glance, heavy with meaning, and then both sets of eyes lock on me.

"Think she's high on the latex?" one asks, as if I can't hear him.

He means Opi Latex. It's common for a Lace Girl to become addicted when we consume it in our tea, but I'm not.

"Talk, girl," the other commands, grabbing my Redwind-mask and pulling it below my chin. "Are you alright? Whatcha doin down here alone without your Ward? Don't you realise the Half-tower is under heavy restrictions now?"

"Are you a mute?" The one on the right presses his hand to the wall beside my head, leaning toward me. He smells gamey, kind of like blood. Has he been hunting in his blue leathers?

Hunting what? We are a fishing tower... *Oh,* it's Common blood.

I swallow as both hover over me, nearly seven-foot-tall dual pillars of authority. They are huge, like all evolved ones are. And arrogant, I'm sure. As is the mindset of a species physically far superior to Common humans like me.

Mute...

I quickly nod my head.

"Mute?" The one on the left has green eyes like the leaf of the La Mu plant. They might be pleasant were they not leering.

"I heard The Trade does that sometimes. Take out the tongue of the smart-mouthed girls," the gamey one whispers. "Or if the voice is annoying or too high pitched."

Green Eyes stares at me. "But you understand us... You're not dumb, are you?"

Not usually.

I shake my head.

"We are in the middle of a civil war. You know what that means?" He palms the rifle in front of him, clanking the metal for effect. "*You* shot in the pretty head. And then The Trade being pissed at us for taking down its property." He touches a rogue tendril of my scarlet hair. "So, pretty little girl, you need to come with us so we can get you back inside where you're safe."

No. Think.

What should I do? What would Maple do? My heart starts to beat so hard I fear they will hear it.

Then it happens—the baby wriggles and whimpers at my chest, over my fretful heart, probably feeling my anxiety vibrate against it.

Both Marshal Blues look at the mound under my leathers. Green Eyes frowns, and the other grins, excited, which seems so much worse. "What do you have tucked down there?"

"You want Opi?"

A deep voice comes from behind us, which can only be from another Xin De male—like them. Their voices are otherworldly deep. Maple used to speculate that when they first engineered the Xin De genus, they made everything bigger and thicker to withstand the harsh environmental changes. Their muscles got bigger. Skin thicker. And they lengthened their vocal cords to the point males would sound more like beasts than a Common man. I don't know if any of that is true.

I follow the sound of the voice as the Marshal Blues turn toward the stranger, clutching their rifles. Ready. "What did you just say to us?" Green Eyes grunts.

But it's too late.

I was too busy staring at the Marshals. They were too busy studying me. We didn't see the second stranger, a huge form, come up the passage from the Redwind.

So, while the officers turn to face the man who spoke, the second stranger thrusts his massive fists into the backs of their necks. Their chins snap upward from the impact, a crack dissects the air, and both officers collapse to a mass on the path. No man should be so strong. No physique so powerful. It's monstrous.

"Maple?" The first stranger speaks.

I sink further into the brick behind me, flattening myself to the wall. Wishing to disappear into the clay and stone.

I stare at the lifeless bodies of The Trade's public law enforcement. They aren't always nice, but they do keep us safe. Safe from...

I look up.

Your kind...

"Maple?" he repeats, and I wince. He thinks I'm Maple. Has he never seen her? My stomach flips. *What have you gotten me into, Maple?*

The crunch of rocks below a shoe draws my attention to a boot. A huge boot. The boot of the second stranger… *I just saw this man kill two officers with the ease of snapping a branch.*

My breath catches.

The large figure steps closer and a metallic tang hits my tongue. His height draws my gaze up from his combat-style boots along dark denim.

He is enormous.

At his thighs, tattooed fists pump, red and calloused across each knuckle, telling tales of violence. His arms are weights beside him, bulked with muscles that form each thick limb.

A long, black hide coat hangs open, the bottom seam skating his thighs. I gaze up to his broad chest stretching a black shirt with a large loose hood bunched at his angular, thick shoulders.

Up to his face. A dark-blonde beard borders his snarl. The same-coloured hair is tied back in a messy knot, revealing something metal on one side of his skull… It's a silver plate that mimics bone just above the curve of his ear.

And his *eyes*… Onyx, almost black. Cruel. Strange. Magnetic.

And beautiful.

"Maple?" The first stranger steps forward, blocking the other from view. "Are you in shock?" He dips to my level, so I look at him. He is painfully pretty for such a big man, with dark hair cut nearly to the scalp, high cheekbones and concerned blue eyes. "I'm Tomar," he says. "Come with us, Maple. The boat is not far."

Tomar…

Find Tomar.

I hear my voice, distant but true. "You found us here. How did you find me?"

"A miracle, I guess," he says, but there is something in his tone that lies. "Come. Is the child well? Are you bleeding from the labour?"

I lift the mask to cover my face again, liking the perceived privacy as his questions weigh heavily on my heart.

Bleeding...

Yes, lots of bleeding.

Too much.

I shake my head instead of answering, shaking the image of my friend and the hazy recall of her last gasping words.

I focus on the immediate situation, on Tomar and the other man. Can I trust these Xin De men? Tomar has designer genetics, perhaps a few generations worth, judging by his luminous blue eyes. But he isn't without humanity like so many Xin De appear to be at first glance.

The second stranger, though—the scary one... He definitely comes from a long line of engineered genes, evident in his black gaze, monstrous size, and the velvety appearance of his tanned skin.

"The baby is fine," I force out, my voice annoyingly fragile. "In my jacket."

"Okay." Tomar offers a wary, tight smile. "Come. You're safe now." He gestures down the passage between tall encroaching buildings. Long vines like wiry fingers dangling from scaffolding and ledges overhead. "I can see you're scared, but we need to move unless we want more paralysed Blues littering the streets of the Half-tower."

"This is a mistake." The scary one speaks, and I swallow. His voice is a bass tone so thunderous and powerful it seems capable of rattling bones.

Tomar frowns at him. "No, it's not a mistake. Would you have the child found instead? Dammit, Lagos, you of all men know what that would mean for it, what they would put it through—"

"We should kill it," he grunts.

We should... Kill. It. Two words like icy bullets puncture my chest, leaving me breathless and trembling. "*No,*" I whisper.

No. Please, no.

"I can't do that." Tomar steps behind me and urges me forward without touching me. "Walk, Maple. Let's get you to the boat."

I amble ahead. As soon as we're safe, I must find a place to be alone with my thoughts and just... *breathe.* I'm like a fish joining an unknown school, heading downstream, hoping there is a sanctuary at the end and not a hook.

They keep a close pace behind me, causing my spine to stiffen. I've got to pretend I'm Maple, at least for a while. She made this arrangement with them, one that surely involves an exchange of some kind... *Oh,* I hope it's stamps or La Mu or Opi; I can do that.

I have to go with them.

Within a second, I've considered my only other option; I return home and secure the flat. Wait out the unrest, wait until the tower is under control—I will be given to another Ward to complete my Meaningful Purpose. The baby will be taken. I don't know where they will take it or what they will do with it, but it is the property of The Trade. It... I mean *him.* I should do that. I was raised in a Trade nursery; they are perfectly pleasant and safe.

That is the rational course.

That is what I should do.

Yet... I inhale hard. Maple's words, *'They cannot find him,'* spur me forward. *'Find Tomar.'*

I halt at the end of the passage, at a howling wall, inches from stepping into a vortex of wind—a dusty, red barrier.

The infant in my cloak doesn't have a mask on... The slightest wind could fill his lungs with sand like an hourglass. But before I can hesitate further, I am wrapped in a coat from behind and guided over the threshold.

My senses run wild.

Practically blind, I blink at dark fabric, but the wind is loud and circling, and my fear is a heavy thud in my neck. Yet, it is the warmth of the hard body I am pressed to and the scent of a Xin De man that seems to overwhelm me most of all with its metallic but soothing tones. As if safety and strength is an odour, like the word impenetrable can be smelt.

And it makes me feel *strange.*

I've never been touched by a man besides my Ward, and the only time I remember being pressed to his chest, I was falling into the Deep Sleep.

I walk when the man behind me does. One step. Two steps. Without sight, I can only trust him.

After no more than a few minutes, an arm scoops around my middle and lifts me from the ground, but before I can panic, my shoes hit a solid surface.

Something is different. The air around me is suddenly still and the roaring wind is muted. Are we inside? No—the floor waves beneath my feet... We are on the boat! I made it.

We made it.

Part Two
The Lace Girl

Chapter Two

Dahlia

I feel like the living dead, mindlessly interacting with the world around me. I'm certainly in shock. Maple's death, The Trade Marshals' murder, and the infant in my jacket are all too much for my brain right now.

So, I followed a stranger because of a name uttered from my dying friend's lips: Tomar. I'm nothing like Maple, not effortlessly confident or spontaneous like her, but I'm not stupid. Naïve, perhaps. Without all the information and with little experience, sure —but I'm definitely not stupid.

Usually...

"Head down into the blade," Tomar says, gesturing toward a set of steps, and I don't look at him as I move down into the hull.

I inhale slowly, steadying my pulse. The air is sharp with salt from the sea and heavy with the whispers of the ten or so strangers hidden in dark pockets inside the blade.

A smuggling boat? By the shape of this space, I would say it is a catamaran. What is the exchange for this passage across the water? What does Tomar want from them? What does he want from Maple—me?

Unasked questions roll around in my mind as I tuck myself in a corner, pull my mask off, and unzip my jacket enough to see the infant's pink face.

He is making shapes with his lips, suckling at the air; he will need food soon. Food I don't have! He has only been alive for a few hours, but he has unknowingly altered the course of my life.

Spero—hope.

In this moment of quiet, my first moment of reprieve from *running,* I feel grief wrap around me and squeeze, making each breath harder than the last.

Grief—I let it surface.

Maple... When she changed her Lace Girl tea, I told her this would happen. If only I had stopped her. If only I had reported her. She may have hated me for it, but she would still be alive. Regret twists my stomach. I failed her.

And then she got pregnant, and we knew it would be a difficult labour, but she had Trade intervention. They were going to deliver her baby. *Oh,* why didn't she go to the Medical Hub? Why didn't I make her? I could have, but I was scared. Fifty percent of births end in a Xin De Maternal Death. The Xin De are too big for us Common humans. Their offspring are larger than we can carry, but I thought—

She's different...

Maple is, was, special and strong. She didn't want to go to the Medical Hub—now I know why. She didn't want them to have her baby.

Life without her seems unimaginable.

Sorrow glides down my cheeks in thin rivulets. I think about her body being discovered by The Trade Marshals, and panic punches me. What if she wasn't dead? What if she wakes, alone, and crawls for help? Will she come to find me?

I shake my head. *No.* She was dead. I am sure of it. The Trade will inspect her injuries and figure out what happened. They will come looking for their property—for us.

She deserved so much better...

The pain in my chest and stomach is nearly unbearable. Through a screen of tears, I gaze around the lower deck to the faces of the other stowaways from the Half-tower. Tracks of ash from the explosions mark their faces. Some have wounds. Most are shaking with fear. They look like I feel—lost.

"How can you see where you're going through that damn Redwind?" A Common man calls up just as Tomar and the monster he called Lagos descend the steps.

"We can't," Tomar answers simply, making his way across to check the ropes that fasten boxes and crates to the hull walls. "We are on a zipline."

The man gasps. "A what?"

Lagos grunts something inaudible and sits in the far corner. I try not to look directly at him but note his position and distance from me. He couldn't be further away without being in the ocean, and I am happy about that. He spreads his legs out in front of him, pulls his hood over his brow, folds his thick arms over his chest, and closes his black eyes.

Tomar chuckles. "It's been taking people like yourself from the Half-tower to The Bite for two decades. Hasn't snapped in the Redwind yet. Trust me, it's better than steering. We have to get through a small gap and without the line to guide us, we'll hit rocks for sure."

The Bite...

Maple mentioned it, but I thought it was another fantastical place that she dreamed up. It's supposedly a cave filled with runaways, both Common, Xin De— and, even, Endigo.

My stomach churns. I've never met an Endigo before, but the tales of mutated Xin De, born with all the undesirable byproduct traits of hundreds of years of genetic engineering and human testing, reach all corners of The Cradle. Endigo men are cast as the villains in most bedtime stories.

We must be moving now as the tip of the boat lifts, climbing a magnificent watery hill.

The feeling of being at sea reminds me of the seesaw at the Trade nursery. Water rises, a billowing of pressure gathering beneath, only to disappear. The trough plunges us into an unknown depth, only for another wave to catch us.

The motion is slow but powerful.

Enough to affect the infant in my arms. He is crying, squeaky sounds that come from an inexperienced voice box.

"*Shh.*" I use the tip of my finger and draw little circles on the baby's back and will my nausea away.

I swallow rising bile.

"You're going to get thrown around, little Lace Girl." Tomar slides down beside me and lifts me to sit in the bracket of his legs, where he locks me in tight.

I stiffen—men don't touch Lace Girls— but then he strokes the fussing infant's cheek and says, "Sing for him."

In front of all these strangers? I lift my gaze and coast the space, shocked to find eyes filled with fragile need waiting for me to sing to Spero. To a smuggling ship filled with runaways and refugees. To melancholy. A goodbye to the Half-tower and everything they have always known.

I clear my throat, gently, then start to sing. "Good first-light, to you, my Collective and friend. We head to the ocean, it's days there we spend—"

Spero stares in the direction of my voice, quietening down. I exhale, relieved, my shoulders loosening as I find as much comfort in the familiar shanty as everyone else seems to.

"Though the Redwind is howlin' with a fist full of sand. We prefer it's hard slapin' to The Trade Master's hand."

A man opposite me joins in, softly singing the song of the Trade Fisher, the song my Ward often sang before he left for the docks each first-light.

"For our Purpose was certain, so on the waves we do meet. Yet we sing with the crashin' as it's freedom we greet."

I sing and soothe Spero as if I've done it a thousand times. And I ignore the fact that I don't know these men.

I look up, noticing all eyes on me. Soft. Sad. Listening. *I just boarded a ship full of strangers with an infant that isn't mine.*

Oh, my.

I cuddle Spero to my chest and close my eyes, singing the shanty to bid farewell to my old life.

As the boat rocks me to the melody and Tomar's legs stop me from sliding, I pretend I'm with Maple. That she huddles beside me, like she did that first day we met when we were no older than ten. When she told me everything would be alright. I am safe.

I imagine it until I fall asleep.

I wake, feeling like no time has passed, but it has. The ten or so runaways are already climbing the steps, and the boat has slowed down. Levelled...

How? There is something odd about the way the boat moves, glides instead of waves, seeming to slide on liquid silk.

Am I dreaming?

"You're awake."

I blink the sleep from my gaze and check on Spero, whose eyes are closed. Little squeaks come through his pursed lips, and my chest squeezes.

"Your baby is hungry," Tomar says, and I bite down on my lower lip.

I ignore it. "Are we... *here*?"

I don't know where we're going, so I don't elaborate, keeping every question ambiguous to not give myself away. To not appear as confused as I am. Even as I go through the motions, I cling to the mindless actions I make because they keep me moving forward and not rushing backward.

Don't let The Trade find him.

Tomar climbs to his feet. "Almost. Go up and see. You don't

need your mask here. I need to help Lagos on deck. I should be up there already, but you were sleeping, so..."

I straighten, realising I was leaning on him. I stuff my mask into my *beibao* and bundle Spero in tight before following Tomar up the steps.

My feet freeze on the top deck when the soft briny mist kisses my cheeks and lips. Peering around in wonder at what cannot be real, my eyes grow.

A dome of stars encompasses us above and is mirrored in the still watery surface below. It's far more fantastical than real—thousands of glowing lights, some bright, others dim, but they are *everywhere.*

No Redwind...

Shocked, I gaze around the cavernous dome of stars, looking for an answer. *Real stars?* They can't be... The Cradle hasn't seen a star in hundreds of years. *Am I dead?* Is this The Crust—the spiritual afterlife?

The further the boat drifts, the more peculiar the stars appear. They move overhead, behind, under. The boat breaks the ones reflected on the water as it moves through them, smudging them.

"No... They are not stars." I spin to take in the beaming spots, a sight mesmerising and extraordinary.

Ahead, I see the end, a rocky grey blockage lit by lanterns and lights from other boats. There are small wooden houses, dozens or more; I can't be sure from this distance.

"Glowworms," Tomar answers, flicking a star from a needle-like rock dripping with moisture akin to wax down a candle.

I gasp in awe. "Stunning."

"They are just bugs," I hear the big, mean one—Lagos—sneer.

"Glowing bugs," I mutter, feeling belittled, but the sight of the cave washes it away. I don't care if my wonder seems juvenile or ridiculous to that man. I don't even know him. And the cave—The Bite, it's real. A community carved with water's hand. And it *is* stunning.

"Welcome to The Bite, Lace Girl," Tomar says, leaning to check the zipline that I can now see rushes between the two hulls.

Tears rise to the backs of my eyes. I wish Maple was here to see this… It was her dream, not mine.

"Why is it called The Bite?" I ask. "This place is not at all vicious looking."

Tomar's eyes lift to the ceiling. "Well, the Endigos say that the sky never forgave us for fucking up the earth, but the ocean did. It took a giant bite out of the ground to give all, Common, Xin De, and Endigo a reprieve from the Redwind."

I hear someone scoff—Lagos.

Tomar ignores him.

And I can't help but smile.

Chapter Three

Dahlia

The zipline ticks over notches as we dock. The hull bumps the edge of a wooden jetty.

The clarity in The Bite is dream-like. I can hear every noise echoing into the depths. Hear the playful trickling of water coming from unseen corners of the cave, and distinct female and male voices. Dock workers shuffle. Boats hum. It is not loud—it's alive, in a reserved way.

I stare into the rocky tunnels, spotting lights from cabins made from both wood and the rock itself. So many houses—they appear small as they cling to the cave walls like starfish are said to do to underwater rocks.

"Off you get, Lace Girl," Tomar calls.

My wonder is cut short when time is up, and I have to figure out what happens next without asking what happens next…

"Give me a few hours," Tomar says to me, unknowingly answering my question, and creating another question: a few hours until what? "Oh, and you know the colours, right? Orange for first-light, yellow for crown-light, and red for last-light. Gets dark down here, but the streetlights will always show you the time."

I nod. We had time-lamps in each room of the Lace House. With the sun always behind a blanket of Redwind, day and night, and everything in between become disorientating.

The other passengers are already stepping onto the rocky ground.

Right, I can do this.

Head high, I cradle Spero with one hand and climb from the boat, my boots hitting the smooth rock.

A few hours.... That is enough time to find Spero some food. Find an Exchange Hub or... a person who can help me. An older woman, perhaps. I roam the faces of people around.

Shuffling so my *beibao* moves on my back, I remind myself I have stamps to exchange. Lots of them. Whiskey stamps are worth five times milk stamps. I am set for a while.

Risking a look back at the catamaran, I find Tomar conversing with another man, and Lagos unloading the boat, lifting each massive crate effortlessly.

A few hours...

I tug my jacket higher, turn toward what looks like a small exchange and stride over to it. Warmth rushes up my spine, so I pause. When I peer over my shoulder, I inhale sharply. Lagos is staring straight at me with those near-pitch-black eyes. And I feel small and out of breath.

Does he know that I'm not Maple? Does he want to kill my—Maple's—baby?

I have to trust them.

I will, but not blindly. A healthy dose of suspicion will keep me and Spero safe.

I lift my chin and continue in the opposite direction toward what I think is an Exchange Hub, a cabin with a sign hanging above the door. It has a fish drawn on it, but I hope they also have powdered milk or, more unlikely, formula.

I enter through a rickety door.

It's a narrow room with very few items on display: crates of fish—half empty—a few items, ropes, gloves, hooks on racks. A small bowl of apples catches my eye, and my stomach rumbles with need.

I whisper, "Apples."

Pulling my *beibao* off, I riffle through to collect all my whiskey stamps and a few tonic ones that I know are also quite valuable.

"Your stamps are no good 'ere."

My eyes snap up to a man with hair as translucent as ice, one cloudy eye, and pinkened skin sagging from his aging face. He is visibly older—in his second century of life, for sure. It has not been kind to him.

"What do you mean?" I ask, blinking at him.

"You got Half-tower stamps." The man walks toward me, his good eye measuring me up while the other doesn't move. "I know your kind." He points to the wad of papers in my hand. "That's worthless. That means nothin' to me. I isn't allowed in the tower."

I almost lose my footing.

What does he mean?

"This is my only form of exchange..." I try to calm down as my chest squeezes. "I- I- don't understand." I force a smile. "I thought stamps were The Cradl—"

"Only worth somethin' in their tower."

My lungs burn. *No.* "That's—"

"Planned." He grins and all his teeth are missing from his wide, gummy mouth. "So you don't go leavin'. And if you do, it ain't easy. They're not gonna give you somethin' valuable, so you can just leave with it. Are they? We get a lot of runaways 'ere."

I don't understand.

"Can you cook?"

What is he saying?

"Can you fish?"

I step backward, feeling light-headed and faint. With no exchange, I'm... I'm stuck, in danger, helpless.

Spero starts to whimper and squirm at my chest. I say, "I can sew and clean—"

"Don't need that. And, nothin' is free in The Cradle," the man says. "Goodwill is a lie. Meaningful Purpose is a virtue. You know that."

Meaningful Purpose...

I grip the counter.

"I'll help you out," he offers, and I lift my gaze to meet his. "I'm generous to your kind, see. You can do your Trade. You can sleep beside me as trade for an apple and whatever it is you need for that babe you tryin' to hide... Milk or formula? Can't make ya own? Is the child new? Are you bleeding still?"

"I—" *I'm dizzy.* "I'm not..."

"I won't harm you. It's a simple trade, and one you were born for. Easy. You don't have to do anythin'. I'm feelin' a bit down these 'ere days. It's a decent Trade, yours is. To relieve and soothe a depressed man. Well?"

"*Sleep*—" Confusion hangs on my tongue. "*Beside* you? Like in the Deep Sleep? In exchange for formula—" I try to breathe. "You have formula?"

His eyes lap the length of my body, and although I'm heavily clothed, I suddenly feel completely naked.

My empty stomach growls, and Spero cries louder. I stifle the urge to throw my arms around myself and him and run from the Hub. Instead, I fist the useless stamps.

"You're a Lace Girl?" he says. "You all smell the same. Like that bloody La Mu leaf."

My voice is small as I answer, "Yes. I am a Lace Girl from the Half-tower."

"Property of The Trade." He leers. "Valuable property. Let me guess, you wanna get to the Common Community up north? Your Ward isn't treatin' you very well? That's why you're ere'."

"Um..."

Maple! She was trying to get to the little girl with the upside-down bird.

A girl she saw in a dream that she swears is trying to guide her. This girl is a phantom with no face or name.

Maple retold the dream, where she followed the girl north through a grey tunnel. At the end, there was no Redwind. She breathed fresh air. She found herself in a farming community between mountains, safe from the wild weather. Untouched and untagged by The Trade.

Is Tomar taking me up north?

"Well?" The old man leans closer, inundating me with his rank breath when he smiles, and my gaze becomes snagged on his mouth. On trenches of gums. He *does* have teeth—tiny teeth. Rows of small, sharp ones that coat the entire cleft of his inner mouth.

My blood turns to ice when a term comes to my mind. *Endigo.*

I fight to hide a shudder.

What choice do I have?

It's a fair exchange, and he said he won't bring me any harm.

"Who will, um—" I clear my throat. "Watch Spero, my baby, while I sleep?"

"If you feed that babe this formula." He lifts a glass jar up from under the counter. It is half full of white powder. "It'll go to sleep for at least a few hours. A full stomach will do that. Mark my words."

I stare at the jar. Relief rushes down a heavy exhale. I can feed Spero for a week or so. A huge weight lifts from my shoulders, and I sigh.

"You only need a few hours?"

He shrugs. "Tops."

"Do you have more formula?"

"No." He slides the jar across the counter to me. "You might start to make your own milk soon. Then we can talk about bottlin' that. There will be lots of interest there." He licks his lips, and I swallow over a lump.

"I won't be here that long," I say, reaching for the formula and accepting the exchange. "I am going to feed my baby first. Do you have fresh water? A bottle or mixing… thing."

He frowns, his gaze dropping to the crying infant, irritation crossing his face, before he grabs an empty plastic bottle from a trash can behind him. "Here." He nods toward the door. "There is fresh water by The House. It's signed. Largest cabin. Three levels. Probably has House Girls out the front waitin' for the travellers. I ain't allowed there. But pretty things like you will be, but—" He shuffles. "We got an exchange, right? You don't gonna steal from me?"

I lift my chin. "I would never steal from anyone."

"You ain't goin' to The Crust if you steal," he adds.

"I'll be back," I assure him.

He twitches. "Soon!"

His tone hits a breath from me. I don't know why. This is life. What I was born for. This is a decent, harmless exchange. I only hope what he has planned for my body while I sleep is gentle. It's soothing to have another person rest with you. Dopamine and serotonin are released in our brains when we have company, stroke someone's hair, or feel their warmth. It is in my studies, and the very Purpose of a Lace Girl.

Usually, we are registered with a Trade man who deserves us, who works hard at his Purpose and takes a vow to care for us. To treat us as special, precious, even. The Endigo man's heated attention stirs through me—this is not how it usually works, but... I gaze down at Spero.

I have to do this for him.

Hiding my anxieties behind a soft smile, I take one final look at the Endigo man, noticing how the pupil in his good eye has enlarged, before heading toward the door.

One task at a time. I need to feed Spero. Need fresh water and a makeshift nipple.

Chapter Four

Dahlia

The House has a small stony frontage boxed with a wooden fence, and beside the single grey door, a tall, scantily dressed woman with black hair is leaning against the wall, scrutinising her long nails.

Jewellery hangs from her wrists and neck, some glistening with beads and some solid metals. An immodest symbol that she is, in fact, a House Girl. Only her kind flaunt jewels in such a way.

I clear my throat as I approach. "Excuse me?"

Moving only her blue eyes, she peers up from her hand, taking a full sweep of my body and mumbling, "Yes?"

That's all I get.

I continue toward her, stopping a few paces from the entrance on the pretty cobbled path bordered by plant pots they obviously care enough about to maintain.

"I don't do girls," she says.

"Oh." I cough with shock. "No. I'm just looking for water." My sentence dwindles to a pause as I consider offering her stamps but stop myself, not wanting her suspicion piqued further.

She stares at the bundle hidden beneath my jacket, her brow rising. She nods with faux indifference toward a metal spout fastened to the outside of the stone building, waterdrops pattering the ground.

"Help yourself."

"Thank you," I say, walking straight to it, squatting, and getting to work. Despite the woman's perceived disinterest, she still glances intermittently from her nails to watch me squat by the faucet.

After cleaning the bottle the best I can, I mix the water with some formula and tuck it into my *beibao*. I need to find somewhere quiet to feed Spero.

Back on the path, I pass a few Common women and men as they go about their lives without so much as a peep in my direction. Before I walk too far, I check the docks. The boat that brought me here is still at the jetty, and Tomar is loading something onto it.

A few hours...

Is he taking me to the Common Community like the Endigo man said? Or am I getting there some other way? Spero cries louder, reminding me I have to feed him first—decipher the details of what happens next after.

I walk along the path between small houses and cabins, searching for a secluded spot to tend to Spero, the small whimpering bundle cradled against my chest.

Although it's dim, small gaps in the cave ceiling, along with the glowworms and lanterns outside each cabin, offer enough light to see.

The alleyways are quiet, yet the air is thick with whispers and transactions.

I thought I would stand out, but everyone else seems just as intent on blending in as I do.

The Bite seems to be a place for living ghosts to gather and converse; their secrets trail to echoes and hide in the rocky quarries.

As I approach a cavity in the hard cave wall, I hesitate. Through the narrow slit in the rock, I see steps that lead downward. I peer into the rocky burrow, where the glowworms illuminate the passage, revealing a glimmering spot of clear blue water at the end. It ripples softly, yet… It feels too isolated.

A wave of unease washes over me, and I glance over my shoulder.

Don't go into a tunnel alone. Don't walk too far from the docks, from Tomar.

Maple and I would explore the Half-tower when our Wards went to their Purpose, but I would never go alone. I am five-foot-two and built small, not equipped to fight or defend myself. Luckily for me—besides my too-many freckles—I am plain. I've been told by many people, my Ward included, that I am pretty but easily forgotten. I never cared. Being overlooked in the Half-tower is a powerful survival trait.

Spero is suddenly quiet, worrying me more with his fatigue and detachment than his demanding cries. Then, a naked woman crosses the small view I have of the water, appearing to be bathing in the cove. A little comfort settles into my wary stomach, so I head down the steep steps that drop me deeper and deeper into the earth.

At the foot of the stone steps, I enter a small, isolated bay shaped like a jagged quarter-moon, walled with encroaching gravelly forms.

If I reach up, I can touch the cool, moist ceiling. It's unlike anything I have seen before, the air isn't like the Redwind or the smoke-drenched tower fort. It is crisp, like the first bite into an apple.

With only the other woman down here, I sit on the concave of a rock, spilling everything out of my *beibao* onto the smooth stone surface. Laying Spero on his back, I unwrap him and check him over. He is still painted pink and red from Maple's blood, and black poo is smeared and caked between his chubby thighs.

I'll clean him after I feed him.

Ripping the linen from one of my shirts, I poke my finger into it to create a nipple shape and loosen the fibres before covering the top of the bottle. This has to work. I don't have another plan. I tip it over and hold my breath. Slowly, the cloth nipple fills with formula and drips through the fabric.

Spero mewls as I pick him up, cradle him in my lap and put the cloth between his lips. He mouths it immediately, much to my relief. I exhale and lean backward against the rock as he softly sucks. His enthusiasm is weak, but so is he.

So am I.

As Spero drinks, I can almost taste the formula on my tongue, my hunger gnawing at my stomach and hazing my mind.

It's not long before he seems to fall asleep. I understand the 'sleep like a baby' saying as he appears almost comatose. I glance up and see another woman has replaced the previous woman in the cove. My eyes scan the small, intimate cavern. There doesn't appear to be anyone else, though there are tunnels and cavities. I don't want to leave my *beibao* exposed to possible thieves, but I need to bathe Spero. And... I will be in the Deep Sleep soon, so I need to wash myself, too.

Right.

With that, I strip off my clothes, scoop my sleeping burden to my chest, and wade into the cool, clear water until my bellybutton meets the surface.

Hairs prickle along my naked body as I squat, the buoyant fluid holding me while I dip Spero until clear ripples outline his face. The water has a scent, cracked salts and moist stone, and I inhale it dreamily. It's real—organic.

Washing him with gentle hands, I smile. He coos in sweet slumber, seeming to enjoy the water's soothing touch. I know I should hurry, but my heart fills with warmth as moments sluggishly roll by.

"Perfect," I say to him. That is what he is, a perfect blank slate.

I think about Maple, wishing she could see him, feel the cool ocean and breathe this crisp, briny air.

That's when my stomach knots. And my breath catches. I snap my gaze up inadvertently. Someone is watching me; I just know it.

Pausing under the feverish lick of attention, I search the rocky quarry and scan the stone steps, finding no one but… My gaze snaps back, freezing on a dark crevice vast and shadowed enough to harbour and mask a large form.

I can't see the person who stands in the pitch-black hollow, but I know they are there, feeling them acutely. Their presence seizes me with tangible hands while my heart pumps for my muscles to move, to escape, but I can't.

I squint into the black void, my eyes creating shapes that are not there, trying to *see* what I *feel* so powerfully.

Who I feel…

Lagos.

His name comes unbidden.

I don't know why it does or why him and I don't know how, but I know Lagos is standing in the shadowed hollow, staring at me.

Is Spero in danger?

His attention feels… wrong, as he watches me bathe from the depths of the impenetrable black hollow. I don't like it. Don't like my shortness of breath, or my hardening nipples, or the way my thighs press together… No—I'm not… not attracted to that brutish male, am I?

I can't be.

I refuse to be.

Straightening with Spero in my arms, I stride from the pool.

The heavy gaze stalks me until the tether of his attention snaps, releases me, and I inhale a deep breath.

~

I have made very few decisions in my life, and none of importance. The Trade and my Ward took that burden from me. So… being utterly alone in my decision to return to the Exchange

Hub makes anxious nerves play inside me. Every step I take toward the entrance is full of effort.

I push open the door.

The Endigo man is trading with a short lady with a hunched back. She is Common, like me. Perhaps if I spoke to her… She could help me. Women are less threatening than men.

I step closer to the woman. She offers the man what looks like herbs, and he trades her a fish with pretty pink scales.

"I wasn't sure you'd be back," he says as I slowly approach, my boots dragging along the floor, my hesitation weighing me down. The Endigo man is uncomfortable to look at, but that is an unkind thought.

But he is...

The lady disappears through the door before I can talk to her.

Ahead of me is the small fruit crate. I stare at the apples, my mouth filling with saliva instantly. I swallow it down.

"I accepted. Didn't I?" I stand strong. "I need an apple." I reach for it, but he catches my hand, holding it mid-motion.

I gasp.

"One apple," he states, squeezing my hand. "Eat it quick."

My heart hammers. "Okay."

His eyes run a lap of my body before he releases my hand. I take the apple and bite into it, replacing his bile-producing gaze with sweet tannins.

"You got enough serum to make your tea?" he asks. "It's not a skill I 'ave. I 'ave never been given a Lace Girl. I ain't offered such prize assets here at The Bite."

"Serum?" I force the apple chunks down my dry throat, never having heard it referred to as a *serum*. What a strange thing to call it. "I have a little of each ingredient to make the tea. I can make a small amount."

His needled smile skitters along my skin, so I add, "Just enough for an hour."

That's a lie.

But an hour isn't enough time to skin me with those teeth, right? Not enough time to hide my body... the parts left?

He lifts another apple. "Have another."

I reach for it, but he doesn't let go, holding my hand and the apple. "For later," he grinds out.

I stare into his one good eye, and his gaze pushes through mine. "Thank you," I say.

"Go in the back. There is a small kettle by the sink. A cup, too. Make yourself comfortable, Lace Girl." He releases the apple, snapping the tension.

Ignoring the screams of my inner voice, 'Don't go. Don't go.' I walk through a door behind him and out of view.

He probably knows nothing about Companion Nights but that is fine. I am well-trained and can prepare myself.

In the back of his Exchange Hub, I see a small cup already waiting on a crate, which appears to be his bedside table.

Just breathe.

Watching myself more than actually being present, I make a nest in the corner with my jacket and tuck Spero into it. Thankfully, he is fast asleep.

I grab the ingredients hidden in the back sleeve of my *beibao* for my Lace Tea: La Mu leaf and seed, Opi Lava, and clove. The Opi is bitter. Usually I indulge in a spoonful of raw sugar, a rare item that my Ward trades whiskey stamps for... I don't have any today.

I walk to the bed. The floor beneath my boots is the natural rock, jagged in parts, smooth in others, all stained in different colours I care little to analyse further.

I sit on his tiny single mattress and slide my boots off, setting them neatly on the floor like soldiers. Orderliness is a virtue.

My pulse is in my neck; I imagine anyone who cares to look at my throat will see my heart beating erratically. See my nerves jumping beneath the skin like scared little creatures.

Just breathe.

Across from me is a large stainless-steel sink covered in blood and slices of silvery skin.

It is fish skin.

Is it?

Yes. It has to be.

A shuddered breath escapes my lips as I stare at the crimson splashes along the metal basin. Beside them, there are thin, dull, and poorly kept knives.

To fillet fish.

This room is no more than a box. Everything he needs to work and live here is crammed into one space; clothes piled in the corner, a small fibreglass shower cut into the wall, concealed by a tattered curtain, and a small, smelly bed.

Ignoring my instincts, I prepare my tea, mixing it into the small cup.

I set it down on his crude bedside table and let it brew. Then, I take a shaky breath and remove my shirt-dress and pants through a trembling exhale.

I'm going to be okay.

Just breathe.

Folding my clothes, I lay them over my shoes. I don't have my lace gown with me—I didn't think I would need it—so I leave my white slip-dress and knickers on. The chill of fear pinches my nipples, drawing them through the fabric.

The Endigo man enters, and I stiffen on his bed, eyes wide with alarm, back so ridged a breeze might crack me in two. The impending moments sink in as he closes the door. And the truth churns my stomach. He is vile. I can't pretend he isn't anymore, and I can't pretend I'm okay with this. I'm not. I don't want this. I want to run.

His good eye drips down my body, a hiss leaving his cracked lips as he stares at my nipples.

"I know you must be nervous," he says. "But I won't harm ya." He looks at the tea. "Drink it and take your clothes off."

I shake my head as tears simmer behind my eyes. "I don't take my clothes off. I leave them on."

"Not with me."

My blood runs cold. "That's not how it's done. I remain innocent of everything you do. I remain modest. Tha—"

"I don't 'ave long, do I?" he spits. "Take 'em off so I can get started with ya straight away."

My mind screams. *Run.*

Panic finds me too late, crawling into my veins and scratching a pattern of terror into my soul.

The Deep Sleep is meant to be peaceful, and a Lace Girl is to be cared for and considered. I am meant to be doted on and adored. Undressed while I sleep and clothed again before I wake.

This is a mistake.

The white-haired fish-man steps toward me, and I snatch the tea. Humming the soft shanty my Ward used to, I find the sound a tiny comfort as I sip— No. No sugar, no care, no clothes, get it done!

I throw the contents into my throat, rip my slip over my head, and drop backward on his bed.

Staring at the uneven stone ceiling, I place my hands on my stomach, feeling my abdomen tremble beneath my fingertips.

I grit my teeth.

I will not cry.

It'll be over soon.

And I'll never know.

Swallowing over a ball of fear, I turn my head and rest my cheek on the rancid pillow, staring at a dull, rusty appliance on the bloody sink. It is shaped like the roof of a house with curved scales like a fish.

I blink my heavy lashes.

The tea works fast.

In the corner of my eyes, the man clumsily removes his clothes, so I train my gaze on the shiny scales that curve upward along the implement.

No, not scales.

Small blades.

It is a grater.

I come to, my mind in a fog. I can feel my chest rise and fall. Feel the dead weight in my legs. Heavy thighs. Sleep is clinging to my muscles.

I feel as though I'm in a dark dream, but it is entirely real, tactile and noisy, except for my vision which crinkles shapes and smudges detail.

I struggle to lift my eyelids. Feeling a heaviness in my limbs, I cannot reach for anything.

I hear… something.

Grunts, maybe?

And smell something… A familiar scent envelops me. What is that? Copper. Safe. Warm. Suddenly, all my weight hits my spine, my legs and arms flopping backward.

Through the slits in my heavy lashes, I make out a face lording over me. Strong features buckled in anger. Black eyes that stare directly into the heart.

Lagos.

What?

His warmth radiates from the hard chest I am pressed against, and arms… around me. Soothing. I've not been touched like this in my life.

My body is floating in them. *No.* I'm being *carried.* I try to speak, but my voice is trapped. Trapped deep. In the Deep Sleep.

I don't know why, but Lagos' presence cracks me open, spilling my strength like a burst dam. In this dream, this deep, sedated dream that can't be real, I start to violently cry.

My lashes beat images in and out of view. I'm moving through the back room of the Exchange Hub. The fish-man's room.

Blink.

The walls are… There is blood everywhere.

Blink.

And a body lying face down on the single bed. I was asleep there only moments ago. The body is sliced from neck to arse, the spine exposed, twisted upward like a wire.

It's a dream.

A nightmare.

My heart pounds hard while the rest of me barely clutches reality, but I find solace in the powerful arms carrying me.

Sobbing so hard my body shakes, I clutch at fabric, digging my fingers in.

Blink.

Slashes of blood web the walls as I am carried from that room.

It's not real, so I don't need to be strong. To pretend I'm capable and like Maple. Maple… My mind drowns in that name, a heavy weight or burden attached to it. What about Maple… Why am I here? Then it hits me in the chest, hard and brutal, beating every wisp of air from my lungs—*Spero.*

Where is Spero?

Chapter Five

Dahlia

“Spero!”

I jolt upright, expecting to wake in the Exchange Hub and for Spero to be bundled in my hide jacket. I blink the La Ma’s heavy hold from my eyes and focus on my strange surroundings.

I reach up and wipe a hand down my face, smearing something thick along with sweat. I realise it’s blood.

Panic floods me.

Searching the unfamiliar room, I find myself on a small, springy bed, wearing a large black shirt, and… Lagos sits in the corner with his elbows on his knees.

My heart pounds.

His presence immediately suffocates me, and a hazy memory tumbles back to light. I was lifted, carried, and his face hovered over me. There was blood on the walls—

Spero!

“Where is my baby!” I bark, scampering to my feet, bracing myself for a fight with a seven-foot monster of a man. I was wrong. I can't trust him. I was wrong, and Maple was wrong to trust me.

Lagos' intense stare pushes me backward until I feel something at my feet. My eyes cut to the floor and when I see my *beibao,* I squat to find the small hacksaw from within it.

"It's not your baby," he says.

Fuck. He knows.

"Where is he?" I fumble with the saw, my stomach clenching with fear.

"Alive," he states plainly.

"I will hurt you," I warn, straightening and wielding the weapon in front of me. And with him sitting and me standing, we are almost the same height. "I will," I repeat, glaring at him.

He huffs. "A papercut."

My eyes grow as I look between the massive Xin De male and the *tiny* hacksaw, reality sinking in.

"Tomar," I spit out. "Where is Tomar? We had a deal." Retorts stack on my tongue, desperate lies and warnings.

"*Maple* had a deal. *You* got on a boat with two strangers, and that fucking Shadow baby. Then the second you're on your own, you offer yourself and the fucking infant up to an Endigo. You lied to us! There is no deal anymore."

Glaring at me, he leans back, unaffected by the way I brandish the shiny, serrated implement.

"Shadow baby?" The term slithers under my skin along with his demand from earlier: 'Kill it.'

I edge away from the bed, gaining a better stance, trying to figure this all out.

"You don't know, do you, Lace Girl?" His dark utterance pours down my spine like liquid ice.

Oh, God. *What?*

What does he know?

"Don't know what?" I ask.

Lagos' onyx-coloured gaze rolls over me. I can barely decipher his pupil from his iris. As he takes in the hacksaw and my defensive position, the corner of his mouth lifts in what might be considered cruel amusement if he were human, but he isn't. Humanity has been engineered out of him, paired with thousands of years of evolution and gene manipulation, and there it is— what he is.

A heartless Xin De male.

"You're a bit feisty to be a Lace Girl."

"Well—" I shuffle, holding the saw higher, feeling the weight of his presence like a blanket that snuffs out the air. "You're awfully brutish to be considered *evolved*," I punch out, shocked by the strength in my tone.

His grin falls. "Evolved."

"What's a Shadow baby?" I demand. He knows something about Maple's baby. Maybe he knows why The Trade can't find it, or maybe Tomar does. I have to know.

He rises to his feet, his sheer, bulking height forcing me backward a step to keep eye contact. Without another word, he walks to the door. To him, the conversation is over.

Oh, no, it isn't.

"Tell me!"

Uninterested, he grabs the handle and pulls. I fly across the room and slam my back to the door. Literally using my small body to block his exit. Between him and the door—I regret it immediately.

My heart thunders in my veins as I peer up at the huge male looming over me like a great forest tree over a single flower in a field.

His growl cuts the thick air, and I lift the hacksaw higher. Warning him. "What is a Shadow baby?" I demand, my voice trembling along each word, but my chin refuses to lower. "I won't just go away. What is wrong with Maple's baby? Why can't The Trade find him?"

He snatches my throat before I can finish. Lifting me until my body dangles and my feet scrape the floor, he leans the rest of the distance. His lips meet my ear. "Listen closely, little Lace Girl. You keep that nail file."

I gasp for air and desperately try to flatten my feet to the ground.

Lagos presses his chest to the serrated edge of the saw and rubs up and down until the blades shred a line through his black shirt but barely graze the tattooed skin beneath it. "Hold it nice and tight." Hot breath hits me, and I swallow in his fist. "Because you're going to need to use it one day, especially if you plan on trading your body to a fucking Endigo again."

A distorted memory comes back. The sight of harrowing slashes of crimson. The crack of broken bones still echoing from the blood-stained walls to the blood-coated ceiling. Lagos didn't just kill the man—he ripped him apart.

The Endigo man was a mutant, sure. A distorted byproduct of the Gene Age, but he was alive. A living, breathing thing, but apparently no more than an annoying insect, insignificant and grotesque, to Lagos, who, even with his leer and dark presence, is undoubtedly handsome.

I try to breathe and be strong, forcing the words through a squeezed voice box. "What. Did. You. Do to him?"

He chuckles cruelly. A throaty sound that presses on my lungs. "I pulled his spine from his back while he pressed his cock between your thighs," he hisses the words, hatred deepening his voice, and I recoil. "You're welcome, little Lace Girl."

"Lagos," Tomar's voice comes from behind me. A knock beats at my spine, snapping the heavy tension between us.

Lagos lifts his head while lowering me to the floor, and when he releases my throat, I grasp it in both hands, feeling the slim column, soothing it.

I gasp for air.

"*Move*," Lagos growls, jerking away from me as if he'd rather fling himself off a cliff than be that close to me.

I know I lied and stole their services—their help—without

offering an exchange or trade, but... His hatred and rage run deeper than makes sense.

Does he think I stole Maple's baby? How does he even know her?

Was he intimate with her?

No way. I am confident Maple was loyal to her Ward, and I can't imagine Lagos having a shred of softness to offer a woman. I can't visualise him pressing his rough lips to hers, or pulling her small body against his, or running his huge hands up her thighs and squeezing— I need air. My lips part as my head spins, and the lowest part of my stomach clenches.

Right, I've decided. I do *not* like him. And it's a contradiction, hating a man who saved me from whatever the Endigo man was going to do, because I did regret it. I did want to run. I'm glad I am not alone in that room with him, but Lagos doesn't need to be cold and monstrous.

He is a murderer, and he clearly has no respect for life.

Adding space for the door to open, I move to the side, expecting Tomar to step in, but he doesn't. Lagos strides from the room and slams the door in my face.

My eyes widen. Then I hear the door lock from the other side.

Chapter Six

Dahlia

I don't know how much time passes as I beat on the door, screaming Lagos' name but it suddenly opens, and Tomar strides in with Spero in his arms.

Relief floods me. "Spero."

I reach for my tiny burden, and Tomar allows me to take the infant. I hold him close. Protective.

I scrutinise his chubby body, checking him over, moving the shirt he's swaddled in. He looks fine and settled, but that doesn't stop the anxious words that gather along my tongue. Then I remember I lied to them and need answers, so I don't spit the nasty thoughts out.

"It's him," Tomar says as Lagos follows him inside, forcing me back a few steps.

He shuts the door, closing the four of us in. I thought that maybe Lagos was alone in locking me in this room and that Tomar would swing open the door and let me leave.

But no.

"I know it is," Lagos states.

"I had to check." Tomar stands in front of me. "Where is Maple?" He folds his arms and frowns. "Go on. Talk."

I don't know what to say or how to explain… Spero pouts, so I draw little swirls on his back with one finger as a knot forms in my stomach, filling with unspoken words, expanding with every passing moment. I'm not Maple—

"You lied." Tomar sighs hard.

"Technically, I didn't say I was Maple," I argue, pulling Spero closer. "You assumed it, and I just went along with it."

Tomar nods toward the bundle in my arms. "But that *is* Maple's baby."

Dammit, Maple, what have you gotten yourself and me into?

I swallow, meeting his blue eyes. "Yes."

"Then…" His pause is loud. "Where is she?"

"Dead." Lagos drops the word carelessly, and my heart squeezes while my mind flashes with images of her final moments, of her screams as Spero tore through her, of her smile when she saw his face and chubby arms.

Tomar pins me with his gaze, filled with concern and distrust. "Is that true? Is she dead?"

What should I say? I chew my bottom lip. The truth? *What will that mean for me? What kind of deal did Maple make? Can I make the same deal?*

I choose the most pressing question. "You answer me first," I demand with false strength. "What is a Shadow baby?"

"You're in no position to bargain." Tomar blocks the door, not that I could leave or have anywhere to go. It's not like I have any options at all. "But fine, Lace Girl. A question for a question. Is Maple dead?"

I nod and whisper, "*Yes.*"

"Who are you?"

"A member of her Collective."

"What—"

"That's two questions," I interrupt. "It's my turn. What is a

Shadow baby? *He*" —I glare at Lagos, my contempt for him unhidden— "called Spero a Shadow baby."

Tomar and Lagos look at each other, sharing a heavy message before Tomar walks toward the bed and sits down.

His eyes soften on me. "It's best if you don't know."

"I have to know."

Tomar leans forward. "You're not Maple. You can leave. You still have time to return to the Half-tower and be rescued by The Trade. The civil unrest will end at some point, and you can return to your Purpose. You will be in danger if you know what he is, and then run with him. It will never stop. They will always come for him, and you will always be in hiding."

"She doesn't need to know." Lagos' jaw clenches and unclenches. "She was born to serve, not to protect or die for others. Kill the baby. It will be a kindness."

"You are not killing my baby!" I hiss, stepping in front of Lagos, pretending he doesn't exist to me—but he does. My body hums with instinctual wariness in his presence. "I *can* protect him—*will*." I focus on Tomar. "I chose him over myself the moment I lied to the Marshals who could have rescued me, and protected me, and offered me a new home, and Ward, and—" The truth rushes to a pause of significance. Tears burn behind my eyes. "I have already chosen him. She was my closest friend. My favourite" —my voice breaks— "person in this world." My lower lip wobbles, my resolve washing away in the twin rivers rushing down my cheeks.

The door opens and closes behind me, and I don't need to look over my shoulder to know that Lagos has left the room. His repressive aura dissolves.

I breathe deeply again.

"Okay." Tomar nods slowly, eyes panning over my distraught expression. "Okay. First, what is your name, Lace Girl?"

I sniffle. "Dahlia."

"Well, Dahlia." He reaches out and wipes the wet trail from below my eye. "You're very brave. The baby, Spero, is a Shadow."

My chest starts to rise and fall, and as Tomar talks, the walls slowly press in on us. Everything goes deathly quiet, as if the air itself is afraid to move.

"A Shadow is an assassin. They operate above the king, directly for The Trade Master. If they find Spero, he will be sent to a specialised training compound where he will undergo unimaginable torment and stress drills."

"A baby," I gasp.

"Yes." Tomar looks pained. "Meaningful Purpose starts in the womb. That is what they say, isn't it? The Trade will condition him thoroughly, brainwash him beyond repair, and train him to kill or die for his Meaningful Purpose."

I cuddle Spero to my chest as a bead of sweat slides down my back.

"At twenty-one," Tomar clears his throat. "The Shadow will be released into The Cradle to join a menial Trade: Fish Trade, Windmill, Mining, or the like. Anonymous until summoned. Spero will be one of the deadliest creatures in The Cradle."

"Why him? How do you know all of this?"

"Maple must have the Xin De genus somewhere in her lineage. The Shadow genus is recessive and extremely volatile. Shadows are bred in the laboratories, not often the result of a missed contraceptive."

She didn't miss it.

She didn't brew her tea correctly.

I can't say this, barely allowing the dangerous thoughts to surface.

"How do they know he's one of these Shadows?" I ask again. "How do you know this? He is just a little baby, just born."

"We found you and—" He pauses, the moment of hesitation worrying me. Is he withholding something? "Let's just say we have connections. We went to the Medical Hub and overheard a man talking about Maple. A Xin De man in a purple tunic spoke Latin to the doctor. I have never seen him in the flesh, but I knew, without a doubt, who he was. Cairo, The Trade Master himself, was in the Half-tower either managing the Marshal takeover or perhaps, just perhaps, he was here for this baby."

I blink at him, trying to absorb his words. "Maple speaks Latin. Her Ward taught her; she would have heard and understood."

Her pleas to keep the baby from The Trade finally make sense, but... "Who are you?"

Tomar sighs roughly, eyeing me, diving in, trying to read my intent. "I help people escape."

"Why?" I ask. Help is not free in The Cradle. Nothing is free in The Cradle.

He lifts his chin. "It's my Purpose."

I huff dubiously. "The Trade gave you Meaningful Purpose to help people escape the—"

"I chose this," he states, throwing me. "I gave myself this Meaningful Purpose."

I don't know how to respond to that. It's not something I have ever heard before.

"Okay." I nod. "But how do *you* know he is? I mean, really know. How could anyone know he's this Shadow... thing, when he is just a baby."

"They know." Tomar nods regretfully. "Spero has excessively high iron levels in his blood, Dahlia. I just checked to confirm this." He pushes back the fabric to show a small red dot on the back of Spero's hand. His blue eyes meet mine again, an apology shiny from their depths. "I was gentle, I assure you. Levels that high would kill you and me, levels that high interact with the magnetic fields in The Cradle. They pull him and push him and control him like The Cradle itself has tethers to his very veins. He has the Shadow genus for sure, and The Trade will never stop searching for him."

Never... The pressure of that hits my chest like a punch. I glance down at Spero. Such a sweet, tiny thing. "Does it hurt?"

"What?"

"The iron levels?" I pause, not entirely understanding. I've been told that The Crust has its own magnetic fields, the planet spins in the sky or something, and that in the old-world, birds used them to navigate and migrate. Is this similar to what happens to Spero? "The… um, magnetic push and pull. Is he in pain?"

"Not right now."

"But one day?"

Sadness fills Tomar's gaze. "It can be painful. That's how The Trade controls them. This isn't something people know, Dahlia. Shadows are the biggest secret in The Cradle."

I can't let that happen to Maple's baby. "How can I help him?"

"For now, you stay here." Tomar stands, his height reminding me how short I am. "At The Bite. Wait out Redwind Whip. It happens every few months and can last some forty days. But"—he shrugs, trying to be light-hearted— "At least you're away from the conflict at the Half-tower. You're safe. The Trade doesn't come here. When the wind settles, we will take you and Spero to the Common Community up north."

I track him as he crosses the room, stopping at the door.

"We?" I ask.

He opens the door, revealing a carpeted, narrow hallway, reminding me of the corridor to the flat back home. "This is your room. Get settled. There are cans of food in the cupboards. Nothing fancy. I'll try to find formula or milk. We'll leave supplies for you outside your door. The toilet is down the hall, but the shower isn't working. Some people bathe in the underground lake, but you can use the water from the sink if you prefer."

Suspicion knots my stomach. It's too much; Spero's identity, the pressure, and Tomar's kindness.

"I still can't comprehend all this altruism from you. Why help me?"

"I'm helping Spero." Tomar smiles smoothly. "It's my Purpose, Lace Girl Dahlia, and now, it's yours, too."

And he closes the door.

I reach for it immediately and turn, sighing with heavy relief when the door creaks open a slither. It's not locked.

I shut it again.

The door isn't lockable from the inside, so after laying a mewling Spero on the bed, I slide a single wooden chair over to the door and wedge it under the handle.

Gazing around the space, I scrutinise it properly. No other doors and no windows, but the overhead light glows red, offering me some concept of time. It's last-light. Having no other entrances actually makes me feel safe.

The room is a plain rectangular shape with a single spring bed, single chair now used as security, a basic two-person table, and a dull metal sink fastened to the wall. It is neat but not fancy, and it will do.

For a month.

I am going to be here, at The Bite, for a month or more... *Oh. My.*

Reality buckles my legs, dropping my backside to the mattress. This is my new life. The weight of my decision to leave the Half-tower suddenly grapples me.

I sit and panic. Every day of my life up until now has been known—one Purpose. Meticulous, routine, and easy... *Each day,* I wake up and accompany, relieve, and soothe my Ward.

And before that, I learned to sew, massage, clean, grow La Mu, make Lace Girl tea, and speak properly until the time came that I was gifted to a Ward.

Tomar's statement chimes between my ears: 'It's my Meaningful Purpose, Lace Girl Dahlia, and apparently, it's yours too, now.'

My eyes drift to the wriggling newborn incapable of anything. It is utterly useless and vulnerable. I'm not sure I've met anyone more vulnerable than a Common girl like me. Until now... My new Purpose.

Crawling up the bed, I settle beside him. *How can you be an assassin? How could any decent human being hurt—*

That's just it; they *aren't* human beings. I often forget. Xin De aren't human anymore. Over time, humans became so useless, with no claws and no flight, fragile and weak. Xin De are their own species, an evolved one, with animal traits engineered into human genes to aid in survival.

Spero is Xin De.

As I feed my finger into his palm, he grabs, holding me. My heart fills, and I smile.

Big, scary Xin De.

We have each other.

"I need to get you more, little baby. Nappies, clothes, and maybe even a toy, because you're special." I play with his hand. "And I don't care if you're supposed to grow up to be a big, mean Xin De assassin, I'll always look at you like this. I'll tell you about your mummy. How clever and pretty she was, how she let me follow her like a lamb, and made me feel…" I sigh. "Not easily forgotten."

Spero squeaks as I talk.

"You don't know this yet," I say through a giggle. "I'm pretty but plain, apparently. Not very special or unique. Not like you, but I'll do my best to raise you."

Looking at this tiny being, so wriggly and new, I am overwhelmed with the urge to care for him. *Oh,* how I wish I had bargained for more stuff from the Endigo, and selfishly—horribly—wonder whether his Exchange Hub can still be entered.

Or is it boarded up?

Will another take over?

It could be lucrative…

I could look after Spero myself. *Do I really need Tomar and, ugh, Lagos?* I could take supplies from the exchange, find my own way across the desert, take my chances…

In my mind, I foresee stepping over the old Endigo man's mutilated corpse and taking items like a scurrying rodent. I couldn't bring myself to *steal* from anyone and stealing from a dead man seems worse than stealing from a living one.

I'm not like that… I couldn't—

Oh, no. The truth finds me in my lonely musings—To make the journey alone, I would have to kill or be killed. Be ruthless and cruel—be like *Lagos.*

The Cradle is said to be barren wastelands, with forests of windmills and the belting Redwind that only military vehicles can withstand. Outside the Trade towers, the land is home to savages. Endigos and Common raiders hide in the desert declines and hills. If I dare try to make my way alone, the people I encounter on the road will ravage me indiscriminately, maybe even feast on my flesh.

And Spero's.

I couldn't kill.

Could I?

Closing my eyes, I exhale a steady breath. I have to accept facts. That even if I knew how to get to the Common Community up north, without Tomar—and by extension, Lagos—I would probably die in the desert.

I need them.

With my eyes closed and my finger in Spero's tiny hand, my chest fills with air before a heavy exhale drags through my lips. Sleep seems to be ready to take me. A few hours on the boat and mere minutes in the Deep Sleep are not enough to appease my exhaustion.

I relax deeper into the mattress, somewhere between sleep and awake, and focus on Spero's light squeezes, little hiccups, and sweet, odd baby scent until...

Chapter Seven

Dahlia

I dream about Maple and wake up crying.

Sleep is intermittent, the gaps filled with feeding and tending to Spero, but as I swing the door open at first-light, and peer down the long, carpeted corridor, it becomes apparent the other occupants are not early risers.

Which explains the noises from last night, moans and giggles, squeaking beds and the thumps of feet passing my door.

During one of my night feeds, I explored the supplies Tomar provided, enough canned food for a week and another huge, shapeless black shirt like the one I woke up in. I presume they are his so I only plan to sleep in them, not wear them out. I have two pairs of pants and a modest shirt-dress. Then again, being attractive is not a priority.

On an exciting note, I realised I could use my linen neck wrap, typically used to shield me from the weather, as a carrier for Spero.

Feeding it over one shoulder and under one arm, I can slide

Spero in at my chest and have full use of my hands. It's not ideal for the desert, not with the Redwind, but it's perfect for the crisp and steady atmosphere here at The Bite.

With Spero secure and well-fed, I close the bedroom door behind me and head down the corridor after convincing myself all night that I would explore and find supplies.

An entire month here, perhaps, and I do not want to rely entirely on Tomar or, worse still, Lagos.

The floor creaks as I pass other doors, heading toward the end where an open stairwell appears to lead downward. So, I'm not on the ground. I have no memory of getting here yesterday, meaning I don't know what to expect.

I take the stairs and when my foot hits the floor at the bottom an opening to my left leads down four ceramic mosaic steps into a ruby-hued room with tables and chairs, but I can't see further inside from here. To my right— *Oh,* I know exactly where I am. I recognise the small grey door and the lovely, jewellery-adorned woman standing at a tall desk.

The pretty House Girl I met yesterday leans over the stone counter, her bulbous cleavage spilling out for the man she is speaking to like an offering and not a subtle one.

The man is scary. Rotund. Light from outside reflects along the smooth, white surface of three parallel scars on his cheek. Perhaps claw marks from an animal or nails from a woman. I squirm, discomfort rising in my legs. I'm not a prude, or maybe I am, but not voluntarily. Being pure and sweet are part of my Trade.

I clear my throat as I approach. "Hello," I say, and they stop talking.

"You!" She turns toward me while a smirk builds on the rugged man's face, his abundance of cheek lifting. "I didn't know it was *you* Lagos carried in here yesterday." Her brow rises on Spero. "That baby best not keep me up."

You're up anyway.

Smart-mouthed retorts build along my tongue, but I simply smile. "He won't."

I walk through the grey door and out into the empty streets. First-light dew clings to the walls and drips down white spikes that lance from the cave ceiling.

The Bite is a ghost town at this hour. As I cross the stony path, I find myself walking toward the Exchange Hub with sick curiosity spurring me onward.

Pieces of wood are nailed from frame to frame, making entering or opening the Hub impossible. I try to shake the pit of guilt my mind wants to drag me into. It wasn't my fault. I didn't murder anyone. I press my hand to the wooden slat and test the structure for possible weakness.

"Miss him?" Lagos' amused voice drifts down my spine.

I clench my teeth and force my legs away from the building, embarrassed. Guilty, also, that I was considering what might be inside.

Then something comes over me, annoyance too consuming to fight, and I spin around to face him. "Are you following me?" I want to say that I felt him the other day at the cove, watching me. That I know he must have followed me to the Hub.

"I have fond memories at this Hub." He looks at me, bored. "Just yesterday, I butchered an Endigo here. You're welcome." Looped over his arm is a heavy wire, similar to the zipline. He is dressed in blue denim jeans with rips at the thighs and an open black shirt that showcases rows and rows of tattooed abdominal muscles.

I swallow and snap my gaze up to his eyes. "You have no respect for life." Shaky legs lock me still while my neck cranes to hold his near-black gaze. "Why? What happened to you?"

The corner of his mouth twitches. "Your baby will kill hundreds of men and women when he is a man. Far more than me if The Trade gets a hold of him."

"Why did you interfere then? Why help us?" I ask, feeling my brows furrow. I hardly recognise the strength in my soft voice. “Did you think I was Maple? What do I owe you for this?

“Nothing.”

I shift nervously as he approaches. He doesn’t merely walk, displaying a gait more predatory, powerful and smooth.

“Then, why?”

He gets too close for comfort. “I went there for the Shadow baby,” he whispers, deathly quiet like his lips are right in my ear. “Not you.”

“But—" I stammer, and step backward. Need space. Air. “You told Tomar to kill Spero. You want to kill him. Why not let the Endigo do it?”

“I draw the line at cannibalism.” He smirks. “No matter how annoying the food on the menu is.”

I swallow. “He was not going to eat u—"

“Are you so sure?”

Cupping the back of Spero’s head, I seek comfort. “He said he wouldn't harm me.”

“Oh, I didn’t know he said that.”

“Are you being sarcastic?” I ask, genuinely shocked that he would be. “I didn't consider you to be someone who uses sarcasm.”

“So you consider me?”

“What?” Embarrassment stabs at my temples. “No. I don't. He didn’t deserve to be ripped apart, that is all. He was born that way. Just like Spero and you. Just because he is hard to look at—"

“No, little girl.” Lagos crosses his thick arms over his chest, biceps bulging beneath his hands. “You were born this way. He’s an abomination, and so is the Shadow baby.”

There is no emotion in his voice.

“And you?” My lower lip wobbles. Never in my life have I been this argumentative, but this Xin De male gets under my skin. “Some kind of supreme being? I don't care what you have seen in the desert or what you do willingly to survive. There is no excuse for kill—"

His huge hand grabs my face, cuts my sentence off, and squeezes my lips to a puckering bow.

"There will come a time, little Lace Girl, while I'm babysitting you across the Great Waste to your Common Community that you'll beg me to kill for you." He steps closer. My body vibrates below his, reacting to strange energy between us, and Spero starts to cry. "You'll breathe with heavy relief, might even wet your knickers, when you hear bones snap, knowing they are not yours."

As I search his gaze for empathy, for a glimmer of humanity, I get lost in empty pits of darkness and hatred.

"Never," I whisper.

"We'll see." He drops my face like a scorching ember and strides past me toward the docks, calling out, "Stay away from that Hub, Lace Girl. What you'll see inside will give you nightmares."

I watch him walk toward the dock at the end of the path, mulling over his words. He means the man is still inside. Will someone clean up? If this were a Trade community then a member would be out to take care of this.

Who does that here?

With a sigh, I turn from him and decide to keep my distance where possible. I don't like the way he makes me feel, not at all.

I'm… *intrigued* by him. What makes his life meaningful? He obviously cares for Tomar, so he's not… void. I don't want to hate him. If I can only see a tiny piece of kindness, a moment of compassion, then I feel I might be able to see past his cruelty. See good in him.

Oh, my. I grip my forehead.

Flustered, I set off at a steady pace.

I spend the rest of the day slowly searching the outskirts of The Bite. Whenever I see people, I head down a path, keep to the quiet corners and shadowed pockets.

If Spero is as special as implied, I feel a discreet presence is what is best, but I won't sit in a room for a month.

If Tomar can pick his Purpose, then maybe I can, too. Can't I?

Thoughts about my new life roll in my mind as I wander. I am following a rocky ledge that cuts straight to the water when I see an old dinghy. Inside, matted nets and tangled pots are stacked carelessly.

Stepping closer, I peer in and see a plastic bottle battered and bent from its life on the ocean floor. I blink at it, getting an idea. If I fill it with shells and rocks, it will make a little rattle.

Spero makes a gurgling sound, so I cup the back of his head before reaching for the bottle.

"That's not yours."

I straighten to find an old man limping toward me, his hands tremor in front of him. He is wearing a plain shirt that was perhaps once white. His jeans are covered in muck from fishing and black suspenders hang like two twin loops at his thighs. "That's my bottle."

I gape at him. "It's trash."

He lifts a bushy grey brow at me, sceptical. "Is it?"

"There are little holes all over it." I wave at it. "You couldn't put liquid in it."

"Still mine. Still not yours." The old man hobbles to the boat, clambering in, his hands convulsing.

I stare at him, feeling sorry for whatever makes his body vibrate like his veins are frenzied. With convulsing fingers, he starts untangling the net.

He struggles, grumbling to himself. His bitterness runs deep. I bet he didn't even look at the bottle, or me, or Spero. He is too blinded by some kind of resentment he holds.

I cringe as I watch him trying to direct the net and weave the tails around. The knots are tight, water and salt logged. The thin, stiff rope is erratically webbed by a wild ocean.

Even though he won't let me have the bottle, sadness slides through my chest. I'm not bitter. I am not hardened by The Cradle, so I really see his situation. Understand it.

I sit on the lip of the old, metal boat without looking at him because I am sure he hates that and start on the other end of the net.

He grumbles. "What you doin'?"

"Helping you."

A sneer curls his lips. "Why?"

I shrug, the word lonely bouncing in my mind, but he doesn't need to hear it. Maybe I'll be helpful, so *maybe* one day, when another girl asks him for something, he won't turn her away. He'll see them as a real person who needs something that he does not.

"I can't exchange! I got no trade for you. Go away." He tries to tug the net from my hands. Even though I'm small, my dexterity is fine, so I keep the rope between my fingers.

I don't look at him as I fuss with the salt-locked webs. "I won't ask for anything." Ignoring him and his dubious gaze, I hum to Spero as I work.

Quietly, I sing.

"Good first-light, to you, my Collective and friend. We head to the ocean, it's days there we spend. Though the Redwind is howlin' with a fist full of sand. We prefer it's hard slapin' to The Trade Master's hand."

I smile at Spero's gurgling, then turn my chin and look around the curtain of my red hair to the old man. He is watching us, frozen in thought. A blank expression has softened his sneer.

"You're from the Half-tower?"

I nod stiffly.

"And the infant?"

Not willing to answer, I return my attention to the net and continue weaving with my fingers around the knots.

"You Trade Fisher?"

"No." I throw a piece of net to the side, needing to untangle a section further down the line to loop it back. "I accompanied one."

"Accompanied? You're not..." I hear him lean back, the boat creaking, as if realisation shoved him to his spine. "You're a Lace Girl. Damn. My sense of smell is rot, or I would have smelt that La Mu shit."

"Shit?"

"No." His voice has softened. Hostility dwindling. "Nice smell," he offers. "Wish I could smell it. Salt burnt my nostrils. There ain't nothing left in there."

"Can you still taste?" I ask.

"Not much," he grunts.

"That's a shame. Food is one of life's great experiences. At least, that is what my friend used to say." What Maple used to say.

"Yep. It's a shame," he says, turning back to his side of the net.

A little smile touches my lips.

While we work like this for many minutes, my mind rolls, entertaining me with ideas and memories. I remember Maple talking about great experiences. Food. Soap. Friendship. And, apparently, sex, but she was never meant to discover that.

It's not for Lace Girls.

It is for Trade men.

She wasn't meant to change her tea, so the Deep Sleep didn't come, and feel what it was like to relieve a man. 'Like exploding while peeing,' she said. Which sounds awful, not lovely, and that is why we Sleep. The man can be himself throughout, enjoy us without fear of judgment, and we exist without impure or uncomfortable memories.

Or worse—egos.

Like the House Girls have.

But… But what if the Lace Girl enjoys it? Like Maple does—did.

Why can't she lie with him while awake, show him her desire? Is that not healing and soothing?

Does this break boundaries? I wish I had someone to ask, but the House Girls have no interest in getting to know me.

Can I make a friend?

With my hand working on the net, I gaze over at the old man. Is there an age limit or gender exclusivity on friendship? I haven't interacted with men much, but I like him; his softer side makes me smile.

Spero suddenly hiccups and then starts to cry. So I quickly finish the last knot and stand. "I have to go feed him. Thank you for letting me help."

The man doesn't look up, but I swear I see his eyes droop. "Very well."

"I can come back tomorrow." I swirl my finger along Spero's back as he cries, trying to distract him. "I could help with the pots. They need new ties."

"No," he grunts.

My heart twinges. "Oh, okay."

I hide the rejection that buckles my brows, turning and heading toward the main path that cuts upward from the docks.

The House is about halfway up on the other side of the stone path. The girl from yesterday and another with blonde hair cross in front of me, eyes following my gait, mouths gossiping.

"That's the Lace Girl. Lagos said she is off limits." I hear as I dart to the side she came from.

"A Lace Girl, *really*?" She sniggers. "Aren't they like pets?"

Yeah, a friend would be nice.

I do my best to ignore them and keep walking. I can see the edge of the fence line peeking out from behind another rocky dwelling.

"Here!"

I spin to see the old man hobbling toward me with the crumpled bottle in his shaky hand. "I don't know what you want it for, but—" He starts talking, and I beam as he places it roughly into my palm. "I used to be a Trade Fisher, and that was a Trade. This is yours. Meaningful Purpose is a virtue. You can take the man out of The Trade, but you can't take The Trade out of the man."

"For a rattle," I admit, smiling.

"Huh?"

"I'm going to make a rattle."

I think he smiles at that, as if he likes the idea, but it's such a flash expression it disappears as quickly as his attention. He is turning and leaving me standing in the middle of the main path before I can ask him again if I can visit tomorrow. He might sift more trash from the ocean floor, and I can find more treasures.

"Thank you again!" I call out to his limping form, and he waves his hand in a kind of shooing motion. I am a fly, and he is playing the bitter old man.

Right, I get it.

I press my chin to my chest, staring at Spero, whispering, "Tomorrow, we will need to find out his name." The infant fusses and squirms. "I think he likes us."

Then, an engine rumbles to life. Movement catches my eye. A stream of salt-kissed air from the docks mingles with smoke and oils. I gaze toward the commotion instinctually, my attention captured.

At the foot of the path, the catamaran bumps the jetty a few times before slowly drifting from the edge, heading away from The Bite.

Tomar is correcting the zipline, but Lagos is a large, looming form at the rear. Statue still. Narrowed, black eyes cut from the bottle in my hand to the direction the old man walked and back again.

I didn't steal it...

If that is what he thinks.

Easing away from the massive Xin De male's tangible gaze, I stride to The House, ignoring the pulsing energy that seems to stir whenever his attention is aimed at me.

~

As I wander downstairs the next day, two men are waiting in a line. The House Girl and the man from yesterday are at the counter again, but this time, his hand is gripping her wrist, and she is trying to tug it free.

"Listen here, bitch—"

Then he sees me. He stops, the hate and hunger within his leer slither down my body, making me shudder. His eyebrow rises when he sees Spero, and his slow grin churns my stomach.

She grabs his face in her hands, redirecting his gaze. Her heavy-lidded eyes and sweet, inaudible words compelling him.

I dart past them.

It's none of my business and nothing unusual. I often saw men bothering House Girls in the Half-tower. Men display little restraint with them. Desire flares to the surface. Unlike with my Trade, where they ignore us. We belong to one man, while a House Girl belongs to no man.

After a small stroll around the town, I trace my steps back to the rocky ledge behind the main walkway.

As I approach the dinghy, the old man is already pulling in a load of fish from his first-light adventures on the ocean. My Ward would leave at night, take on the seas in the dark, and return just before crown-light. So, I was right in assuming the old man did the same, given his Trade background.

Stopping behind him, I say, "I made the rattle. I used shells and a few rocks. He likes it. So, what's your name?" I inadvertently jig, bouncing Spero on my chest. I look the old man over. He is in the same clothing, though his suspenders are pulled over his shoulders, and his shirt seems to have been cleaned.

"Tide."

I knew he would have a geographical name; most Trade members do. Unlike Xin De men and women of importance, they have city names from the old-world, while some girls like me are flowers. "Can I call you Tide?"

"Well, that's my name," he grunts, hunched over in the boat with his back to me, sorting the fish into different buckets.

"I know." I sit down on the ledge and cross my legs. "But some men prefer sir."

"I am not a sir."

I smile, and even though he didn't ask, I introduce myself. "I'm Dahlia."

"A flower, of course. What would you be doing now if you weren't on the run, Dahlia?"

I might have been thrown by that assumption and question were it anyone else asking. For some reason, I feel comfortable with this grumpy old man. "How do you know I am on the run?"

"Everyone here is."

So, that means he is also on the run—or was. I wonder why? But since he didn't ask me what I am running from, I won't ask him. "Well, I would be with my Collective, sewing or sleeping."

"Sleeping?" He laughs once, a husky sound that vibrates around overused lungs. Then he stops, like the sound was painful to make. "At crown-light?"

I like his laugh; it is harsh and makes me smile a little harder. "I mean," I shrug, unapologetic, "I like to sleep. Everyone does, really, or maybe it's just… I miss it. I haven't had much the past few days."

"Well,"—he nods his head toward the net— "you gonna get down 'ere and help me, or just sit there and watch me break my old back?"

I feel my lips curve even wider and climb to my feet. Cupping the back of Spero's head with one hand, I brace the edge of the boat with the other. I climb in and get to work on the nets.

I catch a whiff of lemon from his shirt as I settle down beside him. "You smell nice." I remember he has very little sense of smell, and he's alone on this boat all day, so who is he grooming for today? "You might not know that, so I thought I'd mention it."

"Smell like what?"

I inhale him again, and he pretends to be offended, leaning away. "Lemons and fish," I answer him, picking up the net.

Tide huffs an amused sound. "I like lemons."

I beam, happy to have a friend. "I like lemon and fish together, probably one of my favourite meals, and I used to—"

A tremoring hand touches my arm, cutting me off mid-sentence. I peer over my shoulder at him, this close to him I can make out all his wrinkles, the lovely lines of age that many don't get to wear.

"You're a sweet girl," he whispers, his face tight with seriousness. "You need to stop talking to strangers. Someone will take advantage of you. I heard what happened with The Fish. Got no Exchange Hub now 'cause of it. Lagos and Tomar are still not back. People misbehave when they leave. That's the only reason I'm letting you sit with me again."

Taking a heavy breath, I mull over his warning, trying to understand each part. I want to know who The Fish is? He must mean the Endigo man. Did they call him The Fish? And what do Lagos and Tomar do when they leave? Probably get more runaways or supplies from the Half-tower. Then... are they in danger? If they don't return because they have been shot, what will I do? But I mostly want to know why Tide doesn't want me to sit with him *'for any other reason.'*

"The only reason?" I ask, pressing for a nicer response.

"Yep," he grumbles, turning back to his net.

I swallow my silly sense of rejection and focus on the woven rope between my fingers. "Anyway, I wasn't talking to strangers. I just wanted the bottle, and you were petty about it."

He coughs another raspy laugh. "Petty?"

"Yes." I nod, lifting my chin. "Today, I'll have"—I scan the small metal vessel, from broken pots, to webbed lines, fish, and general rubbish until I see an old hand vanity with a cracked mirror. "I'll take the mirror then as a trade. This is not a friendship, merely an exchange."

"Take it."

"Good." I nod stiffly.

Taking hold of a pot, I begin to untangle it, thinking. A month is a long time to just sit around. Spero sleeps so much, and my room is so small it takes minutes to clean each day, so I need a Purpose. It feels utterly unnatural to exist without one. Risking a look at Tide, I watch him huff and grumble as he counts the fish. I know I've forced myself on him. It never occurred to me that he may truly want to be alone. I saw his bitterness as a façade, perhaps I read him wrong.

Or maybe I just need to try harder? It just seems… human to be social, but then, humanity is slipping away from our species, year by year. Still, I am Common and find myself desperate to engage.

I have never had to *make* friends before, not once. I was given my Collective and my Ward. I didn't choose any of my companions, which has left me without the skills needed to form a friend-type relationship. I'd be happier here with someone to talk to, to confide in. It feels desperate and odd—forcing myself on people—but I don't want to be alone.

I thought maybe Tomar would be around more, but he only drops things at my door, offers tiny conversation a few times, and then leaves.

"So, Tide, you've been around a long time," I chirp, still keeping my tone bubbly. A groan of annoyance leaves him, almost tangible, but I decide to find it amusing instead of hurtful. "How do you make a… a friend-type relationship?"

"A what?"

I smile softly. "A friend."

"Do I look like I know?"

"No," I say. I stare back at the pots and sigh. "I guess not. If I find out, I'll let you in on the secret."

He laughs at that, a rattly old sound that almost causes a coughing fit. There is no way he is as bitter and dark as he makes out to be, not with a great laugh like that.

After a few hours, Spero starts to bumble at my chest. I grab the hand mirror and stand. "See-you tomorrow, Tide."

This time he stops me before I leave the boat by saying. "You're doing fine."

His words have meaning, his tone gentle, and both warm my heart. "Fine at what?"

"You pay attention, and you offer something." He doesn't look at me as he works. "You did fine in making a friend. Some people don't want it, remember that. I don't want it. Some people just ain't made of the right stuff for friendship. I ain't."

"How do I know who is?"

"You don't, so you'll probably end up gettin' rejected, hurt, and that'll shape ya. I'd hate to see that happen."

He likes us, Spero.

"See-you tomorrow, Tide," I say again, my tone sing-song and teasing, earning me a grunt from the old man in the boat.

My not-a-friend friend.

Chapter Eight

Dahlia

One week later

Nights are hard and sleepless with Spero, but The House is always alive. Soft beats come from the ruby-hued room on the lower level, footsteps echo, doors open and shut, and giggles ensue.

And then, as the Missing Moon descends, the night closing, groans and moans take over until first-light.

That is most nights.

I've never stepped into the den, or the ruby-hued room, as I call it. It's empty during the day, so I don't know what goes on there, and I'm too tired to explore The Bite now that I've been caring for a newborn for nearly a week.

Raising the babes of The Cradle is an entire Trade—a coveted one. Being a Sired Mother and working in the nurseries is meant to be the supreme Trade for older women.

I do like to sleep… I mean, I'm a Lace Girl, but babies are like living magic. A new life. A blank slate. So precious.

I want sleep... My eyes feel deeper somehow, wanting to disappear into my head, close and not open again for a long, long time.

Each day is the same. First-light comes and goes. A bag of supplies is dropped outside my room, varying each day—cans of food, often fabric for nappies, soap or toothpaste. Once, a small wedge of coconut and a real baby bottle with a removable nipple—that was an exciting delivery.

At crown-light, despite exhaustion dripping heavily down my spine, I force myself to go outside. I usually head downstairs and avoid the line of men around the front desk. Sometimes, there are two girls on display, other times three. I have been trying to memorise their faces, and I believe at least four young girls live in The House with me. A black-haired girl I heard someone refer to as Beauty, a blonde with grey eyes, a tall brunette who always stares down her lashes at me, and the main girl, who Tide said is named Sweets.

Which she is not.

I would usually dash out to see Tide, and he'd reluctantly allow me to work and keep him company. I won't say we are friends... But we are friendly, and I'll take it. I don't work on goodwill; I leave with something small for my efforts, using the trinkets to decorate my room.

But today is different.

I leave Spero secured in a nest I made for him and lock the door from the outside so I can go to the cove for a quick bath; hopefully, the water will revitalise me.

As I walk down the carpeted corridor, I encounter a blockade of House Girls ahead of me before the stairs. I hear a groan leave me, too exhausted to smile against their disdain-filled stares.

Sweets and the blonde lean on the right wall opposite an open door, robes hang loosely over their shoulders, revealing slim womanly figures and flushing skin.

Down that slither of material, I can see... *everything.*

My instinct is to close my eyes, but I'm afraid I'll fall asleep right where I stand. I want to offer them modesty, yet they don't appear concerned at all that I have an eyeball full of their... female parts.

They draw in deep breaths, and sigh heavy, a kind of longing breezing from them as they stare into the room.

Arousal is thick in the air.

I can't see inside, but I can hear fierce grunts punching through long, unrestrained female sounds.

The hairs on my arms rise.

I prepare to stare straight ahead and ignore whatever is happening in the room, as I have a pretty good idea of what I will see. Maple has told me all about it—sex—so it most definitely is none of my business what they are doing to each other.

The blonde turns her head, her gaze taking me in as I approach. "Oh, it's the Lace Girl. Best close your eyes, Lace Girl. Don't want to tarnish your purity and infect your mind."

There is mockery in her tone, but something else as well. Something vulnerable, which is why I don't take offence.

"Or she can get in line." Sweets trails her fingers across her décolletage, humming to her own attention. "I think she should watch with us."

"No, thank you," I say, darting between them and the open door just as Sweets steps into my path. I stiffen.

In my peripherals, I can see movement that matches the erotic sounds beating from the room. My spine straightens to not allow my head to turn.

I stare up at Sweets, anchoring my gaze in her pretty eyes, refusing to give in to the pull from the room at my shoulder.

"*Oh. Yes. Yes,*" someone moans.

A provocative grin spreads across Sweets' mouth when I clench my teeth to the desperate calls from inside the room.

My body hums just being beside the door, energy so tangible it vibrates around me.

"Look," Sweets teases.

I swallow. "I don't want to."

"Yes." She nods. "You do."

No, I don't.

Too exhausted to fight, my eyes snap to the bedroom before I can stop them, the image flooding my vision and filling my veins with warmth, discomfort, and fear.

He is so much bigger than them. It's even more obvious in their position. Lagos pounds into a girl he has pinned on a slight angle beneath his chest with his face between Beauty's thighs. All I can see of the girl on the bed are her hands reaching from beneath, gripping his muscular flanks, holding on, and slender legs gyrating to keep a lock around his backside. Sat on the pillow, back to the rest, Beauty squeezes the strands of his sandy blonde hair, mewling with her eyes closed.

He is obscenely muscular.

Inhumanly powerful.

And all those tattoos... They reach from ankle to neck, wrapping around and cloaking his skin in ink.

I shuffle, instantly dizzy.

I couldn't visualise this huge man with a woman before, because I always thought sex would be gentle caresses, sweet words, and tender kisses. I never fantasised about this kind of brutal intimacy between a man and woman.

"It's frightening." A voice slides into my ear like a whispering ghost.

Sweets take a step closer. I can feel the warmth from the slip of naked skin between her robe curtains, but I don't look away. From his rippling back muscles. The tensing and untensing of his arse.

Look away.

Look away.

Look away.

"He can fuck for a full day." I hear the passion in her voice, the awe in it.

His grunts seem to circle me, coming from everywhere at once. "We close The House when he's in a mood like this. I've already come twice, but he gets bored so easily. There is no human left in him, Lace Girl, and it's never more obvious than when he decides to fuck you."

My stomach clenches.

I don't care that she's probably trying to upset me. Why else is she so insistent at this moment? To make a point—I am not one of them. I understand.

Sweat mists my forehead.

"Does it hurt?" I ask, wiping the beads before they run and draw attention to my heat.

"Oh, *yes*," she hisses. "It hurts. Being fucked by Lagos the Rogue is the scariest, most unsettling feeling in the world."

The rogue. I haven't heard that before. Suits him. I want to look away. My pulse races and I'm breathless without moving an inch.

"Then why?" I tear my eyes from the scene and meet her gaze. "Because he trades with you?"

She scoffs, an amused sound that I don't understand. "You should go back to The Trade, Lace Girl. Let a man pet you and feed you. Take your tea and lie on your back for a nice belly rub."

"I am not a pet." In a second, hundreds of thoughts rap on my tongue. Arguments for the importance of my Trade, for the mental health of Trade men across The Cradle, but before any can be spoken, I notice the silence around us. The quiet slithers down my back like icy water.

Oh, no.

Slowly, I turn my chin toward the open room, and his suffocating presence wraps around me again. I was too busy staring at Sweets, her too focused on mocking me, for either of us to notice.

Lagos is stepping from the bed, leaving the two girls mewling helplessly on the mattress. His long, hard dick sways above full, swollen balls between his chiselled, thick thighs.

I've never seen anything so male.

I back up as he approaches, the heat and heaviness from his

attention pressing on me. He is the one naked, yet I feel unbearably vulnerable.

I lick my parched lips, tasting something metallic on them. For a flash of a moment, I imagine Lagos dragging me into the room and forcing my legs apart, thrusting into me, hurting me, but then—

He closes the door on my face.

Time seems slow, so I shake my head. Try to feel present.

"Interesting," Sweets mutters, a pleased tone dripping through each syllable. "I guess I was wrong." She steps out of my way. "He clearly doesn't like you at all, Lace Girl."

That sentence shouldn't burn.

It doesn't affect me at all…

"Excuse me." I swallow as my throat thickens. I don't wait for any more harsh truths, heading down the corridor, taking the steps as sweat slides between my brows.

I have to be quick.

Spero might need me.

Usually, I have a few hours at this time while he sleeps, but I don't want to take any chances.

Something strange courses through my body, leaving me vibrating as I stride to the cove.

My fingers tremble as I undress and paddle into the water, soon finding its cool bite soothing. The water laps my flushing skin, and the ocean's body holds me.

What just happened?

Why did I watch that?

I wasn't disgusted. In truth, I wanted to be Beauty. I was born to soothe and relieve a Trade man but never know anything impure myself. Never feel a man's touch, remember it, and even know it is for my enjoyment. What Lagos was doing with his mouth was for Beauty's relief. What could he get from that himself? Kissing her there?

If his gaze can make my stomach clench and his proximity

hums across my skin, I am terrified to know what that indecent kiss would do to me.

I am more than *intrigued* by that brute. So obscenely virile… I… I— I dunk myself into the water, wanting to wash the thoughts away. Drown them.

My hair mimics floating wings of red around my body as I blink underwater. The salt burns my eyes. I close them and see Lagos thrusting into that girl, his back muscles alive with power and energy.

It's too much. I want him. I don't know why or what this is; perhaps I'm self-sabotaging. Trying to prove I am like Maple, clinging to something dangerous. It's confusing, and I wish it away.

Lungs suddenly squeezing, I push back up and gasp the clear salt-pinched air. Breathing hard, I walk from the water, beads sliding down my skin.

Then I notice I am not alone. A strange man stands in the cove, watching me while he slowly removes his dark shirt. I can't distinguish his features from this distance, but his physique, height, and girth lead me to believe he is a strong Xin De male.

Nerves rush down each leg. I'm not used to being alone, this sense of wariness, a perpetual shuttering pulse.

Stepping from the water, I gather my clothes and dress quickly, breathing a sigh of relief when, in the corner of my eye, the man wades out into the water to bathe.

I shake my head at myself, clearly overthinking everything. He wasn't looking at me like that— I've been ignored my entire life. I'm not sure why I feel like everyone is watching me all of a sudden. 'Pretty but plain,' is what my Ward said, and it was a compliment.

'Easily forgotten.'

Chapter Nine

Dahlia

Too soon, I am walking past the House Girls again, cringing internally. At least this time, the door is closed, but the same obnoxious sounds beat through the walls. I can hear every thrust through his grunts and almost feel the fatigued agony in the ballad of moans.

"Apparently, it's Tomar who fancies you, then?" Sweets says, leaning her hip on the wall and folding her arms over her exposed breasts.

"I doubt that." I frown, heading straight for my room only to notice it is unlocked. My heart leaps into my throat as I swing the door open, finding Tomar sitting on the bed with Spero cradled in his arms. I exhale hard.

"He sleeps like the dead." Tomar smiles, gaze lost as he looks at Spero. "Such a sweet boy."

"I wasn't gone long. I promise." Scooping my wet hair to the side, it dangles and drips down my chest, wetting my black shirt. Oh. *His* black shirt. A blush of awkwardness spreads across my cheeks.

"I wasn't judging you, Dahlia."

"You don't mind…" I pause, lifting the fabric of his shirt as my face flushes. "That I am wearing this, do you? I found it with the supplies."

"It is for you to wear. Look what you found." His blue gaze moves around the room, taking in the small mobile I fashioned from shells and rope, the bottle-rattle, and the mirror. "You didn't do anything silly for these items, did you?"

My gaze widens. "No. I helped Tide."

"That old geezer let you near his boat?" He lets out a single laugh, and if I weren't so tired, it would make me smile. "Well, it seems you've managed something none of us have. I've been offering to help him for years, but he won't allow it. Stubborn old bastard."

"Why are you always helping people," I ask, and I hate that kindness is so unbelievable.

"I told you," he says with a chuckle, "it's my Purpose."

"And Lagos," I ask, brow rising, "Why does he do it?"

"It's his Purpose, too."

I scoff helplessly. "Sorry, but he doesn't seem the noble type at all. He is—" I see his leer. "Cruel to me, and rude. Unnecessarily."

"It wasn't the Purpose he was born for, sure, but it is the Purpose he chose. He chooses it every day when he protects me so I can help others."

"Why does he dislike me?"

"I don't think he does, Dahlia," Tomar says. "Helping someone like you is not easy for him. Your innocence bothers him—discomforts him. So he's just," he pauses, "intolerant."

Someone like me?

A Trade girl?

"Intolerant. Grumpy." I lift an auburn brow at him. "Grumpy is a polite word for him."

"Maybe. You don't know him." He nods to a basket on the floor filled with cans and two bottles of white powder. "More food and formula. That formula was not easy to get, Dahlia. It's all Trade stock. It'll be even harder when we hit the desert."

"Milk?" I ask, even though finding milk is hard, surely not as hard as sourcing formula. Reproduction in The Cradle is controlled by The Trade, so anything that might aid a non-authorised pregnancy is scarce-to-impossible to find. The Trade will provide everything needed for a safe birth in exchange for the babe. All babies born in The Cradle are declared Trade property. While the Endigo and Common who live outside of Trade towers are free to do as they please, they are also disadvantaged—on their own to raise, educate, and deliver their young. The Trade will not offer any aid to citizens who refuse the regime. "Just plain milk might do for a while?"

I'm not convinced.

"Powdered milk. Sure." Tomar nods dubiously. "For a day or so, but he'll need more than that. We will be in the desert for a week before we get to the Common Community."

"Can we find a new mother?"

"In the desert?" He shakes his head with a soft laugh, not condescending, more disappointed. "Better luck finding formula than a lactating woman who isn't Trade-aligned."

"There has to be something."

He stands with Spero and lays him down in the nest I made at the bottom of the bed. "What I did find is in that basket." He sits back down and clasps his fingers together. "Might help. If you're willing to try it. I didn't want to be the one to have this conversation with you, but I'm all you've got. I did ask Sweets to talk to you about this, but she's been rather..." He clicks his tongue before settling on, "*Unhelpful* when it comes to you. I wrongfully thought she'd mother you, but I believe she finds your presence uncomfortable."

Annoyance rushes through me. Uncomfortable? How? What have I done? I try not to show my agitation, but it comes through a scoff. "How? I barely speak to—"

"*Dahlia*," he soothes, and I stop talking. "Relax. It's not you. It's her. Just like with Lagos, it's not you, it's him."

"They are both so hostile," I mumble, ignoring a pang of rejection. "I'm alone. Doesn't she realise that? I've never been alone in my life. I always had my Collective, always had friends. Why can't we be friends? I feel like a petulant child asking this, but I'm tired, and—"

"I understand." He smiles kindly, and I sigh, relieved he doesn't think I'm stomping my foot because no one will play with me. "Friendship is a nice feeling, but you can't force it. You and Sweets are very different creatures." He leans forward onto his knees, resting his chin on his clasped hands. "Have you ever been beaten by a man?"

I blink at him. "What?"

"Impregnated and forced to abort it by bathing in boiling water or had your wrist bone broken by a man who was too damn rough?"

My throat thickens.

I shake my head, unable to answer. Not needing to. Tomar isn't asking for a response, and I feel such gut-wrenching sadness for Sweets and the other House Girls.

"She kept working with that broken wrist," he goes on, a sad memory sets in his blue gaze. "Don't worry, that drifter paid with his life. I am not excusing her rudeness." He lowers his hands to his lap. "Nor do I want to make you feel bad. I'm proud of you, of your courage to care for Spero. Just understand what you look like to people like Sweets. You're shiny and new. Beautiful in a way that she can never be. It's not just physical, it is the beauty of innocence."

I shuffle. He offers praise and compliments with such ease that they are almost believable. Do I thank him? Does he want something for his kind words? No; I don't think he does. He seems to say things as he sees them. Pretty but plain, is what I thought, but Tomar says I'm beautiful.

Turning my face, I try to hide my blush of pride. It's embarrassing and obvious.

"You're also *hopeful*. To survivors like Sweets, you have had it too easy. Unfairly easy. She can't relate to you, and you can't understand her. I'm not asking for you to put up with mistreatments by her, but simply understand."

"Okay." I chew on my lip.

"Okay." He confirms with a smile. "So, have a look in the basket."

I kneel on the ground and move a few food cans before finding a bottle filled with little white pills. I can't read, but I can see the symbol of the Trade and the number 1000 printed on the label.

"Nutrients? For Spero?"

"No. They're hormones. Getting my hands on that bottle was a miracle," he says, his tone taking on a more serious edge. "Someone is looking out for you. Those pills could solve your problem."

Shocked, I barely move. Maybe it's the sleep deprivation, but I'm not quite following. "I'm sorry, I don't understand."

"Hormones," he repeats. "The Trade often gives them to the Sired Mothers, the women who work in the Trade Nursery, to induce lactation."

I can feel my frown, because the muscles strain. "You mean..." I have to pause to really sort this information in my mind. "If I take these pills, then I can breastfeed Spero?"

"With those new jars, you have enough formula for another two weeks, tops. It's when we hit the desert that I'm concerned about. Use some of that innocent optimism, and it might just work. We can only try." He stands and brushes his finger down Spero's cheek. "Until next time, Spero. Lagos and I will keep searching for formula and powdered milk in the meantime."

I am blinking slowly at the small pill in my hand, amazed that such a tiny thing can bring about a lifesaving resource, especially in the desert, when Tomar walks to the door. "Wait." He stops. "How many do I take? How often?"

"Sorry, I forgot you can't read. Take two daily. One in the first-light and one before bed. Nothing will happen for at least two weeks, or maybe not at all, but I've heard that just having a newborn close to a woman can induce lactation, so hold him a lot. He is yours now, Dahlia." He reaches out and runs his knuckles down my cheek, the same way he did with Spero. "You look tired. Get some sleep while he does. That's the golden rule."

How does he know all this stuff? He drops his hand, and I wonder what it would be like to be held by him. I clear my throat to banish the thought. "But I need to help Tide and bathe while he sleeps. Or I am just…" I can't find the words in my fatigue.

"A mother," Tomar finishes.

I sigh, walking backward to the bed, dropping down like my bones are mere straw.

"I wanted a toy for Spero. That's how it all started with Tide," I admit. "I wanted a bottle."

I can feel his gaze on me as I rub my eyes.

"If you need things, you just have to ask, Dahlia. If you can't find me or Lagos, then look for Beauty. I think she will be kinder to you. You have more in common with her than others. She used to be a Trade girl."

The sound of the door closing is all that sinks in, my mind already half-asleep.

Sleep when he does…

I lie down on the mattress and curl my knees to my chest. Inhaling and exhaling, finding sleep.

~

Most nights since I left the Half-tower, I dream of Maple's silky brown strands parting as I comb through them. I would groom her, and she would tell me stories.

I miss my friend.

And yet, her comforting brown hair isn't what I see tonight.

During my moments of slumber, I'm brushing black hair, and when she turns her chin, it's Sweets' profile I see.

I wake to Spero fussing and crawl to the bottle. I mix the formula. It's unusually quiet in The House; often, I would be cursed to hear bed-springs and groans, but not tonight.

Lagos wore them out.

I wonder if he is still down the corridor. My imagination slides through the narrow passage to the room. His huge, muscular body is sprawled across the bed, face down, forehead resting on his thick forearms. Two naked girls clinging to his firm body on either side, wet from sweat. Wonderfully satiated. They are safe, warm, tingling, and his for the night.

Uncontrolled, I moan.

Sweets' words ring between my ears. *'He clearly doesn't like you at all, Lace Girl.'* Rejection stings me. Why? Because I'm inexperienced? Annoying? I made a mistake trusting the Endigo man!

Okay… I wish I didn't care what that brute, Lagos, thinks of me, wish his disdain didn't choke, but my body has a mind of its own. Chest tight, skin vibrating, heart sinking, biting jealousy— I care!

Playing with Spero's lips until he sucks the bottle, I lie down with him propped beside me, holding the bottle with one hand.

My mind reels with the vision of Beauty's face in sweet agony and Sweets' awe toward his stamina. He likes them. They share a harsh existence. Find relief in each other. Find an escape. I want that. I'm just surviving, too, and I want something pleasurable in my lonely, scary new life.

The image of that man holding Sweets' wrist in the lobby comes to mind. The way he hissed the word *"bitch."* That image slides to one I made up, of her being held down, her wrist breaking as a man takes her with brutal force.

Not the same man.

'He paid with his life.'

Probably at Lagos' hand.

Or fists...

But no matter the situation my mind conjures, Sweets' eyes are always level and proud. She is tough.

Besides finding my Ward poisoned in his bed, and worse, mere hours later watching Maple bleed to death, I have never experienced anything that might build that kind of resilience and strength.

What must she think of me? She probably believes I'm pathetically simple.

Am I?

I don't want to be.

After caring for Spero, he falls asleep, but I stare at the dark ceiling, finding the quiet uncomfortable. Agitation over Lagos' mean ways gathers in my stomach. Guilt and sorrow toward Sweets tighten my forehead. I wish I could do something to help her. I'm not a weak, fragile Lace Girl. I would have cut Lagos with my hacksaw that first day, and I ran away from a safe life, from Meaningful Purpose and all that I knew to protect someone else's baby. Isn't that character? Does that not hold any value to… I bite my lip at his name—Lagos.

Tomar sees more in me.

Maple did, too.

Soon, I'll show him.

Chapter Ten

Dahlia

I've been at The Bite for nearly two weeks, and this is the first opportunity I've had to approach Sweets without Spero tucked against my chest.

I want her to take me seriously, and I'm not sure I can do that with a babe at my chest, wriggling and fawning.

Luckily, Tomar told me he wanted to show Spero the glowworm tunnels now that he is gazing around, assessing the world with fresh baby eyes, but I think Tomar wants to give me a break.

My upper neck and into my crown have been aching for a few hours, so I massage it as I head down the stairs to the lower level of The House. Tomar said that may be a symptom of the lactation medication I'm taking daily now with my spaghetti in a can and dried fish strips he prepares himself for me. He is a really kind man, and whenever he is near, I am so thankful for everything he does for me—for everyone.

Crossing the lower level of The House, I head into the ruby-hued room for the first time. A slow drum beats through the space, heavy, seductive, and only slightly louder than the murmuring voices. A fire blazes in the den, creating a halo. Men sit around scattered tables while House Girls, dressed in thin corsets and light skirting, dance on top, their bodies arching forward and luring backward to the steady beat.

Outside the glowing centre of the room, a shadowy ring blackens into corners and hides more beings. The silhouettes of men, of women—Endigo, Xin De, and Common, perhaps,— can only just be seen, but I feel the humming energy from one specific area. Lagos. I can't be certain, but my body is suddenly awake.

Instantly hot and sticky, I smooth my shirt-dress down my stomach and flick my red hair over my shoulders, the long ends dangling to the small of my back. I approach a high, long counter and step onto a metal footrest fastened to the bottom to get slightly higher.

"Where is Sweets?" I ask the pretty blonde, who rolls her grey eyes at me.

"You shouldn't be in here."

I sigh hard. "Why?"

"Because it will make him mad if you're here. He seems to want you locked in that room."

Not what I expected. I thought she would mention Sweets... My brows pinch. "Who?"

"What do you want?" Sweets appears from a dim outer pocket on my side of the bar, stopping just in front of me, forcing me to look up to meet her unimpressed gaze. "Not getting enough of Tomar and Lagos' attention, huh?"

Oh my. Even in the dim lighting, the purple and red ballooning around her left eye is vivid.

My stomach knots. "What happened to your eye?" *Who* happened?

"None of your business." She folds her arms over her chest as the salacious scene continues behind her, our voices kept private by distance and the steady drum. "What do you want?"

I clench my jaw, talking through a cage of teeth. "Did Lagos do that to you?" I don't know why his name is always the first to enter my mind. I guess I want to hate him. Want a reason, an incomprehensible reason, so I can convince my body to despise him also.

She shakes her head slowly. "You're so jealous. A girl knows, ya know. You can't keep his name off your lips. And I see the way your breath catches when he's near. He has that effect on everyone; even the men seem to vibrate and get hard-ons in his presence."

She must be out of her mind if she thinks being *taken* and beaten is what I want. I don't know what I want from him. *His touch.* I just know that I wish it was *nothing.*

"I know you don't like me."

She huffs a laugh. "How observant of you."

"I don't care. I have something for you." I dip my hand beneath my shirt-dress and reach into the back pocket of my pants. Retrieving the felt purse, I hold it in front of me for her to take.

She stares at it. "What is it?"

"La Mu seeds and some roots."

Her eyes widen and then land on me, but her entire body language has shifted. "Why?"

Everyone knows that La Mu is rare and illegal to grow or carry. Lace Girls are one of the only Trades besides Doctors who have stamps in the Half-tower to exchange for seeds. "You can grow the plant without soil. It grows just fine in water, but you will need to plant it somewhere down here that has at least a little crown-light. A gap in the cave somewhere?"

She blinks at the purse, unmoving. "Why?"

I know she is asking why I am giving it to her, but I pretend she is asking about the plant. "It is an incredible plant. A little bit of the root, no more than your smallest fingernail, is an anti-inflammatory. But the seeds..." I open the purse and show her the tiny grains. "The seeds are a contraceptive. We mix one into our tea every night. It has to be *every* night. You can't miss one. The plant makes hundreds of seeds for a few months a year so you could have enough for all four of you if you grow four plants." I look at her, at the blackened skin around her eye, and dark anger claws at me. "Use an entire finger's worth of the root next time he visits you, ground it up and mix it into his liquor."

"What?"

I grab her hand and put the purse into her palm. "They all drink liquor, right?" That is the royal, 'they', and she knows what I mean because she nods.

"Yes."

I keep her hand in mine as I say, "Don't let him do that to you again."

With that, I turn to leave the den, feeling better in a way I cannot describe. A way that takes me by surprise. Giving her the La Mu might save her life or get her revenge, just like Isle did with the La Mu she traded for my leather jacket.

Just like Isle... Two weeks ago, I thought what she did was horrific.

Now, I get it.

I didn't think about what handing that precious, rare plant over meant to me, for me. Being a Lace Girl and La Mu are mutually exclusive. We use all parts of it. We even moisturise with the oils. It's why we smell a certain way, men notice and realise we are Lace Girls, that we must be shielded from impurities. I'm letting that go and moving on without it.

"Stop." Sweets' voice halts me mid-stride—mid-thought. "You know Lagos hasn't spoken to me since I let you watch him with Beauty and Naturale. I have no idea why, but he really doesn't like you. He told me to keep you out of his business."

I don't turn around in case she sees my throat roll as I swallow thick disappointment.

"I don't care," I lie. A big fat lie.

She clicks her tongue, seemingly hard up for more mean comments, but finally says, "Thank you, Lace Girl."

"Dahlia," I correct, peering over my shoulder at her, taking in her stunning silhouette set against the deep scarlet background.

The erotic beat hums in my bones. "I'm more than my Trade. I can be anything now."

She scoffs. It holds amusement, but not callousness for once. "Dahlia. A flower." The undertone of envy flattens her voice. "Typical name for a Trade princess."

"A Trade princess?" I feel my brows weave. "I've never heard that term before."

"Some Trade people are named like, river, mountain, right? But you're a prize for a man, like a Silk Girl or the likes. Kings sell princesses to keep the peace and seal alliances. Trade princesses are used the same way. Ultimately, you're a bargaining chip to control the Trade men. A treat for good behaviour. You're all named after flowers."

I never thought of my Trade as a means to 'control' Trade men but as a way to help them. It's therapy. This idea doesn't sit well in my stomach at all, deceit gnawing me to a new perspective. "Yeah, but the Dahlia flower comes in all shapes, sizes, and colours," I point out. "Maybe I could be a House Girl." I shrug before leaving the ruby-hued room, deciding to walk to the glowworms to meet Tomar and Spero.

Chapter Eleven

Dahlia

Pedalling Spero's feet, I pretend he is on a little bicycle. It's slightly cold down at the cove today, but he is warm and pink from our pretend baby-workout.

It's fun to play with him, and he has started to look at me. Really look. And his gaze of wonder… It's something else. It almost overpowers the headache I've been cursed with for days.

Stars could be bright, the moon magnetic, but a baby's awe is magic.

"Tonight, I'm having lemon on the fillet Tomar brings me," I say to Spero, my voice a silly, playful beat. Yesterday, after I untangled four nets, Tide offered me a lemon that a drifter gave him in exchange for a fish. I literally bounce in the air with excitement. "Who's a lucky girl? I am. I am a lucky girl."

I am being silly with Spero, melting against his playful gurgling, when a slither of energy tickles my spine and the hairs on my arms rise...

I look up. *Of course.* Only *he* can make me feel like every part of my body is vibrating all at once—Lagos is crossing the cove, his hair pulled tightly into a bun at the back of his head. The shiny plate above his ear appears to be the shape of a quarter-moon. He is in the same black shirt I sawed a line into, with the hood gathered on his shoulders. It is too small for him; his muscles form shapes beneath.

Guilt hits me. Clothing is not abundant for people like us, and he may be a giant brute who hates me, but he has helped me. And probably hundreds of others alongside Tomar—

"I can fix that," I say, keeping my tone light and casual.

He pulls his shirt over his head, long, thick muscles up his sides tightening, moving. My belly clenches at the display. He drops the ripped shirt to the stony floor, and I consider grabbing it.

"I can sew," I add, hopeful. "I'm good, too. If you wan—"

"It's just a shirt."

He is so cold.

"I'm sorry," I say plainly. He looks at me—bored. "That you have to help me and Spero. I know you don't want to. I'm sorry. I appreciate your help."

"Thank Tomar." He starts to unbutton his jeans, his large hands drawing my gaze down to the thick girth of his hips.

"I will." I stand and smooth my oversized shirt down my pants. I wish I'd worn my shirt-dress, but it was dirty. I don't know what comes over me whenever he is near, but it's equally primal and pathetic. Magnetic, even. A power inequality that throws me over.

Out of the corner of my eye, I notice movement on the steps. Over Lagos' shoulder, three girls I have seen around The Bite descend, their gazes coy as they linger on the massive Xin De male.

"But I want to thank you anyway." I smile at him because he's quite beautiful, in an annoyingly brutish way. "We're not the same. I should just accept your perspective—"

"Save me the sensitivities, Lace Gi—"

"Dahlia!" I spit out as the three girls stop a few metres away from the massive, brutish man everyone seems obsessed with.

Removing their clothes, stripping down to nothing at all, they eye him as they move into the water. Long naked legs disappear into the cool cove bath.

He is still looking at me, a slight grin in the corner of one lip. "Dahlia," he says my name, and I almost lose my balance. "A little flower."

"That I'm sure you'd love to step on. Look, I will stay out of your way from now on. I didn't mean to see... What I saw. You and the, erm..." *Oh*, why is my tongue not working? "If I see you, I will walk the other way. If I need something, I will go to Tomar."

His brows knot in harder as his eyes assess me before he shakes his head with a gruff sigh. "Listen."

Shocked, I square my shoulders as he suddenly strides toward me. Grounding my heels, I refuse to shuffle backward this time. His huge form, a powerful machine now sauntering toward me in only ripped black jeans, open at the top. In the opening, a dark-brown patch of hair makes me feel weird things...

My mouth dries up. My eyes widen when he stops, so close. Too close.

Breathe.

"Tomar said you have been trying to get things for yourself. Why?" I crane my neck to look up into his black gaze, noticing the tiniest slither of grey banding each large pupil.

"It is my fault the Hub is gon—"

"Have we not been providing for you both? You and the infant?" A deep voice like melted steel, and I barely hear the words.

My mouth doesn't work. "What?"

"Tomar wants the burden of this infant, so it is mine by default. And you're his guardian. I'll keep you both alive. Outside of that, you don't need more. I'm not here to pamper you. If you need anything urgently, you come to us." His jaw pulses, and I wonder if he's uncomfortable. He talks like razor blades line his throat, every word expelling with pain. "I'll try to get it for you. Do you need anything urgently, Dahlia?"

"Urgently?" I tuck my lower lip between my teeth, chewing. Then say, "*You* want to protect Spero?" *And me;* my mind screams those two words, but I don't question them in case he didn't mean them. "The baby you said to kill?"

He sighs roughly, a sound similar to the long, low growl of a beast. "If The Trade finds him, you will wish I had killed him quickly, but it's not up to me."

"So you don't *want* to kill him?"

"Why would I *want* to kill a baby?" He reaches out a big hand and cradles the back of my head. His touch is warm, and I try not to melt into it. That scent, safety, shelter—it's him. "You come to us. You need something, you come to us."

"No." Shaking my head, I try to understand. "But… you told Sweets to keep me out of your business. And now you want me to come to you?"

His brows draw in over a dark stare, making me shuffle. "No. I told Sweets to keep you *away* from my business."

Huh? "Is there a difference?"

He steps closer, until my jaw falls open as my head cranes back. A lording form in front of me, formidable, yet it pulls at me. "Yes. There is a difference, Lace Girl Dahlia."

I can't stop myself. Can't keep the words in when he is this close. Can't deny my body or the way it shifts, gravitates toward him. I want to know. "Do you dislike me because I'm a silly Trade girl or because I got in the way?"

"I don't dislike you. I don't think about you at all." His words cut deep, but they betray the energy pouring from him and beating against me.

The dominance in his tone curls my toes into the stone. He goes on, "You're young, fragile, Common, and you will abandon that Xin De infant when you realise the danger that follows him."

He doesn't trust me.

I hold his gaze. "I won't abandon him. I promise."

His already black eyes darken. "If you do, and the Trade finds him, death at my hands would have been a mercy for him. Understand?"

"I won't abandon him!"

Then his focus shifts to Spero on the ground beside my feet, and I share my gaze between them. Watch them eye each other with a keen and strange interest.

"Do you want to hold him?"

Lagos slides his hand from behind my head and steps backward from us.

"You're my responsibility now," he states, his tone deep, his attention still tethered to Spero. "Until you're both safe, you're mine."

You're mine.

Two words.

And I panic.

Not in a bad way— Wait... not in a good way either. In an overwhelmed way. By everything I feel, his words, closeness, and the fact he is actually talking to me. Not just grunting.

I don't move a muscle... Can't seem to convince my legs that the conversation is over, and I should move away from him...

Move away, Dahlia!

Oh, I wish I wasn't attracted to him, but then he drops his jeans and briefs at the same time, exposing the entire, long length of his form.

And he wades into the water.

I can move now. Inhaling the air, the scent of metals from the boats and salt from the sea mingle. I scoop Spero up, not wanting to witness whatever happens between Lagos, and the three girls waiting patiently for him to notice them. I walk away. I'm feeling a little better, knowing he doesn't want to hurt Spero and doesn't hate me, when a giggle from behind me snaps at me like a whip, jolting the truth into my head—I'm jealous.

Chapter Twelve

Dahlia

"I love it," I whisper, staring at myself in the mirror in Sweets' room. Her space is slightly larger than mine, with the same basics, yet it is full of clothes and colourful drapes—an explosion of fabric.

Spero gurgles on her mattress, chubby fingers fumbling with a soft piece of silk. Silk is rare and royal, not an easy fabric to come by in The Cradle. I have heard that Silk Girls wear only silk, a fabric to match their station as the breeding girls for the lords of The Cradle. I wish I could feel it on my skin, all over me; I'm certain it is divine.

Dressed in a cream corset that shows the tops of my breasts, bone structures hold me tight down the curve of my waist, and a frilly, cream lace skirting, I'm something between a Lace Girl and House Girl. My red hair ripples down my spine and over each shoulder, pieces in chunky tendrils. It's wild and uninhibited.

Lagos might like me like this.

"Men like the fantasy," Sweets says, standing behind me, the chipped full-length mirror showing her reflection. She dabs the end of a perfume bottle on my neck, scenting me with citrus top notes and deep base notes of vanilla. Another rarity her trade probably provided her. "Every man wants to fuck a Lace Girl while she sleeps."

"But I won't be asleep." I turn to face her. "And they will know that, right?"

"You'll be pretending, and they will know. It's just a game. You'll bring in a lot of attention, Lace Girl, just like when we first got Beauty. She was our prize. Our little Trade Nurse. She plays nurse with them, and they offer up a good exchange." She smiles, delight glimmering in her eyes. "What do you want? Chocolate? Fabric to make clothes? New boots? A hairbrush?"

I don't have to think long. "Ginger. Butter. Flour. Sugar," I say.

"Really?" Sweets curls her nose. "Fresh butter will be difficult. You don't want a gem," she breathes, "like this." Her delicate hand comes to her chest, fingertips dancing along the fine-linked chain to a deep red stone.

I chew my bottom lip, scrutinising my body in the mirror again. I've never looked like this before. If I saw myself on the streets, I may even be jealous. That makes me smile.

"Can we try?" I offer a little shrug to show I'm not counting on it. "If not, oil will do, but not animal. Vegetable or flower oil is best."

She turns me to face her, hands now on either side of my upper arms, supportive. "Are you sure you want to do this? Lagos and Tomar have been looking after you. You don't need to."

"Yes." I nod. "I'm my own person now. I belong to no man. I want to know what it feels like to be with a man, and to be desired. Lace Girls are ignored. I've watched men grovel for House Girls in the Half-tower. Chase them, need them intensely like their last breath." A flutter of excitement fills my stomach at the thought of requesting butter, of having men offer me jewels, having them drop chocolate between my parted lips, so they can taste it on my tongue… *Oh,* my cheeks burst with pink, my shameful fantasies on display.

"I can choose a nice man for you," —dropping her hands from my shoulders, she faces herself in the mirror to adore her own lovely reflection— "for your first time, but the gentle ones typically don't have very interesting exchanges."

"It's not my first time," I say straightaway, more to myself. The idea of my first time being with a stranger makes my stomach churn. "I've been with my Ward many times. I was just in the Deep Sleep."

"Then it won't hurt as much, your body will open for them, but you have to relax. You'll probably tighten up because you've never felt it before. Remember to breathe." She inhales through her rosy lips and exhales a few seconds later. "Big breaths. In and out."

I follow her as she sashays across the room, her body swaying, seduction carved into her soul. I don't walk like that, so I study her movements, her salacious lilt.

"Do you know a man who can get me butter?" I ask, my lower lip folding into my teeth.

"I only know one man who can get butter, and he *is* a gentleman but does not take kindly to the word no. So, just... be agreeable."

Lagos isn't a gentle man.

The unwelcome thought forces me to swallow. She doesn't mean Lagos. He can't get butter and wouldn't; it isn't urgent.

It doesn't matter. I'm doing this because I want to be independent, feel a man, be adored, and I want something for Tide. He found me lemon, and I don't feel comfortable asking Lagos for something as silly and non-urgent as ingredients to make ginger cookie dough.

"Okay. A gentle man," I accept. "What would I say no to anyway?"

She turns, her brows have hit her hairline. "A lot of things, Dahlia. A *lot* of things. Men do a lot of weird things. I will tell him it is your first time—as a House Girl—and hopefully, he is happy to keep your first interactions vanilla."

"Vanilla?"

"Yes, meaning…" She considers her words carefully. "Standard sex. Cock in pussy. Talking to you is like speaking to a child. How old are you?"

I don't take offence. It's honestly fair in this case. I have skills growing La Mu and sewing, but I'm conditioned to be inexperienced in the ways of men.

Time to change that.

"Twenty-two, I believe, but they changed my birthday in the Lace House. One year I was six, and then a new Wardeness took over, and I was eight. My age went back and forth a few times. I am not sure why. I don't think they actually knew."

She huffs dubiously. "Or they wanted to confuse you on purpose. Men like young women. So, they upped your age without your knowledge."

I blink at her, remembering the moment I was gifted to my Ward. A young girl with red hair tied back in a lace bow. I had breasts and pubic hair, but I remember feeling tiny beside him; it was the first time I'd ever met a man. All Common girls are small in comparison to a man with Xin De genes. My Ward was not Common, though his engineered genus was subtle.

Not like Lagos.

My Ward held my hand in his as they gave him instructions on how to care for me, how to treat me, what I liked to eat, and so on. "So, I could have been quite young when my Ward took me in?"

"But you're not now." She stands behind me again, her head over the top of mine. Turning me, she presents me to the mirror again. "Now, you're a woman, and nothing makes you feel more like a woman than being with a man."

~

I've scrubbed myself with soap from head to toe before dressing in the cream corset, matching skirting, and thigh-high white stocking Sweets found under a pile of sheets. They are too long for me, so I folded the tops and created a neat band around each upper thigh.

Spero is with Tomar for the night, as I told him that I wanted to spend time bonding with Sweets and The House Girls. I didn't elaborate, and he didn't ask any more questions, quite smitten with our tiny assassin.

Across the den, three girls dance on tables, and several bodies are eclipsed by dark corners. Men and women, Common and Xin De, conversing privately as everyone seems to do here at The Bite.

I don't know what to do.

Sweets said I should dance, but I'm not a great dancer… I do sing. I used to sing to my Ward, so instead of joining the other girls on the tables, I sit beside the drum and will myself to sing.

I search the black pockets, trying to see into the depths of each private corner, but I cannot decipher shapes or forms. Still, I am almost certain Lagos is not here. Usually, I feel his eyes like nails dragging down my spine.

Drawing in courage, I inhale and exhale into song, a shanty about fresh air that matches the tempo of the drum.

At first, my voice trembles, so I close my eyes, blanketing the shadowed figures scattered around the room and the gyrating bodies on the tables.

And as I sing the words, I recall the feeling I felt when I first heard them. It's an optimistic song, and yet, melancholic, just like breathing in clean air.

When I was no older than eight, on my first day at the Lace House, a strange girl crawled into bed with me without so much as a greeting but instead with a song. This song. I was terrified to start my studies and prepare for Meaningful Purpose, but Maple was full of peace and strange energy, as if she saw things outside of reality. Somehow, she was a protective force, steady and confident.

I followed her after that night—I would have followed her, my closest friend, to The Crust that day I left the Half-tower.

If not for Spero.

Tears moisten my eyes, sliding beneath my lids, but I don't open them as I sing. It's dark in here; perhaps no one will see my friend's memory punishing me with grief.

Grief is like an old wound, one moment you're moving forward and living in the present, then something happens, and you bump it, or nothing happens, but it flares with pain. It opens, and you bleed again.

I want to cry hard. Weep. To sob each word through my lips, but the song ends abruptly because I forget the last verse…

I inhale and exhale.

Blinking the tears away, I open my eyes to the pressure of every gaze in the ruby-hued room.

My throat goes dry when the silhouette of a man rises from a corner and approaches me, his gait slow and assertive. Coming into view, I see a familiar man but can't quite place him.

"Where did you learn that song?"

Wiping at my eyes, I take a moment to fully emerge from my pit of melancholy. "Um, a friend taught me. Did you like it?"

His eyes crease when he smiles, showing his age, and his height dwarfs me, denoting a Xin De gene along the line. "You're far too innocent to be a House Girl," he mentions, lips quirked. "You're new, aren't you?"

I peer up, meeting his gaze. "Are you a drifter?" Where do I know him from?

If he was from The Bite, he wouldn't need to ask that, though, everyone from The Bite is a runaway, just as Tide said.

"Yes. Just passing through."

"And you're lonely," I say with a shrug.

He laughs as if I wasn't meant to point that out or draw attention to this faux interaction. "Yeah. Loneliness is the greatest misfortune. Are you lonely?"

Yes… I miss my Collective.

I only smile. We both know why he is here, why I'm here. To exchange. It is not different from any formal Trade work, not really. Trading is the blood that courses through The Cradle, whether aligned formally or organised in the desert; it is the lifeforce of our land—what heals it and bleeds it dry.

"I have your gentleman in the corner. Very taken by our new Lace Girl." Sweets touches the man's shoulder, dismissive but polite.

"A Lace Girl?" The drifter smooths his shirt down his chest, drawing my gaze to the tight physique underneath. He was the one at the cove, too far to see any facial features, but... I'm sure it's him. He has a captivating aura. "Well, give a man a chance. What are you asking?"

I lift my chin. "Butter, sugar, flour, ginger."

He eyes me. "To make cookies?"

"Yes!" I beam. "How did you know? Well, cookie dough, really. I don't have an oven to cook the cookies, nor do I know how to."

"Why ginger?"

"Because it is a strong flavour, and Tide might actually be able to taste it. My friend, Tide. He has no sense of smell and can't taste much. I wanted to do something nice for him."

He hums. "What about cinnamon?"

"Cinnamon?"

Rubbing his jaw, a cool grin slides above his hand. "Cinnamon cookie dough would be very flavoursome."

"Excuse me." Sweets grabs my arm and gently pulls me to my feet, guiding me to the side. Her lips touch my ear. "I don't know this man. Are you sure? I have the other option waiting. He will get you butter."

I listen, but feel a pull to this stranger, one that draws my gaze to him again. Eyeing his strong physique, I imagine myself alone with him. Beneath him. Feeling him. Uncertainty nips at my stomach—alone with a strange man. How would a drifter get a spice like cinnamon, anyway? What does he do? Perhaps he'll tell me. I imagine sharing conversation, gazing at each other, our intimacy having smashed the boundaries strangers have. I could sing for him or talk his ear off, and he could care for me...

Oh, no.

My chest tightens.

"I can't," I say. Closing my eyes, I sigh hard. I'm not her… I'm not Sweets. I realise at this moment, while a spice trader and another man with butter cloaked in a dark shadow await my decision, that I don't want to be merely a body. I want companionship. Accompany, relieve, and soothe—my Trade.

Tide's words cascade back in waves of disappointment. *'You can take the man out of the trade, but you can't take the trade out of the man.'*

I open my eyes. "I'm sorry, Sweets. I don't think I can do this." I almost say, maybe tomorrow, maybe another night, I can try, but the words are merely a blanket to suffocate my guilt. I let her down. I don't want to have sex with a stranger, even if it is one of life's great experiences.

Recoiling, I am readying myself for her sneer, accepting it, even, when a loose smile forms on her lips. "Keep the clothes." That is all she says before approaching the drifter with the bad news. I can't listen to her excuses, so I stride from The House.

Can't look back.

I purse my lips and frown. At this point, I couldn't imagine a deeper sense of shame. Eyes cast downward, I cross the stony walkway and head toward Tide's boat. The street lamps glow a deep, moody red, so I know it's past midnight, but I don't fear the eerie night time atmosphere because my embarrassment and guilt are killing me just fine.

Still in my stockings and corset, I approach the old dinghy. Tide is unpacking, throwing the canopy back, ready to hit the black seas and work into first-light. Out there alone on the crashing waves. Haze-suffocated stars probably glimmer behind sheets of thick red mist. I imagine that night time in the old-world would have been beautiful, and people would gather outside just to stare dreamily at the sky.

I sigh, but it must be dangerous at sea now in the almost pitch black with the hungry swelling waves.

I grip my hips and stare at Tide, all alone. *Yes, I am lonely.* But I have him.

The Bite is quiet at this time of night, gloomy and still. I've not ventured outside at this time before. Usually, I would be in bed with Spero, awakened by baby cries or obnoxious groans from the adjacent rooms. This is a nice change.

"I wanted to make you ginger cookie dough." I stop beside his boat. I don't know why I'm here but seeing him floods me with relief. My reluctant friend—my only friend. "I couldn't get any."

He lifts his head and squints, playing at not recognising me. "What are you wearing there?"

"Sweets' clothes." I sit down on the edge of the rock, the same place I sat two weeks ago when we first spoke. "I wanted to know what it felt like to be her," I admit.

He huffs, amused. "You should just be yourself."

"I don't know who I am."

That laugh rattles from his chest; I've become very fond of it. "You're you. Bits of every place you have been and every person you have spoken to. Unique."

"*She* is unique." Fiddling with the end of my skirting, my nails brush my naked thighs, sending goosebumps across my skin. "I'm just my Trade. Even in this," I say, smoothing the pretty cream material over my lap. "There are hundreds of me, of Lace Girls. We are all the same."

"There's already one of her."

I lift a brow at him. "That's a little confusing."

Watching him hunched over the boat, his old body shaky, I realise how much I'll miss him when I leave in a week. He's a grumpy Trade Fisher who can't smell and doesn't want any friends or help, but he likes me. Even if he won't admit it.

"You like me, hey?"

"You're very annoying."

I take that as a yes, revel in it for a moment, and almost miss the way his face falls. His eyes widen on something over my shoulder. Rising to his feet, his mouth moves. It takes me a couple of seconds to make out the words.

"Get behind me, Dahlia."

My spine stiffens, locking me in place while my head turns just as a large black figure approaches like a wraith. Only now do I realise just how dark it is. He is towering over me in an instant, moving faster than my mind can follow.

But I know who it is.

The drifter from The House drags me to my feet with one hand and turns me to face Tide. My eyes widen as my friend's expression shifts from helplessness to horror.

I go to scream, but the man covers my mouth and snarls into my ear.

"Where is the infant?"

"You leave that girl alone," Tide warns, lifting a weak hand and pointing a shaky finger. "She is just a House Girl. We don't want trouble."

Thick, rough fingers pinch my nose, stopping all air from entering and exiting my body. Panic pours through my veins like an icy blade. I need air, thrashing around in his hold as darkness slowly creeps into my peripherals. Losing consciousness.

The man releases me, leaving me confused and gasping for air. I collapse to the floor. The world spins, but I fight the dizzy feeling, desperate to stay on all-fours.

"Say goodbye, old timer."

I crawl on my hands and knees, struggling, and I watch. That's all I can do. I watch as the drifter steps onto the boat and plunges a knife into Tide's stomach.

A choked scream tries to break free as I gasp for air. Tide's trembling hands cover the wound, blood trickling through the gaps of his fingers. He looks past the man to me—looks right into my eyes as though he wants to step toward me, to help me, but his legs give out.

He drops on his knees. Sways. Then lands on his face.

"No!" I manage to scream, but then the man is over me again, moving with a gracefulness a person of his size shouldn't have. It reminds me of Lagos—the way he moves. Lagos. Tomar. I could run to them. Can I run?

"Where is the infant?" My scalp burns as the drifter drags me to my feet by my hair, strands ripping from my crown.

I cry out.

I look back at Tide, unmoving, lifeless. It's my fault. Unable to accept what I'm seeing, I shake my head, shaking the horrific sight. Drowning in guilt, in fear. "No. I don't know what you want." I know there is pain racing along my head, but I'm still wheezing, staring at Tide's body— shock a blanket of disorientation.

"The infant you had at the cove, Lace Girl."

I don't respond. Can't. *Tide...*

The drifter holds me up and punches me in the face, beating a black world into my vision.

I groan, blood trickling from my nose. He's going to kill me. Like he did Tide.

He releases my hair.

My body drops to the hard ground, my hands meeting wet puddles of blood from my gushing nose. I sob on my hands and knees, willing myself to get up, but my legs tremble.

"The infant?"

"I won't—" is all I can spit out.

When a boot collides with my stomach, I jerk to the side. An unyielding heel rolls me to my spine. I cough blood upward, spraying my face with the wet, hot fluid.

Stepping either side of my body, the drifter leans down and takes a fist full of my hair again.

"Tell me where the infant is, Lace Girl," he hisses, face close to mine. "And I'll cut out your tongue so you can't share your story, but let you live. How's that sound, baby? Fair? I think so. If you disagree, I'll get it out of you eventually. Another woman's infant isn't worth the pain you'll experience at my hand."

Another woman... I sob.

Maple.

Spero.

Worth every inch of pain I can endure. I don't want to die, but that doesn't cloud or confuse me. "I won't tell you."

A cruel laugh escapes him, the heat of it slithering across my face. "Yes, you will, baby."

I roll my head on the ground, confused, my ribs aching and nose swelling, constricting air. And the blood. I can taste boiled metallics, iron or… I can suddenly smell it in the atmosphere.

I struggle to stay conscious so I can fight back while he pins my wrists above my head. "You're a mess, baby. You should see your pretty face covered in blood."

Blunt pain hits my stomach.

"Aren't you lonely?" he says, tone roughening. "I could tell you were. I'll send you back to your Collective. Just tell me where the infant is."

Another punch.

He is beating me…

My vision crinkles in the corners. I blink over and over, trying to clear the image of the man hovering over me.

Pain flares through my side.

I don't know what he did to me. I tense up, my body ready for more pain when the drifter lifts his head. "The infant is near."

What?

He can't be. Even though Spero can't be nearby, I reach out a shaky hand and grip the drifter's shirt, trying to hold him to me, to keep him from standing.

"Oh, baby," he chuckles. "Do you want to play with daddy? I can give you attention after."

That's when the atmosphere thickens with fine needles, pricking my flesh and the taste of liquid metal slides along my tongue.

"Did Master send you?" the drifter says over his shoulder just as he's ripped away from me. "What are you—" The sentence is cut to a howl of anguish that embeds in the rocky walls.

I cough blood over my face, feeble in any attempt to move. To escape whatever is happening. I want to crawl to Tide. Check on him. Maybe he is still breathing.

"Close your eyes, little flower."

Lagos...

He's here. A wail leaves me, weakness and fear bursting free. Relief, shock, and so much pain burns to the surface. I want to see him, to make sure it's actually him, not a construct of my dying mind.

I squint. The silhouettes of two huge bodies clash and waves of energy seem to outline them as they fight. The smaller black figure quickly becomes parts, his arms torn from his torso and tossed into the black ocean beside us.

I can't hold my stomach. Squeezing my eyes shut, I turn my head and heave, but can't give in to my broken body.

Tide...

Through a guttural groan, I stagger to my feet and stumble along the boat, crumpling to a heap at the side of my grumpy, old friend.

"Tide." I reach out and turn his face, seeing the smallest of life twitching his lips. "You're going to be alright, Tide. Lagos is here."

"Dahlia," he wheezes, anguish holding his features in knots. "I can smell."

I sob. "It's blood."

"No. No, it's you. Perfume."

Tears rush over my eyes, coating the vision of him clinging to life. "It's Sweets'."

"I like it." And with that, the tightness in his face softens, taking on the same still, peacefulness that Maple's did weeks ago.

Death's serene presence.

I give in then. Lying on my back beside him, a complete bloodied mess, I sigh heavy relief when I hear bones break on the rocky ledge. When I know they are not mine.

PART THREE
THE ROGUE

Chapter Thirteen

Lagos

She is unconscious.

Blood covers her cream corset and stains the pale skin across her chest and arms. Her hair is a red matted mess. I can't identify her injuries in the fucking dark, with all this blood.

I rip her corset down the middle to find her torso swelling on the left-hand side, around her defined ribs. With barely any fat or muscle on her, very little protects her lungs.

And her skin, thin and soft, barely keeps her together.

Fucking Common.

They are unbelievably fragile creatures.

I wrap my hands around her ribcage, encompassing it entirely, and trace the channels between each bone with my thumbs until I feel the breaks. One, at least.

My blood boils. That Shadow fucker kicked her, crushed her nose, split her lip, fuck knows what else. I scoop her into my arms, expecting her to be light, but… She is made of nothing.

Young. Weak. Fragile.

Fuck.

They can't find her.

I stride through the puddles of blood caked across the dusty limestone. All that is left of the fucker who hurt her. Bones and flesh in the ocean. It won't happen again. She stays with me now, until I deliver her and the Shadow baby to the Common Community.

She stays at my side.

Until she is safe.

The rocks crunch beneath my feet as I make my way through the dark rocky corridors and down to the subterranean stream.

In response to my presence, glowworms brighten, illuminating the walls and each lancing stalactite. I take the old cavern stairs with her flopped in my arms.

Check her quick.

Fully clothed, I stride straight into the underground lake, needing to clean her wounds so that I can see the damage I'm fucking dealing with.

A long whimper leaves her split lip; still, even in this battered condition, she is pretty. I noticed the moment I saw her, noticed and hated it. Hated her green eyes filled with fear and sorrow. She looked up at me, and—fuck me—her eyes perfectly reflected my soul. Large, glistening, olive-green orbs of fear and disgust.

Something inside me said, *there she is.* The thing you have been waiting for, the reason for it all. Something pure and gentle that sees you for what you are—inhuman. *Someone* to remind you how real humanity glows and trembles.

Take her.

Fuck her.

She could be yours.

That was pathetic humanity clinging to me— And I felt like killing someone after that. Remind myself who I am and what I don't deserve to touch—Her. Anyone pure and good like her.

Not again.

I followed her that first day because my blood could sense her lie. I watched her bathe and sensed she wasn't Maple. Stalked her to the Hub, where she exchanged her body with that fucking Endigo. No way was I allowing that, even if he'd left her unharmed.

Which he probably would have.

But fuck, did the vision of him with his cock between her pale, flawless thighs fuel my veins for his death. I've never killed a townie before, but I didn't even blink. Red was a mist over my eyes.

Hate their kind.

Mine, too.

Submerging all but the little Lace Girl's face in the blue pool, the water ripples around her perfectly formed figure. It's hard to ignore such a feminine shape, wet and half-bared to me.

She groans as I wipe her face, noting the splits and cuts, the gashes and bloody paint. I see the very moment she comes to. Pain assaults her—cripples her. Her face tightening, auburn brows furrowing above long brown lashes waved over her wet cheeks.

"Tide," she croaks, a throat full of tears.

Dead. He's dead, and grief is not something I waste time on—an emotion without purpose.

"He was old," I grunt.

With her eyes closed, helpless sobs escape her, jerking her entire torso in my arms. She suddenly screams as her physical pain and anguish collide, but she doesn't stop weeping.

"Stop crying over that old fool." I support her body as she trembles. "You're broken."

"Tomar!" she growls, green eyes snapping open, full of anger, disappointment, and betrayal that spear my calloused heart. "I don't want you. You'll never understand. He was my *friend*."

I grind my teeth.

Her need to mourn is a burden. I'm not a soft man. My skin is hide, a thick coat that holds darkness and depravities, but I need her to stop shaking her fragile body around.

"Stop fucking crying!" I growl, trying to scare her into

obedience, and her eyes burn true hatred up at me. The kind the stars feel.

My iron-blood howls, and a fierce self-loathing twists the muscles that hold her.

Should drown her.

Save her from more of this... Pain. Loss. Reality. Death is sweet. A release. An end to suffering. She is too weak, innocent, and vulnerable for this damn world.

Too innocent.

They did that.

Kept her like this.

I inhale hard, close my eyes, exhale roughly, and open them to her glassy, bloodshot gaze. I try again. Gentle. Controlled. "Take it easy, little flower." I keep my voice low and steady. "I need to find your wounds, so I know how to hold you." I pause. She closes her tear-ridden eyes, locking the cold vision of me out, and nods her head once.

Good girl.

I push her red hair from her cheeks and splash the water on her wounds, gauging the depth by how quickly fresh blood swims out into the rippling pool. My chest aches. A real sense of guilt tears through me when I see the bruising waking up over her swollen ribcage.

Could have stopped this.

Guilt is another useless emotion.

My eyes travel over her supple, flat stomach submerged just below the water, and I frown. Is she hurt anywhere else? Why is she wearing this corset?

Don't go there.

Cradling her with one hand, I brush the other across her abdomen, and her muscles tremble beneath my touch. I squeeze the length of each leg, checking for swelling, but I'm pretty certain all her injuries are above her waist.

Internal bleeding creates a bulb at her hip, but blood only leeches into the pool in small, elegant swirls of scarlet. It's not heavy. I lift her from the water, and little fingers curl around the fabric of my shirt. I tense up.

Good girl.

Don't look at me.

"Keep your eyes closed." I can't bear her eyes on me, not this close, as I walk her from the lake and back toward the docks.

Her torso and little tits are exposed—I ripped her corset open. Too close to me. A surge of un-fucking welcome possessiveness rushes through my veins. I lift my head, scanning the area through a scowl. Making sure no one is strolling the roads of The Bite at this hour, warning them not to approach me. She is not like the other girls I interact with.

The girls at The Bite are ruined, broken, and lost. I can work with that. Can touch that. I can be their dark warrior, the monster who keeps their rogue town safe, reaps vengeance for them during the day, and fucks them at night. No expectations, intimacy or gentle hands. They like it. The bloody vendettas and all I stand for.

She doesn't.

I step onto the cat and duck into the hull. Pass Tomar's room. The baby is in there. She'll wake him. I head for my cabin, shoulder the door open, and lay her on the single bed. Water seeps from her damp red hair into the pillow—my pillow.

I stare at her. Still.

What the fuck am I doing?

Her nipples harden, and I squeeze my fists at my side. Freckles dot her chest and over her breasts, with a few on the hard tight beads. I need to fix and cover her and push her the fuck away. Fast.

Reaching for a towel, I lay it over her and lightly dry her through the fabric. And by the time I have the acetone in a sealed bag of water for cool compression, she is unconscious again, breathing deeply. There might be peace behind her eyelids. Might be lies and innocence.

Don't want to disturb that.

I knock twice on the wall. "Tomar." I lay the cool packs on her wounds, nose, ribs, and her left hip. Done. Thank fuck. I cover her again. "Tomar."

When he enters, rubbing his eyes back from slumber, I slide down to the floor beside her, press my back to the bed, and stare at the wall.

He freezes. "What happened?"

Keeping my position beside her, like a damn guard dog on the floor, I manage to convince my body to lean aside, allowing Tomar access to her.

He dashes out and returns with his med kit, and I glare at the wall, molars clenching in my jaw, while he checks her over.

"So?" I bark, firmer than I meant to.

He is hovering over her. "Her nose is fractured. Lip split, but not enough to warrant stitches. Swollen. Everything is internal."

I thought so.

"I could realign her nose by hand, but it'll hurt like Hell, and I don't have any Opi for her."

I nod. "She will have Opi."

"But *I* don't."

"Then don't touch her." *Don't hurt her.* Her nose was perfect. "A little imperfection would do her wonders," I grunt. I'm an arsehole.

Tomar steps back from the bed and stares down at me. "I'll see how she feels about it when she wakes up." His eyes lock on my face, suspicion and concern obvious in their blue depths. "What happened to her, Lagos?"

"We have to leave." I growl, fighting back my anger, and look up at him. "They found her."

"Who?"

"A Shadow."

His shoulders sag. "That's why you ran out of here like a bat out of Hell," he states to himself, not me. Probably wondering why *I* saved her, why I was the one. Why she is in *my* room.

He likes her.

Can't blame him.

"Is she naked under the towel?" he asks, voice tight.

Calm. I stay very still. "Almost." I don't have an honourable reputation when it comes to women, and one like her… I'd never tarnish with my murderous hands. He must know that about me. After everything we have been through, he knows the pleasure I allow myself—women—is a basic necessity. Not romantic or intimate. An animal instinct that brings me to pain without it.

She's too human for me.

"Any injuries to her body?" he asks, and I hear him shuffle.

Is he reluctant to look?

"One rib is broken," I answer, because I don't want him to look. "Others fractured, perhaps." I direct my attention back to the wall and stare at it, hiding my thoughts. "Swelling around her abdomen. No skin tears. No stitches are needed. He wasn't trying to kill her or do too much damage. Or she'd be dead."

"He was going to take her back to The Trade." Tomar closes his eyes, shaking his head, before opening them again. "Poor little thing. A broken rib will make travel painful." He strides toward the door, saying, "She needs to be cleaned, and cool compressed, and—"

"I did it."

He stops. Looking back at me on the floor by her bed—my bed, *my* fucking bed—and then to her unconscious, he tries to read the situation. "You're happy to give up your bed for the girl tonight? When she wakes, I'll move her into mine with Spero if she wishes. Let her decide where she is most comfortable."

"Fine."

Fuck, that was hard to say.

He exhales with satisfaction, the single word that struggled along my tongue filling him with relief. Makes more sense for her to be in his room. Fucking Lace Girl Dahlia, with her pretty eyes and perfect skin, needs to stay the hell away from me.

"We have to leave with them tomorrow. We can dock for a few

days by the fall, but then we have to get away from The Bite. If they send more Shadows, they'll find us. They will sense us."

I grunt. I know.

"You'll get the cat ready? We need to give Sweets, the other girls, and the townies all the supplies we have for the month. We won't be back again for a few weeks."

I nod. "I'll do it at first-light."

He stops and the weight of unspoken words thicken the air between us. An inevitable message twitches in my veins. It is a constant reminder.

He finally says, "We can't risk me being out of action for a day. Not with Dahlia and Spero. Tomorrow, while we are at the fall, we need to drain you. You need to be in control, in top condition while we drive across The Cradle."

My eyes cut to the little flower, wary of our privacy. "I know."

"While I'm out, you'll need to listen out for Spero. I'll feed and change him and put him to sleep. Just listen. I might not wake up straight away, and she needs to rest and recover." I stiffen, so he adds, "It is only for a day, Lagos. He's incredibly sweet and easy."

Turning to leave, he pauses at the threshold of my door with his back to me. "You won't hurt him, brother. Not everything you touch breaks."

A cruel smile slides into place.

That's where he's wrong.

Chapter Fourteen

Dahlia

Water lapping, a motor humming, the scent of oil and liquor and blood all seep into my senses in slow waves of consciousness that pull me from the dark, peaceful space I'm in.

Then pain.

Along my abdomen, sharp agony throws a cry up my throat. I try to sit but scream and fall backward, hoping the flare of pain will stop if I lie still, but it doesn't.

It continues now that I'm awake.

I squeeze my eyes shut and block out reality as it tumbles back. The image of the drifter beating me and the helplessness I felt.

"Don't move, little flower."

Lagos.

When I hear his deep, otherworldly timbre, relief floods me, bringing with it the hazy recall of his sharp jaw and black gaze. Of his face over mine. Of his big, rough hands washing me in the cove, carrying me through the streets, and…

That's all I remember.

My eyes flutter open to see him cross the room to a table. He is shirtless. Bulky muscles roil beneath tattooed skin.

I peer down my body, seeing a loose black shirt, the neck scooping lower than my collarbone and hanging off one shoulder—the thing drowning me to below my knees with a hood flap at my back.

But it's the rip in the middle, exposing my hip, that catches my breath. It is *his* shirt. The one I tore a few weeks ago.

"Lagos," I beg. I didn't mean for his name to sound so desperate, but every muscle hurts so intensely that I can't feel the ones that don't.

"I've got you."

He returns to the side of the bed, leaning over me; his warmth is a blanket of safety. That's his presence. I don't know how a man so cruel and cold can somehow make me feel the safest I've ever felt.

A cool glass touches my lower lip. I part my mouth, and as he pours a familiar bitter liquid along my tongue, I blink over the rim at him. At his rugged and brutally beautiful face so close to mine. I thought his irises were black, but they are dark grey, like steel, a strange colour that I cannot tear my eyes away from. As if gravity resides within that hue.

I swallow, and he leans back, saying, "Opi."

I know.

I nod. "I know the taste."

"We found it in your pack."

"Spero?" I feel odd, my throat rough, voice hoarse from overuse, but I can speak without pain.

"Safe. With Tomar."

I sigh into the mattress, my body sinking. Heavy eyelids beat my vision away. I don't fight fatigue. Warmth curls inside my stomach as the Opi works, a serpent of blissful ignorance coiling around the pain, *hiding* it.

It works quickly, sporing into the bloodstream through every vessel. It's small molecules that ride red blood cells. Less than a minute; that is how long it takes to reach every corner of the body. Such things I learnt in my studies. To make sure we don't drink our tea and then decide to stand.

Grief hits me. "Tide."

Lagos rises. "Sleep."

Without thinking, I reach out my hand for him, wanting his warmth, fingers lingering in the void of his body, just before everything goes black.

Everything is hazy, my memories, senses and the feel of my own body, but time is rolling while I am in and out more often than I can recall.

I have nightmares.

Reliving the beating.

Crawling to Tide...

Too late to save him.

When I open my eyes again, they sting with tears. I blink. I see a large circle of light reflected opposite me on an unfamiliar door. Was that always there? I blink at it. Where is that coming from? Where am I?

Lifting my chin, I manage to look over my head at the wall behind me. There is a small window filtering muted light. Like the portal ones on a boat...

Am I on a boat?

Tomar and Lagos. *Spero.*

The names come back with clarity. Just as I lift my hand to rub my eyes, something slides along my forearm like a thin snake.

I look down at my body. A black shirt swallows me. Oh, that's right—it's Lagos' shirt. Did he... undress me?

A tube, with a clear fluid, lays over my arm. I follow it to the back of my hand, where it disappears beneath a strip of tape and into my flesh.

Panic surges inside me. "What is that?"

I follow the other end until I see a bag hanging from a rail. Whatever is inside it is going into my veins. I've seen this before… The memory helps me settle. In the Lace House, a girl named Banksia was mauled by a cat, and they administered medicine directly into her veins.

Then I hear, "We could have taken the infant to the Common Community without her."

That's Lagos.

Stilling my every muscle and breath, I wait silently and listen to the voice outside the room.

I don't feel the slightest bit guilty for eavesdropping. Spero is mine, so any conversation involving him is mine to hear. I try sitting again, but a pang of pain strikes just below my breast, warning me to make each move with grace and caution.

"We could have left her with the Marshals. Now we have an extra burden with a damn broken rib and annoying voice."

Broken rib?

I cup my side and wince.

Annoying voice?!

I scowl at the closed door. And I know I should be grateful to him. He didn't have to help me, didn't have to put himself in danger for me. But he did. He saved me.

He's still mean.

"She was *meant* to be the mother," Tomar states, his voice flat… *Too* flat. Is he unwell? "She was meant to be lactating, so he would have food as we cross the desert." His sigh is heavy, and I can almost feel it from here.

"But she isn't the mother, is she?" There is a heavy pause. "Go rest. I'll check in with you tomorrow." With that, footsteps fall outside the door just before it opens.

I am glaring at the gap that Lagos now fills, burning a hole into his bare chest.

"Just the welcome I expected." He smirks. "Are you in pain or just that pleased to see me?" He strides in, all those muscles rippling with each step. It's male—so very male, and I despise how much I want to feel them beneath my fingertips.

I hold my rib and cut my gaze to the bag on the rail. "What is in there?"

"Fluids," he grunts. "And Opi."

I glance at the needle under my skin. "Did you put this inside me?" A shiver rushes along my spine at the thought of him caring for me while I sleep. Of him touching me gently. Of his hand on mine.

Removing my soiled clothes…

"No." He slumps to the floor, severing that unwelcome vision.

Through a slight wince, I peer over the edge of the bed to find a green, thin rollout mattress on the floor.

"Tomar did it," he adds.

Lifting his knees, he makes his huge body somehow fit into the space on the floor.

I watch without moving. "What are you… What are you doing?"

He cups the back of his head. "Resting."

"In my room?"

And closes his eyes. "It's *my* room."

I huff—my annoying voice. "Well, can I go back to my room? I have things in there. My *beibao*, my… things." My sentence trails to a whimper. *Oh...* Sorrow claws at my abdomen. "Things *Tide* gave me."

He hums, indifferent.

Anger burns through me. I see Tide's body bleeding out, hear his rumbled chuckle in my heart, and wish I didn't go there that night. Tide. Maple.

Who is left?

You're alone.

"I want Tomar!" I don't know why, but I want to wound Lagos. To reject him. Lashing out at him feels mean and… *good.*

Unaffected, he rumbles sleepily, his voice darker, deeper. "He won't be available today. Give me an hour to sleep, Lace Girl, and I can be at your beck and call instead."

"I don't want—" I groan, my face growing hotter and hotter with irritation. Breathe. He saved me. Be gracious. "I don't want him at my *beck and call.* Just…" I lift my hand and cover my eyes, wanting to cry from pure emotional fatigue. "Where is Spero?" I drop my hand. "Who is watching him?"

"Tomar just fed him. He's asleep."

Well… I stare at the ceiling. My skin prickles with the need to jump up and do something, walk, wash, anything human, but every other part of me protests. I'm exhausted. Fatigue holds my muscles. Holds my mind. I am not ready to face the world. A place less wonderful without Maple and Tide… I stifle a sob, not wanting Lagos to hear.

"You didn't hand him over." Lagos' sudden utterance crashes down on me.

I swallow my tears and clear my throat. "What?"

"You took that beating, little flower, and you didn't tell him where the infant was." And he sounds angry, disgusted, even.

"Of course I didn't," I say, and to my horror, my voice shakes at the memory. I thought I was going to die, but in the moment, I recall only wishing it happened fast. Spero's whereabouts would remain a secret if only I die fast…

A dark chuckle leaves him. "Like it's what anyone would do in that situation? You're wrong. This is The Cradle. Women sacrifice their young all the time to save their own skin. You're foolish. The infant isn't even yours. Isn't even human."

Neither are you.

I breathe, only half in control of what I say or do due to the Opi in my system. So much Opi. More than I've ever had before. I'm sinking into exhaustion even as we speak.

And his crumbs of concern are wiped away by blatant prejudice, making me want to curl into a ball. People I care about are dying, Maple and Tide. My heart presses further into my chest, hiding. I lost Maple, lost Tide. I will not lose Spero.

"I don't care *what* he is. He is mine."

Without looking at him, I sense his disapproval. Feel the air around me still... freeze... My declaration hangs in the atmosphere, then he finally growls, "Don't do that again, little flower." His voice is dark and gruff with an authoritarian edge that accepts no argument. "Don't save his life if it means risking yours."

I sniffle. "You saved me and risked yours."

"It's endearing that you believe I was ever in danger. I told you that you're mine until you're safe. Take every word from my mouth as a certainty. I don't lie."

But who will protect me from you, Lagos?

Chapter Fifteen

Dahlia

I blink and then focus, only to realise I must have drifted off again because Lagos is no longer on the floor.

Cupping my rib, I sit, unable to spend a moment longer in this bed. In this room. I sway in place; my brain is loaded with Opi. But I want to get Spero and go back to our room at The House. Stay inside and behave like a good girl.

My heavy head sways on my neck for a moment, and though I don't feel pain, I can tell my lip and nose are swollen.

Then, something beside me moves. I peer over and see Spero in a nest of blankets, staring at his hands, quietly getting to know each digit.

A wave of joy moves inside me, my heart singing, 'You. It's you. All of this is for you, sweet baby.'

Right, it's time.

Steadily, I swing my legs around and find my feet dangling, a foot from the floor at least.

I look at the ground, knowing I have to slide off and take a little drop. The bed is high, which makes sense, seeing that Lagos is a behemoth.

Indecision suddenly stops me from taking the small plunge. Maybe I should call out to Lagos for help. Common sense inside me says to ask for a hand down. Pride holds my tongue.

Lagos might be rude and a bigot, and I want to hide my heart deep inside my chest when I am with him…

I clear my throat. But he *has* always helped me when I needed him. If only his caring actions matched the words spouted from his lips. He just… infuriates me.

I peer down at his shirt, a curtain of black that rolls over my knees to my calves. My nipples pebble inside the oversized fabric, and I blush. My body reacts to him, betraying me—eyes refuse to look away from his sculpture form, fingers knead to feel the fluid movement of his muscles.

But my heart will toughen.

He is a forty-something-year-old Xin De monster, and I am a young Common girl born for lace. We are not the same. He will never feel and love the way I do or be vulnerable and curious the way that I am.

"Don't you dare."

I look up to find him standing in the open door. A formidable force like him should come with thunder, not silence.

Bury your heart.

Still feeling my nipples beading, I swallow as he stares at me in his shirt. His brows draw in, and he moves to the bed, getting into my space. His warm magnetism moves me, pulling, pushing.

"Arms around my shoulders." His deep voice caresses my ear. Abruptly, he scoops me from under my backside. I hold my breath and his neck as he takes my weight, before carefully setting me on the floor.

His hands are still on me. So close. My chest touches his, his warmth embraces me, his scent becomes the only thing I can smell, and we don't let go.

Time… just… slows.

Does he like his hands on me? Do I feel nice beneath his rough fingers? Do I smell nice?

I like your hands on me, Lagos.

Or maybe it's the Opi.

Quietly, I peer up the massive torso above and against me. I stare into his intense steel-coloured gaze. "What happens when we get to the Common Community? You leave us there, and then what should I do?" I don't know where that comes from… I know the answer; I take care of Spero. My Purpose. I raise him. That's what I do.

His hums. "Live with your kind." When he straightens, my hands slide from his shoulders. "They farm." His voice flattens, closing off emotionally. "They are all Common. They'll teach you how to live like your own kind."

With what seems like a great effort, he edges backward, adding space between us.

I want to reach out and grip his shirt, pull the big brute in and kiss him. I wonder what it would be like to have him kiss me… To kiss me like he kissed Beauty—where he kissed Beauty.

My head lolls.

But I stand taller.

He's looking at me. I like it. Now he can see all of me looking like a pile of red hair and slim white limbs. I shuffle, my knees rubbing together nervously. I pinch the bottom of the shirt drowning me, and shrug. "It's a bit big."

His dark eyes dip down my body, stopping at my bare feet and flicking back to my face. I blush under that sharp gaze.

A smooth grin pushes his lips out. "Well, I am a bit bigger than you."

I flush deeper. I don't know how to react to him today. Hating him is easier, but when he grins like that… A private place between my legs seems to awaken, making me squirm in front of him.

And he watches. *Notices.*

"I need to pee," I blurt out. Cringing, I close my eyes to block out his face.

"Opposite this room."

I peek one eye open.

"Do you need help?"

Both eyes open to his smirk.

"No," I say straightaway. I don't know why he seems gentler today, but I appreciate it.

And hate it.

And feel weaker.

"Thank you. I can manage. I'll go slow." I chew my lower lip nervously. "Any chance I can wash up before I go back… How long has it been?"

"Come up when you're finished." He ignores my question. "I need to see you eat something. You have Opi in your system, so take it easy. You'll see where to bathe on the top deck."

On the top deck?

"Wait." I straighten, feeling my brows pitch with confusion. I am missing time. "We're not at The Bite anymore?"

He turns to leave. "No."

What about Sweets?

About my silly things?

Through my hazy mind, a terrible thought surfaces. Where is Tide's body? We left it there. Maybe he's alive.

Dread hits me.

Perhaps he found aid or is still bleeding out on his little dinghy. How long has it been? Hours? A day?

No, no, no. I want the images and thoughts to go away. He was dead, no, he *is* dead, and I had to save myself—for Spero.

And I was so scared…

I clutch at the ache in my stomach. Feels like it will fall out. I was just whisked away from all the chaos my baby caused, and—

Lagos suddenly leaves the room, and the questions in my head mash together. A drone of fear and truths.

I stand opposite the door. Blink at it. This is what Tomar warned me about. I will always be in hiding. If I choose to care for Spero, people might die, and I will leave them for him.

Chapter Sixteen

Dahlia

Leaving Spero swaddled safely in a nest, I take the small steps up the centre of the catamaran to the top deck. Using the rail, I'm cautious. Though the pain is not too great, swapping my weight from foot to foot makes me aware of my light-headedness.

I hear a hiss of cascading water. Then, through the white noise, a conversation presses through, tones and inflictions, but not complete sentences. Only words: impure, fucking, her, something about needing a fuck.

The deep voices pause, probably hearing my footsteps, and I quicken my pace so they don't think I was trying to eavesdrop—again.

"Coming up." I step onto the deck and freeze. Gaze around in awe. We are definitely not at The Bite. A screen of water to my left and a rocky structure blocks my right. Overhead stones and the mouth of a spilling waterfall collide. We are hidden behind it—inside it. And it's a wonderous white curtain that encloses us, hiding us from view.

I close my eyes and sigh. I would have never seen such a thing, such a beautiful part of The Cradle if not for Maple and Spero. Great experiences… food, soap, sex, and I think I have my own to add… I smile. *Nature*.

Trade citizens are herded into towers to protect us from the Redwind, given Trades to offer us Purpose, but at the cost of discovery and adventure. Of finding who we are in our mind.

And it isn't simply our Trade.

I open my eyes. "It's so pretty." I revel in it. The waterfall mists the air with cool, briny droplets that sheen my skin and dot my eyelashes.

"It's falling water," I hear Lagos grunt from somewhere not too far away.

"Well"—I smile at his grumpiness because it's stunning and he must know that. Deep—deep, deep, deep— inside that thick skin, he knows. "Some things must be prettier when they fall."

"Hm."

I blink, breaking the small clear orbs on my cheeks. How I wish Maple could see this… She deserved so much better. My heart twists, and I suddenly feel as though I owe her for this.

For all of this…

For this glimpse of The Cradle beyond the Half-tower, outside the regime.

"Please come sit with us." Tomar's voice catches my attention moments before the top of his head appears on the far side of the ship. He waves me over. "There is no spray over here."

I inhale and try to clear my thoughts. "What were you talking about? Please don't stop on my behalf."

I begin toward the back, careful not to trip over the ropes and frames of the catamaran. It is pieced together rather than designed—each element appears salvaged. Mismatched and tarnished but strong.

Slowly, Tomar comes into view. His skin is ashen, with thin blue veins visible beneath his cheeks. He looks unwell. "You look pale, Tomar. What has happened?"

"A little off." Even his voice seems distant. "I'll be fine. How are you? Your nose looks much better now the swelling is down."

I don't care about my nose or the dull ache in my side. I take a step. This area of the large cat is obviously where they spend their time above deck. Fishing rods are set in holders, and large, old tackle boxes are fastened to the edges.

Lagos suddenly appears at my side, his hand on my elbow, helping me over a lip in the frame.

I peer up at him, at his dark-blonde beard and serious gaze. "If you keep this up," I tease, "I'll start to think you have a heart."

"That would be a mistake," he states, cold, letting go of me the moment I am on the flat. "Bathe, eat, and go back to my room."

My room... I wish I didn't feel those two words inside my stomach.

"Fine." But it isn't fine. I'm not fine with that. I don't want to go back to *his* room. Turning to Tomar, who smiles softly, I find myself grinning lazily at him. "Were you talking about sex when I came up? Is that why you want me to leave?"

Tomar coughs out a "No!"

I lift my chin. "You said something about needing a fuck. I can handle it." I move around and carefully sit on a small, fold-out chair opposite him.

"Is this the Opi reduction effect?" Tomar asks Lagos, forced amusement in his tone.

Oh, he's right. Heavy doses of Opi can yield a sluggish and dazed aftermath. I have never taken it twice in twenty-four hours, though I know many Lace Girls who have. Their Wards enjoyed them often, but mine only required me once a month because he was older, much older than me. Though I liked him as a person and a man, I was never attracted to him.

I glance at Lagos once, just quickly.

He is stiff-backed as he moves to a box fastened to the back wall and opens it. "I said give a fuck," he clarifies. "Not need a fuck."

I frown ahead. "I want knowledge of all the great experiences in life." I didn't mean to say that aloud. "What's a better way to learn than from two men like yourselves." I apparently have no control over my own mouth right now.

I don't gaze across at Lagos again, but I don't need to. I feel the air beat with disapproval, ripples of energy coming from him, but he says nothing. Does nothing. Am I imagining his tension? I try to push further, testing. "I don't want it to be a mystery to me. Why are these conversations so private?"

I focus on Tomar, a beautiful man who is almost too kind to exist in a world like this. Warm gratitude moves inside me. I do like him. He is a much safer and quieter option to Lagos as a companion. I only wish my body agreed.

He rubs his jaw, hesitation challenging his response. "To be honest with you, I don't know anything about sex, Dahlia. I can assure you, that's not what we were discussing."

I scrunch my nose. "I don't believe you."

Tomar chuckles, but his brows draw in. "I think you should eat something, Dahlia."

"Why are you laughing?" Shuffling on the chair, I adjust myself, wincing once when a needle prick of pain hits my rib. I continue with a breath, "I'm not a child. I'm a grown woman."

I'm not sure why I felt the need to clarify that, but the words come out with a defensive snap.

Lagos' body is warmer than the air when he stops at my side. I don't look at him. Don't need to. I seem to be able to feel him, even without touch, achingly close to me.

A tattooed hand holds out a piece of dried fish in front of me. "Eat," he demands.

Tomar nods to the food, and I take it as he says, "I'm not laughing at you, Dahlia. I would never. I am more like you than you realise. You were protected from depravities. In an echo chamber of *specific* information. I don't want to discuss this—"

"Tomar is abstinent," Lagos says, sitting on the side of the boat. He crosses his feet at his ankles, and it's any wonder the catamaran doesn't tilt under the mass of his muscular body.

I cock my head. "What?"

He smirks. "He doesn't—"

"I understand the word, Lagos!" I shoot him an agitated look but find his eyes dark with warning, like he doesn't want to talk to me about sex. I take a breath and look at Tomar. "Why?" I don't get it. "Why would anyone abstain from something so healing and therapeutic?"

Tomar glances at Lagos and then back at me again. I think he hates this conversation, or it makes him uncomfortable, but he says, "It's distracting." He shrugs. "And I have a Purpose."

Lagos seems to find time for it. The thought comes fast and unwanted.

I clear my throat. "But… It's meant to relieve, to soothe, to bring peace—"

"And it can." Tomar points at the fish in my hand, and I take a bite. A flick of pain reminds me of my split lip, so I nibble the fillet instead.

He continues as I slowly eat. "But it is also addictive. A temptation. Remaining celibate, abstaining from sex, avoids inner conflict. I can't choose a woman over my Purpose."

I blink at him. I have no idea if he's being honest with me, but it doesn't make sense. It goes against everything I have been taught by The Trade. "And you believe that if you have sex, you'll… be distracted from your Purpose? That is the opposite of everything I was taught."

He smiles gently. "There are different kinds of Purpose. Mine is entirely consuming. It's a chance I am not willing to take, Dahlia. Neither should you."

I'm struggling with this information. "But it must be a good experience to have such a positive effect on men. Right?" I find myself needing a clear answer. Digging for one. I was conditioned to believe my Trade saved The Cradle from decades of depression and suicide. That's all true, isn't it? The nausea of deceit sinks to the pit of my stomach. Is it all a lie? To what purpose?

My pulse beats in my neck. "What about lowering blood pressure, loosening muscles, clearing a man's mind?"

"Sure." He sees right through me. Leaning forward and holding eye contact with me. "If a man is in love and it's kind and consensual, then it can be a great experience. A loving one."

"Don't soften this." Lagos uses his shirt to open a bottle of liquor. The kind I'm not familiar with. "Tell her the truth." He drinks from the spout. It fizzles. "Tell her—"

"If a man is without it," Tomar cuts in, his voice strangely hard. "Or denied…" He struggles with his message before admitting, "This is very unpleasant to explain to a young woman such as yourself, Dahlia. It is the most basic of needs for a man. Primal. Wanting it is—"

"Wild," I finish, thinking about the way Lagos' body moved over that girl, the way Beauty mewled like a feline, the erotic sounds, grunts, and groans.

"It can become an obsession," he confirms.

"But women like it, too?" I see Beauty's face twisted in pleasured agony. What was he doing between her thighs… Lifting my chin, I stare straight at Tomar. "I'd like to try it."

"Lace Girl, quiet now," Lagos says, tone deep and gruff.

"Well—" Shock lodges in Tomar's throat, and he coughs into his fist. "Well, I think it will only distract you from Spero."

My cheeks flush. "Maybe when I get to the Common Community, I will find a boyfriend, and I'll have sex with him." I can't seem to stop my mouth. "While I'm awake. Both of us. Would be awake." I lock my lips, halting the provocative nonsense. But feel the current of disapproval on my cheek. I risk a look at him—Lagos—finding his eyes have darkened, his attention pinning me to the chair. "A farmer's son, maybe," I say to Lagos as I stand, and his jaw pulses. "To teach me how to live like my own kind." I walk to Tomar, stopping at his side. "Will you listen out for Spero while I bathe?"

He doesn't move, looking strangely stiff in his seat. "Of course.

You can access the cave around the side." He stands awkwardly, perhaps because he's unwell, preparing himself to guide me.

"Please, I'd like to go alone."

His uncertain eyes sweep the length of me. To convince him I'm capable, I straighten my back and ignore the tightness in my side.

After a few moments, he relents. "Okay. We have lowered the ramp for you; it's only a slight gap anyway. You'll see a hole in the overhead formation where the fall trickles through; it collects into a small pool. You can shower there. Are you sure you're alright to go alone? What about your rib? I could face the opposite direction while you bathe but be within reach..."

My pulse flusters to the vision of Lagos watching me shower like he did that day at the cove. Though, I could have imagined that... *Oh,* I probably imagined it. "I'll stand under the water. I won't use the pond, so I should be fine."

"Yell out if you need me."

I nod at him. Impatient to escape the heavy gaze setting my skin ablaze, I set off toward the private rocky space.

Chapter Seventeen

Dahlia

Under the soft glow of worms, I pull Lagos' black shirt off with one hand and cup my side with the other, supporting it. I ache, but I'm slow and careful as I move and stretch.

I leave my knickers on.

Prickles race across my thighs and arms; every little blonde hair stands to attention as the salty air kisses my skin.

There are rocks to get closer to the careening ceiling of the cave, closer to the downpour. I have always liked a bit of pressure when I shower. I take the steps and shiver as the cool ocean water blankets my body.

My breasts draw up, nipples stiffening on the small mounds. I am sure my body feels healthier than it should, thanks to Lagos. A hazy memory of his hands cleaning me in the cove, applying cool compression to my wounds, comes back in flashes. With them, guilt. I yelled at him. Lashed out.

I shouldn't have.

I should thank him.

Sighing, I wash my arms and chest. The water pinches at my

open wounds, reminding me that salt and minerals mingle in the clear fluid. That's good. The Cradle's natural antibacterial source.

Pulling my red hair forward over my shoulders, I work my fingers through the wavy tangles. I flick my hair back, the long, water-soaked strands slapping my spine. I feel good for a moment and forget, twisting to clean my backside when the pain in my rib roars.

A cry breaks my lips seconds before the thundering of heavy feet approaches from behind me.

"Flower—"

I turn around and freeze. Lagos is only a few metres away, staring at me naked and dripping with water.

The cave shrinks, a narrowed world that includes only his gaze and me. His eyes fall to my toes, lazily travelling upward, lingering at my trembling thighs, over my belly to my breasts.

His attention snaps to my eyes.

I blink at him. *Speak. Say something.* "I'm fine. I just… twisted in a..." I swallow as he strides toward me. "Strange way."

"*Mine.*" The depth of his tone rumbles through me, and I can't breathe. As he stalks into the downpour with his clothes on, he adds, "To keep safe," in a way that seems forced. As if that wasn't what he meant at all. That '*mine*' was the word urged up his throat, cut from a deeper thought he wants to deny.

He stops a stony step lower than me. I peer up at him, standing so close that his massive body blocks me from the downpour, offering me only the rush of water that touches him first.

It is overwhelmingly intimate.

And I see his nictitating membrane for the first time. The third eyelid swipes from the side, clearing the tiny beads of water from his near-black irises. It is a unique Xin De trait that humans engineered. The gene was originally copied from birds or some other beast.

His warm hands grip my hips. "Turn around slowly." He eases me to face the other direction. My heart races up my throat while I oblige, now staring at the rocky formation.

His body isn't touching mine, but I feel the entire length radiating from my ankles to the last red hair on my head.

"I didn't like that," he states.

My brain is mush. "Didn't like what?"

With one hand holding my hip, the other slides across my belly and up between my breasts. He washes across my chest lazily, possessively. "Filth coming from your sweet lips."

I can't move. Parts of me want to tell him to leave, and much stronger parts want every inch of him to stay. Close. "That's a *you* issue, Lagos," I manage to say, and am so proud of myself.

But he continues, unfazed. "You talking about sex and getting fucked—" His hand lowers, huge and warm, caressing my belly. "By some Common boy." Every tiny muscle beneath his touch clenches and awakens. "Most of fucking all," he grinds out, "I despise the way Tomar looks at you."

I moan uncontrollably.

"Your moans are so fucking sweet. I wonder if you moaned in your sleep or if these are also mine." His praise is a deep caress, and I want more. When his firm torso meets my back, the long, hard surface is like a wall closing in. I shiver. *Oh my,* I'm caught between massive hands and his body. *Caught...*

I feel a private place between my legs clench and unclench, restless. Demanding. My feet shuffle apart on their own accord, welcoming him. A big hand moves down into my knickers.

My heart thrashes in my neck, between my ears, beating all over my skin. It is any wonder I can hear him, but his voice is clear and depthless. So deep it might be spoken directly into my mind.

"Do you want to know what a Lace Girl is to a Trade man? What they really are?"

His hand cups me between the thighs, and it is so big that his palm holds my pelvis while his fingers thread under me. Unable to stop myself, I rock in the cradle of his hand, my head spinning with confusion and something else...

"A tight cunt to fuck his sorrows into each night. She stays sweet. Stays pure. Humble. And she doesn't see the effect she has on him. How she makes him vulnerable, unravel." He presses something hard into my lower back. As I realise what it is, my eyes widen on the rocky structure ahead. "How *obsessed* he is with her. The Trade doesn't want her to realise how much control she ultimately has. *Fuck* no." He grinds against me and his long, thick middle finger skims my slit, drawing a whimper of need up my throat. "They can't let her have it. It's *their* control."

"*Lagos...*" I should stop him, but then two strong fingers slide up and down messily, touching me. I grind against his palm, and he hisses, grabbing me *there.* Hard.

"Stop, little flower," he rasps, his timbre like gargled gravel. "You're hurt. Let me play with you while you're fragile and can't stop me. Stay still. It's not your fault. You're not giving me your innocent mind. I am taking it from you."

I drop my head back, meeting his hard torso as he awakens nerves that I didn't know I had. He builds them up, up, up. Then there is no cave. No water. No pain. No salty spray. Just his fingers sliding up and down, and then—

He edges one inside.

My mouth drops open and long moans escape my lips.

"Are you okay, Dahlia?" Tomar calls from around the corner.

I panic.

"Lagos!" I squirm.

"Answer him," Lagos orders.

"What?"

"Answer him, or I will. And I will tell him exactly what I'm doing to your sweet body."

"I'm... I'm fine," I call out.

"Do you need me?" Tomar's voice sails from behind a rock.

I feel Lagos' chest rumble with annoyance, so I quickly spit out, "No, I'm a bit naked at the moment. A bit..." *Vulnerable.* "I'm fine."

"Alright..." The word plays along a dubious tone, tight with suspicion.

Lagos growls, and his hard length beats against my spine like a threat. "Good girl. There are many things you should despise about me. But the way I make you come with my fingers isn't one of them, little flower." He slides two long fingers inside me but stops at his first knuckle.

"Oh!" I squeeze my eyes shut, fending off any more stimulation, waiting for him to push through but—

His body turns to stone at my back, and he pauses, stopping my mind from spiralling. Stops the pleasure, the build-up, the brewing of something explosive—

A huff leaves me, my lips pursing. Sulking. I am pretty sure I'm sulking.

"What…" I pant and squirm. His fingers are still through my slit but not moving. "Why did you stop? Is it over?"

I don't mind.

That was nice, but—

Dark energy rushes from him right before he growls, "I'm sorry." The hand on my hip releases me, moves to cover my mouth, and it all happens fast. Like a bolt of lightning. Energy that fizzles out of control. He adds a second finger and spears them both deep into me.

I cry out. "Ah!"

"I'm sorry," he grunts from low in his chest as pain assaults me. Then he spears me again. "I'm sorry, little flower, I couldn't stop myself."

I'm crying behind his hand, his fingers catching my tears and whimpers as sensation assaults me with pain and—so much pleasure.

I am reeling. And he doesn't stop for a moment or allow me to resist, fucking me with two fingers until the pain lessens and pleasure rolls forward, taking its place.

"You're tight," he rumbles at my spine. "Too tight for me. It'll hurt every time."

I'm out of my mind because I want to moan that I don't care. At this moment of frenzy, I don't care. How do I possibly say that?

Who would desire such a thing? That I want the pain if it means I get the pleasure—one of life's great experiences. That I want his warmth at my back, his voice vibrating through my spine, and the way he stirs me inside, thickening my senses.

"I want it," I admit.

"Good girl."

There is a direct line from his fingers to my lower belly, and he coils it until it's so tight it strains and stains and—

Snaps.

I arch my back on a cry, and his hand covers my entire chest, supporting me while something infinitely wonderful floods my body. My rib protests the shudders, but I barely feel it. Barely feel anything else besides Lagos.

I pulse around his fingers. It does feel like exploding while peeing... Just like Maple said.

"Mine," he grates, restless. "Falling apart. Falling into depravity. I suppose you were right. Some things do look prettier when they fall."

Tightness grips my thighs and holds on. Shudders of energy spark through me.

As it all eases, I slump against the rock-hard body behind me, my eyes fluttering open for the first time since it all started.

I stare ahead.

Lazily, Lagos' hand moves from inside my knickers and slides over my body in the slick water. The skin of his fingers is rough, calloused, hot, and impossibly virile. At this moment, I finally understand what *I* like. My desires. What *I* am attracted to. What draws me, impresses me. It's rough, hard edges, excitement, and strength. It's everything I'm not used to, and what he is at his core.

Exhaustion closes in on me, but he massages his big hands over my body, igniting every cell, keeping me awake and aware.

My breasts rise and fall as I pant. They are tight, nipples beaded while big palms roll over them, wash them. Wash *me*. Everywhere.

"Mine."

I'm touched and stroked with a kind of possessive dominance. His grip is firm, his reach without bounds, authoritarian—claiming.

I'm nodding—*yes.* I'm yours... *until I'm safe. Yours.* One of his hands slides between our bodies, and he grabs himself through his jeans, hissing. For just a moment, I feel him palming his erection. Releasing it fast, his hand descends to my backside and slides between my cheeks.

"Lagos?" I hold my breath as his forefinger and middle slide over my hole, the muscle puckering against the attention.

"I can do that," I gasp.

I mean wash myself, though I'm not sure that's all he's doing. My toes curl when his index finger circles the rim. Heat floods my face, cheeks set ablaze by his dark touch.

"Mine."

His hand disappeared from that special place, and I find the courage to turn around to face him.

"Time to get you dry," he says, voice hoarse with restraints.

"Okay." Due to being on a few rocky steps above him, I don't need to arch my neck to the point of pain this time. So I stare directly into his steel-coloured gaze, comfortable.

Lagos softens, as I gaze up at him. "Little flower. Look at these bruises..." He touches my cheek, and his jaw pulses as his eyes linger on each bruise.

"Do I look ugly?"

"Not possible."

Warm affection swirls around inside me, giving me a little more bravery. Enough to say, "That was... an experience. I'm sorry I was too tight, that it... was hard to get inside me." *Oh, my.* Am I saying this all wrong?

"You're apologising." The softness dissolves instantly, his hand dropping, my words landing a blow unintentionally. "I hurt you. Took—" He bites down, locking words inside a cage of teeth. "You should be running from me, little flower."

I blink at him, feeling sad. *Just let yourself smile. Be kind, Lagos. I can see it inside you. Why are you fighting it?*

"Doesn't it always hurt," I say, "a bit?" Sweets told me it hurts... I reach for his hand so naturally—almost like I've done it many times—and hold it. He lets me. Across his fingers, the sight of blood makes me blush, prickles of embarrassment moving up my neck and over my face.

"That's my blood." I swallow, that embarrassment burning beneath my cheeks. "Is that normal?"

His frown deepens.

"Well..." I start. His fingers are twice the length and width of mine. I turn his hand over and over, studying the tattoos and scars that mark him, that tell tales of pain and hardships. "Your hands are a bit bigger than mine are." I smile up at him, desperate for the softness to return to his features. I need it. I'm naked and vulnerable while he's slowly emotionally shutting down. "Remember," I press, "Like the shirt? You're a bit bigger than me." *Oh, stop talking.* I'm trying so hard it's humiliating.

A muscle in his jaw tightens, but my tedious lips won't stop, won't listen, *won't* take his hints.

"Do you ever smile?" I breathe. "I won't get used to it if that is what concerns you."

A corner of his mouth softens. *Yes.* "You've seen me smile, little flower."

I beam. "When?"

He steps backward and reaches behind his neck, pulling his shirt over his head. "After I killed that Endigo."

Before I can frown at that, he uses the half-dry side to pat me down. I'm distracted by the smooth muscles that ripple across his shoulders as he moves. I don't move like that; my body doesn't operate like a machine, built and designed. His ancestors were engineered, after all—all Xin De were.

"I've seen you grin and smirk," I argue, gripping his shoulders, dizzied by the thick and powerful way they respond. He dries my legs, one at a time, and I try to keep my balance.

"There's a difference?" he grunts, not looking into my eyes as he finishes patting water from me so that I don't have to twist. That is the only reason for this care and consideration. Surely.

"Yes."

Straightening, he reaches for his other shirt—well, my shapeless dress—and helps me into it, minding my wounded rib. "And that is?"

"Grins are..." Annoyance hits my temples. "Ugh. I don't know. It's in the shape of the lips."

"Please, little flower, tell me about my not-smile."

"A smirk and a grin are..." I make patterns with my hands. "Like, shaped odd and tilted..."

"Yes..."

"Cruel," I punch out, dropping my hands.

"Shaped odd and cruel?"

I glare at him. "And mean."

Finally, my arm feeds through the hole of the shirt, and I'm free of his intoxicating hands and attention.

"A grin isn't always cruel, more mischievous," he states. "Isn't it? A smirk can be cruel and unpleasant."

"What?"

A huff of amusement leaves him, and my walls of annoyance and frustration crumble. It's deep. So deep I feel the timbre thrum between my legs.

"Never mind," he says. "Stupid conversation with a silly girl."

He doesn't always talk—loves a good grunt response—but when he does... It hits me—I can't believe I didn't see it before. Through his rugged appearance and rebellious attitude, it never even crossed my mind. Lagos is too educated to have been born in the waste, to be an outlaw. He studied. Suspicion sets into my gaze as I measure him up again.

"You're educated," I state.

He stiffens. "Hm."

I beam at him. "Too educated to be a rogue brute."

With what could be a chuckle but too controlled, he repeats, "A rogue brute?"

"Yes." Smoothing the shirt down my body, I feel clear and level and buzzing from my first-ever… climax. A great experience, Maple. Truly.

And I'm getting to know him; if he's educated, then he has a Trade. If he has a Trade… then he must have a Trade name!

"What does Lagos mean?" I ask, eyeing him, watching tension build through his muscles, pump into them. Warn me—I shouldn't ask. I should stop, but I'm mindless with what just happened between us. "Is it a geographic name?"

He stares at me, his third eyelid flicking across. Thick tattooed arms the size of trunks fold over his broad chest, pressing each bicep out further. "Lake."

"It means lake." I nod slowly. "In which language?"

"*What* language?"

"That's what I said."

"An old one."

"So..." I wiggle my brows, excited to be talking to him like this, to finally see a glimpse of the man inside the brute. "You were born a Trade man!" That sentence falls out with warm joy because he was once like me. And looking at him, it's hard to believe he has ever conformed, or that anyone could tell him where to be or what to do, but only Trade men and women have geographical names. "What was your Trade?"

Then it all changes.

His demeanour stills the air.

Cruel, unyielding detachment claw into his black gaze, severing my mood. I swallow and shrink backward, but it's too late.

"I'm not a man at all," he bites out, sharp like the crack of a leather belt, harsh and final and powerful enough to make me flinch. To flatten my smile and hurt my heart. "Stop humanising me! Just because your pussy has been wrapped around my fingers doesn't make me human. Just because you want me to be won't make it happen. You'll be disappointed, *Lace Girl.* Stick with cruel and mean and add further substitutes if you wish, perhaps brutal and vile and murderous."

He called me Lace Girl...

My lower lip trembles. "Just because you hate yourself doesn't mean I have to!"

Suddenly, he snatches my throat and possesses me, leaning down until we are nose to nose.

"Your hate for me was the only thing I liked about you."

If he punched me, it would hurt less. "You don't mean that." My chin dimples as I hide my need to cry. "I never really hated you, Lagos. I was afraid and lost, and you were mean, but you have shown me you care. You don't have to pretend that—"

"You're embarrassing yourself! I just wanted your soft, young pussy on my fingers, Lace Girl," he growls, releasing me with disgust. "I don't care about you." He turns from me.

I wrap my arms around my stomach, holding myself. Long legs take him away from me. I watch his naked back, muscles roiling beneath tattooed skin.

The cave around me fades and I'm suddenly alone with the weight of this moment pressing on my heart. I let him touch me.

Let myself enjoy it.

I can't forget it.

Sleep it away.

And I don't want to.

I watch him in silence, waiting for him to disappear from view before slowly heading back to the boat, because where else can I go? Nowhere.

My steps are slow, like my heart. By the time I get back to the room, I'm ready to burst into tears. I see Spero is awake but not making much fuss. He must have been fed by Tomar.

Absently, I scoop Spero into my arms. Gritting my teeth, I ignore the pain and manage to get onto the bed with him. I lie down on my good side, which happens to be with my face to the wall, and tuck my tiny burden in the curve of my torso.

My skin still hums from Lagos' rough, possessive touch, while between my legs, a heavy pulse resonates as if blood rushes to a fresh wound.

A tear slides down my temple, nesting in my ear. I don't know what I was thinking, asking him personal questions, wanting to get to know him. He is just a brute, nothing more. Not a Trade man who I can maybe relate to, but a rogue. A Xin De monster with no heart, no kindness at all—

I sigh. I can't convince myself. Sobs fall heavier because it's not true. There is kindness, sweetness, and a gentle touch. I have felt it—seen it.

Why is he like this?

Chapter Eighteen

Lagos

That was a damn mistake.

Surrounded by jagged rock, I press my palm to the limestone wall. Hidden in a private alcove, the same one we hide extra supplies in, in case the catamaran is found and sacked. I rip open my top button with the hand smeared in her blood and fist my cock.

I shudder and growl. Fucking hell, I need this. After that. Fuck.

If I had a slither of humanity for every time I pushed her away and yearned to hold her, I'd be human enough to deserve her.

But the fact I just took her virginity without consent, punctured her so thoroughly there was no chance she wouldn't bleed for me, attests to my lack of anything decent.

And I won't tell her. Not that she was a virgin. That her Ward never claimed her. For whatever reason, he didn't touch her pussy while she lay drugged beside him.

And not that I—stole it.

It's why I preferred her look of fear and disdain. That fits. It fits my leather-like skin, the beastly muscles that ripple beneath it, and the charred heart that serves to pump my iron-blood.

I can't bear her sweet gaze.

Don't deserve the look she just gave me after she came on my fingers. Not the loved-up awe or the naïve hope that we aren't worlds apart.

Yes, I'm a Trade man.

And no, I am not.

It's not that simple.

I can accept gratitude and lust from townies at The Bite, House Girls, and the nomads, but not her.

Not a sweet, untouched girl who took a beating from a Shadow. Woke to take on the world again, her trauma tucked in deep, sure to surface in her nightmares when this is all over.

She deserves more.

Deserves peace.

A kind, warm heart.

I pump my cock. Hard. Punishing. So hard it hurts, with no teasing or lingering for enjoyment, only a single-minded determination to blow my fucking nuts so that I can think straight.

The crown of my cock goes blood red, precum licking on the cave wall. I come a lot when I blow, it's not a small mess, it's a fucking flood, but this time, it's going to be another level of intense.

I look down. The hand I used to claim her, covered in pretty scarlet stains, jerks up and down my throbbing cock.

Dahlia's little body flashes in my mind, and I shuffle and groan through clenched teeth. Bearing down on my hard length, I don't try to blink her away.

I speed up.

Thinking about her.

About stealing her virginity.

Losing control.

My head drops back, shoulders bunching up as I work my cock harder, faster—fierce.

I imagine visiting her in her sleep and covering her face with a pillow, holding it down just enough that she can breathe but not see or move.

I'll whisper that, "I need to feel you. Hold on to the sheets. Be a good girl for me. It's not your fault that I'm doing this to you. It's mine."

I'm the monster in this story.

I imagine dragging her lace knickers down trembling white thighs, spreading her open, and pushing inside her.

Fuck.

My legs shuffle wider, restless. Fist flies over my cock. Need it out. Groans crash from my lips as I envision *taking* her, but then…

Fuck me— I imagine she removes the pillow and stares up at me, big green eyes, freckles for days, with a slight bump in her almost perfect nose, a message about her inner strength and courage.

And she smiles.

Images flood me; I don't fight them. My release grabs my balls. My fist tightens. Hot, fierce blood rushes to my cock in a wave that makes me momentarily nauseous.

And I come, growling and spurting over the pitted limestone wall, letting in the despicable reverie of her enjoying each thrust, taking each inch, and squeezing my cock with her inexperienced pussy.

Heaving, I lean my forehead on my bicep and brace myself harder against the wall. My chest strains. Cock is in agony—good. I need it to hurt. Or I'll be ready to go again too soon.

Fuck. I have to stay away from her. I have to keep my damn hands off her. Have to. But I… I fucking can't.

Chapter Nineteen

Dahlia

The following day and night are spent hiding in *this* room with Spero, feeding, cuddling, and talking to the chubby assassin.

After a few hours, I find my *beibao* tucked in the corner which makes my stomach flip with guilt. Someone went back for it. Someone risked their safety when they returned to The House.

Are people coming for us?

To The Bite? I thought The Trade didn't know about the cave town. It was safe. Forgotten, perhaps. Ignored, maybe? Until we placed a prize that was too valuable to keep them blind.

It is my fault.

And it is where Sweets and the others live—I find the pressure of that thought too much to handle, my mind awash with concern and sadness I will never be able to say goodbye to them.

It's not new to me—unspoken words. I'm used to doing as I am told and leaving without closure.

Following.

Obeying.

From the nursery to the Lace House, to my Ward's home. The

Trade has the ultimate power over everyone, and it is a certainty that we all accept.

As the Opi drains from my system completely, all come-down dwindling to normality, and pain returns. I prefer it to the muddled haze I have been in the past few days. A haze that has obviously made me do silly things, say embarrassing things, and believe impossible things—like Lagos the Rogue might actually enjoy my company.

Inside my *beibao*: the hacksaw, the items from Tide, most of my belongings are accounted for, but a few items are missing. A pair of underwear and the rest of my Opi, which was probably used the past few days. And the knickers were likely left on or under my bed. I only have two pairs now, so...

That's unfortunate.

I pull out the cracked mirror and stare at myself. I look awful. The bridge of my nose is swollen on one side. Tiny veins are visible along my nostrils. Bruising moons the underside of my left eye, and my lower lip has a small scarlet slit. I lift my hand, tracing the warm flesh and stroking the red and blue bruises.

What a sight...

Not at all pretty.

I'm pulling on my own clothes, my shirt-dress and pants which are now a size too big for me, when a knock comes from behind the door. It can't be Lagos. He doesn't announce himself before he storms in—presumptuous, rude, and controlling. *Brute.* He doesn't own us. I am not his!

"Come in," I call out, trying to keep my voice level. Pulling my red hair over one shoulder, the waves roll over my chest to my waist. "Tomar?"

The door opens and Tomar appears, his stunning face full of colour again and his eyes smiling when they land on me.

"Good first-light, Dahlia," he says. "I hope you're well."

I relax. "You look better."

With a nod, he moves straight to Spero and strokes the infant's pink cheek. "Good first-light, special boy." He looks me over and pauses… for… too long. I shuffle with uncertainty.

We haven't spoken since— An uncomfortable feeling sinks into my belly when he looks at me, brows weaving.

"Are you alright?" he finally says, and I exhale. "It's been days since you were hurt. I'm… I am so sorry, Dahlia. I swore you were safe, and I—"

"It isn't your fault."

"I said I would help you. Keep you safe." He shakes his head, almost at himself. Striking blue eyes coast a path from my split lip to the swelling at my nose. Suddenly, I feel my wounds, tight and healing, his gaze somehow igniting them.

"And you did." I smile softly. "I'm alive, and so is Spero."

He exhales, heavy regret coasting the air. "I'm truly, deeply sorry about Tide."

My breath catches, having been suppressing this— Every time I speak Tide's name, Lagos slams cruel indifference on me. "People die in the Half-tower, and we do not even know," I admit, forcing a shrug. "They just disappear. The Trade carve a line into the Peace Steeple. We aren't meant to mourn. It is an interruption, I suppose, from our Purpose."

His brows weave. "Grief isn't something we control."

I exhale relief; he gets it. He is far more human than Lagos. "I know." Pressing my hand just below my chest, I cradle the ache that moves through my stomach. "I feel it here. Feel Maple and now Tide."

He touches his chest, palm over his beating heart. "And here."

I nod, staring at him. I am so thankful he is allowing me to feel and share this. Lagos doesn't have an ounce of compassion for the dead. It is so nice to have someone who processes death similar to me. "*Yes*. I feel it there, too."

"I don't meet girls like you often…" A moment passes while his eyes seem to roll to every inch of my being, even sliding in somehow, making my insides flip. "I see the allure of your Trade— you're so sweet and endearing." He flushes a little before clearing his throat, his eyes have a strange fragile hope that doesn't make much sense to me. "We have to leave, Dahlia." His voice rasps with effort.

I inhale hard, and he snaps his gaze to the ground. I'm glad he isn't gazing at me like that anymore because I'm not sure how to respond. Or why my belly knots.

Men give that look to House Girls but not to Lace Girls. Not usually.

I ignore the ripple of unease in my shoulders, squaring them instead. "What do I need to do to help? Or prepare?"

"Have you been taking the hormones?" he asks delicately.

Dread sinks in as I try to recall the last time I took the little white tablets. "I missed the days that I was asleep." I swallow. "How much formula do we have?"

"Enough for a few days," he says, his eyes shifting as he contemplates. "It'll be okay. We'll be able to get some powdered milk at the first stop."

I know that's not enough for Spero. He needs vitamins. Minerals. More than powdered milk. "Okay," I say, reluctant.

"Are *you* feeling strong enough to travel?" He stares back at me. "It will be rough. Lagos is getting the truck ready above ground, but it has been months since we used it, and the first stop is a day's drive away. It will be a rough drive. It's still windy as all Hell, even for The Cradle."

The peculiar look in his eyes transforms into concern when he assesses the area over my ribcage. "Can you handle it? Do you want more Opi for the journey?"

"No!" I blurt out and then force myself to back up and calm down. "No, *thank you*," I repeat softer. "I wasn't myself with that much in my system. And the lack of sleep..." I pause, trying to hide the regret evident in my gaze. "I feel much better now. More myself."

My heart beats between my legs, betraying my words.

I shuffle, my eyes losing focus as the feel of thick fingers inside me, pain and pleasure and his arousal at my spine—

I snap out of it to see a strange kind of suspicion playing across Tomar's expression. Concern and maybe even... *anger?* Or —I don't know. I can't read him at this moment.

"Did he touch you, Dahlia?" he asks darkly.

I gasp and step backward once. "No!" Quick to deny it. Too quick. It was obvious because I didn't ask who or what or press for an explanation.

He moves forward, filling the space I left. "We have spent a fair amount of time together over the past few weeks, haven't we?"

I blink at him. "Yes."

"And in that time," he says, watching me with disappointment that unsettles my stomach. "I've... Well, I've seen some changes in you that... *worry* me."

"Like what?" is all I manage.

"First, the clothes you were wearing when Lagos rescued you. Then, the conversation yesterday about sex. You have a new Purpose, Dahlia. A pure one. Suitable for your s—" He clears his throat again, clears a word or message his mind won't release. I hate it when people do that. Suitable for my what? "Suitable for *you,*" he finishes.

His tone makes me want to apologise, but I'm not certain what for. For changing? Being unappreciative, maybe?

"I'm sorry if I've somehow disappointed you," I mutter, my voice lowering.

"No." He touches my cheek, causing my breath to hitch again. "I'm not disappointed, just worried. I didn't think I would have to worry about you and Lagos. Not with your conditioning. I've known him a long time, longer than you have been alive. I saved him. I care for him, but his..." Tomar clenches his jaw, and I see the muscles beneath dancing with agitation. "*Ways* seem to corrupt everyone."

"Corrupt?" I repeat, not at all liking the two syllables on my tongue, or the shift in the relationship between Tomar and Lagos, or the intimacy between *us* right now... Or the way his hand is still on my cheek and his eyes are taking me in with confident familiarity and—ownership?

"He is not a soft man but is an incredible warrior, and *loyal.* With glimpses of compassion only..." He pauses before saying, "He's not good for someone pure and gentle like yourself. He can have anyone." He laughs without mirth, the message straining. "Not you. He grows bored of people and places so quickly. I don't want to see him ruin you, sweet Dahlia."

Am I ruined?

For enjoying his touch?

And I realise what the look in Tomar's eyes is now, what he feels behind them. I've seen it, and it won't go away. *Jealousy*. It isn't anger; he is jealous.

Of what?

Of Lagos.

"Stay with me," he suddenly blurts out, and I freeze.

What?

"Close to me," he adds.

I hold my breath.

"In my room at night so I can protect you. Keep you safe. Keep you pure and—"

"From being corrupted?" I blink at him, eyes agape with shock. My heart is thrashing in my ears now, discomfort dripping down my spine.

"Did he touch you?" he repeats, gaze heavy on mine.

Startled wordless, I lie through a slow, hesitant shake of my head.

As if regret rears up inside him, his eyes widen, and his hand drops from my cheek. "My apologies. Of course not. Excuse me, I have to pack the supplies."

~

I repacked my *beibao*. My mind spiralling from the conversation with Tomar. I am already second-guessing myself. He only wants to keep me safe and protect me from pain. The anguish that a man with the reputation of Lagos can easily cause me. I get it. I'm naïve, but not stupid, just inexperienced.

He was helping me.

Guiding and protecting—

But… I sigh.

Sometimes, people speak with words, and other times, they speak between them. He spoke between them. And… I can't decipher the message, but I sense withheld intent. I have always felt comfortable and safe with Tomar.

Now… I'm not so sure.

My stomach turns with uncertainty.

All I can go by are his words; he doesn't want Lagos to touch me. Tomar cares for him and saved him once but doesn't want him to *ruin* me. I wish I could dissect what he means by *ruin.*

By having sex? I already have. By enjoying it? That seems unfair; Maple enjoyed men. She wasn't ruined! Was she? Is that why she died? All the terrible things that happened to her, was it punishment? I know The Trade would consider me somewhat spoiled if they knew I felt a man's fingers inside me, but… Tomar isn't Trade-aligned, and I'm no longer a Lace Girl.

None of it is clear.

Then there is the jealousy; Tomar's stifled but obvious jealousy. Which makes no sense as he has a single-minded Purpose to help people. Why would he feel jealous? Women—and me by default— are a distraction, he said so himself. So why was he looking at me like… like he wanted to… to be closer to me. I don't know.

Unable to hide down here any longer, with my clouded mind recalling our conversation, I decide to face him—them. The one who wants to shelter me, and the one who touches me when I can't see him and hates me when I face him.

With Spero wrapped to my chest and my *beibao* slung over my shoulder, I head to the top deck. Tomar is pulling in a rod, and delight sparks through me when a shiny pink fish appears, flapping around on the hook. Its dorsal fin is split in two. Very pretty but odd-looking creature.

"You got one."

He jerks around, his blue eyes brightening when he sees me. "Hey. Come over here. This is Salmonskip. Rare and tasty. You'll like it. Do you, ah, do you want a turn?"

Looking at the webbing on the boat deck, I nod eagerly. "I have seen my Ward use nets."

"Give it a go." Tomar reaches for Spero, then realises the tiny bundle is literally attached to me. "I can take the boy if you want?"

"It's okay." My chin hits my chest as I peer down at Spero, snuggled up and blinking heavy lashes at me. "He's nearly asleep." I look back at Tomar, pride in my face. "I use my neck wrap, and it keeps him fastened to me. And I can use my hands. It's how I helped Tide..." I swallow over the lump his name causes. "It is how I helped Tide untangle his nets."

"Clever," he offers.

"Thank you." Dropping my *beibao*, I take a big breath and move to the nets, getting straight to work.

The cascading waterfall creates white noise. It helps the silence that ensues between us to be relatively comfortable.

We aren't discussing Lagos.

And I'm thankful.

Recalling what my Ward taught me once when I accompanied him on the river, I repeat the process until the nets are in the water. I sit back down on the fold-out chair and wait, feeling pretty proud of myself. "I can take care of myself, I think. What do you think?"

Tomar smiles. "Sure."

"Doubt it." Lagos' deep timbre thrums through me, settling at the base of my spine, just to remind me what my body does when he is around.

Squirming, I hide the warmth that hits my cheeks. I don't turn to acknowledge the great Xin De brute, but every hair on my body rises, so he must be close behind me.

"Ignore him." Tomar turns back to the fish and starts cutting it down the centre, removing the insides and replacing them with salts he has drying on a silver plate. "The truck ready?"

"As it will ever be."

As quickly as Lagos entered, he vanishes, leaving a heavy silence that not even the splashing waterfall can soothe.

"I apologise for our earlier conversation, Dahlia," Tomar says. "I... I don't know what came over me."

My stomach flips again. Why did he have to continue this? We could have pretended it never happened. "It's fine." My voice shakes so I gently chew my lower lip, feeling the small split. It doesn't hurt much today. I stare at the white screen of water all around us.

"We'll just forget about it, then?" he states in an easy tone—maybe too easy.

I nod anyway. "Sure. Hey, what do you do with the catamaran when you go above ground?"

His gaze hits the cavernous ceiling and pans the tent of water around us. "We leave it here."

"Right here?"

"It's a secret." He winks at me, and I let myself smile at him again. "It'll only be for a few weeks. Lagos and I will return, and you'll be at the Common Community, safe."

"So..." I find my lower lip again, worrying it between my teeth, as I think. "You'll be back to check on Sweets and the others? To make sure they are safe and provided for?"

His brows draw in over a serious gaze. "Why wouldn't they be safe, Dahlia?"

My forehead tightens as unease grips me, and after a long moment of silence, I finally ask, "Aren't they in danger of The Trade now that... That they found me—us? Didn't they? That is what happened at the cove. That man..."

"Ah." He nods. "Lagos didn't explain. Of course, he didn't. Sorry, Dahlia. He isn't a talker. I should have known he wouldn't have. They sent a Shadow after you. That man, he was Shadow."

My jaw drops. "Like Spero?" I sink further into the chair and hold myself, my fingers creating little circles on my arms. It soothes me. Even though the man is dead, my lungs begin to squeeze. He was fast, strong, and... charming. That is the worst part. He was clever. I even liked him. Panic turns to acid in my chest, burning me, tightening and squeezing my lungs. I'm scared of him, of them. That is what a Shadow is, what Spero will be if they take him. The kind of being that kills an old man and beats a girl bloody. "That man was a... was a Shadow?" My voice wobbles even as I try to hold it steady.

"Yes." He looks across at me, freezing with one hand on a fish and the other on a knife. "He is dead, and I won't let you out of my sight again. You're safe."

I breathe out steadily.

Safe. Safe.

And Spero is, also. I can't allow that night and that man to be venom permanently in my veins. Not a wound that can be opened. I won't allow it. "And Sweets? Is she safe?"

"They won't send Marshals, not to The Bite," he says. "They'll send more spies, and they won't find you there. I only hope they leave The Bite alone after that."

"You hope?" I whisper. "And if they don't?"

"I don't know." He drops a fish into one of the tackle chests. "We will keep you safe... Shall we check your net?"

I sense Lagos before I see him. He is a warm lick of energy moving through my body but also an unwelcome stir low in my belly.

"No one will hurt you again, little flower," he states, and I almost believe the fierce conviction in his depthless timbre.

He won't let anyone hurt me.

Not physically... I almost say it aloud but instead move to the net, eager to prove the giant brute wrong. Dragging the webbing over the edge, I find it full of… of trash.

I slump down, my nose scrunching up. Sulking, I stare at it and then at Tomar. "Nothing."

"Next time," Tomar offers, trying to lift a large tackle box.

I watch him attempt it, taking hold, but he strains and growls before dropping it with a thud.

Then I see fragile pride furrow Tomar's brows as Lagos lifts the bulky tackle box with ease.

"Leave it with me, brother."

Lagos stops beside me with the hefty trunk in his arms. He's so strong… My pulse leaps. I gaze up at the long, thick length of him. My mouth parts when I meet his steel-coloured eyes staring down at me through his lower lashes. "Check the net again, little flower."

I blink up at him.

Why would he say that? To taunt me? I am not going to allow him to mock me further. The net was full of rubbish.

Diverting my gaze, I focus on Tomar instead as he packs and stacks, emptying the boat, fastening crates and preparing to vacate the catamaran.

The silence extends and lingers, and I want to say something to distract my silly curiosities, but instead, I grumble. Reaching for the net, I pull it over and…

There it is. A little fish struggling for breath on top.

It wasn't there before. Maybe it was buried underneath? Perhaps it flopped its way to the very top of the discarded collection of goods.

No. It wasn't there.

"You did get one," Tomar says, glancing over his shoulder. "You *can* take care of yourself."

We both know I can't.

He isn't patronising me. There is a difference between encouragement through optimism, and appeasement through praise. So, I nod in agreement with a light smile touching my lips.

But no, I can't fish.

I reach out and brush my finger over the silvery head, stopping at a small bloody hole in the left cheek. A hole from a hook.

A spark of deep affection shoots through my body.

It would have been nice to have caught the fish in the net, but *this* fish has a message for me. One I do not wish to ignore. A meaningful message—I think it is a peace offering from Lagos.

Chapter Twenty

Dahlia

Sad melancholy sits quietly in my lower belly. Leaving the catamaran is strangely emotional, knowing I will never see it again, nor The Bite.

Maple told me once that we have three deaths. The first is when your mind is void, the second is when your body decays, becoming The Crust, and the third is the last time someone speaks your name.

Maybe… just maybe… we have hundreds. Like Tide said to me the day he died. We are bits of every place we have been and every person we have spoken to. So, every time we say goodbye to a bit, we have one little death.

Goodbye, Tide.

Goodbye, Bite.

Two little deaths.

On the surface again, it feels as though I am emerging from a dream. From years underground. Yet, it has been less than a month. So much has changed; I have changed.

Mere weeks ago, my world was huge and safe. At least, that was the veil The Trade fitted me with. I had a Collective of friends, a nice, warm flat, and Meaningful Purpose. Now… my world is tiny and unstable. A blotch of dye on the vast canvas of The Cradle.

I'm excited *and* scared.

Redwind pummels the large, red truck, rocking it as the road disappears between the two front tyres.

A Redwind-mask hangs in the crook of my neck, and Spero snuggles on my lap instead of in my hide jacket. The restless assassin wriggles around, and the jerking movement of the truck is too much pressure for my broken rib.

Belongings and supplies are stacked in the back, placing the three of us together in the front seats. Somewhat close.

I sit between them, all too aware of Lagos' thick leg touching my outer thigh. The desert is ominous, a vast, never-ending vortex of nothing and everything.

Tomar and Lagos discuss the route and possible dangers, but the conversation falls silent when we bump over a hole in the road, and I outwardly wince at the pain shooting through my side.

"Are you alright?" Tomar asks, flicking his eyes between me and the road above the steering wheel he holds steadily.

"I'm fine," I assure—lie. It hurts so much, but I remember my Ward once telling me that things hurt the most while they heal. I hold that as true, as a tether to my resilience.

"*Flower.*" There is a warning in Lagos' tone, challenging me not to lie to them.

I grit my teeth, not wanting to be this fragile and vulnerable. I was born a Lace Girl. Common and small. All things I cannot control. I decided to leave the Half-tower, to help Tide, and to revel in new experiences.

To have control over… some things in my life. What I can control now is how I respond to this pain—this healing pain. I can be tough. "I'm fine," I repeat.

We head toward the horizon, a sliver belt that divides two hues of hazy red.

The truck jerks, and I'm unable to swallow my whimper. My body tenses involuntarily, ready to react and to protect myself from the next violent movement.

Lagos stiffens beside me.

"You're in pain," he basically snarls the words a heartbeat before he scoops me up. But his touch… It is firm yet gentle.

Careful.

He braces me on his lap and becomes cement columns around me, unmoving and steady.

My breath stutters. Physically, we are close. My body is cradled by his, his warm skin humming like electricity, but his emotional reluctance is like a tangible wall that separates us.

I peer up for a split second, but it's enough. His eyes are on me, roaming and soft, and… he looks away. The silent interaction is crowded with longing and uncertainty.

Does he have affection for me, too? Why do I feel this way?

I stare out the window. Large objects lurk in the dusty-crimson haze.

Suddenly, they are upon us. A towering pillar, and then another, and another. I gasp. *Wind turbines.* I can only make them out when they are imminent—it feels like the turbines are literally jumping out, lunging and alive.

It takes my breath away.

"Remarkable," I say, awe playing along each syllable.

"Yes," Tomar agrees. "The Redwind gives energy and takes it away. The windmills cover nearly half of The Cradle and power most civilised towers."

Lagos grunts. "They are just big fucking fans."

I blush and say, "Maybe the bigger the thing, the more remarkable it is."

"The more destructive."

"The more powerful."

He sneers. "That isn't always a good thing, little flower."

"It has the potential to be a very good thing if used correctly," I argue. "I like big, powerful things."

Tomar glances between us. "Are we still talking about windmills?"

I sigh, wishing I had brought a hammer instead of Maple's little hacksaw. Maybe I could chip little holes into Lagos' walls. I know we are different. Human and Xin De. Common and evolved. I still wish for more for him, happiness and beauty and peace.

For miles and miles, windmills leap into view, the farm stretching on and on across the hazy landscape.

We drive in silence.

And drive.

And drive.

Hours later, Spero begins to cry, so we stop the truck for a break. Lagos and Tomar climb out, braving the chaos, using the truck to shelter them from the Redwind. I lay Spero on my lap and feed him from the bottle he eagerly sucks at.

I need to try to feed him tonight, need to stimulate my nipples, probably fail miserably, and try again and again.

Until it works.

It has to work!

The truck is still, my rib sighing with relief, but outside the metal vehicle, it is anything but calm.

Through the side window, I watch the wind churn in angry gusts. I remember Tomar saying that the sky has never forgiven us for 'fucking it up.' I wonder if the Redwind is a punishing force from a being greater than us?

From The Crust itself?

I guess it doesn't matter. It's too late to repair. Redwind is The Cradle's temperament.

I'm staring at sweet Spero when Lagos and Tomar's voices join the aggressive storm. I look up but can't see them. They are shouting at each other, gruff voices clashing. I cuddle Spero closer. I can't hear what they are saying. I can only take in the tones and tension.

It's about you.

I don't know why that thought surfaces. It's silly and untrue… only… the energy between them has become icy and uncomfortable to be around. Now, they are arguing outside the vehicle, so I can't hear them.

I finish with Spero and rap on the window to get their attention, only seeing that dense red air and no shapes beyond. Lagos appears first, and then Tomar on the driver's side. They climb in and shut the doors fast.

"We're going to stop early," Tomar states, starting the engine and pulling onto the main road. "To give you a break."

"I said I was fine."

"Bullshit," Lagos grunts.

"I don't want to slow us down, I want to ke—"

"It's not open for discussion." Lagos lifts me again to sit on his lap and glares ahead. Two tight lines pinch between his weaved brows. I wish I could smooth them with my finger and see the softness I know hides within him.

"Clearly," Tomar mutters. "Not much is these days."

Lagos growls out an inhuman sound that makes the hairs along my skin rise and prickle.

Brute.

With a sigh, I curl into him, pretending that he isn't a huge, mean Xin De male and, instead—a friend.

I can feel his heartbeat beside my cheek, its thrumming soothes me, drumming affection into me whether I want it or not.

His thighs are stone beneath me, his stature just as solid around me, and I can tell he is absorbing the jerky movements of the truck so that I'm not thrown around.

"Thank you," I whisper, honestly, but secretly hope he doesn't hear.

Then his heart speeds up beside my ear. And I think he tilts his head, his lips meeting my hair. It's subtle. I'm not sure it happens. If it did, it's probably because he hates my appreciation.

That would mean he is gentle. It would mean he cares about me.

You care, Lagos.

Chapter Twenty-One

Dahlia

A peculiar sight emerges on the silvery belt ahead.

As we near it, I make out the shape. A building—a roadhouse of sorts—a dot of eerie civilisation set against the hazy highway.

The rumble of various engines permeates the air as we pull alongside a row of mismatched motor vehicles.

All made with madness.

Salvaged parts and faded paintwork, horns curling from the large front lights, pipes cracking.

Preparing, I pull my mask up to cover my nose and mouth. I try to open the door, but the pressure of the wind wrestles with me. "How do—"

Lagos pushes it open.

I close my eyes as the sand whips inside the vehicle.

Lagos stands with Spero and me in his arms and walks us through the Redwind to the porch, his legs unfaltering, stature pressing through the dense atmosphere.

The howl of a turbine reminds me that they are all around us, but I can't see them anymore.

The weathered brick walls bear scars, chips, and cracks from the cruel gale but protest the damage by remaining robust.

And lively.

Walking into the derelict roadhouse, I see girls scantily dressed in worn stockings and ill-fitted corsets. I understand why Tomar was reluctant to stop here. It wasn't because he didn't want to stop early, but that he didn't want to stop… here.

Lagos thumps over to a long bar that runs the entire length of the room, a flock of women already on his heels. Hands slide down his back, stroke his spine, desperate for his attention.

"Hey, big boy."

"We *missed* you."

Too focused on the petite hand on Lagos' shoulder, I startle when the old door slams behind me, shutting the howling and gale outside.

The bar falls quiet.

Spero gurgles in my arms.

It's dim here, shadows and shapes scattered around, and the slow dancing of smoke from lit cigarettes becomes flags above each figure.

"Wait here with me." Tomar's voice comes from beside me.

Lowering my mask to the crook of my neck, I shake my hair loose, the red ribbons cascading around me.

And the air thickens.

Several eyes snap in my direction. All from large Xin De men spread out across the room.

"Take her to the back," Lagos orders Tomar, returning to our side with a large rusty key. His onyx eyes hit me. "You stay in the fucking room, little flower."

A man with his back to us, sitting further down the bar, suddenly slams his drink on the wooden top. "I can smell her from here, Lagos! What the hell are you doing with a Lace Girl in my house?"

Lagos keeps his back to the man, eyes sliding across my face. "She's not a Lace Girl." He brushes my hair over my shoulder, such a gentle, uncharacteristic show of affection. My knees buckle. "Not anymore."

"Who is she, then?" One of the girls poses, tone tight.

A brunette leans backward on the bar, facing us. "You used to be a Lace Girl? I never understood that Trade. The point of it, that is."

Another girl with too-blonde hair positions herself next to her, and I glance over at them, readying myself for the usual disdain.

"Tell me, Lace Girl, because I have always wondered," the blonde starts. "When you wake up from being drugged and fucked, and his cum is leaking from between your thighs, do you feel pure and wholesome then?" Her blonde eyebrow cocks in a display as provocative as her words.

Past me would have tried to be friendly, even worked to change her opinion of me and my Trade. What is the point? I would have once felt sorry for her, but I'm wary of the perpetual tolerance that conditioned my Trade.

"That has never happened to me," I state, straight-faced.

She scoffs, and it's angry—bitter. "*Ugh.* Of course. He cleans you up." Her hands clap in a sloppy way. "Well fucking done. What a fucking gentleman."

Lagos is striding toward them, face tight with barely controlled rage. Before I can stop him, he is grabbing each girl by the throat and lifting them from the ground. Unfathomable fury ripples the muscles beneath his shirt.

"Lagos, no!" I step forward, reaching for him, but Tomar catches my elbow, stopping my hand in the air.

Lagos goes very still.

The girls claw his forearms, chins to the ceiling, mouths open in choked screams.

I cup the back of Spero's head and circle my fingertips against his crown to counter the rapid rate of my heart. "*Lagos.*"

Lagos glares at them as the brunette slowly turns grey, and the blonde has a wet patch spreading out between her legs. "Don't say my name like that."

What? I swallow over my fear for them. "Like what?"

"Like I care what you think." Lagos' voice is cold and detached. "With that long, pleading tone. It won't work on me, Lace Girl."

I panic, my heart beats between my ears and with nothing better to say, nothing more convincing, only another, "*Lagos...*"

"Fuck!" A low, inhuman growl breaks from him. When he opens his fists, the girls drop to the floor.

The blonde gasps for air, palming her neck, while the brunette crawls away on her hands and knees.

My body twitches to go to her and help her to her feet. Check her over and apologise, but I find loyalty rooting me to the ground. Loyalty to Lagos.

That thought shakes me.

I clutch my heart, inhaling hard. I don't know what that was about or why he reacted so viciously to mere words. I am used to the scornful ways of House Girls. Or was it their interruption that bothered him, not the words they said?

It doesn't matter.

I don't need to agree with his ways, having already accepted that we are very different, but it doesn't feel right questioning him in front of others. In private, maybe.

If he will tolerate it.

Lagos spins around with his arms open wide. "Anyone else have anything to say?" He pauses, and everyone in the room tries to melt into their chairs. "No? *Good.* No one comes in the back room. We will be occupying it for the night."

"B-but." The man who first slammed his fist on the bar now wipes the sweat from his forehead. "I need an exchange for this—"

"I will leave you a crate of dried fish as. Fucking. Always!" Lagos booms, rounding on him. "Don't insult me."

The man visibly trembles, head lowered and hunched forward over the bar as though he wishes to disappear into his own shoulders. "Easy, Lagos."

"Come with me," Tomar says, his voice clipped and tight, guiding me through the bar to a door set in a far corner.

It opens to a narrow hallway, lit from above with a flickering light and walled with aged paper, the top corners folding over like bunny ears.

As we shove open a door and walk inside, the shift in pressure lifts dust particles from various boxes and furniture. The back room is chaotic. I sneeze.

Crates are stacked carelessly along one wall, each balancing on the cusp of toppling over. I scan the space, spotting a single bed buried under bags and suitcases. Some unzipped and open, others layered on top of each other. The room is cluttered, and I wonder how the space is used.

"Take the bed. Get some sleep." Tomar waves to a couch buried by clothing. "I'll sleep there."

I stare at a strange stain in the centre of the bed. Just the sight of it makes me want to throw up. "I should be getting used to this." Discomfort tugs at me.

"*Oh*, Dahlia."

"I'm sorry. I'm being unappreciative."

"You're not supposed to be used to this." Tomar moves toward me and touches my cheek. Stroking the corner of my mouth, he says, "Smile more. You have the loveliest smile." I appease him with a subtle smile. "You'll be at the Common Community soon. A safe place to raise Spero. Far away from this violence. I know that his brutal ways are hard to stomach, but those girls shouldn't have spoken about you like that."

I wasn't even thinking about Lagos or what happened in the bar at that moment, but apparently, he was. And now, I don't want to appear insensitive or disappoint him with my selfish concerns.

Deep breath. I nod with assurance, holding his gaze, but notice a huge dark shape in the doorway behind him.

Lagos is frozen in the gap, brows drawn in tight, spearing his black gaze at Tomar's hand. "Have I interrupted something, Tomar?"

Tomar drops his hand from my cheek. "I think Dahlia needs some privacy to feed Spero." With a quick turn, he starts toward the doorway, having to shoulder past Lagos, who refuses to move an inch.

After Tomar leaves, there is an uneasy pause, almost like the room itself takes a sharp breath in and holds it.

Alone with Lagos…

Swallowing, I divert my attention to the bed. A dull ache in my side reminds me how utterly useless I am. And yet, I need to move these cases.

Behind me, I hear the sound of Lagos' boots drumming the floors as he approaches. "I have a clean sheet and spare clothes. Used but clean." He stops behind me. I spin around, forced to arch my neck to meet his sharp, dark gaze. "I made sure of that."

His closeness makes me silly.

"I'm missing underwear." I can't believe I just said that. So I add, "I mean. I only have two pairs. Do you think we can find some somewhere?"

"Missing?"

"I mean, they were left in my room, I think."

"Hm." Then he turns his hulking body to leave.

Panic lodges in my throat.

What if he goes to one of those girls for company?

Is affection sickening? Because nausea rolls through my belly as the memories of Lagos thrusting into that girl, needing her, inside her, all over her. And Sweets' words of admiration and esteem; *'He can fuck for a full day. We close The House when he's in a mood like this.'*

What mood is that?

Angsty feelings hammer through me. "Stay." I grab his thick wrist, and he stops midstep. "Stay with me." The desperation in my voice makes me cringe, but I hold his wrist tighter.

With his back to me, his chin turns until I see the outline of his profile. Dark eyes contemplate my request below deeply furrowed brows.

He looks… tired—open.

Funny, I always thought of him as this grumpy free-ranger, a rogue without a care in the world, but I was mistaken. *So* mistaken. Just because he doesn't share his emotions doesn't mean they are not painful. His thick, muscular body is ripping with silent burdens I didn't see.

Each scar.

The plate on his skull.

The sneer.

All bloody secrets.

And something inside me flips around. I realise it's not just my body that wants him anymore. Not just primal and instinctive. Not merely longing in my muscles—no.

There is warm affection in my chest. The pure kind. As though, I want him over me, his body covering mine, his thick muscles loosening because I don't want anything from him. He can just be. Can relax. And his world will become a little less… heavy.

If only for a moment.

"*Lagos*." When I breathe his name this time, it holds a heavy message. I want his gentle side. I say it aloud, because maybe no one ever has, and maybe no one ever will. "I don't want to hate you," I whisper. "You said my hatred was all you liked about me, but I don't want to hate you. And I don't. Not even when you're mean, so you don't have to be. It doesn't change anything. It doesn't work. I don't hate you," I repeat. "And I won't. Not even if you want me to, so please don't punish me for it."

My face goes bright red—I feel the embers of embarrassment. I may be a silly girl, but my declaration isn't made from soft, naïve thoughts but from a genuine, deep appreciation for him.

He slowly edges around, tight unease twirling in the dark depths of his almost black gaze. I feel his body burning as he stands before me, a looming form.

He reaches for the back of my head, fingers feeding into my

red hair this time, supporting my neck as I peer up at him. "I will not be cruel to you again, little flower."

I try not to whimper. He *was* cruel. "Okay. Thank you."

Warm fingers make circles at my neck and crown. "Why do you want me to stay?"

I get lost in his gaze for a moment. "I don't know," I answer honestly, just as Spero starts to fuss, severing the thick tension between us. I blink, and it seems to release us.

My foot shuffles backward once, and I turn to cringe at the bed.

"Stop." He removes the bags and suitcases and strips the sheet for me in one movement before covering the mattress with a new sheet.

Once he's finished, I grit my teeth and amble up on the bed, setting my back against the bedhead. My rib pangs, but I endure it. I need to get Spero used to the feel of my breast, to— I don't know… rehearse for when we have no food left.

I need to try breastfeeding him.

Apprehension finds little nerves inside me and picks at my courage.

"Will you stay while I try to feed him?" I don't know what I'm thinking, but my vulnerabilities lunge for him. "I don't want to be alone while I do this, and you are entirely the wrong person, and yet I can't imagine anyone else being here—" *Stop talking.* "For some reason."

He stares at me for a few heartbeats, and my lungs fill with anxious breaths…

Until he finally nods.

He crosses the room and lowers his massive body to the floor in front of the door, creating a heavy barricade with his form… For privacy. I didn't even think about that, but he did. That's why I want him here, to share this responsibility.

I should be embarrassed to do this in front of him, but I'm not. Should feel ashamed. This doesn't seem like the kind of activity a normal girl does in front of a Xin De male like Lagos.

I should change my mind.

Ask him to leave...

He won't mind.

A heavy sigh leaves him, and he drops his back to the door, his eyes level. Frown fixed.

I watch him for a moment, trying to pick up on a small sign that he doesn't want to be here. That he finds the entire thing distasteful and strange.

Without moving a muscle, his dark gaze meets mine. "I'm here."

He answers my insecurities.

Spero is crying, a needy sound, so I position my own little burden on my lap and drop one side of my shirt-dress and bra, exposing my left nipple. It tightens to a point.

My eyes lift to Lagos, wanting to know if he has looked away. I find his gaze unwavering—grounding. His attention seems to carry support, giving me air, offering me comfort, normalising... We are in this together.

I should want him to look away, but his gaze and time is dedicated to me, somehow making the weight of my uncertainties a little lighter.

Don't look away, Lagos.

With a steady breath, my eyes fall to Spero. I've no idea how to do this. None. It should be pretty straightforward, right?

I position my nipple between his little lips, cradle the back of his head, and just... wait. His chubby hands pat and palm my breast, entertained by the new feeling.

Nothing happens.

He doesn't even suck. Just sits babbling with the nipple between his lips. It might take time.

I sigh heavily. "I was breastfed by a Sired Mother," I say, making conversation, looking up at Lagos. "Were you?"

He stares at me, dark eyes eclipsed by serious brows. Silence sweeps over the room then, and my pulse pitter-patters in my throat. I thought the question was innocent... But I was wrong.

Something deeply emotional drowns inside his gaze. "I'm certain I wasn't," is all he says.

He answered. That is... *huge.*

A small smile touches my lips. "It'll be in your file. You were a Trade man, so you'll have a file. It has everything in it." I chance the subject again, but don't push for any details.

"Hm."

I use my finger in Spero's mouth, then try my nipple again. Filling the personal moment with words. "Do you want to know what's in *my* file then?"

"Yes," he answers so quickly, my heart soars. Even if he only wants to help me through this, even if his attention is fleeting. Just for today. Just for this moment. For the milk. I don't care.

My heart soars anyway.

"It said that I liked bananas," I start, smiling down at Spero and moving my nipple in his mouth. He sucks a little. This is good. "But I haven't had one in years, so I can't confirm that. And I used to draw patterns on everything, not pictures, just swirls, but I used to do it for hours and hours—" I smile and take a big breath. "Or so it says. What do you like?" I gaze up from Spero, finding Lagos still watching. "Or *did* you like, when you were a child?"

"I don't remember," he states, firm but gentle. "Tell me more about baby Dahlia."

"I like this side of you." *Too much.* I clear my throat. "I, erm, I first laughed at four months old. And I loved gazing at myself in the mirror from five months old and apparently never stopped as a child." I shake my head, amused by myself. "I don't know why."

His eyes soften on me. "I do."

My breath catches.

Does he mean... is he implying that... That he thinks I'm worth gazing at?

"Have you..." I falter. 'I do' stirs inside me, making me feel silly. I need to move the conversation along, or I will drown in those two words. "Have *you* ever read your baby file?"

He doesn't move a muscle, his features schooled. "No."

"I wonder if you used to smile as a baby," I say, my tongue getting the better of me. "Or if you— Maybe you just didn't like the way it felt... Or something."

"I doubt I smiled as a baby."

A knot forms in my belly. Lagos is irrevocably sad. I want more than anything to hold baby Lagos and make him smile. "But *everything* is wonderful when you're a baby," I try.

"Not for everyone."

My throat thickens, forcing me to look at my little assassin. I sigh. "It will be for Spero."

"Thanks to you."

"And you," I add, but that makes his frown deepen. "I'm not lactating," I admit as Spero starts to scream with hunger, fussing for the bottle. "What if we can't get him food, Lagos? I have to make this work. If he went hungry and was in pain. I couldn't bear it."

"I won't let that happen."

I stare straight at him. "You're in this with me then? Protecting him? What has changed?" Whether it's the hormones, my failed attempt at breastfeeding, or baby Lagos with no smile, I feel heat prickling the backs of my eyes now.

"You took a beating for the Shadow baby." Lagos rises to his feet, rolling his shoulders like a beast after a long sleep. He approaches me. "That changed everything, little flower."

A tear pinches the corner of my eye as I lay Spero on my lap and retrieve the bottle instead—defeated. He sucks on the bottle, eager. I failed.

Feeling Lagos' warm, magnetic presence standing over me, I look up at him just as a single tear slides down my cheek. "Can you tell me one thing you like then?" I wipe at the insolent tear. "Just one?"

His dark eyes track my tear. "*You*."

I inhale hard, my lungs drawing in the word, wanting to hold it inside my chest and keep it forever.

He likes me.

The door pushes open, Lagos steps to block me, and I pull my sleeve up to hide my breast. Sniffling and wiping carelessly at my wet eyes, I look across to find Tomar is standing in the doorway.

He shifts his gaze between Lagos and me. "Why are you crying, Dahlia?"

"Knock," is all Lagos says.

"Given I knew you were in here, I didn't think that was necessary." Tomar folds his arms over his chest. "My mistake—"

"Yes, it was." The possessiveness in Lagos' tone stirs the air, brewing a storm that scares me.

This has to stop.

I breathe out in a rush. "It's okay. I was trying to feed Spero. We didn't know it was you." I attempt to soften this entire situation, adjusting my clothing. Careful not to move too quickly and trouble my broken rib, I climb slowly to my feet.

There is something unspoken between them, making my chest squeeze and ache.

It's my fault.

"I have food for you." Tomar walks across the room, and Lagos disappears from it, fists tight by his sides. "Here you go." The door closes, and I force myself to look at Tomar, not the door.

I'm handed a small bowl with what looks like potatoes and a few strips of meat. "It's snake," he says.

My eyes widen. "Snake?"

"Just pretend it's fish."

I cringe. "It's fish." A roll of nausea moves up my throat, so I swallow it down. Looking at the door, I find myself longing for Lagos. He might have lied to me and said it was fish, but Tomar is honest. I should want honesty, shouldn't I?

Protection from unpleasant truths that won't actually hurt me seem pathetically nice.

Picking at the potato with my fingers, I sit on the bed while Tomar prepares the room, ready to sleep in.

In a quiet kind of limbo, we spend time eating and preparing the beds, and finally, Tomar lies down on the single sofa. Resting his forearm on his head, his knees lifted so he can fit on the cushions, he inhales deeply and exhales everything—surrendering to his exhaustion.

I spend the following few hours on my back with Spero tucked between me and the wall, blinking at the ceiling, listening to the muted but provocative conversations outside the room.

Is Lagos having fun?

Is he being… *entertained*?

I cover my face with my palms and groan, needles of jealousy prick at my insides. This may be the last time he can 'fuck' things. I roll to face the wall, my lungs squeezing, withholding precious air. I can't breathe.

He said he *likes* me.

Apparently, I like bananas, but that doesn't mean I won't enjoy other fruits. I bet this roadhouse is open all hours, so he can really get the urges out. One girl after another.

I close my eyes and feel tears pressing through my lashes. *Why?* I clutch my stomach as it twists. Why is it physically hurting me? He isn't my lover. He's merely my guide, a reluctant one at that. Just helping me escape.

That is all he owes me.

I focus on serious matters: This might be the last stop with food and company. The further north we travel, the further from civilisation, the more savage and unpredictable The Cradle will become.

I peer around the room. This may be one of the better stops. I swallow at the thought.

Chapter Twenty-Two

Dahlia

I wake to the sound of deep breaths so close I can almost feel the sound cascading directly into my ear.

A shiver rushes down my spine, and all my hairs stand on end. The breathing is endlessly deep, rumbling in my bones and pulling me completely from sleep.

I peer over my shoulder and down the length of the bed, squinting through the dark to see a large body lying horizontally just below my feet.

Lagos.

And that breathing is him… asleep. So, deeply relaxed.

I sigh heavily, pointing my toes to brush the side of his form. The room and the roadhouse seem to disappear, or maybe its shelter is no longer significant. I have him.

Help me; I'm completely and utterly falling in love with this emotionally unavailable, inhuman male.

After quickly checking Spero, I sit with a quiet wince and stare down at the huge Xin De monster at the foot of my bed. His knees hang off, legs bent, and feet planted on the floor—he's massive.

It's dim here, but I can see that he is bare-chested, only wearing briefs. I can't tell the colour, but a long bulge lays over his thigh like he grew a forearm from his groin.

I swallow.

Snap my eyes up.

Deep shadows and subtle highlights contour his strong features. His long, dark lashes lay on his cheeks, and, somehow, he is even more striking when he sleeps.

My gaze slides down his face, revelling in this stolen moment. He has high cheekbones and a perfect nose, straight but not too prominent. His half-parted lips look soft, surrounded by a neat brown beard that is so male.

Kiss him...

My eyes drift to where Tomar sleeps soundly and back to Lagos again. My mouth suddenly dries.

I part my lips to breathe, finding my chest tight from the overflowing nervous energy as I lean forward.

Oh my, he is stunning.

Not like a flower or a painting.

His beauty is too unforgettable to be simple lines and perfect patterns. His beauty is a forest fire, wild and unpredictable, rugged and fierce. You get lost in it… Or burnt.

Without thinking, without a drop of sense, I hover my lips above his, drawing in his warm, deep breath.

"What are you doing, little flower?"

I gasp. "Please don't move or wake up." My lips brush his while I talk, and I nearly collapse for more. "Please, keep your eyes closed. I want to be alone with you. I want to pretend you won't throw hurtful words at me."

He is humming as I speak, ignoring my words, as my lips touch his, his hand feeding between my hair and neck. He grips the nape of my neck with gentle dominance and pulls my lips to meet his.

I. Melt.

Energy skitters along my skin.

He tastes sweet and metallic, and his eyes are still closed as his mouth moves over mine slowly, leisurely. Perfectly. Lagos tastes my lower lip, groaning through me as he sweeps his tongue in to taste more. And more.

My eyes flutter shut.

I don't know what to do. I've never been kissed like this before. It is so much, so intimate, so personal. I want to bounce and giggle, but that would break the kiss. The kiss I never want to end.

My pulse buzzes in every cell and my hands fumble with where to be. On the mattress? On his bare chest?

I end up leaning with my palms flexing on his hard chest, supporting myself and my torso so my rib doesn't cause a scene and ruin the moment.

This moment.

The moment Lagos kisses me.

He lifts his free hand to the other side of my neck, thumbs sliding under my jaw, one stroking my pulse up and down, both guiding me against him.

My core clenches.

I can't stop the moans rolling from me now, can't stifle them, then—

He breaks our kiss and presses my forehead to his. "*Shh*, little flower. I don't want Tomar to hear your sweet moans. They are mine."

I pant in the darkness of my eyelids, senses stolen, along with all the air in my lungs. "Please." I don't know what I'm begging for.

More.

So much more.

His hum of amusement strokes my face. "It's not fair, is it?"

"What's not fair?" I whisper, every muscle frozen on a cliff's edge, wanting to leap off but not to die, to feel something.

Something *explosive.*

"The way your cunt begs for me." The pulse of his dark, vulgar utterance hits my lips, matching the one that flurries in the column of my neck.

I nod, my forehead moving against his. "Yes. It's not fair."

"At the next stop, I will take care of that warm, tight place between your thighs. The last time I touched you, you were weak and drugged. This time, you can pretend I made you. Forced you. I will make it all better in secret. In the dark where you yearn for my depravities."

Oh, my. "Yes."

He chuckles darkly. "You can guard your soft heart, but your pussy will weep with pleasure when I touch it. The monster inside me will come for you, little flower, and it'll claim every inch of your purity. Are you sure you want that?"

I squirm on the mattress, uncomfortable, wet heat gathering in my knickers. I'll do anything for that.

Anything.

I breathe the word, *"Yes."*

And then he slides out from under me, leaving me bent over an empty space that vibrates with his warmth and scent.

Intoxicated by my first kiss with Lagos, I slowly straighten and open my eyes to the shadowy room. *Oh, my;* he woke up. He woke up! He woke up while I was stealing a kiss. Mortified, I imagine dissolving into the mattress, a puddle of silly goo.

And now he's leaving?

He didn't want that.

Rejection washes over me.

I search the cluttered, dimly lit room to find Tomar a sleeping silhouette in the corner, and Lagos pulling his jeans on.

His huge length slaps his abdomen as he has to physically tuck it in to get the zip over it. A rock-hard outline forms. It is any surprise that it doesn't tear the seams.

I can sew…

I could fix that.

If it did.

Groaning at my silly thoughts, I cup my forehead. I have a fever. I'm sick. Hot. Clammy. Help.

Questions churn in my mind but don't find their way out. Why… Why are you leaving the room? *Who* are you going to see? Did I put him in *the mood*? The one Sweets spoke about.

"Lagos?" is all I end on.

"Where are you going?" Tomar is sitting up in the dark, and I instinctively drop to my spine. Pain slides between my ribs like a knife through butter. I cry out and cup the area.

"Are you okay?" Tomar asks.

"Flower…" Lagos pauses by the door, looking like he is about to lunge for me, but then Spero starts to fuss, and Tomar is sleepily standing.

"I'm okay." I cut the air between us with my hand, defensive. Lagos was going to leave. He should just go.

He stills. Stares.

"Out," he finally answers Tomar, disappearing from the room, leaving *me* with a pool of need between my thighs, perspiration misting my skin, and the hammering of neglect crushing my chest into my lungs.

"I'll feed him." Tomar rubs his hand down his face, ambling over to me. "You can get some more sleep, Dahlia. We have a long drive tomorrow, and you look wrecked."

Wrecked.

That's a very accurate word.

Chapter Twenty-Three

Lagos

Raging for a fuck after feeling her hesitant lips on mine, tasting that sweet, young breath inside my mouth, I storm from the roadhouse and out into the deadly Redwind with no more than an upward glance at the low-life patrons of this cast-out roadhouse.

We stop here because it is where I belong, with the broken women and the vile men. We were not meant to stop here this time. This… This slum is not the place for a girl like my little flower.

My little flower?

Well, fuck me.

"Lagos! You'll bleed out there," I hear called after me. The voice belongs to a nameless, faceless no one, though her pussy would know my cock.

I may bleed—it's the least I deserve for touching her again. Tainting those sweet, inexperienced lips.

The Missing Moon is vengeful tonight, leaving The Cradle in stark, deathly darkness as I pace. Feeling the wind lash my hide-like skin, I beg for more. More lashes. More violence.

I open my arms, pulsing my muscles, wanting them to rip free of my skin. Show me I'm human! Prove it! Make me feel. Give me agony. Regret. Make me feel just a slither of what she makes me feel so I can be worthy… So I can be worthy of her touch.

There has to be more sensation than this left inside me. I feel nothing until she looks at me, and then too much too suddenly. I can't keep it.

The feeling.

It comes and goes with her.

Why her?

I don't fucking know. Perhaps it's that tight, untouched body—I am a fucking beast after all. Innocence is like honey. But I've seen innocence and beauty before, tasted it, fucked it, killed it. But her…

Being with her as she fights the pain in her ribcage, strong upper-lipped. As she explores her new freedoms, her own thoughts, her sweet awe.

Perhaps it was watching her stifle tears to breastfeed another woman's child, a Xin De, at that. A creature, not a human, and then to watch her… *fail.*

To. Watch. Her. Fail.

I felt more than I've felt in decades, almost more than was bearable.

I wander around this land like a mere part of the landscape, acting on impulse, owing my life to Tomar, so I serve him. But I'm not experiencing anything anymore—agony, happiness, joy, devastation. It's all been bled from me, drained to a husk of male flesh.

I inhale the wind, daring it to shred my nostrils as it should, fill my lungs and drown me, blind me—

Nothing happens.

Inhuman—the gills in my nostrils activate, filtering and removing the shards from my indestructible body, and my nictitating membrane slides to shield my irises. And the numb…

the numbness I feel in response to a gruelling Redwind is enough for me to abandon the idea of her.

And me.

And us.

I know what I said, what I want, what her body wants, but I won't take more from her than I already have. I should stop this now.

Because I'm not fucking human, not organic, not real—I will not taint her further with my bloodied hands.

I rear to the left and head back inside, heaving, chest pumping.

My eyes dart around, landing on a girl by the bar, petite in stature, with medium length, red hair—she'll do. I can turn her around, wrap that red hair around my fist, and rearrange her guts, never looking at her face—pretend it is her. Get my fix—*calm the fuck down.*

"Yes?" The redhead slinks from the bar as my hot gaze burns through her, my intent ripping her clothes off. Hopeful stupidity quirks her lips.

"Are you clean?" I stalk forward. The little thing caught in my snare flushes across her chest and to her cheeks.

She nods. "Yes, Lagos."

I smell her heated arousal in the smoky air.

"I know what I look like to you." I stop in front of her, forcing her to crank her neck back just to hold my sharp gaze. "I know you like what you see, but I'm fucking ugly on the inside, believe me. Are you ugly on the inside?"

A little smile hits her lips. Like a fool. A damn fool who thinks I am playing a game. I'm not. I'm warning her.

"I'm *disgusting* on the inside," she purrs. "Aren't we all?"

Her last three words... Those three words nest into my guts and spawn. Aren't. We. All...

No—not her.

I am.

You are.

Tomar is.

My head snaps up to the door as that last thought pounds like fists beating at my chest, a threatening display. The man I call brother… He has been acting wildly out of character around her.

He likes her. Too much.

A sweet girl, and he is ready to fall from grace. Well, not while I'm alive.

Not with her.

Without another word, I stride to the door and return to the room, unwilling to leave a pure little flower alone with a starved man.

Chapter Twenty-Four

Dahlia

I sleep through the night, vaguely aware of Lagos coming and going from the room, his dark outline crossing the space only to leave again, but never for long.

Tomar tends to Spero, and I let him. Guilt is ever present, but in the end, exhaustion wins.

Between slumber and wakefulness, at some point during first-light, I am somewhat aware of a conversation.

Lagos saying, "She needs more sleep. She's still healing."

Tomar agrees, but says, "There is a doctor at the Common Community. If we can just get her there, he will help her recover."

"Fine. I've fuelled up, and unloaded the crate for our stay, so I've made room in the back seat for her and the Shadow bab—"

"Spero," Tomar corrects. "So she won't be in your lap this time, brother?"

It is all a hazy montage of shuffling and voices as I dip in and out of sleep. Never moving or fully opening my eyes because every time I do, I relive the kiss, the dark promises, and the moment he left—again.

When I finally get up, we hit the road straightaway, leaving that little *bit* of me behind forever. The place of my first kiss.

Goodbye, roadhouse.

One little death.

Right now, the truck throttles down the long desert road, the Redwind and mist-covered sun clashing around us like a wildfire. I blink out the passenger window and thoughts cascade in. Fester.

Why did he leave?

Am I a bad kisser?

I tell myself—chant, even—that none of this is about us, it is about Spero. My new Purpose.

Spero is my priority.

Not Lagos the Rogue.

Forget about Lagos.

But my silly affection-nausea kicks me while I'm down. A sinking feeling in my stomach taunts me with, 'was he with another girl?' While my heart balloons saying, 'no, he likes you.' So, I'm both heavy and light, and the two pull me apart at the centre.

Love and sex *are* distracting; Tomar was right. He said that if a man is without *it* or denied *it*, it can become an obsession. I think this applies to women, too.

It is not fair. Our days together are numbered. Doesn't he know, doesn't he care? Soon, I'll lose another friend, companion, or person I care for.

Lagos and Tomar.

All I now know.

I like Tomar and will miss him dearly, but I am… I am lost in Lagos.

And we only have a few days together, then he'll leave, and I will never see him again… Realisation presses on my chest, and suddenly I can't breathe—

I. Will. Never. See him again.

With a sigh, I gaze at the front seat. Lagos is driving this time, his broad shoulders bulking out from either side of the chair.

Tomar has his shoes up on the dash, arms folded across his chest, resting but not asleep.

Reaching to the seat beside me, I place my hand on Spero's warm chest and tap lightly. "Will you both leave as soon as we get there? Or... will you stay a while? Until I'm ready." I feel completely pathetic, childish, and vulnerable asking this, but I do it anyway. I add, "I trust you." My heart pauses for the answer. "And you'll miss Spero, right?"

"I will miss Spero." Tomar peers in the rearview mirror, soft eyes meeting mine. "We aren't allowed to stay, Dahlia. I'm sorry, that can't happen."

What?

Used to navigating my broken rib, I straighten in a smooth and careful way. "What do you mean?"

"Only Common know where it is. Xin De aren't even allowed past the tunnel."

I chew on my lower lip, trying to create an image in my mind of this place. "The tunnel?" I check.

He nods, blue eyes still on me in the mirror. "Yes. The Doctor, Robert, will collect you and Spero at the front of the second tunnel. He will take you into the Community and give you a room."

"So..." Struck by a horrible truth, I blurt out, "You have never actually seen the community."

He sighs. "No."

I huff, shock and fear racing through my tone. "What if it's a trap?"

"It isn't." Tomar slides his boots off the dash and turns in his seat, facing me, settling me with his kind eyes. "I've— Rather, *we've* been taking people there for decades, and I've seen some of the escapees since. Met with them to check in, offer aid, and exchange. They are happy."

"So..." I ponder on this... How many people have they saved? How many girls has *Lagos* saved? Is he rude to them all? Does he kiss them and touch them between the legs?

I shut down my incessant jealousy, reaching for the highlight of the conversation.

"So… I can leave?" I confirm.

"It is not a prison, Dahlia." Tomar chuckles at my surprise, twisting to the front again. "You're free to do as you please, but to be safe—"

"Don't leave," Lagos barks, his thunderous tone kicking me in the chest.

"Why?" I challenge, just to retaliate. "I'm free. I belong to no man." I know why—it's not safe. The Trade are hunting Spero, and I'm his guardian. For life. Forever. It is what I agreed to weeks ago at The Bite. It is what I want.

He growls that inhuman sound that flares heat through my core and warns the provocative words on my tongue.

Brute.

"You shouldn't growl at people," I say through a smile. "They may mistake you for being antisocial."

Tomar snorts with a sudden burst of laughter, not at all trying to smooth over my obvious teasing. Instead, adds, "That would be a real travesty. They might think you're unapproachable, brother."

Laughter fills my throat. "It'd break your little heart—"

"To be left out," Tomar finishes.

"Take it easy." Lagos grunts, eyes fixed on the unclear road ahead, but I think that maybe a small part of him enjoyed the breeze of light conversation.

A very, very small part.

I chuckle quietly and realise this is the first time I've laughed—properly laughed—since Maple died.

Lifting my eyes, I meet Lagos' gaze in the mirror. He pauses on me, looking at my smile, and softening before returning to the desert terrain.

My heart pitter-patters.

Casting my gaze through the window beside me, a bright smile rests on my lips. This isn't goodbye forever; Tomar said he saw people again, outside the community.

And they are happy.

Maybe it's the dopamine from the laughter or the fact Lagos almost played a role in a joke, but for the first time in what feels like forever, I'm a bit excited for what the future holds for me. I look at Spero, *'And for you.'*

If Tomar meets me one day in the future, will Lagos come? Are they always together? Suddenly, my mind plucks at a word spoken: *brother*.

I suppose when you travel together for, what did he say, decades? That person would feel like family.

How did they meet? I don't want to ask anything that might dampen the easy mood or affect the smooth brow above the brute's steel-colour gaze.

Things have been.... *tense* between them. I'm glad whatever it was seems to be loosening.

I love that expression, Lagos.

I know Tomar saved him... which in itself seems highly unlikely as Lagos is a behemoth, huge across the shoulders and monstrous hands, a giant. And Tomar is only slightly bigger than a Common man.

I'm deep in thought when Lagos suddenly curses, throwing the steering wheel to the left, jostling my body. I cry out but lunge to brace Spero. We churn up an unsealed road, and I try to stifle my whimpers. Red dirt storms around us as we drive away from the main highway, and then—

He slams on the brakes, and I wince as we jerk to a blunt stop.

"What was that?" Tomar spits out, panting as though he has been running.

"Flower, are you okay?" Lagos reaches a big, warm hand out to me, placing it on my thigh... I feel it everywhere.

I nod fast, questions buzzing on my tongue but silenced by the abrupt rumbling of an engine in the near distance.

And getting closer.

Through a wince, I twist in my seat. The demonic sound

grows, and a distinct pounding, almost like metal chewing dirt, echoes from every direction.

"Fuck." Tomar turns toward the main road, and we all watch vehicle lights filter through the Redwind. "Why aren't we getting the hell out of here?"

"It's not Marshals, not military," Lagos states, his tone blunt and impatient.

Tomar's unease strikes me. I freeze, not sure what to say or do. My mouth drops open, eyes wide, looking between them for answers.

Tomar searches the red mist. "What do you mean it's not—"

"Wait..." Lagos points to the ceiling just as something screeches above us like lightning striking. "Odio."

"Who?" I ask, gripping the passenger handle. Two huge tanks appear on the highway, and our truck vibrates as The Cradle quakes beneath the colossal vehicles.

We watch them pass.

I hold my breath.

One after the other.

Three armoured tanks.

Tomar says, "Not the military, huh?"

"No." Lagos shakes his head, fierce eyes assessing the red waste. "The Guard."

The Guard? The special military personnel that protect royalty, lords, Trade officials, and the like?

"Are they gone?" Tomar darts around, surveying the road behind us for more encroaching vehicles. "Do you think they saw us?"

Lagos sighs roughly, his black eyes meeting mine. "That bird doesn't miss a damn thing."

"What?" I breathe. "What. Bird?"

"Why aren't they stopping, then?" Tomar asks, a thread of deep discomfort in his tone, reminding me of the dangers we face out here.

"Because"—Lagos swings the car around, heading back toward the now empty highway— "That was the king."

I stammer. "Like... Rome. *The* Rome. Like, Rome of The Strait?"

Nerves rush through me.

The Cradle's Monarch, Rome of The Strait, has legendary status throughout the land, being ruthless, unbeaten in combat, and sworn to fiercely protect The Cradle and ensure each Trade citizen has the chance for Meaningful Purpose.

He is a deity.

There is a screen in each building in the Half-tower, and we used to congregate around it once a week to watch the Trade updates—invasions, rescues, and celebrations. Rome is featured in almost every update. And we are required to watch them—all Trade-aligned citizens, but then...

I'm no longer one of them.

I'm... I don't know. Trade girls say, Fur Born. As in, girls who live in their fur. Not for Purpose but as animals. It is a derogatory term that I will not accept.

"The one and only," Tomar answers, his bright blue eyes sweeping over me as Lagos continues down the road slower than before. "Rome the Heartless. Are you okay? Is Spero okay?"

"Yes." I tuck the tiny assassin back into his nest on the seat, but he's awake now. Wide-eyed and staring at a spot on the ceiling. "So, that was the king... King of The Cradle? How do you know?"

Tomar drags his hand down his face, exhaling heavily. "That screech must have been his eagle, Odio. It never leaves his side. Which means he was inside one of those tanks." Tomar looks at Lagos. "And he must have more important things to do than check our vehicle."

Lagos' jaw pulses. "They'll be back for us. They know where we are. We have to take a different route."

I place my hand over my heart, feeling the racing organ beneath my palm. "Luckily we got off the road when we did."

Clearly shaken by what just happened, my mind ticks over blank thoughts as Lagos turns onto the highway and into a red abyss.

My breath catches to behold the endless red nothing in front of us. Being dependent on them is difficult and easy for the exact opposite reasons.

I worry my lower lip. I trust them to know what to do, to get us there safely no matter what obstacles we hit head on— My brows furrow… But we didn't hit this one, did we? We avoided it.

How *did* we avoid it?

I lift my head and stare at Lagos in the tiny mirror, dread creeping in on suspicion's heels. "How did you know they were coming, Lagos?"

Tomar's eyes shift to Lagos, and the lingering pause has a pulse of its own, sending icy fear down my spine.

Can I… *Can* I trust them?

Did he see the tanks? No.

Did that thing, that bird, did it screech before or after he pointed at the sky? I can't be sure. I didn't focus on the sequence of events at the time, but I feel in my belly that he pointed before… How did he know? Am I going crazy?

"He saw the tank," Tomar answers, smooth and controlled. "Xin De eyesight is something else."

No. Shaking my head, I look down and frown, my eyes losing focus as my mind clouds with thoughts. "No. There was no tank when you turned off the road, Lagos. I'm sure of it. And there was no way you could have known that thing, that bird, was above us. So, how?" My eyes lift and hit his in the mirror. And there it is, in his gaze—a secret. A lie. "Lagos?"

My voice shudders out. "Where are you taking me?"

"*Dahlia.*" Tomar turns in his seat, but he's not as comforting this time; in fact, his attention shrinks me backward. "We are taking you to the—"

"Don't lie to me!" I grab the door handle and squeeze it. "I'll jump out!" And for a split second, I consider doing it. Jumping out into the waste, fuelled by the anger of being deceived more than by thoughts of survival— But then my tiny burden fusses beside me.

Spero.

My heart sinks.

Panic carries bile to my mouth. I'm stuck. Trapped.

Tomar holds his hand up. "Woah. *Dahlia,* let go of the handle. You're not in any danger with us—"

"Tell her," Lagos grunts.

I gape at Lagos.

"That's not a good idea," Tomar says.

And I look back at him.

"Tell her!" Lagos snaps.

Back at Lagos.

I growl. "Tell me what?"

The silence screams.

Tomar straightens in his seat before leaning back with a heavy sigh. "We have never done this. Telling you puts Lagos in danger."

The truck slows—deathly slow—and as it does, my heart races into my ears, echoing like my head is empty of anything else.

The truck stops.

Staring forward at the red-swept plane, Lagos says, "I sensed the bird. I felt the tankers on the terrain." He turns, showing me his side profile over his wide shoulder. A near-black gaze shifts to me, and the tang of something metallic slides along my tongue. "Because I'm a Shadow."

Chapter Twenty-Five

Lagos

Twenty-five years ago

My heart thunders between my ears as the sirens ring out, the Desert Dogs snap and snarl at my heels, the Redwind moves the small foliage, and floodlights circle the rocky quarry that cups the metallic compound.

Light and dark move on the ground, making it hard to navigate and avoid holes or loose rocks. The wind whips around, slicing my arms. The dense Redwind has a life of its own, lancing rocks and sand at me. Attacking me. Indiscriminately.

I can't look back at the metallic fortress. I have to keep running.

My brain is on fire. Trapped deep inside my body, I propel my muscles forward through the magnetic fields. It feels like hooks pull my veins, drawing them out through my spine.

Vomit fills my throat, so I spit some out and swallow the rest down.

Panting, heaving, running, jumping, the treacherous terrain shuffling, I press through the resistance of the field.

Can't stop.

All the beacons surrounding the Shadow Training compound are on, surging through me. Demanding my compliance. Ordering me back to my room, to be tortured, to be trained, to be hardened and charred.

I can't go back even if I wanted to—they would kill me now. Knowing that I can fight the agony and push through a wall of pain that should be unbearable. Death is meant to come first, suicide, even. To make it stop. Not resilience, not against the *Iron-Draft*.

Go back.

Go back.

Make it stop.

I don't know where that slimy voice comes from, but I growl at it—ignore it. No, I won't stop.

My thighs burn, my arms draw my torso onward, and I climb the rocky quarry walls, pound the ground, then suddenly—

I hit a road.

The Redwind, a deep storm of crimson, swirls up the clearing, the absence of rocks and concaves, an opening for its unrelenting wrath.

I run. And run.

Hundreds of metres down the road, an old car suddenly flies by, too rickety to be Trade-aligned. I race after it, waving my hands. "Hey!"

But they aren't going to stop for a half-naked beast of a man like me. Even at fifteen, I am more man than evolution ever allowed. My ancestors were designed. Built. Engineered. With traits of the beasts in the human formula.

I've got at least four different lives smeared on my torso, lashes of scarlet and bile, and sweat. I have wounds and scars up and down my skin; each holds a tortuous memory and pairs with a conditioned response.

The hands that cave skulls. The feet that stomp through bone. I'm terrifying.

Adrenaline pulses through me. I sprint down the narrow road. No one will be out here. No one will be close.

Goodwill is a lie.

No one would stop.

Suddenly, energy pours down my crown, blanketing me in sheer agony. My body convulses, but I growl and fight through the pain. Run.

They are trying to bring me down from the inside out, overwhelming my iron-blood. My legs threaten to collapse, but I thrust through it as if it were a tangible wall—I bash the bricks, the fibres, the cement down, baring my teeth. Nothing should hurt this much. No one should endure this. Every pain receptor inside me detonates.

Kill yourself.

It'll all be over soon.

Just kill yourself.

Chapter Twenty-Six

Lagos

Now she knows.

I told her she should run from me—warned her. And now she is mine, and I'm in deep. Feeling greedy. I am going to finish what I started with her. I don't know who I was trying to be—moral, I suppose. Tomar…

And seeing that hating myself and my kind is a plague that never ends, why not fuck her? Why not fuck her tight, inexperienced body and be the vile abomination I am.

I shove the truck into gear and take off down the unsealed road, burning up the red dirt as we pick up speed.

"Dahlia? We are the good guys. We are not going to hurt you or Spero. You must know that." Tomar cranks his neck around to look at her, her cheeks losing colours, her body stiff. Fight and flight always have a challenger in Common humans. And it's freeze.

Most little girls freeze.

Shadows do none of the above. They do not react; they act.

I don't have time to console her or explain. I have to get as far from the place we were seen as possible.

If I have to choose between the sweet looks she gives me, the gentle smile—I clear my throat— or her safety, then I will fucking choose her safety.

Every. Fucking. Time.

I will go west.

As far west as I can.

"He's not operational anymore." Tomar studies my little flower as she wilts and hides, tucking herself into the corner of the truck. Petrified.

Not operational...

Fucking perfect choice of words, like I'm a homicidal machine, made of killer edges, coils and joints, a branded engine, fuelled up and ready to be activated.

For murder.

I lift my hand and tuck my hair behind my ear, my fingers skimming the metal part of my skull. Not operational, indeed. Unable to be destroyed by the Brain-Interface coil they had in my head, but still drawn to every fucking beacon—the devices The Trade use to control us—and every other Shadow. Including the Shadow baby sitting behind my seat.

I sensed him while he was still in the womb. Tomar made the connection and communicated with Maple through her Ward, unknowing the civil unrest would take him as a casualty, and she would die in labour.

Then... I sensed the baby in the Half-tower and found a redhead with an infant cornered in a laneway by Marshal Blues.

I feel him now—behind me.

My blood literally surges in response to other Shadows, not unlike a thousand tiny lightning bolts trying to escape from inside my veins.

And I know that if I held him, time would warp, but I would be in control. It would stretch, but I would understand it. And so would he.

"Lagos has no ties to The Trade anymore," Tomar continues, "His life is at risk if you tell anyone what he is, even in the Common Community. You cannot trust anyone. Dahlia?"

"Leave her!" I bark, angry at myself and him for being so careless with our information. We should have never told her about the Shadow baby. We should have taken the thing to the Common Community ourselves. Dropped the little Lace Girl back at the Half-tower to be a Trade man's unconscious fuck toy.

She would have never crawled into my mind. Never made me feel.

I fist the steering wheel, hearing the plastic crack under the pressure of my ragging possessiveness. Memories of her assault me. Of her bruised and naked in my arms. Of her virgin blood on my fingers. Of her soft, inexperienced lips trying to find a rhythm above mine. Mine. Mine. Fucking Mine. That's all I know, and I can't think of anything more dangerous than a little flower plucked and kept by an iron-blooded beast.

My eyes drift up to her reflection again, muscles rippling along my arms and over my shoulders in response to her withdrawn expression. Green irises shuffle as she panics internally. Fingers drawing swirls on her knees. Her bottom lip is tucked between her teeth, gnawed and worried. I want to hold her.

Fuck. I force my eyes back to the road and keep driving toward the Horizon.

West.

~

A hot electric outline comes into view along the hazy horizon belt. The shape of an old farmhouse in the middle of nowhere. Nothing abnormal alters the flow of my blood, which doesn't mean it is abandoned, only that there are no Shadows, and no military with beacons.

It is strangely still. I sense very little through my iron-blood.

I glance in the mirror for the hundredth time these past three hours on the road. My little flower is cradling Spero in her lap, holding a bottle to his lips, and staring out the window. She hasn't spoken, and after my warning, neither has Tomar. And I'm not eager to converse at the best of times. Silence is usually pleasing, but somehow, when she is in it, it's painful.

Painful and frustrating.

The farmhouse expands as we drive through a set of rickety fences, once surely for game or live meat before the Trade banned all independent ventures. Quality control issues. More likely to be simply *control* issues.

"What is this?" she speaks, and I swear my lungs draw in my first full breath in hours.

"Looks like an old farm." Tomar pulls his shoes off the dash and sits up. "Is it safe?" Twisting in his seat, he surveys the area. "We should go in first."

I've already noted everything; there is a barn locked with thick chains that I'll check first; a window open on the second level; an old white Ute with the front screen blown out, eaten at the tyres by grass and roots, that might have fuel; the mountains are far enough away that I'll spot invaders if they attempt to approach the home while we are inside.

"I will," I state, pulling up right alongside the vine-woven veranda. Opening the door, I step out and shut it in one movement, not waiting for a response. My body cuts through the Redwind, parting it as I walk to the old barn. I fist the chains laced around the twin doors and snap them.

After I've checked the barn and the scrapheap of a car, I head toward the truck. As I break through the dense crimson wind, beelining directly for her door, she is staring wide-eyed at me. My third eyelid closes against the sand. To her, my irises will appear near white. Her lips part and her startled gaze tracks my every step — Then I open the door and scoop her and the infant into my arms.

She grips my shirt.

My blood pulses and each nerve ending reaches for the child at her chest. He starts to cry, but it isn't from pain. It's change. Just a change like any other, a sudden bright light, a splash of cold water. Our blood interacts much the same. A sensation attached to a sense that no one else possesses.

I kick open the front door and walk her into the farmhouse. Lowering her carefully, her body slides along mine, and her tiny hand unpeels from my shirt as if reluctant.

I check the switch at the door, my keen ears picking up a hum of electricity. It's wired, but the bulbs must be burned out or non-existent.

"Wait here."

Leaving her by the door, I search the rest of the farmhouse; three empty rooms each with closets, dust rising as I move around.

I follow the narrow hallway past them, my shoulders brushing the walls. Ducking under the doorframe, I enter a large kitchen that overlooks an old garden now weaved with foliage that thrashes around in the wind.

This house has been empty for a long time. I check the taps. A rattle begins above the ceiling, banging and racing to the spout. Water spits out and then flows. *Interesting.* There must be a mill around here somewhere. I wet my hands and stroke the water through my beard.

Then I head back to her.

"Safe?" Tomar calls through the house to me. My boots stomp on the wooden floorboards.

Despite the fragile fixtures and ancient furnishings, and the narrow passages only suited for Common, the farmhouse is perfect to hoard up in. Not for me—I roam, not settle—but for her. I could see her on this porch swing with the Shadow baby, making little swirls with her fingers on his back.

Singing.

Smiling.

Fuck.

What am I fucking thinking about? When she is around, I don't know who I am anymore. Soft. Pathetic.

Just as I return to the front door, Tomar shoulders in with her pack and a crate. "All good? We should mark this place down for next time." He exhales hard, setting the crate down, still weak. "Yeah?"

Out of nowhere and without moving an inch, she whispers to the dusty house, "You said Shadows have excess iron in their blood..."

She pauses.

I stop in front of her.

Tomar hands her the tiny pack of her personal items. "Go on, ask anything," he says encouragingly.

"That... That it tethers them to The Cradle?" She blinks over and over as if these questions have been rolling around her mind for the past few hours, and only now does she have the strength to say them. "Magnetic fields or something? So... How then? How can you be—" She shakes her sweet head, disbelief in her flat expression. "*Free* from The Trade?"

"That's a complicated question," I state, not ready to share this with her.

"I'm so glad you're asking questions, though," Tomar pushes forward. "This is good. We can tell you whatever you need, Dahlia. Let's get settled for the night first..." He *smiles* at her, and my forehead tightens. "It hurts to see the distrust in your eyes." But then he lifts his hand to her cheek, runs his knuckles down the soft curve, and the control in my head pops.

I. Don't. Fucking. Like. It!

I step into his heels, my much larger body looming over his back. My presence burns him with a warning so deeply volatile I don't know what I'll do if he doesn't take his fucking hand off her fucking cheek. Before I can grapple my possessive rage, I grab his hand and pull it from her face. "No."

That's all I say.

Her breath catches.

Tomar stares at our hands for a long time, betrayal drawing his brows in. His expression curls into something deeply disappointed.

"Dahlia," he says, frowning, "go pick a room for the night—"

"Don't tell her what to do." I squeeze his hand in mine, capable of crushing the bones inside.

"*Lagos...*" he stammers. "Fuck, brother, what are you doing?"

"You're lucky I don't break it," I snarl, tugging him around by his hand, holding it up like he is a petulant child I am ready to flog for misbehaving. "Do you have her knickers?"

She gasps.

The Shadow baby cries.

"What?" He falters, guilty eyes shift between us. "Her what?"

He does.

He fucking took her knickers.

"No, of course not," he snaps.

I glare down at him as his shame hides inside feigned shock.

Fury builds and builds within me. I've ignored it enough, allowed enough between them. No more. It ends now.

"Don't touch her." I hardly recognise my voice, it's too vulnerable, too angsty, feelings that have been shackled, coming through with no experience or control. "She is mine." I cut my attention to my little flower, frightening her with misdirected fury. "The room on the right is yours."

She doesn't move.

"Go. Now," I bark, and she takes off down the corridor with her pack on one shoulder and the babe at her chest.

Like a chunk of burning wood, I drop Tomar's hand and storm into the room opposite hers, slamming the door to protect Tomar from the insanity rippling through me.

Can't be trusted.

Kill him.

Take the girl.

My brain is on fire.

My heart is throttling.

Muscles contracting.

I care— I care— I want.

Humanity rears up.

I set a torch upside-down on the floor in the corner. There is power, but the lines must be fried somewhere. Rodents, probably.

Flipping the tiny spring bed over on its side, I settle on the floor on a mound of thick duck-feather blankets I found sealed in an airtight box in the cupboard. The people who lived here had affluence at one point.

I glare at the ceiling like the anger inside me can crack the age-old timber rafters, curl the roofing out—

I growl. Carving through my brain are ideas of her and me, and her knickers with Tomar, and my deep, rooted, agonising need to peel his skin from his flesh so no part of him has touched her.

My brother.

My saviour.

At the sound of a soft sob outside my door, I jerk upright. I have never moved so fucking fast. Lunging to my feet, despite my half-naked state, I wrench the door open.

She is there.

At my door.

She collapses against me—half pulling, half pushing—and bashes the blunt of her fists against my abdominals in a weak, heartbreaking display of anguish and confusion.

My chest aches. "Did I do this?"

Sobbing, she beats me with her fists. "It's… It's too much." She wheezes. "It's all been too much. That man beat me, Lagos! He beat me, and you're— You're like him." She can't get the words out after that, her throat filling with emotion too large to breathe through.

"Breathe, little flower." I scoop her into my arms, her long red hair rushing over my forearm. The white slip-dress she is wearing flows, soft and feminine against my body. My cock thickens in my briefs, jutting out of the grey fabric.

"I care for you!" she sobs. "I like you!"

"You shouldn't." Kicking the door shut, I take her to the bedding and lay her on the blankets.

I'm not a decent creature, not a kind or considerate man, not—what I need to be for her. I don't know how.

I just have to try.

"I would never hurt you," I growl, my voice deepening, tight and angry.

She turns fetal; her soft, petite body sinking into the blankets, and my arms encompass her, drag her to my torso, and hold her there. *Fuck.*

I stare ahead at the cupboard, at my reflection in a full-length mirror. My jaw clenches. The abomination glaring back at me is twice her height, and easily three times thicker. My eyes dilate, blackening. I'm staring at a malevolent canvas, a beast crawling over goodness in human form and defiling it.

My cock leaks.

Fuck her.

Trying to get a fucking grip, my iron-blood burning through me, detonating my pulse, I look away from our reflection. My heart thumps on the other side of her head, and I'm seriously concerned the violent organ will scare her. Scare her away—I tighten my arms around her because I can't allow that to happen. Not now. Not anymore.

I have to admit it. I have to relent to the unyielding talons of her presence. I've tried to ignore it. Fought through each feeling as it bubbled inside my mind. Attraction, then intrigue, then consideration, possessiveness, obsession, and ultimately the feelings keep coming, stacking on top of each other, fucking burying me.

She *is* too sweet.

Too good for this world.

Too pure for me.

But I want her anyway.

I'm already everything that is wrong with the world today, everything that is wrong with genetic engineering and the black age of the Gene Wars.

But I want her. And like a bullet to the head, I realise I decided she was mine weeks ago at The Bite. When I held the back of her head and called her mine aloud for anyone—for everyone—to hear. Mine until she is safe. Mine today. Tomorrow. Even the day I leave her at the community, to be safe from everything I am.

Even then.

Chapter Twenty-Seven

Dahlia

His body is so warm around mine. I am lost in long, thick arms and a wide, sturdy chest. A tingling sensation rushes along my skin. I should be more frightened as his mere presence strokes shudders through my body.

Hairs rising.

Toes curling.

It's him.

He pulses unlike other Xin De men because he is a Shadow. I didn't see it before.

He awakens energy in the very air around me, sending skitters of it across my skin like dancing veins of lightning. That is why every man and woman is obsessed with him. It's more than the obscenely muscular form, and those black, menacing eyes that silently growl heated, depravities—He arouses the atmosphere.

I want it.

This is a harsh existence. We live like mere animals in the desert. Pleasure is not easily found out here. I want to find relief from the truth of who he is, find an escape from my feelings of deceit. Just like Beauty and Sweets. I want to disappear into the electrified aura of Lagos the Rogue.

"Show me," I say before I can stop myself. "What you talked about last night. What you were going to do to my body, to me—"

He growls, making a dark sound that seems to thrust inside my core, making my muscles clenching around it.

"Do you want to feel a Shadow deep inside you, little flower?" he asks.

Oh, my.

"You're already there," I squeak, a helpless sound, both terrified and desperate. "You've been inside my chest, in my belly, for weeks."

"I'll be much deeper than that."

I gaze up at him, instantly caught in the snare of pitch-black eyes. Lagos isn't fighting it anymore, he's decided.

"Let's get you nice wet for me." He looms over me, forcing me to my spine. "Gentle," he warns. "You're still fragile."

Hot lips touch my mouth, and I prepare for more pressure, breathless for him, but he trails to my chin.

"You make the prettiest sounds when you gasp," he murmurs darkly between kisses of deep possessiveness, tracing the column of my neck down to my clavicle. "So fragile." He kisses the thin bone above my chest. "So soft."

I lick my lips.

Anticipating.

Already panting, I peer down to watch this beast of a man. Excruciatingly slow, he mouths my breasts over the fabric of my white slip-dress.

He sucks on my nipple, and my hands fly up to the back of his head, nails weaving into his wavy dark-blonde hair.

I lie like a stick, straight up and down, stiff and awkward. My skin blushes with embarrassment.

"Stop." I don't know what I'm saying or why I'm saying it. It's my final attempt to protect my heart. If we do this, if I let him do this, I know that's it. For the warm affection inside me will spiral out of control. "Stop."

"Stop?" he repeats and licks my achingly hard nipple, groaning.

I shake my head, dizzy. "No."

"No?"

"I..."

Lagos trails down the ladder of my ribs. "You." And breathes hot air against my belly button. "Say it again." Groaning, he rubs his face on the supple part of my lower belly, and even through my dress, his rough beard reminds me that every inch of him is hard, coarse—male. "Mean it. Say stop and mean it." His hips thrust in the air. Even without the pressure of his body on mine, I can feel him tightening against his instincts. Restless with restraint.

I can't say it again. I don't want him to stop, but I need to catch my breath.

When I don't answer, he hums. "Don't open your thighs for me." I roll my hips up to the sound of his raspy timbre, a sound steady with control yet somehow volatile.

Prowling down my body the last few inches, his nose meets my knickers. He inhales and growls. My toes curl and my back arches, my body obeying the beast's unspoken commands.

"You have no idea how much I need this," Lagos states, hunger a raspy phantom in his tone. Needy.

This *need*, a man's instinctual desires and emotional burdens, is what my Trade is all about—to accompany, relieve, and soothe.

His tongue laps at the material, then down my closed legs. He teases a wet, hot trail down the valley between my pressed thighs.

I squeeze them tighter.

"It's not your fault. Remember that, when you dream about what I did to this body, remember it's not your fault," he snarls and shoves my thighs apart.

My heart thunders in my chest.

Exhaling heavily, he stares between my legs. The white material, barely covering me, is damp from my arousal.

I can't look any more, dropping my head back, brows tight, staring at the ceiling, and gripping his hair tighter.

"Do you still want to know what I like?" Lagos ducks, his mouth on my knickers, heat exploding across the sensitive area.

I hold his hair, my tether to the moment, or else I'll fall—plummet.

Oh, that feels good.

"Yes," I whisper, my eyes rolling back when he licks over the fabric and buries his nose at the very top, inhaling, it's erotic and wrong, and…

Rolling his nose against me, he purrs, "I like the smell of this soft red hair between your thighs. Strawberries and cream. What a delicate flower you are."

Spreading me further, pinning my thighs open, he fills the space with his large shoulders. One hand on my thigh, the other feeds under my knickers so a long, relentless finger can slide all the way, deep inside me.

I moan wildly. There isn't any pain this time—only pleasure.

Until he hits something, shooting me with an unnatural sensation like someone massaging my bones from the inside.

"Not very deep, little flower, but so fucking tight. And pink…" Sliding his finger in and out of me, my arousal makes wet sounds. "Everywhere. So much pinker in here."

Oh, he's looking *there.* Embarrassment becomes a blanket of pink and perspiration.

My backside tries to pulse off the blankets, to work with his finger, but he has me locked beneath him.

"Lagos..."

"Gentle. Your hips don't know what they're asking for is dangerous."

Unbridled moans cascade from my throat. *There.* There. Close. To that feeling… The same one I felt at the waterfall. The same one… *Oh.*

His tongue glides up, stopping at a collection of nerves and circles, and circles. And circles.

My head makes the same motion, my mind coiling with pleasure.

His finger moves in and out, too constant, controlled. Then he sucks, and I tighten everywhere, hands in his hair, legs around his face. The clash of his finger's steady penetration and the violent sucking forces all my blood to that area. He might as well be licking my heart, because every inch between my legs pulses with its frantic beating.

"Good girl, come for me."

Crying through the climax, my thighs tremble beside his cheeks, the delicate skin scrubbed by his rough beard.

His forehead presses to my lower belly, and he pauses there while I mewl with unbidden control. Pulling his finger from inside me, he crawls up my body, forcing my thighs further apart.

I look down to see his packed shoulder muscles rotating. Dragging with him, the long, hard length between his legs. It beats against my thigh.

Then he stops over me, and I blink at him. Blink. Blink. Nerves play on my tongue, not allowing words through.

"Things I like..." Lagos hums with his lips inches from mine. "Your green eyes filled with soft nerves and sweet lust."

I part my lips, drawing in thick, buzzing air. It's happening. He is going to... "I'm scared," I admit. "It hurts. Doesn't it?"

The movement of his warm fingers sliding up my side, collecting my hand, makes me shiver. "Do you want me to hold your hand through it?" Lagos entwines our fingers.

I nod. He *is* gentle. A gentle man with me. For me. The sickening affection in my belly swallows me whole—I love him. "Yes."

His fingers bar mine to the blankets above my head. Eyes unwavering from mine, anchors for my nervous energy; he reaches down with his free hand and grabs hold of his dick. "Don't look."

"I've seen... it."

He drags his lips up my face to the inside of my upper arm,

peppering kisses on the soft tissue there. Intimate. Sweet. Contradicting what he is doing with his other hand, removing his briefs and using the crown of his dick to slide my knickers into the crease of my thigh.

I'm still in my little white dress, with my knickers bunched to the side, flushing across my chest and up my neck. While he is over me, completely naked like an animal—like a beast. It's the image of being defiled.

And he is too big to kiss me while he does this. His head is clear over the top of mine. I press my cheek to his heart and pant. Ready.

Lagos notches his dick at my opening, and I freeze. Tense. The hot bulb isn't going to get inside me.

No way.

"*Yes.*" He grabs my thigh and thrusts into me.

Short. Steady. He squeezes through the layers of skin and muscle, and I cry out, digging my fingers into his hand, mewling wildly but to no end. He is everywhere. The pressure of him. The weight. The electrified air.

I wish I could see his face, but feeling a rumbling growl in his chest is warning enough. "*Tight. Mine.* All mine."

Fear curls inside me.

He pries me open.

"You're doing *so* good," he groans, edging out only to squeeze in further. "Such a tight fit. You're going to feel me deep inside you. My cock is going to throb against your cervix, do you understand?"

I nod against his chest.

And he thrusts in until I feel something punch at bone, at the end of me. He tucks me under him further, bundles me into the position he needs, ready, and starts to really move.

The air around us seems to spark and sizzle. My mouth opens, cries and moans soaring together. I let this massive man use my body to work out his carnal need.

In. Out.

Oh.

A restless hand paws my thigh.

Grunting with each inward thrust, he groans long and deep to his outward draws. Over and over.

Pleasure stirs inside me.

"That's it," Lagos rasps. "Take your Shadow's big cock, little flower. It's too late now. You're defiled. You're mine."

Climbing up my trembling side, his hand stops in the crook of my neck. He juts his hips in a way that strokes over the little nerve ending above my entrance.

"Come," he demands, and my ears burn as if he bit down on them.

The room melts away again. Nothing but us. Nothing but him inside me. Making my body his. Making the space between my thighs shaped for him. Shaping me so thoroughly, I'll never feel right without him, not between my legs, not in my lungs, or low in my belly.

I climax again, the muscles enclosing his dick spasming, my legs jerking at his backside, cries pummelling through my lips. He will feel me—feel me *pulsing.* I bury my face further into his hot, hard chest, mortified by that.

"Your pussy is so *good.*"

This Xin De male was designed to murder, but every inch of him seems built for this. To completely unravel a girl. Even with the pain—the stretch—his rhythm is flawless and exact, his attention to detail unwavering.

His thrusting continues.

He slides along tender places inside me, over and over, coiling me again and again until I'm a cluster of pathetic yearning. Feverish. Stretched.

"That's a good girl," he praises. "Come for me again." And I tremble through another climax.

"Please..." I paw at him with my free hand. He doesn't appear to be slowing or growing tired. Panic fills my chest.

I don't know how much time passes or whether it's night or first-light, but my body is no longer mine.

My body pulses on the blanket to his rhythm. In my peripherals, I see a blur of activity. Dropping my cheek to the blanket, I meet my own gaze. Caught beneath the huge body of the male, my legs jerking at his backside, but it's him…

I climax again, watching him.

The sight of him over me, in me, is the most impossibly erotic sight. His hand still holds mine above my head, his arse clenching and unclenching, biceps bulking out, and his eyes… closed below brows weaved with agonising pleasure.

"I'm going to fill this little body," he warns. "You're going to be swollen and sore tomorrow, with my scent all over you, so there is no mistaking you're—" He growls, "Mine."

Soon, his pace falters, his hands paw restlessly, and every part of him—arms, back, shoulders, neck, dick— tighten and build over me.

"Fuck." He bundles me even closer as he beats his hips, cum shooting into my depths. "Good girl. My very good little flower… *Fuck*."

I close my eyes. Tingles set to race across my arms and up my thighs. The air is thick, magnetic, spinning me. I think I lose time, but…

His dick slides from inside me; his lips meet mine and we share heavy, exhausted breaths.

Heaving, I barely kiss back as his lips take over, tugging at mine. That is what he does. He takes, and I give. And I never want it any other way.

"Look at me," Lagos demands.

I force my eyes open.

"You're mine," he says, daring me to object, engraving his claim into my mind while the feel of his hot cum drips down my thighs in thick rivers. "Say it."

My voice is soft. "I'm yours."

"If Tomar touches you—"

"Lagos."

"Listen!" He grabs the side of my neck, forcing my eyes to him. "If he looks at you in a way that would displease me, I need you to tell me."

"Do we have to do this no—"

"Yes, we have to do this now! Because right now, I've claimed you, split you open, and I'm…" He shakes over me with barely contained rage. "I'm feeling violent." I swallow. His eyes turn black. "I'm feeling like I need to hurt him. Say you will tell me everything, and I will not leave this room until I calm down."

"I will tell you," I whisper, pressing my lips to his and talking against them. "Are you mine, then?" I tease. "Lagos the Rogue. Are you mine, if I am yours?"

A strange expression softens his eyes, and a small grin plays in the corner of his mouth.

"That is why," he mutters, almost to himself, almost to an incessant question reeling in his mind.

"What is why?"

"You somehow—" He shakes his head, confusion darting around his now lighter, steel-coloured gaze. "You get in my chest. Settled me. With four fucking words." He huffs. "To control me, I've been brainwashed, iron coursing through my very blood, but you… You do it with four softly spoken words. How the fuck did you do that?"

My heart expands, but I just shrug, trying not to fall any further, to not lose my figurative footing entirely. "I don't know."

His subtle grin slides wider. "Do you *want* me to be yours, little flower?"

Pop goes my heart—a bloody mess everywhere. "*Yes,*" I whisper.

"Then I am yours."

Chapter Twenty-Eight

Lagos

Twenty-four years ago

You're an abomination.

The stench of blood, cum, and sweat burns my nostrils. I sit on the edge of the bed, the mattress sunken beneath my weight, with my elbows on my knees and my eyes level with the door ahead.

Any minute now...

He will come.

And I will kill him.

Sweat pours down my forehead, and chills rush along my skin. Strange images and shapes plague me.

I've been like this since I escaped, burning up from the inside out. My brain is trying to kill me with shock, sensation, fever, thoughts... So many fucked up thoughts that I swear are not mine but come from inside a chamber embedded in my cranium. One I can't touch or talk to but communicates with me.

But I'm awake.

And in a nightmare.

I don't know anymore.

Strange words knell in my head from voices that are both mine and somehow… not.

I am locked in a body that is not human though something inside me roars with humanity. Weeps for what I have done.

Continue to do.

You're filth.

My eyes fall to the dead girl on the bed, my cum leaking from inside her, red finger marks painting her slim throat. I fucked her and choked her to death.

They made me do it.

Kill yourself.

It is the only way.

"I am coming in." A deep voice rumbles from behind the door, and I rise to my feet like the perfect predator I am.

I roll my shoulders and pump my fists at my side as the door cracks open, and *he* walks in…

The Xin De man who has been following me around the Upper-tower port M. Shorter than me but bigger than a Common man. Blue eyes that glow, a distinct Xin De trait, and softer features, angular, fine, and clean. I'd place him in his second decade of life.

We all grow up fast.

Innocence is dead.

This clean-cut Xin De man thinks he can sneak up on an assassin.

I sneer. "I expected you."

"Easy…" He closes the door behind himself, and the fool locks himself in with a literal human-bear. "I can help you. If you will let me."

Don't trust him.

"Why are you following me?" I demand, my pulse fierce, ready, fuelling me with blood to reap violence.

He clasps his hands in front of him in a comfortable move that pisses me off. "Because you're hurting people, Lagos. And I want to help you."

I snarl. "Lagos?"

"You don't have a name yet, right?" He edges over, respectfully hesitant but getting closer. "I'd put you at... sixteen? Am I right? You would have been given one in five years when they released you, but for now, you're just a number. Still in training. Still a lot to learn. What is your number?"

Zero Zero Six.

Just Six.

"How do you know all of this?" I ask, suspicious, before defensiveness drips down my spine, bringing hot wrath to my forehead. I clench my fists. "You're one of them, aren't you?"

"Trade?" He laughs, and it's the strangest sound I have ever heard. "No. I'm a priest. Do you know what that is?"

I lift my chin instead of admitting I don't know what the fuck that is.

"That's fine. I'm not Trade-aligned. I assure you. But I do know what you are."

"Then you know I am trained to kill, remove, and dissolve, so you're either very brave or very stupid."

"Do you like the name Lagos?" he asks like I didn't just threaten him. "I thought it suited you. You leave rivers of blood for me to follow. Something you wouldn't do if you were fully trained." He touches his chest. "Please, let me introduce myself. My name is Tomar, it's an old-world name. The word lagos comes from the same old-world place. Seeing we are to be brothers."

He's fucking insane. "Stop following me, or I will kill you, and no one will even know we met."

"You're getting more and more sick." His blue eyes study me, and I want to pull them from their sockets so they can't. "You're getting very careless. I can help you. I want to help you."

I lift my chin while my knuckles ache under the pressure of my clenching and unclenching fist. "You can't help me."

No one can.

No one has.

No one cares.

"It's the iron in your blood," he says. "It hurts, doesn't it?"

"*Now*," I hiss, a dark disturbance wrapping around my tone. Taking one big step toward him, I make him flinch, make him show his true hesitation—a healthy fear of me. "How. The hell. Do you know about that?" I finish.

He is Trade.

Kill him!

"It isn't just the iron!" He shuffles backward, adding space between us. *Smart.* He must know I could lunge—grow bored of him—and rip his head from his shoulders.

Do it. Kill him.

I grind my molars to the insolent thoughts. Sixteen or not, I am twice this fool's size. I lower my head, glaring at him through my lashes.

Kill him.

"There is also a coil in your brain. Did you know that?" He rushes out, and I freeze my muscles just as the thoughts compound and growl.

Kill him. Kill him. Don't trust him. He is lying. He is lying. Lying. Lying. Fuck.

The man named Tomar nods slowly. "Yes. I can help. It will drive you mad until you listen to it, and then when you do, when you let it control you, it will make you kill yourself."

I lock up my body, fight the impulses, the conditioned instinct to remove obstacles, to dissolve threats. "I don't need anyone. Never had anyone. Never team up. It's not in my design."

He gazes across at the girl on the bed, her skin already turning grey, her glassy eyes resembling a taxidermied being. "You're killing innocent people... I don't think you want to."

"Why not just kill me then?" I dare—desire—but will fight to the last drop of blood, to the final twitch, to my rattling death encore. I will fight.

"Because we can help each other," he admits this time.

Ah, so he needs me.

"I need a man to protect me while I fulfill my Purpose," he adds.

"So," I sneer, "you want to *use* me? Want your own assassin. I am not available. Too busy killing innocent women,"—I jerk my chin toward the dead bitch— "as you can see. I'm booked up."

A knowing expression smooths his features, and he tilts his head. "Please, you can't convince me. You ran. You ran because your heart wasn't in it; it is stronger than their conditioning. I help people. Let me help you first."

Kill him. I snarl at the voice snapping in my brain. "How?"

Tomar smiles calmly at me, and taking a big breath, he says, "The excess iron compound was engineered into your bloodstream to activate a Shadow. The coil was designed to control one. *But* as progressive as The Trade's tech is, as advanced, the brain in its organic form will always be more complex. And more powerful.

"The coil doesn't do what it was designed to do, but after nearly a century of testing, they found it did serve a purpose. To destroy a rogue Shadow. To send them mad, activate sickness that isn't there, signal a virus response—have the body fight itself.

"*And* implements voices. Thoughts. Whispers. Shadows have thrown themselves off cliffs. Died when organs have spontaneously shut down. It will kill you one day, and until then, it will torture you."

Fuck. How does he know about the voices? The accidents... My body nearly forced me into a burning truck yesterday. I didn't give my legs permission to move, but they did. It was like something else was momentarily in control.

And her— I look at the dead girl, black hair winged out around her on the mattress. I only imagined choking her; it was a fever dream, but there she is.

Real.

Fucked.

Dead.

He's telling the truth. Rage for my kind and for The Trade bore into my guts, festering a hatred like no other.

He is lying!

I frown. "What can you do?"

He exhales hard, almost relieved I'm talking, listening—considering. "I can have your Brain-Interface coil removed."

Chapter Twenty-Nine

Lagos

Fuck.

Dahlia.

Little flower.

I roll her to her side, careful it's the side with perfectly intact ribs. She must be in pain, but she holds the ache with such demure grace.

I wish I'd killed that Shadow slower now. If I had the chance to go back, I'd take my time—enjoy it.

Careful with my little flower, I slide my palm down her thigh, to her knee, and back again. So fucking soft. So fucking untouched. So fucking mine.

She smells like sex.

And me.

My cock leaks, ready to fuck her again. I could have kept going the first time, could have blown my nuts inside her, and continued immediately. I never need downtime. I can keep going. Can be hard most of the day.

I stroke my knuckles down her spine over the fabric of her white slip-dress, and she arches to the gentle pressure, little hairs rising along her arms. Spine bowing, her arse lifts toward me.

Sliding between the crease, I stop above her little rim, where I circle the taut muscles but don't touch them. She moans, then stops with a gasp, perhaps not ready for that. "Do you want that, little flower?"

"You shouldn't," she pants. "It's... Strange. Too strange."

"I'll do whatever I want with this little body now," I growl, but listen. My muscles always listen to her for some fucking reason. I don't have time, lubricant, or patience to loosen her up for me anyway.

I continue down to her wet pussy and slide two fingers through her hot, swollen lips. *Fuck.*

So tight.

Too tight.

Hungry need drives my hips forward. I finger-fuck her swollen channel until she shudders and drips with my cum and her slick fluids. And her moans... Fuck me, so fucking loud and heedless.

"This pussy"—I speed up, skirting around the flat muscle inside her that insists I press back— "is mine."

Darkness cloaks the room, it must be late or early, so I'm certain Tomar will hear everything.

With my bicep tucked under her head, I wrap my arm around to possess her throat with my fist. Hold her to me, support her body from jerking too violently as I work the first five inches of my cock into her from behind.

"*Lagos*," she says, my name a needy moan in the base of her throat.

"That's it..." I thrust into her, holding her body like it's mine, not hers, restricting her movements and taking. Taking. Taking. "Take my cock."

I grip the root of my cock while I fuck her, squeezing the thick base that doesn't fit inside her tight hole.

Groans rumble from my throat, animalistic and primal as her pussy clenches and squeezes me, milking my shaft in a frantic inexperienced way.

"I- I…" Long moans roll through her lips to the sweetest cadence. "It's happening again."

She comes.

"That's it. You're so responsive," I praise her.

She comes easily for me, the sweetest sounds of pleasure purring through her lips. I'll forever lock them in my mind, in my iron-blood, to keep for when she is at the Common Community.

"You like your Shadow's thick cock?" I growl, possessive as all hell over this little flower and her sweet, tight pussy.

I know I'll have to go easy on her, not fuck her or touch her every second of the next few days on the way up to the community, but it'll be hard.

I'll be hard.

That is all I have with her—two or three fucking days before I leave her forever. I must leave. They don't allow Xin De in the community; even so, I could never be a part of a… A fucking Collective. I wasn't designed for companionship. I was engineered to be a loner, able to leave at any moment, drop everything and take an assignment for my Meaningful Purpose. I may no longer be an active Shadow, but it is what I am made of.

She has to be safe from… The outside world and the deep, volatile darkness within me. It's all I care about anymore. All that truly matters.

My new Meaningful Purpose is to ensure she is safe. And perhaps, it always has been. Leading up to the moment I met her, all the events formed a path before me. *A way to her.*

The hell I endured at the hands of The Trade, the breakdown, the fall, the deaths, cum and blood, and Tomar, fucking Tomar with his will to save people—all of it. All I am and all I've done have been stones in the bloody path that led me to the Shadow baby and to *her.*

To find her.

Not to keep.
But to save.

Chapter Thirty

Dahlia

The comfort of his warmth is unparalleled. The heavy drum of his heart against my cheek is grounding, a reminder that I am alive and that there is another caring for me.

A resting smile moves to my lips as a sense of security bundles me up. I understand sleep better than I ever have before. I am never the one awake while another person sleeps beside me.

I see now that the embrace of slumber is when we are most vulnerable, quietly existing inside our bodies, not outwardly living in them.

Lagos is stunning when he is asleep, and even though I can feel him inside me—inside my heart and a pulse between my thighs—right now feels even more personal.

Deeply personal.

I reach up and coil his chest hair around my finger, following the thick black patterns of a tattoo.

Spero fusses from the room opposite this one, and so I try to lift the heavy arm embracing me, but to no avail. "Lagos…"

"No," he murmurs, voice gravelly and hoarse.

I smile, and a little ease passes over me. He doesn't want to pretend that last night didn't happen.

"I have to go to Spero," I whisper, nudging him again.

A sleepy groan of annoyance rumbles from him, but he lifts the weighty arm, allowing me to slide out.

I go straight to the bathroom, pee, and quickly wash my hands. There is a rectangular bar of soap on the basin, which is already wet. Lagos has used it. So, I feel quite comfortable that it's not old or last used by a stranger. I wash between my thighs with cold water from the faucet and the bar of soap.

Within a few minutes, I'm a tiny bit cleaner, have changed Spero's cloth nappy, and am walking into the dusty old kitchen with him in my arms.

My breath catches when I see Tomar's hunched back bent over, his head in the cupboard, hands sorting through cans and items.

Did he hear? *Yes.* I heard Spero, so he definitely heard me last night. The conversation between us, the one I rammed down and said I would forget, comes crashing back on waves of discomfort.

"Tomar?"

He bashes his head in the cupboard, trying to pull it out. "Fuck." Rubbing the back of his skull, he stands and faces me.

"Hi," I manage to say.

Unspoken words ride the tension between us as we stare at each other.

My eyes drop to a container in his hand, and even though I cannot read, I know what it is from the picture on the side. "Is that?"

"Not formula." His voice pulses, blue eyes deeply sad—betrayed. "No. But it *is* powdered milk."

I take a step forward through what feels like an invisible wall of resistance. "Thank you, Tomar. You have saved us. I will never forget that."

"So..." He clears his throat, deflecting. "How is your rib feeling?"

I shrug a little. "It's okay. It doesn't really hurt that much anymore. It's not like I'm doing anything strenuous—"

Tomar's eyes drop to the container in his hand, fingers idly turning it. "You should have come to me… last night." His gaze meets mine. "You should have come to my room. I wouldn't have touched you."

I inhale hard, the bite of tears behind my eyes. I don't want to hurt him, but I don't feel that way. I almost wish I did; it seems to make more sense.

I chew my bottom lip. "But—"

"She didn't." Lagos finishes, suddenly a furnace at my spine, his intimidating presence boring through me.

"Oh, Hell." Tomar shakes his head, glaring over the top of mine. "Put some damn clothes on."

A warm hand slides across my chest and up to my throat, possessive and authoritarian. "Get the milk and go back to my room, little flower," the dark voice behind me orders.

Tomar's brows weave with utter repulsion. "You touched her."

Lagos presses against me from behind, his hard erection bruising my back as his free hand slides over my hip and down between my legs.

I want to swat his hand away, but I can't, both arms bundled with my tiny assassin.

"I didn't *just* touch her, Tomar," Lagos booms. The heavy weight of his tone knocks the air from my lungs.

I swallow in his tight palm. "Please, please don't do this—"

"I split open this virgin cunt with my fingers last week," he growls. "Jealous, brother?"

Wait… I blink.

"She was— She'd never… Her Ward didn't touch her?" Tomar's tone rises and cuts the air, severs it.

"My what?" I whimper. I watch his lips move, blinking at them. Hear his words and tone. But the meaning eludes me until…

The blood.

Virgin…

Clarity breaks through.

"And looking at her face, she didn't know." Tomar turns bright red with fury. "You took her virginity without telling her, Lagos!"

"Little flower." Lagos releases me and turns me to face him. His hands come up to cup my cheeks. "I shouldn't have said that."

I gaze up into his near-black eyes set below weaved brows. Soft. Concerned. "What do you mean, Lagos?"

"Lagos!" Tomar barks. "Damn you!"

"I was a… I was a virgin?" The word echoes in my mind. "No, no, no. That's not— That can't be."

"She had a choice!" Tomar is yelling at my back, my eyes lost in the depth of hot-steel grey. Gravity eyes. Eyes that lock me in place. Capture me. "It was her choice! It could've been—"

"You?" Lagos snaps those eyes up to Tomar, set ablaze with anger.

"No," Tomar deflects quickly. "That's not… That's not—"

"It'll never be you!"

I hear Tomar swallow. "I didn't—"

"Don't fucking lie!" Lagos roars, his palms still on my cheeks vibrating with restraint and burning my skin with rage. "At least I don't hide my depravities. You're just like everyone else. You want to sink inside her, and—

"Don't, Lagos," Tomar warns.

"Tell her what you want to do to her," Lagos hisses. "What you dream about doing to her sweet, young body. Tell her what you do with her knickers at night. Do they smell like her pussy?"

"Stop," I whisper, feeling choked, but Lagos can't hear me over the craze rushing between his ears, the thump of his pulse is a tangible threat in the air. "If I didn't owe you my life, I would have ripped out your guts the moment you looked at her like—"

"I am a fucking animal!" Tomar barks, defeated. "Dammit! But I am trying to be better."

I sniffle. *"Lagos..."*

His eyes, tunnels of relentless grey fury, drop to my face. They soften in an instant as he says, "Little flower?"

I'm so confused. "I don't want to be here." I shake my head through hiccups, feeling the walls press in and the room shrink. "Let me go back to my room."

"My room."

A cloud of confusion sits around me as I walk to the room. I hear Lagos say something to Tomar, and then he is behind me, shutting the door.

Feeling like I may collapse, I lay Spero on the blankets and place my hand on the wall, steadying myself.

I'm hungry. Dizzy.

Clues crumble my composure. The blood on Lagos' fingers that day at the waterfall. Words from the girl at the roadhouse. *"—fucked, and his cum is leaking from between your thighs. Do you feel pure and wholesome then?"* I was never sore the next first-light.

Why?

No. Please, no.

"He never touched me… *there?* Why?" I murmur to myself. A tear rushes a cool path down my cheek. "I never soothed him. I never relieved him."

"Good."

I turn my muddied ire to Lagos. "You knew! You have known since the waterfall. What have I been doing for the past five years? Why didn't he… *want* me?"

"Perhaps he was a good man. Perhaps he wanted a daughter. Not a fuck thing."

"A daughter?" I swallow but feel like I am choking on jagged rocks. "My Trade is a health-care initiative. I know you have no respect for it, but I grew up believing in it, Lagos. I truly believed in the good we were doing."

He stands completely naked before me, long, thick, and muscular—every inch of him. And his dick, half-hard, I've never seen it another way.

"I don't know what he was thinking," he says, his voice otherworldly deep. "But I am certain that you did your duty to that man."

Duty...

No. My lower lip bunches and wobbles as I try not to sob. "I didn't. It was my Meaningful Purpose."

He is in front of me, his hand sliding between my hair and neck, gripping the nape. "To accompany, relieve, and soothe? Correct?" His thumb slides under my jaw, pushing my chin up. My eyes meet his, and I try to blink the tears away. "Your *presence* is soothing; your silly awe is a great relief in this fucking dire land. I'm certain you meant everything to that man."

The vision of Lagos clears as I continue to bat the tears away. Gazing up at him, I feel weak with confusion.

"It pains me to see..." His eyes follow a cool tear as it rolls over my lips. "Tears. But I am pleased he didn't touch you. You're mine."

Every cell in my body wars—I'm glad it was Lagos', but I'm deeply lost. "You were so... so vulgar about it."

"I shouldn't have been." His dark eyes map a course across my face, soft.

"Was it vulgar?" I ask.

"No." His jaw pulses. "No, it wasn't. I will hold that memory forever. I told you it wasn't your fault, what I took from you. I don't regret it. I'd do it again."

Blinking, I let all the information settle in my mind. I nod slowly, half-accepting his words while burying the unease. This isn't a fairytale. This is life in The Cradle, and he isn't human. He won't always act the same as me or think the same as me. "I have to feed Spero," I say.

"Fine." He gazes at me for a moment longer than usual, and I almost see the affection pour from him. The same kind I feel when I look at him. Not just animal instinct, nor pleasure and possession, but wholesome, selfless affection.

He sighs hard before shifting his eyes to the door and striding toward it.

"Don't hurt him!" I blurt out.

He stops with his back to me, shoulders bunching, tension stalking across them.

"*Please.*" I swallow. "Tomar cares for Spero and me… and *you*. Please."

"I'm not going to hurt him," he says, reaching for the door handle.

"Where are you going, then?"

He edges around to face me, a slight grin touching his mouth. And that somehow makes him appear a decade younger. "Is this how it goes now?" he asks, his tone deep and gravelly. "Do you have my balls? Do I need to inform you of my comings and goings, little flower? Have I made my obsession too obvious?"

Obsessed.

With… with me?

Warmth moves through me. "No. Sorry."

His dark gaze drips the length of my body, before he huffs an amused sound. Almost to himself. "Because I am. *Obsessed.*" His eyes meet mine. "So, if that's what you want… I'm going to shower, then take apart the cars out there and salvage the pieces. Is that acceptable to you, *little flower*?"

I hiccup a short giggle, my cheeks full-blown furnaces, and a little piece of unease drops into oblivion. "Very acceptable, *brute*."

He nods toward Spero and says, "Don't just feed the Shadow baby—"

"*Spero.*"

"Feed yourself," he finishes curt. "Properly. There is fish, and it looks like Tomar found cans. Could be spaghetti. Eat, or I will force-feed you."

Chapter Thirty-One

Dahlia

I'm not sure at what point I turned into an animal. The desert has transformed me, unravelled me. I understand the appeal of being a House Girl now. The endorphins of lust and love. It is addictive —the excitement of maybe he likes me, the angst of maybe he doesn't, the visceral memory of him thrusting into me, flooding me with emotions. I can feel the absence of him… inside.

Before I left the Half-tower, I was sensible and preoccupied with sewing and singing, but now I find myself gazing at Lagos as he pulls apart the old vehicle in the barn.

Only occupied by him right now. By his shoulders as they expand with each breath. By the sweat that follows the thick curve of his bicep and the way he uses his forearm to wipe at his brow.

My temperature rises.

My eyes are lost in the virile vision ahead of me as I sit on a bench in the barn with my legs crossed. His huge black shirt is pulled over my knees. Underneath, I only have knickers on. My mask is beside me on the ledge, but I don't need it in here. I chew absently on a protein bar Tomar found. It's chocolate, sweet and bitter, but my mouth waters to know what Lagos' skin tastes like right now. While beads of salty perspiration collect along his muscles. I have never seen a man working outside of their Purpose. My Ward was an old Fisher with small muscles and simple, plain features.

I shuffle, my swollen core and lower belly clenching. "How long will this take?" I ask, embarrassingly breathless.

Concentration draws his brows in when he glances over his shoulder at me as he works on removing a tyre. "Lot to get through, little flower. Another car. Rooms full of boxes. We left The Bite early; we have time. We should stay a few extra days. Things might be raided by the time we pass through again."

We.

Tomar and him.

Not me.

Not you, Dahlia.

That truth makes my stomach roll. He has *needs,* and I understand them better today, despite my entire Trade being about servicing said needs. Physical needs… The kind I didn't really understand because I wasn't supposed to. Lagos—my Lagos—has needs. When I'm safe, he is going to find someone else, like Beauty and Sweets, and the girls from the roadhouse that clearly knew him…

"Were you with any of those girls the other night?" The question cascades through my lips like spitting lemon. "I mean… at the roadhouse?"

He pivots on his haunches to face me, signature frown in place, but tighter with disapproval. "You kissed me that night," he states, voice roughening.

I clear my throat, blushing at the memory. "Yeah. That one."

"You kissed me," he repeats, "but you still ask that question."

Yes? I'm confused. I shrug, then roll one shoulder, hiding my scarlet-hued cheeks. "I wanted to kiss you."

"Don't do that."

My shoulders flatten. "Do what?"

"Kiss a man who has been with other women the same night. You're not a House Girl. You're not an afterthought or a first choice. You're the only choice."

I beam, and the knot in my stomach tightens because the love and affection in my heart blooms further, spreading out and weaving through my insides. I look down at the barn floor and gather my emotions before quickly returning my gaze to him. "Is that a no?"

He pivots back to the car, back to work. "They are not my type."

Right. I scoff, raising a brow at his back, dubious. "They knew you, Lagos."

He pulls the tyre off and lays it on the floor beside him. "I didn't know I had a type until recently. Until I was nose deep inside your pussy. That'll change any man."

His words make me hot all over, my nipples hardening, poking through my dress. I glance hesitantly at the barn door—closed. And listen to the howling wind outside, both things offering a sense of privacy.

"Lagos…" I say his name in a breathy way that causes him to stiffen with his back to me. I press my hand over my racing heart, feeling the frantic, nervous thudding. Looking at Lagos—all man —I am inundated with an urge… to move lower. First, to my nipple. Even beneath the fabric, it buzzes with sensitivity, so I rub the point in circles. Hairs on my arms lift, and wet heat gathers between my legs.

Lagos slowly edges around to face me, rising to his feet. "Careful, little flower." He drinks me in. "That look will get you in all kinds of depraved trouble."

"I can't imagine doing depraved things with anyone else but you, Lagos," I whisper, needier than intended.

He doesn't move a muscle, but heated dark energy rolls from

him. "You better not imagine doing *anything* with anyone but me, little flower."

With even the slightest shift of his gaze up and down, my entire body shudders. "Keep going," he demands, his tone raspy and depthless. "*Lower.*"

Slowly, I trace between my breasts down my trembling belly to between my thighs. I lean back, becoming limp, as I press my palm over my knickers to cradle that hot, wet place.

A dark, determined gaze tracks my movements.

Feeling every inch of his attention like tangible pulses through the air, I moan and begin to grind on my palm.

His eyes meet mine.

"I feel hot." I pant. "Help me." When he pauses, a wave of nerves flush through me, but he is striding toward me now.

I gasp when he scoops his hands between the bench and my backside, lifting me. I can feel the volatile strength he possesses in the effortless way he carries me, but he is so careful. Gentle.

He sets me on the car's bonnet, his hands on either side of my body. As he drags his lips down my chin, travelling to my chest, belly, ending between my legs, I moan and arch at the sudden excitement. A small ache flares through my side from my own eager movements, and I wince but don't want to stop.

Lagos' gaze snaps up to meet mine when he hears my discomfort. "Flower?"

"I'm okay." I pant, lifting my hips again, careful this time. "Please, please don't stop. Please, Lagos."

"No." He grips my hips and slides me down from the car, but before I can protest, he turns me around and bends me over the bonnet. "Relax."

Huge, warm hands journey up my naked thighs, drawing the long shirt to my hips, then dragging my knickers down to weave my ankles together.

Exposing me.

My cheek meets the cool metal machine. A large, muscular

arm tucks under me, supporting my torso, as he lays over me on the bonnet.

"Don't fight me. Let me take this body. I'll be careful with it," he whispers in my ear. I can smell his sweat and oils and a musk that is all male. And the heat... so much heat blankets me.

I hear the shuffling of his pants, feel the warmth of his dick between my thighs. The crown presses inside me from behind, reminding me how swollen and used I already am.

"*Oh.*" I moan long and hard, and he holds me still, safe, as he slowly moves in and out. His dick is thick, so thick and so long, soon it rubs me to a hot, wet, shuddering mess.

I squeeze my eyes shut as pleasure becomes a bundle of sensation in my belly, circling and circling.

"You like that?" He stays deep, rocking his hips, my arousal making wet sounds to the slow, rolling motion. "*So* wet for me. I thought a sweet thing like you would be too afraid of the monster to drip for him. I was wrong, wasn't I? You want me to mount you, fuck you, feed on your innocence."

I moan at his dark words.

Lagos starts to groan as my clenching channel works around his thrusts, seemingly urging him to speed up and paw at my thighs.

"*Oh*, Lagos."

"Fuck, *yes*, little flower. My sweet untouched girl with her lovely wet pussy that holds my cock so perfectly."

His words, his filthy words...

That hot bundle of pleasure gathers and grows, spreading to my inner thighs and lifting to my belly and everywhere in between.

"This is mine. You know that." His lips touch my ear, heat rushing me like rivers of molten lava. "So I need you to learn how to come. Do you understand what I mean by come?"

I am barely breathing as he pulses softly inside me. "Yes. Climax."

"*Yes.* I need you to learn how to make yourself *climax*. Because when I leave, the only hands allowed on this sweet, young cunt will be your own."

I open my eyes to the barn wall and his hand beside my head on the bonnet, bracing his body over mine.

"*Okay*," I breathe.

He rolls against my backside, stroking the muscles inside me, gentle but thorough, never drawing out completely. "Before we get to the Common Community, you will play with your body until you understand it the way I do." He stills, and I moan—sulk —needing more friction, more stimulation, more... Just more.

"Please, Lagos. Move."

He hums, throbbing against my clinging insides but not offering the friction I am desperate for. Need.

"You will show me how well you're learning, perform for me, and you will do it over and over again until you're so attuned with your fat, little clit and your perfect, tight cunt that I know you can look after yourself."

"Okay, brute." I roll forward, trying to use the bonnet to cool the hot agony screaming at my wet centre. "Please, please move. I need you to move."

He chuckles, a deep timbre that rumbles against my backside and through me. "Easy, little flower." He lifts up and pets a huge hand down the length of my spine. "You're fragile." He draws out excruciatingly slow and pushes in, inch by inch, driving me insane. "So pretty." I rock back and forth against the car, my backside hounding his pelvis for more. More.

Two hands circle my hips, fingers pressing over my pubis and thumbs digging into the dips at the base of my spine. With a grunt, he starts to pound into me, holding me with steady authority.

I barely move as he slides in and out of my slick core, rhythmic, relentless, determined.

"Oh..." My eyes roll, and I gasp for air, stamping the shiny surface with my heavy breath.

This man has a way of making me feel taken, even as I beg for it. He makes me feel utterly defenceless, completely vulnerable—at the mercy of his powerful hands and hot, deep drives.

"That's my good girl. Defiled and fucked, and *so* mine." He hums, the sound deep and delicious.

My core clings to his length, wanting to keep him deep, and locks on as he draws out, leaving me in a frenzy.

I mewl and moan, my pulse fluttering inside my neck. "Lagos…"

"I've been so gentle with you, little flower," he says, groaning as he pounds into me. "I've been soft. Usually, I'd need my mouth full of pussy and my cock stuffed in one to feel satisfied, but there is something about your trembling body that feeds me in ways nothing else ever has."

I like that. That I'm enough. That he desires me as I desire him. From the moment I saw him, I knew. I'd never seen anything so... male. And I wanted it, to my core, to my most primitive cell—I wanted him.

Mouth gasping, I begin to come undone as his dick thickens, so long, so hot, so wide—inside me.

Stretching.

Rubbing.

Stroking.

How does he do t-that— *Oh...* Stars burst behind my eyes, and my mouth twists in sweet agony.

"Mine." He grunts. Thrusts. "All mine. Fuck. *Yes*."

Deeper.

Harder.

Thrust.

Then he brackets my legs, restlessly pawing at my hips, and pumps and pulses into me, shuddering and growling, the sound rivalling the dominant Redwind outside the barn.

Lagos works outside throughout the next two days while Tomar ransacks the kitchen cupboards and storerooms. They keep their distance from each other, even eating separately.

Guilt coils in my stomach.

I did this. Maybe that is why The Trade offers a man a Lace Girl? To stop the conflict between men?

I want to help Lagos or Tomar gather items, but Lagos grunts and says, "No," and Tomar declines, telling me to focus my efforts on Spero.

So, I try to breastfeed the tiny Xin De assassin several times, cry when nothing happens, and then offer the bottle with powdered milk.

I don't know if I am doing this correctly, but I am helpless and inexperienced, and it is hard not to blame myself.

When I get a chance, Lagos and I talk... Well, *I* talk, and he listens. Even having been around The Cradle and seen things I can't even imagine or dream of, he doesn't share. And I wonder whether he has been going through the motions, even being free, his existence, to his core, is still geared for Meaningful Purpose.

It starts in the womb.

Whereas affection is attached to my words and stories... I tell him about Maple and my Ward, but Lagos has no one to speak of. Only Tomar, I suppose.

At last-light on our second day, I watch Lagos shower in the barn. He holds a hose over his head, the water lapping along his muscles. Between his thick thighs, his balls seem heavy, and his dick sways as he washes himself, the water rushing the long length of it and licking from the tip.

His body is unnaturally—unfairly—virile. Every muscle is long, lean, and formed around a heavy frame.

I don't wash outside.

It's inside for me. As I am scrubbing my clothes and knickers in the sink, the bar of soap gliding over the fabric, lathering it with frothy cool water, Lagos hunts around the house.

And he finds something.

Behind a cupboard is a large door. And down the seven steps is an underground shelter. The walls are lined with rough-hewn stone. There are two more rooms and a second kitchen and bathroom, both neat, clean, and stocked with more supplies.

And, best of all, the bathroom. It is beautiful, far more elegant than my bathroom at the Half-tower, with a ceramic tub that curves gracefully, its surface smooth and inviting.

These people had a plan, a future. I wonder what happened to them. This home could have been empty for decades, maybe even longer.

Maybe they just died.

I am gazing dreamily at the bathroom, considering all the possibilities, and without being asked, Lagos uses the car engine to boil water for a bath.

He pours the water in, bringing the temperature to a comfortable level for Spero and me.

I beam, strip off, and dip my toe in. The water is tepid, in a soothing way.

Right, get in, Dahlia.

When I climb into it, I feel a bit like my old self. *A Trade Princess.* I suppose, in comparison to this life, being in The Trade does seem like the royal treatment.

Leaning back in the bath water, my body half-submerged, breasts and knees above the surface, I place snoozing Spero on my bare chest.

Lagos doesn't fit at all; he sits on a stool behind my head with his long, thick legs open and his rough fingers massaging my scalp. Small aches have been moving across my temples for the past few hours, which I hope is a symptom of the hormones.

My chest squeezes when he is kind and gentle like this, with his fingers in my red hair, massaging my scalp. I never imagined this man, this entirely rough man, to be this… attentive.

Though, this side of him only emerges when we are alone. When Tomar is around or near, Lagos' entire presence hardens.

"You once said you wouldn't pamper me," I giggle softly,

humming as his firm, consuming touch rubs down the nape of my neck and back up my scalp.

"I said a lot of things I now regret."

He *did* say a lot of mean things... Picking up the soap, I dot Spero with it, and then do my best to wash myself without disturbing him too much. I enjoy this moment, musing to myself.

The only thing missing is a story.

Maple used to tell me stories while we bathed or groomed each other. Lagos must have more to share. He must have experiences filled with awe, tasted things that explode with flavour, done things, *anything* that might be considered wonderful and tell-worthy.

I try to get more from him, posing a leading question. "Maple told me once that food, soap, friendship, and sex are life's great experiences." My voice is hopeful. "I added my own. *Nature.* Do you have any to add?"

He hums. "No."

My chest tightens, wisps of air leaving with a sad sigh. I want more, so much more from him, but getting anything from Lagos the Rogue is like pulling teeth from a skull. I would know. My Ward needed his tooth pulled out by a Trade Doctor once because it was aching so badly, he couldn't eat.

It isn't easy to pull teeth...

"It isn't easy to pull teeth," I say, the thought bumping through my lips clumsily with an awkward chuckle.

"Yeah. It is."

I roll my eyes. "You are impossible to get to know, Brute. Please, try. Do you have anything? Anything you can share with me?"

"The world doesn't look the same through my eyes, little flower."

Something about that sends knife-like stabs to my heart. "I've been so scared to like you," I admit, especially because I don't know you! "I was scared of how attracted I am to you, because I'm truly, truly terrified of the sick feeling in my stoma—"

"I make you feel sick?"

I laugh once. "Yes… We are *so* different," I breathe. The truth of that statement is in every inch of us, physically and emotionally.

I recall the sound of his inhumane growls, the strength no man should possess, the sight of his third eyelid sliding across, and the vision of his naked body. Too profoundly sculptured— I saw a picture of a stallion once. The long, lean muscles and the way the skin seemed to display each, seemed to mould to the figure, and… Lagos and his kind are not human.

And I let him inside me.

My thighs squeeze together, already wanting the space there touched and filled, insatiable for him—terrified of him, too. Intimidated each time he looms over me, but a willing victim to his lust and desires.

For a little while.

He is mine.

For always, I am his.

"I'm going to miss you," I whisper, instantly hoping my words disappear into the cool bath water, never to reach his ears and display more vulnerability. I've shown him my body but not my entire heart—not yet.

A heavy, rough sigh rumbles from behind me.

I stroke Spero's back while he dozes on my chest, half submerged in the water.

"I'll be sad," I say. "Never seeing you again will— It'll… hurt, I think." My throat tightens, just envisioning the moment he turns his back, and I am forced to watch his powerful body stride away for the very last time.

"Hurting you would be more pain than I could endure," he states, voice a serious bass tone. "And I have endured a great deal of pain."

At his words, at a glimpse of his past, I quickly swallow the lump expanding in my throat. Is this an opening to ask him more questions? I don't want to ruin the peaceful energy; not like I did last time at the waterfall. But we don't have years to share stories, don't have the luxury of bonding over months, growing together —growing older… We only have now.

"I want to know you, Lagos… before you leave me." *Oh, my.* My voice breaks. "When I think of you, remember you, I want to know who you are."

"I don't want you to know."

"What about what I want?"

His hand slides around my neck and down to my collarbones before caressing up my throat again. "You might find it easier if I tell you."

I don't believe that, but I offer, "If that is true, then tell me, tell me so it doesn't hurt so much when you leave."

"What do you want to know?"

I hear the tense shift in his voice, but soon, our time will be up. I need to know now. Everything. I want to know everything. "Tomar said The Trade controls Shadows with magnetic fields… Or something? Can you explain that?"

"Hm."

I blink ahead, absently stroking the baby at my chest and listening to his breathing deepen. I wait.

Lagos finally says, "I'm not a Trade Scientist, little flower. I don't understand the complexities of what they did to engineer my kind, but I do know that I'm my own magnetic field. All Shadows are, including the infant. When I'm at full strength, it's basic attraction and repulsion, like any magnetic field. The Trade uses this to steer us, or at least, guide us if we are willing to follow. That is, if we have an assignment."

I exhale hard.

That is heavy.

I've heard of many things in my short life. Of a streaky, colourful arch in the sky called a rainbow and an animal called an elephant with a nose like a hose—wild concepts that are hard to imagine. But this is still a lot to absorb and accept.

And I'm not highly educated. It wasn't necessary for my Trade to be so. But I know what a magnet is, and I have heard of birds using The Cradle's magnetic fields to navigate, but to think we changed Common humans *so* much…

To suit a Purpose.

The Trade's Purpose.

"That is…" I try so hard to absorb this information. I turn my face, peering up at him. "You're incredible."

He narrows his eyes at me. "No, little flower. *You* are incredible. *I'm* an abomination."

My heart drops, so I return my gaze to the tiled wall. I peer down at Spero. In his light slumber, he is making shapes with his mouth. Spero *is* incredible.

They are remarkable. Lagos is literally a force, pulsing energy, rippling muscles, powerful, stunning, but I can feel his self-hate, so I don't say that aloud. I will tell Spero what I think, though. I will tell him every day about how miraculous he is. And when he has questions about his kind, I will have the answers. So, for him, I have to keep pressing Lagos for information.

I need to know more.

"Willing?" I say, pushing on. "You said, if you're willing? So you have a choice… in a way?"

"You don't need to know—"

"I do!" I cut him off, desperate to keep the conversation going. I think it has to be now. If I stand, leave the tub… I might not get another opportunity. "If not to know you, then to understand Spero," I add. "I need to know. You are the only one who can tell me. If you care about me at all, about Spero, then you will tell me everything. *Please…* Do you have a choice?"

As a weighty pause circles me, I lean back into his big hands, seeking the soft, gentle version of Lagos the Rogue.

"We can move from it, but it is... unpleasant." His hands move around my neck and crown again, through my wet hair. "If it's too powerful, it's like pushing through a physical wall."

"Is that the pain Tomar spoke of?"

"There is more pain in *making* the Shadow," he says, voice detached.

A tear slides from my eye. "How do I protect Spero from the magnetic pull?"

"Tomar has told me that there is a doctor at the Common Community." His tone becomes flat, factual. "He knows you're coming. He knows about the infant. If the Shadow baby wants to leave the community one day, when he is a man, he risks coming into contact with a field or beacon, and if he's at full strength that will tear him in two."

"Oh." My breath hitches.

"The doctor will drain his blood if he wants to leave. The iron regenerates after several weeks, but it will help."

"Wh- what?" My eyes widen, but I don't dare turn around and display my horror.

"It's been a practice since the old-world, little flower. It will lower his sensitivities, but not eliminate them."

"How do you…" I falter. "How do you drain blood?"

"Through the vein," he says. "When needed. It'll help him later in life. We move around a lot. Doing this lowers my sensitivities to The Trade's tech."

"Will it…" I close my eyes. "Hurt? Wait—" My eyes snap open again. "*You* drain your blood, too?" I twist slightly, gaze hitting him over my shoulder.

"I just sit back and pump my fist. Tomar does the actual procedure," he states. "It's only necessary when we are on the move. He drains about a quarter of my blood and gives me some of his, which leaves him feeling shit, but I recover faster. I'm *his* burden."

"And then you protect him. You're co-dependent." I look at the ceramic lip beaded with water. Exhausted by concepts I cannot grip. They are *co-dependent.* Just another reason why he will leave me. Leave with Tomar. "Is that how he… How Tomar *saved* you?"

"And this."

I look up to find Lagos has his finger on the metal plate above his ear, shiny silver peeking out from between his sandy-brown hair.

"What's that?" I ask.

His eyes drop to the sleeping infant at my chest. "What we are trying to save the baby from. They implanted a coil in my brain to interfere with my thoughts, infiltrate them. If they get their hands on the infant, this is the first thing they will do to him."

The first thing...

"Lagos..." Tears stream down my face, and the sight of them causes his jaw to clench and unclench.

He wipes a salty bead from my lip with his thumb. "Don't feel sorry for me, little flower. I've done unimaginable things to sweet, innocent girls like you. I've crushed Trade flowers with my hands."

As he says that, nausea rolls in my stomach. I gaze into the steel-coloured eyes I have come to adore, seeing darkness and trauma. It wasn't his fault. Can't he see that? He didn't choose to be a Shadow.

I stupidly let the thought free. "You didn't have a choice, Lagos. No more than Spero does."

"I did." His eyes dilate, sending icy fear slithering down my spine. More predator than man in an instant. "I escaped when I was sixteen. I killed more men and women than I can even remember while I was in the training compound, *preparing.* I remember what they called them—Desensitisation Drills. But I could have stopped killing after I escaped. Couldn't I?" I lower my gaze. He grabs my jaw and forces me to look up at him. "But I didn't. I killed *more.*" His pitch-black glare bores into me, warning me. His voice drops, but his whispers only seem more visceral. "I killed pretty things like you while my cock was still inside them —" His hand falls from my jaw. "Think of that when you miss me, little flower."

Oh, Lagos. My lower lip wobbles and more tears roll down my cheeks.

Shallow breaths leave me as I try to fill my lungs again. I only seem to care about how these deaths affected him. What does that say about me? I used to think straight—he is a murderer with no respect for life. I remember thinking that, but now… I only feel the suffocating shroud of compassion and love for him.

I only want to hold him closer, to shake his self-loathing away. "You can't make me hate you."

His frown deepens. "The water is getting cold," he states, his voice equally as chilly as the bath.

In heavy silence, he pats me down gently, and I dry Spero, and we get ready to lie down for the night.

Chapter Thirty-Two

Lagos

Twenty-three years ago

I thrash my head from side to side. The sandstorm outside roars, roars, roars, building the ache in my cranium.

Behind my eyelids, I see… *her.*

The last girl. My last innocent kill. The one on the bed, with cum and blood dripping down her thighs and my finger marks marring her slim, white neck.

I hiss, wanting the disturbing vision to go away, desperate to be released from her, from whoever she was, and the incomplete memory of what happened. What happened? What fucking happened? I fucked her and killed her—that's what happened. *Why?* Because of the coil. The coil. The fucking coil…

I come to… Tormented and half-conscious, my heart continues to break against my ribs. I'm in the back seat of the truck... Not in the room anymore. I realise this.

Half-asleep, I lift my hand to the side of my head, feeling the tender skin around my metal plate. It's been there for five months now, but they removed bone and sliced into my grey matter—Healing is taking its toll.

It's gone; the coil is gone.

I open my eyes. The sight of the girl dissolves, but the self-loathing stays in its impenetrable fort within me.

"Lagos." Tomar opens the truck door and slides in the front seat, his face filled with excitement at first. He stops, his expression dropping. "Another nightmare, brother?"

I blink the sleep away, clearing the vision of him, only then realising there were tears. I had fucking tears in my eyes.

I jolt up and wipe at my face, fixing my features into hard lines, defiant of emotion. "What do you want?"

"Well,"—he lifts a brow— "good first-light to you, too."

"Leave me," I snap.

"No." He dismisses, and I try to focus and awaken. As I fully align myself with reality, I realise there is no sandstorm. There is no noise at all.

So used to the constant noise torture I endured at the compound, my mind fills my dreams and nightmares with riotous sounds as a default. Similar to any other standard of life: grass is green; water is clear; rocks are grey, and the skies fucking roar.

It's just more torture... More torment. I remember what they called it, Noise Conditioning.

Tomar twists to face me. "I have something to show you, my young Xin De Shadow."

I drop my head back. "I'm only eight years younger than you, Tomar." Vulnerability over his sharp gaze on my tears churns into anger. "Let me sleep!" I snap defensively. "I was dreaming about pussy, something you'll never understand, or you'd weep, too."

He hums, momentarily unimpressed that I taunted his beliefs. Archaic beliefs almost long forgotten—*almost.*

God. Jesus. Mary.

Just more fairy-tales.

But it is this belief system that secures him connections and loyalties across The Cradle. Other believers are present in almost every pocket. The doctor who removed my coil—a believer. Trade men, even lords, many who keep this faith in secret.

"I have something to show you," he repeats. "Wake up."

And I snarl, closing my eyes to block him out. "Why is it so fucking quiet?"

"Because…" His voice fills with enthusiasm, my mood washing off him like it always does. He has a twenty-second rebound rate, and he's back to his Purpose. "I parked the truck in a fucking *cave*, brother. No Redwind."

My eyes cut open, and I straighten. "What do you mean in a cave?" I get a good look at him—bright—as if he has been solving problems and dealing with people all day while I slept in the back of the truck. Through the window, I study the jagged rocks on all sides of the vehicle. My heart slows down, but thumps deeper, heavier as if the organ draws in a breath and relaxes.

"You remember I told you about the Half-tower? How it's The Trade's most neglected tower? How there are people who want to escape? People we can help, people *you* can help, heal your soul—"

I snarl.

It's too early for this.

"What fucking hour is it, Tomar?"

"It's first-light." He waves his hand, way too eager for my liking. "I drove through the night. Now listen. You remember the underground town? *The Bite.* The one near the Half-tower. The one we thought didn't exist…" He nods his annoying head, his lips drawing out into a huge smile. "I found it! We're here!"

Here.

His words find their mark inside me, joining my anger, self-loathing, and disdain for life.

Help people.

Heal your soul.

Chapter Thirty-Three

Lagos

I grind my teeth in my sleep.

The roar of the storm outside carries a familiar nightmare on its sand-laden back. Single quick flashes of a scene appear in my mind.

Flash; a dead baby on the floor of the compound laboratory, head crushed into the clean white tiles. Flash; bloody grid marks beneath my boots.

Flash; running, running, my lungs burning… And then a girl sprawled out on the mattress, her neck twisted and crushed.

Flash.

Dahlia.

Dead Dahlia. Crushed little flowers covered in blood, green eyes staring up at me, betrayed and in love… In love.

Dread weighs me down.

"Lagos… The storm is scary tonight." Somehow, her small whimper reaches into my mind and pulls me out of there, thrusting me back into her arms.

My eyes snap open to the ceiling of the farmhouse, my body

instantly turning to pull her close to me. To protect her. "It's just the wind. You're safe with me, little flower. I'll take care of you."

I lie still, staring ahead, but part of me feels tethered to that place, the compound, and the years that I spent training, killing, and studying. So, I hold my little flower, focus on her breathing, her scent, and easily shake away the dark images of my past.

"But..." she murmurs sleepily. "What about tomorrow and the next day and the next? What about... Spero."

The Shadow baby...

She yawns, tucking her little body into the cave of my torso. I gaze down at her. The room is dim but slithers of light from the torch slash her profile and body.

My gaze follows the bridge of her nose, straight but for the slightest curve from the attack. To her lips, full and parted as she breathes. Soft bruising paints the corner of one eye. And freckles —freckles fucking everywhere, with a few on her upper lip.

"The milk..." She sighs sleepily, sadly. "I've failed him."

I'm not sure if she's awake or tormented in her slumber by that fucking Shadow baby and its needs, but I don't like it.

I'm certain I wasn't breastfed. Why does he get her? He only burdens her, saddens her. I hate that. Just put it in a damn box and feed it every few hours.

That's how it's done.

I recall the rows and rows of incubators I saw that last day before I escaped. Shadows fed through tubes, hooked up to machines, barely organic. An awakening moment... That was me —*is* me. I am not human.

I'm an abomination. Made of the same material as a human but built in a laboratory.

I gaze through the dark, across to the sleeping infant in the corner, tucked in, covered, kissed goodnight. This fucking thing...

This infant is... *lucky.* Not a word I would usually use, but I can't shake my contempt. Though I know it is pathetic jealousy—I have to share her...

I don't like sharing her.

But no matter how powerful my possessive demands are, her misery strikes me harder—

The need to taste between her legs burns through me, and within a minute, I have her on her back with her thighs either side of my face.

"Lagos…" she complains, sleep clinging to her husky voice.

As I rub my nose and lips against her knickers, inhaling, she moans. Finding the back of my head, her little fingers feed into my hair.

"You smell *so* good." A possessive growl vibrates from me. As much as I want to chew her knickers off, I don't. She only has a few pairs. I saw her washing all her clothes in the sink earlier. She needs more. I need to provide for her.

I drag her knickers off her trembling legs and brace myself on my elbows with my palms holding her little thighs to the blankets, spreading her wide for my gaze.

Even in the dim, I get an eyeball of perfectly shaped pussy lips, slightly open, revealing luscious soft internal flesh. So vulnerable. So fragile. This is what a man dreams of after death.

I lick her from arsehole to clit, and she jerks off the mattress, rasping out startled breaths.

"*Oh*… Lagos."

My name… Is it? A strange need growls through me. Unbidden, unwelcome, fucking dark, because I wonder what it would feel like to be called Six. Would I like hearing that from her? Or would I despise it?

Would I choke the word from her lips… Dark rings eclipse my vision until her pussy is my only focus.

I lap at her, up and down, her salty juices coating my tongue. Squeezed between my abdomen and the blanket, my cock thickens. Precum pumps to the tip, smearing and leaking.

Her hands paw at my hair.

She moans when I dip my tongue between her swollen lips. Rimming her entrance, her flesh ripples against the onslaught of my attention.

She squirms and mewls, her backside trying to shift and join the movements.

I glide one rough palm up her trembling stomach, over the ladder of her ribs, careful not to hurt her. Covering both small, pert breasts, I knead them firmly but also pin her the fuck to the blanket so I can eat her without interruption.

"I know where to lick you, little flower. How hard. How fast. When to stop. *Fuck...*" I never want to stop tonguing this perfect cunt.

Supple thighs rub against my beard while I mouth her pussy, fucking her channel with my tongue and thrusting my hips into the blankets.

Groaning… *Fuck.*

Too turned on.

Groaning harder…

Dangerously turned on.

I snarl viciously as I eat her, hearing fragile uncertainty pitch her whimpers, but that doesn't stop her from coming. Doesn't frighten her pleasure away.

Her pussy clings to my tongue, her climax tearing through her quickly. She pulses in my hold, her moans belting the room with sweet, wild abandon.

I didn't even suck her little clit.

I drag my tongue slowly up and then latch onto the tiny hood, pushing with my lips to bring the little pink member out so I can flick it with my tongue.

"Oh!" Her legs spasm. "Lagos… Please, it's too much."

I hold her the fuck still. Not unlike holding a wounded animal as it thrashes to keep from the clutches of pain, she thrashes as I force her to come again and again, despite her sensitivities. I want her twitching with sensation.

As she comes apart for the fourth time, I lick down to her entrance again and hum. I lick her for my enjoyment. Only mine. Messily and hungrily and without consideration.

I squeeze her left nipple and roll it between my thumb and

finger— *Fuck.* Then, I nearly blow my load on the blankets when the tight bud weeps with a thick fluid. She is lactating into my fucking hand.

I bet she doesn't even know.

Arousal hits my temples. I don't stop stimulating and squeezing as something—some kind of emotion—spreads warmth through my chest. *Pride.* It's fucking pride. I'm *proud* of my little flower.

Crazed with need, I'm prowling up her body, trailing my tongue over her wet, shuddering skin as I move.

Dropping my elbows to the blankets on either side of her, I stare down at the way her milk glistens in tiny rivers from each nipple.

Fuck. Me.

My tongue darts out instinctively before I can stop myself, and I lick the milky fluid from her. As I take her small breast into my mouth, drawing in, her nipple squirts. Warm, sweet liquid streams down my tongue. I swallow hungrily, humming and greedy for more.

"Lagos!" She yelps, panic and embarrassment ripe in her sweet voice. It only fuels me.

To get away from me, she tries tugging at my hair, and the small sting fuels me.

"I'm… I'm… Stop," she pleads. "You don't understand. You have to stop."

Hell no!

Drinking from her, my mind in a haze of pleasure, I fist the blankets by her head and fuck her leg, losing control momentarily, but then stop… Because she needs me to stop. She needs to feed the fucking infant.

I tear my mouth from her nipple, heaving because I forgot to breathe. "You need more food." It's the first thought to axe through my arousal.

Her needs… She needs more food if she is to let that infant suck nutrients from her body. "I'll be back with food."

Without a second thought, I am standing and walking from the room.

The hallway is almost pitch-black except for the glow of one of our flashlights in the kitchen.

I enter to find Tomar sitting with his elbows on the kitchen table, his face buried in his hands. Darkness crinkles around the edges of the space, but the torch in front of him beams upward, creating a dot on the ceiling.

Stirring displeasure digs claws into my thick skin. "Were you listening to her come on my tongue?"

He lifts his head, a pained gaze hitting me, before snapping away with a hiss. "Get some clothes on, Lagos!"

I look down the long, hard slope of my body to my cock, thick and steeled against my abdomen, painting me in precum that won't fucking stop flowing.

"She is lactating," I state plainly.

"What?" He rises to his feet, eyes bugging out with shock. "That's— That's brilliant news."

I cross my arms. "She needs food."

"I agree." He moves to a crate and grabs a large cardboard box. "Full of military-grade rations," he states. "The people who lived here must have raided a Trade vehicle or something."

Cold, I grab the box and turn my back on him, walking away.

"Why is her innocence so attractive to you?" he blurts out.

I stop dead in my tracks.

"I know why I like it, but I don't know why you do," he goes on. "Is it because you're depraved? You want to break all the pretty things?"

Some fucking honesty from him in relation to her—for once.

Slowly, I edge around to face Tomar, the torch offering enough light to really study his exhausted demeanour.

"Tell me how you really feel, brother?" I glare at him. "I thought I won't break everything I touch?"

He closes his blue eyes and shakes his head. "I didn't mean that. I know you don't *want* to break anything."

Perhaps it's because I know he cares for her, because he cares for me, or maybe it's because I know men can't control their instincts… I offer him honesty. "Maybe to start with."

"See it from my perspective." He opens his eyes, levelling me. "I have spent the last two decades watching you hate the world and yourself, kill hundreds of men and sleep soundly. I have tried to show you peace. I have tried to show you joy. I don't want her to be broken… You will find her annoying and boring. And you will hurt her."

"Annoying... *Yes.* She is fucking annoying, but that says more about me and my bitter view of life than about her." I clench my teeth, already hating that I called her annoying. "And boring? The opposite. Everything is more when she is beside me. Things I've seen a million times are more remarkable, more beautiful. Her innocence sees the world the way I want it to be. The way it should be. It's not a big fucking fan... Is it?" I cross the room, shadow him, and grip the side of his neck with one hand, squeezing. I think I'm warning him or showing him affection. Perhaps, I want to snap it. I can't tell. "It's a fucking remarkable fan," I admit, voice rough. "And I want to see more with her so she can open my eyes."

He frowns up at me, locking his jaw. "I tried to open your eyes many times, Lagos. You wanted to be blind."

I release his neck. "Not anymore."

"You found God in her." He laughs without mirth. "I see The Cradle as remarkable because I know God made it, designed it, and I see God everywhere. In all of it. Even the punishing wind. Even in you. I see His incredible power and will."

"I only see her." My tone deepens, a threat thundering in my chest. "Don't test me when it comes to her, brother. Bury whatever feelings you have. If I so much as suspect your hand is on your cock while you dream of the sounds I pull from her, I will remove your hands and your cock."

"Vulgar," he grumbles but saves further feigned disgust. "I was wrong to let myself feel that way. I see that now."

"It's not wrong. You're a man after all. It took her for me to feel humanity. It took her for you to feel primal." As the words growl through my teeth, the urge to kill him intensifies. I don't want anyone feeling primal, or anything else for that matter with her.

Fuck.

I pause, lording over Tomar as moments roll by. Killing him would hurt her and pain me to an early grave, so I stride away from him.

Focus on my little flower.

Chapter Thirty-Four

Dahlia

My breasts are tingling with sensation, milk rolling over the curve.

The torch is on, so I put a shirt over the spot to filter the beam. Outside the farmhouse, the Redwind howls and prowls, shaking the glass in the frames.

I sit naked on the blankets, with Spero cradled in my arms, his mouth latching onto my nipple almost immediately. Awe curls around me at the beauty of nature and life—the violent weather beating at the windows of the secure room where I breastfeed Spero for the first time.

We did practise before I even had anything to offer, and now he seems eager to explore this new sensation.

He swallows.

"He *did* it."

"You did it."

I look up to find Lagos has returned to the room, standing naked in the open door, holding a box of sorts as he stares intensely down at us.

He is magnificent, with his rough, battered skin, rippling ink from neck to ankle, and long shadows carving each muscle. Thrumming on his abdomen, a hard, smooth dick, the underside licked from root to swollen crown with protruding veins.

Arousal and something sweeter, *happiness,* fill my chest, and it is bittersweet, given this moment—Lagos, me, and Spero—is destined to end. Soon.

I am not ready for it.

Lagos closes the door and leans against it. A steadfast guard. "I have food for you, little flower. You need to eat."

"Okay."

He studies me. "Your rib?"

I sigh at the small talk. "It's fine. Can we stay another day?" The vulnerability in my voice scares me, but I don't have time to hide my emotions. It's now or never. Time moves even when we wish to stand still.

Oh, how I wish to pause it.

"*Yes,*" he says.

I hold Lagos in my sights, unable to tear my gaze away from what appears to be affection and softness blazing so outwardly in his gaze.

"The Shadow baby is lucky to have you," he rumbles.

"Spero," I correct, though I know he doesn't really think Spero is beneath him. On the contrary, it's self-loathing that haunts his tongue, that expels punishing words. "If you keep calling him a Shadow baby, I'm going to start calling you a Shadow daddy."

"Okay."

My breath catches from the seriousness in his deep timbre, and I smile, gaining reluctant courage.

"Do you think that…" I swallow, nerves fluttering in my neck. "If things were different… That we could live in a place like this?"

He watches me. "Yes."

"Together?"

"Yes."

I exhale hard, retreating my gaze to Spero, flooded with

emotions too sad and sweet to bear. It's too much. We are doomed, but I wish to drown tonight. It's wonderful—and painful. It has to end, but we have now. Tears fire behind my eyes, glossing them over.

Wild fantasies are not virtues.

"Can we pretend that we are from the old-world?" I gaze up at Lagos the Rogue, huge and formidable, a guard dog at the door, and he stares back at me, naked and breastfeeding. "And I am yours, and you are mine. Can we pretend that this is our home and that Spero is our baby?"

"Yes, little flower. You can pretend."

"Lie with me?" I hold my hand out for him. "*Please*. Lagos."

He stares at my small hand, his throat bobbing, before he walks over to me. I was once afraid of the way he moves, stealthy but lording, too graceful for a man his size.

He takes my hand in his, his warm, coarse fingers wrapping around me. He follows me down as I lie on my side with Spero at my chest. My nipple is between his lips, but slumber makes his eager sucking slow and intermittent.

Lagos settles down opposite me, facing me, and we just… look at each other. His eyes map my face, and mine study his. He has small scars on his cheeks, tiny clear white lines.

I lift my hand and brush a dark-blonde strand behind his ear, my fingertip skimming the metal plate.

"We could make a real cot for Spero." I almost choke, not sure why I am torturing myself with this. "I saw wood in the barn."

Watching intently, his attention is searing. His big hand lifts so his index finger can draw a line down my nose as if he wants to remember the slope, the bump, the feel. "I could."

We map each other.

I run my finger across his forehead, scooping dark-blonde strands to the side as I go. "And we could fix the wiring."

His brows weave. "I could."

I smooth the pinched crease between his eyes. "We could be happy here."

"I would."

A few tears squeeze free. "You wouldn't be bored, brute?"

Lagos uses his thumb to brush the little drops away. "Not with you, little flower."

The heavy weight of this fantasy swirls around us, changing something on a deep level. I gaze at him, disappearing into steel-grey eyes so bright against the dim of the bedroom that we've made our own.

I show him my body, share it, but now he sees my heart that pours through my gaze. "I like the farmhouse, Lagos." I smile, remembering. "Tide told me that we are little bits of every place we have been and every person we have met. I would be content with just this bit."

Lost in his gaze, I have to forcefully tear my eyes away, blinking through the shadows to where Spero sleeps at my chest. I tuck the infant under my arm and steadily climb to my feet. As I walk to Spero's tiny nest in the corner, a cavity made with blankets and pillows, I feel Lagos' watchful attention.

Returning to my place opposite him on the river of blankets, I whisper, "Show me how to do it. Show me how to touch myself. The way you touch me. I can dream of this place, your fingers, and your strength, and touch myself."

"Lay on your back for me," he says, and I watch his mouth move around the dominant words, memorising.

As I do as I'm told, he lifts to his knees beside me, over me, looking down on my face and torso like a puppet master.

So close, I can feel the heat from his thighs. His balls hang and his dick fists up from them, throbbing.

My breath skitters out.

Intimidated by this monster of a man, but also… breathless with arousal, gasping for his warm touch.

As if he understands, he smooths my hair down my head, calmingly, at the same time reaching for my hand. "Use both hands, little flower. I would have my hands everywhere. Not an inch left untended."

He guides my hand to my breast. "Like this." He flicks my nipple with his thumb, warm milk sliding from the moist tip, dripping down my side.

"Fuck. So vulnerable for me."

Leaving my hair, his other hand takes my free one and glides it down my trembling stomach, excruciatingly slow.

My chest pumps hard, though my breaths still seem shallow.

While cupping my breast, I let him dip my other hand between my thighs.

"Here," he purrs, using his fingers to lead. I'm warm and wet, and the skin just inside responds to our touch, rippling and flushing. The world spins, stars suddenly skipping through the air.

"So warm, so wet." He is a predator hovering over me, seconds away from sinking his teeth in. "Appreciate this pretty flesh, little flower. You're sweet. Nervous. It's so fucking beautiful."

He called me beautiful...

I shudder as our fingers work together, rubbing between my tight folds. Messy. Abandoned. *Safe.* He helps me explore my hot centre.

"Such a good girl. Don't be too shy to go deeper." He pushes two of my fingers deep inside, his long digit mounting and guiding mine through my clinging muscles. "Like this."

"*Oh...*" I moan, lifting my backside from the blankets against that *full* feeling.

"And out again," he orders.

I copy his rhythm. His larger finger moves inside me while two of mine try to match his pace and depth.

"Oh, *Lagos.*"

My eyes roll back.

"Feel how soft your pussy is, how supple and delicate it is. You're so fragile here. A man could sink his teeth in. Lick hard enough to taste blood. You're sensitive. So fucking vulnerable." He groans, leaning over me to lick the milk sliding down the curve of my breast. "Mine. Remember who you belong to when you fuck your fingers at night."

He pulls his hand from between my legs, placing it on my thigh, pinning me down for his dark gaze.

I try to concentrate on both of my hands, but it's hard. And while my eyes roll back to the thrusting of my fingers, back arching and pelvis lifting, I seem to paw impatiently at my wet breasts.

I become a desperate mewling being on the blankets, squirming and trying to finish myself, edge closer.

"This is your clit."

Then he is there. His hot mouth is above my fingers, creating suction as his thick, ardent tongue licks hard at what feels like hundreds of tiny nerves.

I pulse off the blankets.

Crying and mewling, I struggle to keep my hands on their task, finding myself careless, rough, thrusting harder, deeper, to match the buzzing of his mouth.

"Oh, Lagos… I can't— I need—" I don't know what I need, but he does, so when he pulls his lips away from me, gazing down with predator-like intent, I whimper at the loss of heat, suction…

A chill sweeps across my core.

"Make yourself come, little flower." He moves my wet fingers to a knot above my entrance.

Lagos fists his dick as I nervously circle the sensitive area. He looks down at me while I play with hesitation and uncertainty. Already aware of the powerful pleasure this special place can offer.

"That's a good girl. Don't be shy. Rub around the hood and feel your little clit inside rise for you."

I get closer to the bundle, my circles tighter, a noose around the bud. *Oh...* I twitch. So strange, my legs spasming when I press down on the very peak.

Sweat gathers on my skin.

"There she is." He rasps, breathless. "Good girl. Keep going. Rub that sweet, little clit. Good girl. That's my girl."

Milk beads on my nipples.

My mouth dries and tingles, and parts of me—toes, thighs, ears—come alive with sensation without ever being touched.

"Eyes on me," he growls, pumping his dick hard, the flushed head dripping and engorged. Massive. Intimidating.

The air in the room boils.

Working myself to the point of tiresome agony, it is the sight of him so violently thrusting into his own fist, abdominal muscles bunching, virile beyond anything human, that finally throws me over the edge.

Groaning, I come shuddering and bucking, my legs kicking out and toes curling. I feel like speared prey, and I realise how closely pain and pleasure are experienced.

"Will you think of me?" My gaze slides up to his, hazy with pleasure. "When you touch yourself?" *Or when you're with other women...* I think the horrible truth but don't say it, despising it.

"Like this. Just like this," he says darkly, black eyes dragging across my exposed figure, tight fist sliding up and down his length. "With milk dripping from your breasts and your body flushing from a sweet orgasm."

He drops his head back, baring his teeth as he comes, spurting white ropes across my chest and chin. Grunting as his dick visibly pulses in his fist, his eyes stalk over the claim he paints on my skin.

"This is the image, little flower," he pants heavily. "I'll play over in my mind each night."

Chapter Thirty-Five

Dahlia

We spend the entire next day in the bedroom, *pretending*. Well, I pretend while Lagos humours me.

He takes my body.

He *can* go all day.

We have been intimate, many times. We never stop, only to eat and feed Spero.

Inside me with his fingers, or mouth, or dick, he rolls me around, so even while I fight to stay awake, I sense his hands on me. Spreading. His eyes on me. Gazing. Memorising.

The day ends too soon.

And then we leave at first-light. Tomar locks the house up, saying he hopes to visit again in the future as there are more supplies than we can fit into the truck.

Goodbye, farmhouse.

One little death.

Now, Lagos is driving, and Tomar has his feet on the dashboard, his hood pulled down, and deep, rough snores coming from under the brim. I don't think he slept much last night… And

Lagos and I didn't come up for air either; all three of us are exhausted.

"He snores," I half-laugh.

"Hm," is all I get from Lagos.

Spero is in my lap, feeding from my breast, and the feelings of bliss coursing through me has a wide smile rushing along my lips —I did it. *We* did it.

My cheeks heat, and my lips part as I remember what I let Lagos do to my body last night, how I let him lick me between the thighs and suck milk from me while I was half-asleep.

It is so wrong.

So, so wrong.

And yet, when the milk comes down it feels like a release. When Spero is there, there is nothing but wholesome peace, but when Lagos is there, the sensation seems volcanic and strange and overwhelming. I'll never say it aloud; I'll never admit that I enjoyed it.

I look up from my tiny assassin and peer out the window to watch a curtain of red sand beating the glass between me and The Cradle.

I can make out the hazy outline of a mountain. We have been following it for half a day. The desert burns like wildfire. We haven't seen a windmill or any sign of civilisation for many hours.

Lagos watches me in the mirror, every time I lift my gaze, his eyes catch mine in that moment. As if I might disappear, slip through his fingers before we have a chance to say… goodbye.

Goodbye to a little death.

"You're you. Bits of every place you have been and every person you have spoken to. Unique."

But he doesn't feel like *a* bit… Saying goodbye to him doesn't feel like *one little* death. It feels like all of them.

My throat tightens.

Accepting the unacceptable— Lagos is not a part of my future. I swallow, and my breasts tingle. My pulse, or emotions, or heightened state, seem to stimulate the milk production.

I inhale hard and exhale.

Thick Redwind blankets the bonnet, dusting the truck in sand and debris as we head north this time. Further north than I thought The Cradle went.

There is a place at the top of the border called The Horizon. It's the end of civilisation, the end of life, a capricious, uninhabitable death zone. Or at least, that is what we are told.

You get lost.

Sucked in.

Into oblivion with Lagos... A sad smile moves across my lips. Maybe that wouldn't be so bad.

"We're close to the tunnel." Tomar looks across at Lagos, reading the volatility that I feel in my bones.

The creeping tendrils of anguish make themselves known, moving into my belly and flailing around. I don't want to say goodbye.

I love him.

I inhale hard and look at Spero, using him to ground myself in our reality. He is fast asleep, so I place him in his nest beside me.

"There is promise for your future," I whisper to him, stroking his chubby cheeks with my finger. I sing a few words, curling new rhymes around my tongue as I go. "Your eyes full of promise... *dreams* yours to chase, you'll have freedom to grow, at your own pace, with no Trade control, you'll...you'll..." I can't think of another word. "I'll work on that shanty for you, Spero."

"That's lovely, Dahlia." Tomar sighs, and I know I'll miss him, too. "Your gentle voice will be missed when it's just us men again. Sing another for us. *Please.*"

Abruptly, Lagos veers the car to the side of the road, tyres spitting red dirt up at the windows until the vehicle comes to a jerking stop.

"I want to provide for you," he states, the words punching out with fierce determination.

I blink at him in the rearview mirror. "What do you mean?"

He turns, staring at me in the backseat. "Even after this. I know how to care for you now. What a young Common girl needs. I want to provide for you. You're mine."

"Lagos?" Tomar looks between us, brows furrowed into deep lines.

I press my palm over my heart as it frantically pitter-patters. Don't say things you don't mean. Don't… I can't bear it. "What do you mean?"

"I don't want to..." His deep voice trails to a dark sigh, one filled with brittle helplessness. With emotion so rare to outwardly hear from him, and in front of Tomar. "Things I like… You and me. The farmhouse. The bath. I liked it."

I close my eyes, shaking my head as I hold them like that. Fending off his words as they slide in deep. Too deep. I can barely breathe around them.

"I know you did," I choke, my throat containing emotion, my will stifling hot, needy tears.

"I'll come back."

My forehead pinches as that statement rolls over me. I open my eyes to find his pinning me in place. "Please don't say things you don't mean."

"I'll come back," he states adamantly. "And I'll meet you when it's safe. Outside the community, somewhere close. Do you want to meet me, little flower?"

I splutter, demanding tears falling, my head nodding and nodding, unable to stop because yes, yes, yes. "Yes!"

"I'll provide for you."

I try to catch my pulse, slow it down so I can hear him over it. "In what—"

"In every way." His steel-coloured gaze holds me arrested, his tone dead-serious and inhumanly deep. "I'll give you anything. *Everything*."

These are just words. Goodbyes. Niceties to sugarcoat the end, a cloak of pretty lies, and then I'll simply never see him again. "I thought you weren't here to pamper me, Lagos?"

"I was wrong," he growls. "That's exactly why I'm here. I want to give you life's great experiences. I want to see them through your eyes."

Oh, my. Is he serious?

Tomar fades away. There is no truck, no howling wind, no beating red sand that rushes the bonnet. Lagos the Rogue is the only thing I see, feel, hear.

A sad smile touches my mouth, tears falling everywhere, their salty kiss reminding me of The Bite. "Will you bring me bananas and chocolate?"

The corner of his mouth turns up, a half-smile. A lovely one, framed by his neat dirty-blonde beard. "I'll find you bananas and chocolate, little flower. All your great experiences. I will provide them all."

He *is* serious. "Will you kiss me?"

His eyes roam my face, mapping, tracing—imprinting. "Every inch."

"When it's safe?" I confirm, believing him. I believe him. He will. My lower lip wobbles so hard it's nearly impossible to keep smiling at him. "How long will you stay with me each time you visit?"

"A day." He looks down and then up again, and my breath catches. That's it? My heart squeezes. "Perhaps." He growls, thinking. "I'll find a way. A place close, but outside the community."

It's not enough.

I gasp for air; hope is drowning. Scary. It can end in ruin. "How will you get the information to me?"

"Nothing can stop me, little flower. I've broken through The Cradle. Nothing can stop me. No one can stop me from getting to you."

Stupid feelings rise and bubble over. The ones I have been burying, the ones not fair to Tomar or his loyalties, but they spit out with desperation anyway. "Then why can't we do that now! Find a place. Stay together, and we can have new, great experiences. We can kiss, and I will protect you, and you can protect me, and we will be together."

Pain scores a path across his features, his half-smile falling away. "I have to go with Tomar."

I can't look at Tomar right now, afraid he'll see my misdirected hatred and jealousy, but that isn't fair. It isn't…

I nod slowly but don't feel it. "Because you owe him—"

"My life," he finishes.

"And you need to save people." My voice breaks. I try to smile harder, forcing it, but it's crooked, and now I am not sure it is a smile. I'm not sure how to smile right now. "That's because..." I inhale a shaky breath. "You're *good,* Lagos. I have to share you."

My words are just as desperate as I am. I need him to know. A sea of unshared affection swirls in his steel-coloured gaze. Then he swallows, his throat rolling before he turns back to face the road, jerks the wheel, and continues down the highway.

I risk a glance at Tomar, who is staring contemplatively out the window, seemingly unfocused and distant.

We drive in silence.

Staring at Spero in the nest beside me, he smiles at my attention. He knows me—I am his person. I will care for him.

Lagos cares for me.

Even though no one cared for him. I think about baby Lagos with no smiles, trapped in a cell. Did they cuddle the babies? Rock them? Sing? In my mind, the babies are in metal cages, but that doesn't make sense. If they are highly trained, educated, and skilled, Shadows are probably held in fancy facilities, with gymnasiums, the best educators, and modern technology. A clinical setting. White cells, clean sheets. No personality.

Spero will have colours.

Messy sheets.

Too much charm.

I can't bring myself to smile back at Spero right now. I have so much I want to say to Lagos. Most important of all—I think I love you. But I have no breath left to say it. I feel I'll need all my strength to say those three words aloud.

Last-light sashes the horizon with red, and I wonder how we will find a tunnel in the dark.

I am drawing little patterns on my thighs, envisioning the farm and the Common men and women, when the truck slows down, the taste of metal slices at my tongue, Spero starts to hiccup and cry, and Lagos hits the brakes right in the middle of the road.

Then he puts it in reverse.

We fly backward. Air rushes into my lungs and my rib flares with pain as the car spins to face the other direction. I grip the handle as we are thrown to the side, and Tomar does the same—

Then we stop.

Which is worse...

I pant. "What is going on?"

A glint of last-light reflects off something in the distance, red dots like eyes in the Redwind.

"It's too late," Lagos growls.

"What is too late?"

The sound that follows is a subtle bell, but it quickly builds into a sharp, piercing ringing, slicing through the air like an unwelcome presence.

I cup my ear with one hand while the other tries to shield Spero from the riotous noise, but I watch on in horror as Lagos and Tomar argue in the front seat, their mouths moving fast, eyes fierce.

Palpable energy seems to pound and bleed around Lagos until—

Time stretches, making each moment feel like hours.

Lagos twists to step from the car, but Tomar lunges for him, taking a fist full of his shirt, desperation and sorrow crumble through his expression.

Lagos turns back, his eyes narrowing on something in Tomar's hand. Tomar is holding my knickers in his fist. Lagos snatches them and, with the same fist, strikes Tomar right in the nose.

I clutch my heart as thick blood sprays the truck, painting the windscreen and seats. Tomar grips the bridge of his spitting nose as he slides into the driver's position.

"No. No! Fuck!" I think Tomar chants, but I can't hear the words, drowned in the screams of metal on metal like a force surrounds us, bellowing.

Scanning outside, my frantic gaze searches through the dense red vortex, despairing, struggling to find an anchor.

Then I find one.

Then he is here.

My car door suddenly opens, and Lagos leans in, his hot lips touching my ear as he says, "You were my great experience, little flower."

He closes the door.

My insides wilt as I watch him walk down the centre of the road into the Redwind, parting it with his huge body until he is swallowed entirely by the crimson fortress.

No.

I grab the door handle.

No, no, no.

And for a moment, I almost throw myself after him so we can kiss goodbye, so I can tell him I won't remember it, won't remember what he did before me, only all the wonderful things he did *for* me—

Time snaps back.

Tomar turns the car around to face north again, beating the steering wheel with his fist and sobbing outwardly.

My face has a veil of tears, but I have no memory of when I started to cry.

As I press my palm to the glass, gasping for air, the ringing is suddenly sucked into the direction Lagos left.

Spero's cries are painful to hear now, so I scoop him up and hold him close to my breasts, feeling the cool kiss of milk seeping into my shirt-dress. "What… What just happened?"

"Trade found us," Tomar says.

I knew. I *guessed.* Still, hearing it sends despair racing to every cell in my body. "What?"

"He is giving us time." He nods and then shakes his head. "He had to. They knew there was a Shadow close. The beacons went off. They would have kept coming. Now... Now they'll think it was him. Now... now they'll leave us alone."

"But... I don't..."

"You're safe."

I'm safe?

One little death.

But Lagos doesn't feel like one little death, one little bit of me. He is too massive, too consuming, too much a part of the Dahlia I chose to be. The one I became at The Bite, the one who became a mother, who experienced life's greatest things, all with him at my side.

He feels like *all* my deaths. None of the other bits exist without him.

Chapter Thirty-Six

Dahlia

The Redwind isn't incredible, windmills are not remarkable, glowworms are just bugs, and Spero is not hope.

He is just a baby.

I stare at Tomar's hands gripping the steering wheel; the stretched skin over his knuckles is white, and his fingers have his blood smeared across them.

The rearview mirror holds the fading image of Lagos, although he is long gone, and we are miles away now. I am terrified that if I look into the mirror long enough, I will see him standing there.

What if he ran after the truck?

What if he killed them all, broke their bones like he promised he'd do, knowing I would sigh with relief because they were not mine or Spero's… And now he's trying to get back to me. To say goodbye… That is all we were going to do anyway.

Say goodbye.

But he did say goodbye.

"You were my great experience, little flower." His depthless timbre echoes between my ears.

"He will live, right?"

Tomar stares ahead. "I don't know."

"He will escape, and you will find him." I don't ask this time—I state. I demand. Demand The Cradle, The Crust, our very existence to abide by my words.

"This was the only way. Trust me."

Trust is such a fragile thing, because when it's paired with something unacceptable, like grief and loss, then it becomes flimsy. And I hope Tomar is wrong. I don't want to trust him because I want him to be wrong.

I stare out the windscreen again, but everything seems… Bad. Sad. Wrong. The whirlwind outside is just a horrible vortex that swallowed up my heart when it consumed Lagos right before my eyes.

Every moment that passes drags me further from him, like a chasm opening up between us. The Redwind blurs as more tears rush down my cheeks, then sobs break from my lips, and I shake violently, no longer holding it inside—I love him. I love him so much that I pretended it wasn't happening. I wasn't prepared for a goodbye, least of all one like this.

All this time, I silently clung to the idea something would happen, a new development, a magical safehouse for us to grow old in— My world tilts. I quietly hoped that Lagos would choose me over Tomar and the people he helps… When all along, The Cradle had a sadder fate for us.

"You love him… Oh, *Dahlia…"* Tomar chokes my name out. He tries to speak, but each word barely breeches his lips. "I will look for him. I will look for him, and I will bring him to visit you. I promise."

It feels like The Cradle is crumbling around me, and I am willing to be buried.

"Take me back to the farmhouse!" I cry. As I say it, I know it's just a broken plea. It's too late. I just want to curl up on our pile of blankets and inhale his scent, disappear into the memory of us and forget reality. I could waste away in that memory.

Wracked with sorrow, I barely notice when we enter a large tunnel.

Rushing grey concrete blurs through every window. The Redwind has disappeared, but last-light dots a distant exit. A portal to my new life.

'To be with my own kind.' His words. *'Learn to farm.'*

My heart drops.

I want to throw myself from the truck and run back, but I don't. I have Spero. I need to keep myself together for him.

Just like I did with Maple a month ago, I ram the sorrow down, force through gritted teeth the perpetual imagery of him stepping from the truck, press his last words into the back of my mind, lock Lagos The Rogue into the sad chambers of my heart.

The truck slows down, rolls, and then stops. From the gullies of the tunnel, five human silhouettes cross in front of our vehicle. Even in the shadowy channel, I can make out the shape of rifles in front of them. I might have been scared once, but now I feel very little.

"Only the girl and the infant." A female calls, her voice crystal clear. A perfect drone of authority.

Tomar turns in his seat; one of his nostrils is plugged with congealed blood, and his shirt is stained around his collar and spotted across his chest.

My wide eyes meet his glowing blue ones, and I realise this is it—the last time I will see him. *What should I say?*

Nothing is enough.

"It's happening too fast," I whisper, my voice a quivering mess.

I watch his throat roll as he tries to hold himself together. "I will look for him. I will die looking for him."

I nod. "You're my friend." It's a silly thing to say, but… It's everything.

"I hope so," he says and leans back to run his knuckles down Spero's cheek, "Goodbye, special boy."

I can't do this. Fear seeps in like ice, so I have to move, act, or everything I feel, grief, sorrow, despair, will solidify and leave me paralysed.

I grab my *beibao* and bundle up my tiny burden before I slide from the truck. Clinging once again to the motions of merely moving forward, I walk toward the strange woman.

One step.

Two steps.

Goodbye, Tomar.

One little death.

Chapter Thirty-Seven

Dahlia

Five months later

My nightmare is becoming a dream. Sometimes, I change it. Sometimes, I mindlessly follow it. It is no longer a place I wish to escape, but one I plunge into, achingly familiar with every word, every action and response, eagerly awaiting the finale that never comes…

"I won't tell you."

A cruel laugh escapes him. "Yes, you will, baby."

I roll my head on the ground, disorientated. Struggle to stay conscious.

"You're a mess, baby. You should see your pretty face covered in blood." Blunt pain hits my stomach. My face.

He is beating me... But then the drifter lifts his head.

"The infant is near."

He can't be. He isn't.

I know now... It's Lagos. Even though Spero isn't nearby, I reach out a shaky hand and grip the drifter's shirt, trying to hold him to me, to keep him from standing.

"Oh, baby," he chuckles. "Do you want to play with daddy? I can give you attention after."

"You're dead," I growl...

I jerk upright, the sounds of a rooster and my sobs thrusting me to wakefulness.

Gasping the earthy air that still seems so strange and raw, I gradually level with reality. Somewhere in the distance, through the window behind my head, I hear the lowing of animals, their deep first-light calls echoing from the barns and hutches.

Outside, a door shudders on the hinge, chickens chatter, and the rooster heralds the first-light again.

This is real.

At the farming community.

That was a nightmare...

I should feel relief, but instead I burst into tears.

Every. Single. Night. I wake up at the same point, right before Lagos arrives to save me. Right before I see him. Hear him say, *"Close your eyes, little flower."* I can't hear his voice anymore...

I draw little swirls on my thighs with my finger, soothing myself, aligning myself, gaining enough composure to release the burning pain, letting go of the anticipation of his arrival and his words. I am still waiting for him.

When I am awake, quietly planting seeds and tending to my little plot, I imagine him prowling through the greenhouse with booming predatory grace...

And when I sleep, I suffer the fists of the Shadow that tried to snatch Spero and hurt me. I endure it with bated breath, waiting for the moment Lagos rescues me. Maybe tonight will be different? Maybe tonight I will sleep long enough to see him… Why that night? After that night, I barely left Lagos' side.

"Good first-light, Dahlia." Robert's soft voice comes seconds before he raps at the front door. "Are you dressed? Can I come in?"

I gaze down at my huge black tee-shirt. The hood creates a flap at my upper back, and the tear at my hip is my favourite part.

"No," I whisper and then clear my throat. "One minute." Standing on shaky legs, I stride over to Spero's cot.

A head full of dark hair peeks over the top rail, and chubby hands hold tight. Two big brown eyes watch me slowly approach. No sleep lingers in his beady gaze. He's been awake, probably watching me toss and turn, for a while.

A cozy little sanctuary surrounds him, padded and arranged with linen toys from the community. Little animal guardians to keep him safe: an eagle, a bear, a dog, and a snake.

"Hello," I say, my voice as lifeless as the void in my chest. I scoop him up, and he babbles as if he understands me and doesn't blame me. By crown-light, I will have a small smile for him.

I promise.

Planting Spero on my hip, I head to the front of my quaint two-bedroom cabin and swing the door open.

Robert's hazel eyes drop down my body, considering. "Ah… The community gave you a closet full of clothes, Dahlia. A nice nightgown, too. Why don't you throw that away?"

My heart twists—his words are unacceptable and terrifying. I can't remember Lagos' voice, but this shirt… It lingers with his scent.

"Oh." I forgot. I meant to wrap myself in the pretty, white nightgown they gave me to avoid the pity in Robert's eyes.

"How are you feeling?" He clasps his hands in front of his neat beige pants, his stethoscope hanging loosely around his neck like a trophy he refuses to take off. Shoulder-length dark hair frames his sharp jaw, and hazel eyes beam from a perfectly kind face—unassumingly Common. Approachable. Welcoming. The women in the community swoon whenever he is nearby. He is always presentable, with a shaven jawline and hands clean of farm work as he spends his days in a clinical setting.

He is the kind of man I should want… And nothing like Lagos.

I shrug. "Fine."

"Anything I should know? Any discomfort?" His brows pinch in tight over those assessing hazel eyes.

"Why would there be?"

"Dahlia…" His voice drags my name through puddles of concern. "It took us a while to get you to accept this…" He places his hand on my shoulder, and I don't flinch from his touch. For the first time, I force myself to allow his compassion. "You're pregnant."

I chew my lower lip and place my palm over my swollen stomach. "Oh, is that what this is?"

"Okay. Very funny." He drops his hand from my shoulder with a knowing chuckle. "I was worried. For a second, I thought you had relapsed. See, most women have a hard time with pregnancy. Heartburn and such. The fetus is growing fast, Dahlia."

I know. The baby inside my womb belongs to the largest man in The Cradle, the most powerful, stunning, and magnetic man in existence. I know what is inside me; I feel the weight, joy and sorrow of it each and every day. "Any news from Tomar?" I ask, my voice almost retreating.

"Nothing since you asked yesterday." His bright smile twists, becoming contrived. Hesitation and unspoken words flow to an awkward silence, so he adds, "Should I leave? Do you need more sleep?"

I close my eyes and sigh. "Yes. I'm… exhausted. Spero was fussy last night."

He nods. "Of course."

As he turns to leave, I blurt out, "If you hear from—"

"Tomar," he finishes. "You will be the first to know. I assure you."

Any day now…

He will contact them.

They have a group of Common that visit a Hub every second day where they meet with men like Tomar. Men who help Common, like me, escape. *If they want to escape.* Many citizens appreciate The Trade, their protection and the simplicity of Meaningful Purpose. Others do not.

My hand was forced.

By Maple and Spero.

Watching Robert stroll away past the other cabins, I bounce Spero on my hip.

Guilt trickles through me.

I wish I could be happy, at least enough to smile with appreciation. They accepted me into their community—a secluded village protected from the Redwind by mountainous walls—and gave me a little cabin all my own, freedom, and my own plot in the greenhouse.

It should be perfect.

I close the door, mindlessly walking to the second bedroom that I use as a playroom. Placing Spero on the mat, I crawl down beside him, lying flush on the floor.

My fingers make patterns on my swollen belly, tangling *his* shirt over the swell, achingly familiar with the moment—me lying here, making swirls and sobbing.

For months.

Jerky, shuddering breaths expel as I fight internally. Not to cry. Not today. His absence, his unborn baby, Spero, and the throbbing between my thighs that begs for him is too much, but it's the unknown that won't relent. The questions that canter through me—they destroy me.

Is he dead?

Are they hurting him?

Does he love me?

Was it real? *Us...*

Or did he just pretend?

My mind swarms with memories.

. . .

"Can we pretend that we are from the old-world?" I gaze up at Lagos the Rogue, huge and formidable, a guard dog at the door, and he stares back at me, naked and breastfeeding. "And I am yours and you are mine. Can we pretend that this is our home, and that Spero is our baby?"

"Yes, little flower. You can pretend."

We seemed to start and end at the same time, going through the motions of survival, never really allowing ourselves to grasp the concept of love… Of us.

Now it's too late.

I bunch the fabric in my small fists and lift it to my face, smothering my mouth and nose, suffocating in the black shirt that still hugs his wild, magnetic presence.

I sob and wail.

When will it stop?

Chapter Thirty-Eight

Dahlia

I leave Spero in the community play school, where we take turns working. Though, I haven't been asked to take a shift. One day, maybe, when I can smile and sing for them.

The air is warm and thick. The kind that holds and deepens odours, rich with the scent of flowers and soil.

With my tiny hacksaw in one hand—my nail file—I cross in front of the community cabins toward the greenhouses.

Today, the Redwind merely stirs my hair, the sky-high mountains screening the community from the deadly gale. Dense red fingers creep down from the clouds above, trying to reach for us, but we are too deep in the valley. I don't even wear my mask some days—most days.

At my shoulder, a sheer mountain wall looms, and a small stream seems to disappear into a gap. The mountain overlays another behind it and another, a hum sailing from that direction. The drone of technology, cars or engines—the community's defence force.

I've never seen it.

Most of us don't have clearance to see it, kept in an old-world state, simple and minimalistic.

But I know that the community has their own Community Protection operations and that in the gorge between peaks, less than a kilometre away from where I stand now, a small base hides vehicles, weapons, and trained personnel.

We are self-sustained—mostly—but since The Trade and The Crown control all factories and mines, a lot of equipment is raided and salvaged. If we're completely honest with ourselves, Common Communities are raider encampments. No different to the Endigo or raiders hoarded up in the ruins.

Slightly more sophisticated.

What other choice is there? To conform to The Trade. Live Meaningful Purpose and return to The Crust. Or raid?

I enter the greenhouse in my new ankle-length linen dress, passing two Common women around my age as they pick from the rack of shovels and rakes.

I channel the Dahlia from the Half-tower. The one desperate for friendship. I remember my first week at The Bite, how eager I was to find someone to call a friend… Anyone…

Even an old man.

Even a reluctant House Girl.

I hope Sweets is safe.

Reaching out, I trail my fingertips over the trays of seedlings that line the walls in grids. Hundreds of them. The baby shoots grow, reaching up toward the overhead artificial lights.

"Your seeds have sprouted!" A girl named Lucy stands from between two rows of small tomato bushes, a soil-stained blue apron covering her from chest to knee. Her brown hair is pulled back into a ponytail that flicks when she moves, while my red hair hangs in tendrils all around me. Wild. *Rogue.*

"I didn't touch them," she says, "but you should check them out. You *do* have a knack for plants."

I squat at the little plot that is mine to tend to and pat the ground. Healthy baby greens rising from a bed of lush dirt.

"I grew La Mu at the Half-tower," I mutter to her.

"Never heard of it." Her voice comes from directly behind me now. "Is it pretty? What does it look like?"

She has never heard of La Mu? The divide between me and the others here grows with each passing day.

I straighten. "It's not pretty." It's poisonous and potent and medicinal, but not pretty."

Distracted, I gaze across the vast green prism, willing myself to feel the awe of new life and growth all around me, but I can't catch the beauty of it, the promise and serenity, as if awe is a little wisp of air as elusive as a dream.

I didn't fit in at The Bite, and I don't fit in here. The Common Community is filled with optimism and collective grace. A concept I no longer feel a part of.

"Dahlia."

I look over at Lucy, feeling absent inside and out. "Sorry. Did you say something?"

"I want us to be friends." Her big blue eyes hold me in a gentle embrace. "I've been trying for months. Is it me? Or… Are you too hurt?"

Her words knock me backward, ringing a conversation through my mind with bitter melancholy.

"You pay attention, and you offer something." He doesn't look at me as he works. "You did fine at making friends. Some people don't want it, remember that. I don't want it. Some people just ain't made of the right stuff for friendship. I ain't."

"How do I know who is?"

"You don't, so you'll probably end up gettin' rejected, hurt, and that'll shape ya. I'd hate to see that happen."

. . .

"Did he hurt you?"

Her question snaps me to the present.

"I'm sorry, what?"

"The man who put the baby inside you?" Her voice softens, laced with uncertainty, as if the very question might shatter something delicate between us. "Did he hurt you?"

"Not on purpose," I whisper, each word fragile and raw. Just the thought of his body over mine, thrusting inside me, *taking* me, is agonising. But… things hurt the most while they heal. I'm not sure this applies to broken hearts.

Lucy looks at the hacksaw that I grip with deadly yearning. "Can I borrow that?" she asks. "To cut the tomato stems?"

I clutch it to my chest, and she studies the silly response.

Right, of course, you can.

Clearing my throat, I hand it to her. "Sure. It's more of a nail file."

Suddenly, the baby inside me rolls, warping my belly and making it difficult to hold back the tears that threaten to spill.

"Wow." Her eyes widen as they travel over my pregnant belly, which stretches the fabric of the pretty dress I received when I first arrived at the Common Community.

I curl my toes inside my boots, grounding myself in the present. Forcing my attention back to her, I weave a mask of perceived contentment over my true feelings, a veil that hides and guards my broken heart.

"Would you like to feel the baby move?" I ask, the gentle invitation spilling out.

She brightens. "Ooh, yes, please!"

I take her hand, guiding it to rest on my belly and watch as her eyes sparkle with wonder as she feels the little movements beneath the surface.

"Amazing," she breathes.

In this moment, I can't help but think, it's just a baby… *It's merely a bug, just falling water, a big fan.* Nothing remarkable…

"You have a lovely smile," Lucy says, her gaze on my lips.

I touch my mouth, fingertips tracing the curve that feels so unfamiliar.

The thought of him, my brute, who left this inside me, manages to make me smile. What does that mean? What does that mean?

Is time healing me?

Am I forgetting?

I don't want to forget.

"Dahlia," Robert's voice soars through the greenhouse, drawing my gaze to the entrance. He is walking down the narrow path, greeting everyone he passes, his hazel eyes anchored on me. "You have a visitor."

His words are a hot flame licking out, forcing a visceral response from me. "What?"

Tomar?

"An old companion of yours." He looks concerned, but I can barely see straight as my adrenaline spikes. "Are you emotionally ready to see—"

"Yes!" I wipe my hands on my dress, tiny crumbs of soil dusting my pregnant belly. "I'm fine. Lucy and I were just feeling the baby move." I don't know why I say that. It is a feeble attempt to convey my healthy mental status.

Making friends.

Everything is fine here.

Everyone is happy.

Let me see him!

We look at each other. And I wait… For five full heartbeats and one baby kick, during that moment of apprehension, the air stiffens so much that it is hard to inhale.

"Please," I gasp.

He nods stiffly. "Alright. I will get us clearance to enter the tunnel *together*."

Shock. Excitement. Fear.

My heart thunders, pulse shuddering in my neck as I sit beside Robert, with two armed women—they call themselves Community Protectors—driving us down the tunnel that feeds through the mountain to the entrance.

I vaguely recall the drive through this cement channel months ago when my stomach wasn't swollen.

Steep grey cement chases the car on all sides, the centre of the road pinned by the headlights. I draw swirls on my leg, aware now of this habit. One I've had since I was a child and used to draw swirls on everything.

I wonder how high the mountain above us goes, reaching past the Redwind into the sky. Can the peak see the stars and Missing Moon at night? How strong must the tunnel's foundations be to hold a mountain on its back? Who built this tunnel? Is it from the old-world?

I find myself on the cusp of hysteria, breathless and jigging but stifling it, instead filling my mind with mundane questions.

Robert stares ahead, stern eyes watching the light at the end of the tunnel steadily grow. "Let me go first, Dahlia."

"I'm free to go any time I like," I state, adamant, still keen for confirmation because if it's Tomar, I am going with him.

I'm going rogue.

"For your protection. Do I have to remind you that when you arrived five months ago, you had a fractured rib and contusions across your nose and eye?"

Tomar won't hurt me.

Then I see it.

Leaning to the side, I stare between the two front seats through the windscreen. A black dot appears in the glowing exit ahead, the speck growing as we approach, taking form, becoming a figure. A man.

I grab the door handle, tensing my body to prevent my eagerness from throwing me out of the vehicle too soon. It's him.

It *is* him.

With the car barely at a stop, I jump from it and run at him. My body hits his. I throw my arms around Tomar, and he envelops me, rocking me like no time has passed.

"You came! You came back!"

"Dahlia..." My name rushes out through a startled gasp. When he pushes me out in front of him, his hands slide down to my hips and his eyes follow. "You're... You're..."

"Did you find him?"

"You're pregnant?"

On my tippy-toes, I take Tomar's stunning face in my tiny hands, trying to direct his gaze to mine but it's arrowed on my swelling abdomen.

"Tomar! Did you find him? Is he alive?" My eyes burn, tears boiling behind them, quickly finding an escape as I lose control. "Please, *please*."

Something changes in Tomar's expression as he stares at my pregnant belly, blinking. Something shifts...

"No," he murmurs, his mouth fumbling, eyes deep in thought, before he adds, "I mean, yes. Yes."

"Yes, what?" I shake his head, and he grips my hands, pulling them from his cheeks. I search him, eyes darting across his frozen features to decipher his unnerving intent.

Tomar swallows over thick hesitation, and then his blue gaze lifts slowly from my belly. "I found him," he states.

My chest squeezes. "Is he alive?"

He pauses for what feels like a lifetime, an entire rotation of The Cradle...

Then says, *"Yes."*

Lagos.

My Lagos, my Shadow with no smiles, with one great experience—me—is alive.

I close my eyes, holding them like that as tears wash my face, as my mind accepts the moment, and my lips work to form words.

"Is he coming for me?"

"No."

I open my eyes.

It takes a moment for the word to sink in, blinking, and blinking, and blinking at him.

"Wha- what do you mean?"

Tomar shifts on his feet, checking over my shoulder. "He wants you to move on with your new life, forget about him, don't look for him."

A short, painful scoff scratches up my throat, seeming more like broken glass than air.

"I... I can't." I huff a mirthless laugh, my brain throbbing with anguish. "I have his child inside me. Won't he want to know?"

"I'm sorry, Dahlia. He won't."

I step backward. "Stop."

"I told you he grows bored of people, and that he would ruin you," he says, brows knotting above a stern face. "It was just... You meant nothing to him."

"Stop." Short breaths chop from me. I reach out a shaky hand, looking for something to grasp, but find only empty space. "I don't believe you."

"I'm sorry, Dahlia. You should—"

"Stop! I don't believe you. He said he wanted to provide for me. You were there. You heard him." I shake my head—stop, stop, stop, please stop—fighting anger, wrestling with anguish that digs into the chamber Lagos the Rogue resides in.

"He doesn't want you," he whispers.

"You're a liar!" I launch myself forward and lash out, punching him and wailing, beating my pain against his chest. "You're a liar! Why are you lying? He loved me!"

"Did he tell you that?"

Tomar catches my fists, and from behind, someone grabs my thrashing arms, hauling me from the man I don't know.

I don't know you, Tomar.

"He loved me!"

"He barely knew you, Dahlia!" he spits out, voice shaking because he *is* lying, the effort of his deceit weighing on his tongue. Or is it sadness… Is it goodbye?

I hate him.

"I hate you, Tomar!" I cry at him as Robert handles me, possessing my upper arms and pulling me back to the vehicle.

"Gentle with her!" Tomar barks at Robert, pretending to care, taking a single step closer, seeming distraught.

Which is another lie.

You're a liar, Tomar.

"I will be," Robert says curtly. "She's pregnant. She needs to settle down. I've got her. You should leave now."

"I can't. I have to speak with you, Robert," Tomar calls over to him. "I can't leave like this."

"No Xin De in the community!" Robert booms. "Leave."

"It's not safe."

"*I* will come back to speak with you. Just me. Wait here." Robert forces me into the back of the vehicle, belting me in while my body vibrates and my lungs heave.

I lose focus to my unrelenting anguish. In a bleak haze of misery, I feel the car moving, but I focus on my lap, trying to keep a grip on the truth. Hold it. For dear life.

"Even after this. I know how to care for you now. What a young Common girl needs. I want to provide for you. You're mine."

I mutter his words to my knees, rocking back and forth. "It's been different. Different he said. *He's* been different. You and me. The house… He liked it. He liked me."

I cover my face with my palms and sob into them, because it doesn't feel right. A deep, drowning disorientation drills into my brain, damaging it. Making me second-guess *everything…* Lagos. Me. What happened? I didn't make it up.

We connected.

It was real. Deep. Beautiful. Wild. One that affected me irrevocably. His possessive touch, his warm lips, his claiming words. The roadhouse, the farmhouse. And the gentle way he touched me when he could so easily have broken me beyond repair…

Like now.

Like right now.

Chapter Thirty-Nine

Dahlia

My brain feels like a weight inside my skull, holding my head to the pillows.

How did I get here?

Muddied consciousness.

Strange sounds.

A scream cut short in a throat.

It takes several heavy beats of my lashes that seem to thunder on my sensitive cheeks for me to remember what happened.

Robert gave me a sleeping tea to help me disappear for a while, to numb the pain, to temporarily fill the hole in my chest. To mute the cruel, haunting words. *'He doesn't want you. You meant nothing to him.'*

Fatigued, my palms slide around the swelling between my hips. A tug deep inside my heart fills me with an insatiable need to cry and wail, but the tea seems to dowse the pain.

Why is it so dark?

Rolling to my side, I feel around the sheets for the edge of the mattress, fingers seeking through dark, empty space for the switch to my lamp. Finding it, I sigh and flick it over, but nothing happens.

Sluggishly, I lift myself to a sitting position and blink against the dense dark.

"Spero?" I squint at his cot cloaked in darkness, unable to make out more than a vague shape.

Outside the cabin, something bangs, a single loud pop that echoes around the mountain, ricocheting off earthy walls, and then stopping. Seems to have disappeared into the canopy of the Redwind above.

That sounded like…

It can't be. Memories of my final few nights at the Half-tower, of war, of unrest, come tumbling back.

Was that a… a gunshot?

My heart lurches.

I jerk off the mattress, hitting the floor with a thud, forgetting about the tiny human inside me. Staying low just in case, I crawl to Spero's cot on my forearms and knees.

Squatting, I lean over the edge to scoop him up, finding his chubby body in the dark. Heavy relief washes over me once I have him cradled against me.

It wasn't a gunshot.

Couldn't have been.

It is so quiet that every slight sound seems amplified. I trail my fingers on the walls as I feel my way along them. My feet shuffle as I amble into the main room.

Focus. I take in the pitch-black space. Between the open front curtains, I can barely make out my neighbouring cabins.

There is no power.

In the distance, I hear a wooden door swing open and close, and a man ask, "What was that awful bang?"

"Everyone stay inside." I hear a woman answer him, loud enough to warn us all. "Our windmill is down. The batteries will kick in soon. Go back to sleep."

I bump Spero on my hip as he gurgles and bumbles. When I

lean against the wall, peering through the front window, I watch dark figures, outlined by the glow of their torches, spread out, searching for… something.

I shuffle backward and walk away from the door, my mind still in a fog from the tea. Feeling my way, I head back to my room and lay Spero down in his cot.

I can't quite tell, but I think his eyes are wide open. I touch his cheek reassuringly. "You're okay."

By the bedside, I kick something weightless. I pick it up and stare at it; time draws out as I notice the brown-blonde fur and the small frown, immediately wanting Spero's fluffy bear for myself tonight.

Such a grumpy bear.

There is a creak in the main room, followed by my own unbidden gasp in my ears. I follow the sound to the front door, my body tensing, going completely still as I stare into the dark void. "Who is there?"

My pulse beats in my neck.

"Lucy?" I think I see… something. A figure… And it is like I am getting drawn in, sucked into the black space while trying to find a shape. "Robert?"

A metallic taste swirls around my tongue, and as I lick my lips, the black void moves forward, becoming solid. Energy borders the form like black dye seeping into the air.

A huge male figure.

In a hood.

Towers in front of me.

But before I can scream, the male drags his hood back and the smallest of light from a torch outside slides along a shiny metal plate.

"Hello, little flower."

Chapter Forty

Dahlia

"Lagos…"

The ground beneath my bare feet seems to tilt. "Is it you?" I say, my voice a fragile whisper.

He is so still.

Too still.

His hood tilts toward the cot. "Thank you for helping me find her."

It's him!

I don't wait for him to answer me, launching myself at him, crying, "Lagos… it's you," before throwing my arms up so I can grip his thick neck muscles.

I practically climb him with his help, his big hands catching me beneath my thighs. My lips meet his, tasting the sweet and metallic essence that is him, that belongs to the man who I love.

Who does want me.

Who came for me.

Why would Tomar lie?

A growl rumbles from his chest, purring against my body as he strides to the bed. He crawls on with me, already bucking his hips and bruising my core with his erection.

I wrestle with his hooded cloak and shirt, drawing the material off his torso, immediately met with warm, hard flesh.

Tilting my chin, I can't breathe as his lips move around my face and neck, lingering on my throat, where he sucks until whimpers spill through my lips.

I close my eyes.

Just feel him.

He mouths me. His tongue laps the new welt before following the curve of my chin while one hand removes his jeans and his feet kick off his boots.

We are restless hands.

Gripping and desperate.

Removing our clothes.

Unwilling to part our bodies, or break our lips from sucking flesh, or open our eyes, or wait a moment longer to be together.

And he is *rough*, pinning me beneath him, heavier than he has ever been before. He brackets my head with his forearms, his body covering me entirely.

"Lagos..."

"Is this mine?" His tongue rims the shell of my ear, and his hand spans out over the firm mound between my hips.

"Yes," I whisper.

Unwelcome fear pours down my spine when he slides two fingers between my thighs—too fast. And he doesn't prepare me further, dragging his thick, hard dick up between my slick folds.

He thrusts into me.

He practically snarls as he drives in deep, hitting the end inside me, beating a yelp through my mouth.

"Lagos!" I gasp for air.

Then his fingers curl in my hair, tangling the red strands, and his hot breath blows down over me. "Call me Six."

I don't understand.

Tears spring to my eyes; he has suffered something... terrible.

Something that is manifesting right now. His usual pulsing energy is darker, a palpable need, greedy, and vicious.

He groans. "So tight, little Lace Girl."

Helpless yelps beat from me. I curl away from the severe fullness, the painful friction that fringes on too much.

"Fuck, *yes*," he hisses, grabbing my thigh in a bruising hold, yanking my hips up to meet his hard pounding. His balls slap the private place beneath where he enters me, sending pleasure through my core.

I moan, long and hard, trying to hold on as he *takes* me. I paw at his flanks. Unlike before, he doesn't consider my fragility, or small muscles, or tiny bones. My body absorbs his devastating pumps.

My head spins with sensation as he takes me from full to empty. Over and over again. I try to keep up with him, my hands pawing at the thick, rippling muscles at his sides, my legs pulsing behind his.

"I missed you." I sob into his chest. "It was real. *We* were real." All my emotions—loss, grief, need—burn at the front of my mind as I let him use me the way he needs, the way he demands.

I don't know what he has been through, but it's dark presence fills the room. Even though it is punishing, the motion, speed, and power, my climax rushes through me before I realise it, gasping his name. "Lagos."

His fist tightens in my hair.

"Six," he demands.

No. "I don't want to call you that." I shake my head, trying to bury the terror creeping into the room and circling me, warning me.

"Say it!" he growls, hammering his hips into me, knocking me up the mattress.

I'm in the most vulnerable position, naked, being taken, when a profound sense of dread swallows me whole.

Am I in danger?

His knuckles bite at my scalp, so I relent and sob *the* name, "Six."

That sets him off.

Every thrust takes him deeper, driving me from pleasure to pain and back again until I have whiplash from one sensation to the next, and then he rears up.

Glaring down at me, his shadowed face is in full view for the first time since I saw him standing in the cabin. His dick pulses inside me, and a big hand moves from my hair to my throat. He wraps long strong fingers around my neck.

I stare into eyes void of… anything.

He squeezes my throat. *Hard.* Pressure. So much pressure. I open my mouth in shock, heaving, but my lungs burn with each empty gasp.

My vision warps. The sight of his lost, onyx gaze narrows to a single point. I reach up and claw at his hand, tugging it from my neck, but he doesn't inch, doesn't flinch.

Still thrusting into me, his panting and growling become muffled as I choke, but my heart is loud. It pounds wildly between my ears as it strains to feed my body sweet, sweet oxygen.

"Lag—" I choke. "Lag—" As my vision blurs, his face becomes a silhouette with electric edges.

My body vibrates with sorrow, shoulders quaking beneath his heavy mass. This is worse than my nightmare, than my memory of the Shadow because Lagos isn't here to save me. He is the one hurting me.

Then— *Crack.*

What happened?

Lagos collapses on top of me. His death grip on my throat doesn't release immediately. I swear his fingers grip harder, getting it done, killing me…

I can't move.

His body crushes me.

Then his hand goes as slack as his body. The pressure

disappears from my throat, so I gasp and gasp, filling my burning lungs.

And I hear—

"Flower…" A pained gasp.

Is he okay? Lagos?

He is shifted from on top of me, rolled to the side with a careless thud.

When I have drawn in enough oxygen, my vision returns, and I blink. Fear and relief and anger mash into panic.

Tomar is standing over me with a solid lead pipe, fresh blood smeared on the cylinder, and Robert is lowering a gun to his side, expression fierce with concern.

"Breathe, Dahlia."

Just breathe…

Part Four
The Shadow

Chapter Forty-One

Lagos

Five months ago

I must have blacked out.

My fists ache. I recall beating heavily armoured Marshals to death on the roadside, the Redwind a phantom that held us in a cloak, hiding all from sight. My skin shielded me from the razor-sharp sand, my third eyelid closed, making my entire eyeball a milky colour. I've been told it's fucking terrifying to see the way my body activates against The Cradle's lashing weather. Then, I recall the pain. Each blood cell plucked from my veins by tiny hooks, the sound of my roar, and…

I've lost track of time.

Now… it's quiet, but a recognisable scent fills my nostrils… I inhale.

Beaming lights carve through the gaps in my eyelids, forcing me to open them to a familiar room.

The compound.

The air seems to lick every inch of my skin—I'm naked and strapped to a steeply inclined bed, not quite standing but definitely not lying down. My cock is erect and near flat against my stomach. Placed around the room, screens further immerse the white space with lights and the humming of internal fans.

Directly across from me is an expansive, shiny wall that partially reflects my own form. My blood roars instinctively, the sensation of eyes on the other side provoking a predatory response.

Lines stem from my veins to bags of fluid hung on either side of the elevated bed frame.

Gritting my teeth, I curl my hands into fists and test the restraints, growling and snarling when they only tighten, cutting into my wrists.

"It's been twenty-four years since we last saw you." A voice comes from behind me. "Zero Zero Six."

I tense up. "Twenty-five."

An older Xin De man is circling me, his tongue clicking as his feet rap smoothly. He is near my height, dark-haired, in a white shirt and white pleated pants.

"We barely recognised you, but your blood introduced you," he says. "And we know your fingerprints, your DNA. It's nice to have you back."

He reaches out and grips my bicep, squeezing the thick muscle. Hard. "You're a big boy now."

A snarl hits my lips. "Lower."

"Soon," he replies easily, and my mouth flattens into a tight line.

For a moment there, despite the restraints, I was still Lagos the Rogue. A construct of the past twenty-five years, not the conditioned beast they engineered before it.

The sixteen-year-old Shadow in me wouldn't have joked about such a thing. It wasn't a joking matter. Not that.

He sees the shift in my manner. "Oh, you remember, then? You remember all the ways we will help you focus on your assignment. We don't need to taunt you. You're a very impressive Xin De male."

It doesn't matter. None of it does. I remind myself as I lick my dry lips, clinging to the subtle taste of her, to the memory of her… At least she is safe.

You're safe, little flower.

They will believe the Shadow they were chasing was me, not the infant. But then the man smiles— No. *Smirks.* And I am reminded of my little flower and a ridiculous conversation we had, one that makes my chest ache with need as angry dread sinks claws into me.

Why is he smirking...

"We know," he says.

I clench my teeth.

"We know about Tomar."

My heart fucking races.

"We know he has the infant."

Blood pulses in my temples.

Then he reaches into his pocket. My iron-blood boils as he retrieves small, white knickers. "We know about the girl."

Rage eats my control. Sparks of energy detonate inside me, firing through my cells, grabbing hold of my muscles and bulking them. I thrash in the restraints growling and hissing, lunging forward toward him, needing to get my hands around his throat and bend it, collapse his trachea so he drowns on the blood pissing from his twisted arteries.

He hums, almost disappointed in what he sees. "You're very reactive. Too much Common-time in the red waste will do that to a Shadow."

I want to bark at him like a rabid dog, but the words won't form around my thickening tongue or press between my gnashing teeth.

"You're no good to us with a temper." He smiles, and I continue to jolt around, unable to stop myself. This is my humanity. Feeling… This is feeling. I have too many for her. I am drowning, drenched in Dahlia. I will inhale every sensation, hold it, and care for it. I don't want the humanity she has given me to go. I don't want to lose it. Again.

"I'm going to enjoy working with you, Zero Zero Six," he states with genuine satisfaction riding his tone and disappears behind me. "See-you soon."

Chapter Forty-Two

Dahlia

Murmured conversation moves around me, the deep voices finding me in my unconscious daze. A dull ache grips my neck when I swallow, clearing bile and fluid—waking up.

"You interrogated him?"

Robert...

"He is here for Spero."

Tomar...

"He told you that?"

"He didn't tell me anything," Tomar says. "He's a damn Shadow. They don't break. I just know."

"Did you know, Tomar?" Robert asks, his voice dripping with accusation. "All this time? That he was one of them."

"He is not one of them."

"Why did he do that to Dahlia?" Robert's voice is odd, deep and angry. This is his community, and I've been nothing but trouble. Two Xin De finding their way into the community, searching for me, here *because* of me. "Why not just take the child? Why touch her? Why did he do... *that*?"

Why did he do... that?

That. That.

Take me and choke me.

I roll to my side and smother my face with a pillow. Finding false privacy, I curl my knees up and gasp through my sobs.

"Is he awake?"

Robert.

"It's unclear."

"And Dahlia?" Before Robert can finish his question, I am bolting upright.

He is awake.

Alive.

My Lagos.

Disorientated by the unfamiliar room, I take a moment, scanning the area, my gaze moving from a monitor to the door.

I rush to it. The thin gown I'm wearing sways open at the back, but I don't care. In the hallway, I dart to the only other Patient Room, away from the small lobby and the men conversing too loudly.

The community only has one Common Medical Cabin, and it is unassuming, just like the Community. It's no bigger than the two-bedroom wooden cabin I live in, but the Trade technology they have managed to raid and salvage is beyond anything I ever saw at the Half-tower.

Flinging open the door, I freeze in the gasping gap when I see Lagos strapped to the bed, thick leather cuffs wrapped from wrist to bicep.

A painful smile slides across my lips as I wonder how many times he snapped the restraints around his wrists before they realised he needed more. A lot more. All the way up his arms. He is just so... remarkably strong.

His blank stare breaks my heart.

Slowly, I walk over to his bedside. He doesn't turn his head, eyes fixed on the ceiling—open, white, and void. The nictitating membrane over his eyeball looks thin and glossy, with a translucent sheen that is as beautiful as it is frightening.

I look him over. White material bands his head, covering a wound that I can't see, leaving his blonde-brown knot of hair in a gap at the back. His neck and shoulders are perfectly aligned and stiff. The sight of his bare chest absolutely destroys me— it breaks a dam inside my gaze, blurring the vision of all those new scars and slices. They are already healing, but in parts, the tendons and muscles are only covered by thin, clear tissue—*scar tissue.* They skinned it, skinned him, or...

I cover my mouth but fight to stay strong. Wiping my face, I glance down at tubes snaking beneath the restraints, passing fluids. One of the tubes pulses with blood, and one drips with something clear. That's good.

They are caring for him.

He will get better.

Instinctively, I reach for his hand, and my heart drops when my skin meets his. Sensation buzzes through me. His flesh is so warm and hard and still as if he is a mere heated stone.

"Lagos..." My voice wobbles. "Brute?"

What did he call himself?

Six?

I ignore the way my chest aches at the fact he won't look at me, won't acknowledge me. *After that.* After what happened.

He must be asleep, but it is hard to tell with his third eyelid closed. Another predatory trait to filter the sand and debris and to stalk. I understand why they aren't allowed in the community. They have unfair engineered and evolutionary advantages.

"Oh, *Dahlia.*" Tomar's voice soars around me, and I stiffen with rage, glaring at him over my shoulder, at the man who lied to me. "What are you doing here?"

"You knew," I hiss.

He shakes his head. "I had—"

"You knew, and you lied!"

"Dahlia," —he thrusts his hands toward the bed—"I needed you to run from him. Not look for him. Not go to him. I saw that you're pregnant, and I just… I had to think quickly. It wasn't like I planned this on the way up here, but… I needed to keep you safe. As I was holding you…" He looks at his hands. "Holding your unborn child. At that moment, I thought only your hatred was powerful enough to shatter your love."

"It wasn't…"

I get a flash of a white coat as Robert enters from behind me, and I turn my cheek to look at my catatonic brute.

"Tomar was trying to protect you," Robert says. "Don't be too hard on him."

"I've been following him since he left the compound two weeks ago," Tomar admits.

The truth slices in deep. "You were never going to tell me, were you?" I scoff with anger. "If he didn't come to me."

"I was trying to protect you from this." Tomar is still gesturing to Lagos, maybe assuming the sight of him will have me cowering. He has no idea how much I love that man. "From all of this."

"I don't give up on the people I love. There are so few of them!" I admit, squeezing a stone-like hand. *I love him.* I swallow hard, emotions lumping in my neck, the swollen column struggling. "What is wrong with him?"

"He's…" Robert sighs as if stifling hollow words. "I want to be honest with you. It's called Brain Interruption or Mind Washing. Basically, torture and conditioning."

"Why won't he look at me?"

"At the moment, he is sedated," Robert answers. "I'm using a lot of Community resources for this. We've just removed his coil, but his brain has been through a shredder, and I am not that kind of doctor. I have never removed a coil before. It's an entirely different kind of surgery, and I wasn't trained for it."

"They let him leave," Tomar states, "And I just knew… I knew he was sent to finish this. I know a man who knows a man who is a Trade Tech. He told me that they sent a spy to get a stolen Trade baby. I lied and said I heard a man lost control and killed a runaway Lace Girl and a baby in the Common Community. He seemed too interested in that story. Hopefully, that gets back to The Trade Master."

"And you think they'll just forget about us?" I shrug. "Isn't Spero a weapon? Isn't Lagos worth something to them?"

Robert places his hand on my shoulder. "Better a broken weapon than one in the hands of a Common Community."

With a sneer of derision, I turn my chin, glaring at Tomar. "What now for you? You fix him up and take him away with you? Your own mindless bodyguard and soldier?"

I know I'm not being fair, but I can't help it. He lied to me. Made me second-guess everything between Lagos and me.

Tomar's usual face of kind superiority crumbles. "I thought I was your friend, Dahlia. Isn't that what you said? Can't you understand why I did this?"

"I understand why you did it." I look back at my brute. Last time, I accepted that Lagos was destined to save people. I was willing to let him go. This time, I can't do that. This time, I want him to choose me. "I understood then, too. I don't want to anymore. I want him to pick me."

"There might not be anything left of him now." Robert looks at my swollen belly. "At least not in the way you want or need. Wait until the sedation wears off."

At the sound of his words, something deep inside me wilts to dirt and soil. So close to getting him back, so close to the farmhouse, and the pretty picture we played in where we are happy and raising our child. So close...

"Where is Spero?" I ask, my voice absent and flat, barely a whisper. "I want to stay here, so he needs—"

"He might not—"

"Don't." I lift my hand, cutting the lies and excuses in the air, finding my spine and it is as strong as the man lying beside me. "I want. To stay. *Here.* Where is Spero?"

A long pause simmers between us, testing my resolve and his steadfast authority.

"Safe," Robert finally answers. "He is with Lucy. In her cabin."

Hm. "Why Lucy?"

I hear the suspicion in his tone as he says, "I thought you were friends?"

"Sure." I feel his eyes on me. "We are."

"Give her some time," Robert says to Tomar and leaves the Patient Room.

With a sigh, Tomar turns to leave. "I won't be far away. I'll check in on you."

"He keeps fighting them," I rush out. "You did that. You gave him hope all those years ago when others in his place jumped off cliffs and hung themselves. You gave him companionship and purpose. For that, I will always be grateful to you. I could feel him fighting them last night in his mind. You know what you said about the brain, how it is just too powerful to fully control?"

"Yeah. At the end of the day, a man has to submit to Meaningful Purpose. It needs to be the heart and soul of him. Lagos… What did you call him?" He laughs sadly, walking away. "He has always been a *rogue brute*."

I don't know how long I stand by Lagos' bedside, watching his third eyelid swipe from one side to the other, a small sign of brain activity and awareness.

But after the time-lamp turns red, I'm too tired and crawl onto the bed, tucking myself into a small gap between him and the rail.

That is when his heart thuds harder, and that suffocating presence that used to scare me, rolls over me, soothing me, sending me a message. He is inside.

A hot tear rolls down my cheek, and I close my eyes to catch more. Inhaling his sweet, metallic scent and listening to the deepest, strongest pulse in The Cradle, I try to sleep.

Chapter Forty-Three

Six

Three weeks ago

Pain.
There is a man named Tomar.
He is an enemy of The Trade.
A killer.
Dangerous.
He is to be dissolved on sight.

Pain.
There is a girl.
Her name is Dahlia.
She is an enemy of The Trade.
A thief.

She has a Shadow infant.
You need to take the infant.
Dissolve the girl.

Chapter Forty-Four

Dahlia

For the past two days, I haven't been home, and despite talking to him, Lagos hasn't moved an inch. Not when I kiss his cheek or when I hold his hand.

I don't want to leave him, but my heart yearns to hold my tiny assassin. We haven't been away from each other this long, and due to the nature of the Shadow connection, Spero can't be anywhere near Lagos.

Exhausted and aching with grief, I wander back to my little cabin on the other side of the community to bathe before I go to Lucy's.

I am walking through the front door, focused on getting in and out quickly, when I hear the babbling of a baby coming from my room. He shouldn't be here…

"Hello? Lucy?" I call out just as I enter, finding Tomar leaning over the cot, waving a stuffed animal in front of Spero.

"Hey," he greets.

"Oh." I stop, blinking at them. "I didn't expect to see you here."

My eyes dart around, taking in the messy sheets and an unfamiliar bag on the floor.

Unease sweeps through me.

Tomar straightens, appearing confident in my personal space. "Robert told me to stay here until we have more answers about Lagos."

I lift a brow. "No Xin De in the community, remember?"

"I think I'm the Xin De they want here just in case the other one wakes up and ruins things." His choice of words find a mark in my stomach, further stirring my restless insides.

He waves at the bed. "I didn't sleep in your bed if that's what you thought. I slept on the foam mat. I presume it's Spero's playmat."

Suspicious, I move over to scoop Spero up and cuddle him to my chest, inhaling his sweet, weird baby scent. "Hello, baby boy." I jig him and twirl around, smiling for him. "I missed you. Did you miss, Mummy?" I lean in and rub my nose against his.

"You're so beautiful."

I lift my head to look at Tomar, startled by the conflict in his eyes and the way they pierce right through me. And I know what it means now. I've seen it in him before. The last time we were alone… He makes me wish I was still pretty-but-plain-easily-forgotten Dahlia.

"Don't look at me like that."

His fingers twitch at his sides, seeming to be uncomfortable. Stiff. Waiting. "You're such a special girl. I watched you become a mother and now look at you… Even after it all, you're so sweet, pure, loyal—"

"Stop." I turn to leave. I can't do this. Every slither of emotional strength I have is quickly draining from me.

He rounds on me and Spero, blocking the bedroom door. "I can take care of you," he presses, taking a single step toward me, forcing me backward.

I gape at him.

"All three of you." His eyes narrow as if trying to puncture the layers of denial that surround me. "He'll never be what you need. Even if he gets better."

"Do you want him to?"

"Yes, of course!" he bites out. Then pauses, too quick to answer. Too quick for his heart it seems…

He exhales hard, a painful truth riding his breath. "And *no,* because no matter what he does, you're basically blind to it."

"I am not blind to it."

"I can't stand this." His voice swims with admiration as he says, "And now that you're so pregnant, so damn beautiful…" He falters, resentment taking hold. "I *hate* that you're with him. I can't stand it. Three nights at the farmhouse. Three nights I had to listen to him fu—" Inhaling steadily, he seems to bridle his emotions. "I hated it. I sat in the kitchen and listened, tortured myself over you. And then, that last night, I let myself sin. I pretended it was me. I closed my eyes and pretended I was the one inside you. I don't want to share you. I hated when Robert grabbed you from me, and I despise Lagos for coming for you."

I swallow. "You're my friend."

"Am I?" He crosses his arms, puffing out his chest as he stares down at me. "You don't treat me like a friend. The way you threw your arms around me in the tunnel didn't feel like we were *just* friends."

That hurts. I was desperately happy to see him. So utterly overwhelmed to see the man who was safe and kind to me. "I care about you. That is why."

"See"—he shakes his head, not accepting the truth— "I think you do love me. I think you just can't see it. I would be so good to you and Spero, and the baby. I have already worked it all out with Robert."

Worked what out?

"Well, it is not up to Robert. This is… This is that thing you spoke of." I walk to the cot and try to hide the way my hands tremble as I lay Spero inside. "How men become obsessed when they are denied." I straighten. "Just stop, Tomar. I don't feel that way about you."

"Do you remember when you asked about sex?" His breathing becomes strange, fast and unsteady. "About finding a boyfriend and experiencing *it*. See, I think he just got to you first. You were so easily manipulated by him. Girls fall in love with the first man who they let touch them because they have been vulnerable. I saw him hurting you, Dahlia. I wouldn't do it like that. I would be gentle with you—"

"Stop!" I punch the word at him. "He isn't usually like that. That wasn't him. That was the coil. You know that."

Too many feelings muddle my head, and I decide to push straight past him before we both say something we'll regret, but he grabs me around the upper arms and shoves me to my backside on the bed.

I stare up at him in horror.

He looks down at his hands, shocked. "I'm sorry. I'm so sorry." He lifts his gaze to where I am on the mattress, bracing myself on my hands, and a darkness coasts through his glowing blue eyes. "*God*, you're beautiful. If you were with me, *vulnerable* with me, just once, I could show you. I am a good man."

"You're scaring me," I admit, feeling exposed and defenceless on the mattress, but unable to move. My muscles fill with heavy fear that locks me in place.

"I'm scaring you?" He spits out, still standing over me at the end of the bed. "*I'm* scaring *you*. Me? When you have let him inside you, and I am the one who scares you?"

I don't know what to say.

"Just tell me this,"—he clasps his hands together in front of him — "If he's brain dead, if he's broken or volatile and has to be destroyed, could you learn to love me?"

Destroyed?

He isn't a machine!

Even crawling with unease, I answer him honestly because he is my friend. A little *bit* of me. "You remember when you said that you can't control grief?" I recall a time when his presence was comforting and safe. "Remember, you said you feel it everywhere, in your stomach and chest. This is like that. I won't ever love anyone else like this."

He chuckles, but it's unfeeling. "You will. You could. I could show you. If you let me touch you, you'll see what it's like to have gentle, loving hands on you. That's all I want."

The taste of metal slides along my tongue moments before, "Time to visit your God."

Lagos' inhuman voice booms from behind Tomar, the depth capable of shaking the small cabin to pieces, splinter by splinter.

"Lagos."

Tomar's eyes widen.

My heart leaps—I have seen how quickly Lagos can kill a man, seconds, within the blink of an eye, the beat of a heart, he can have a man bleeding on the ground.

So when he grabs the back of Tomar's neck, lifting him beyond the safety of his feet, I know he is fighting his own internal battle to not kill his brother, his friend, his companion.

"Brother," Tomar gasps.

"I warned you," Lagos seethes.

I blink up at my brute, dressed in grey pants but naked from the waist up, fierce, possessive rage thundering through every inch of him.

"Lagos, please. Put him down."

Lagos growls. "Why are you in her room?" His black gaze cuts to me, blazing. "Why are you on the fucking bed with your legs like that?"

"Don't hurt her," Tomar begs, taking me by surprise. He's still protecting me, so misguided and confused, and protecting *me.*

I hear a crack.

I think it's from Tomar's back as he hangs from his neck, his heavy body like a weight on the narrow channel of bones.

"Lagos, *please,*" I beg again. Sliding from the bed, I take hesitant steps toward the seven-foot-tall Xin De assassin, reassuring him. "Nothing happened between us."

"Bring those sheets. Let me smell your lies, little flower."

I sob. "I swear it."

"I can't trust you," Lagos snarls at Tomar, the statement final, a bullet to the heart. "I was locked-up, inhaling the knickers you stole, beaten, abused, altered. I've been through hell, *brother*. Would you like me to send you there?"

"*Lagos*." Beside him now, I touch his shoulder, and he freezes. His eyes slide to my hand, brows furrowing. "I love *you*." I blink tears, wishing for everyone to disappear, fade away, and leave me alone with him.

Him.

Lagos.

My brute.

With darkness and cruelty and trauma. A vicious killer. More monster than man.

And mine.

As I am his.

"Do you trust *me*?" I whisper beside him, my voice trembling with emotion. I reach for his other hand and place it on my swollen stomach. "Trust me. There is only you. There will only ever be you."

Growling, he drops Tomar.

"You're on your own," he states, voice deep and flat, cold. "I paid my debt to you." Lagos stares at his hand, cradling his unborn child, hypnotised—subdued. "Stay away from me, brother. I want you to live, so stay the fuck away."

Tomar scrambles to his feet but stills at the door, risking a moment so he can memorise the sweet boy in the cot—Spero. The boy he showed the glowworms to, who he cuddled and sang to. Tomar's blue gaze glosses over, and pain spears me right through the chest.

Then he leaves.

And I feel like...

It is for forever.

Goodbye, Tomar.

One little death.

Maple. Tide. Now Tomar. I am losing friends faster than I am making them, but I will not lose Lagos.

Peering up, I find his gaze locked on my pregnant belly. Steel-coloured eyes, open and soft, focused.

My Lagos.

"Is it you?" he asks, voice a deep whisper. "I felt you beside me just now, and then you were gone. I thought I was back there."

"You felt me?"

He kneels in front of me to get closer to the second heartbeat beneath my skin, his head level with mine but tilted to track the movement of his huge hands on his unborn baby. "You made this for me? That's why."

"Why what?"

"Why it didn't work."

What didn't work?

"The conditioning," he adds more to himself than me. I don't understand what he is saying, but his eyes lift to me, painful memories stirring within them. "My little flower."

Emotions—too many at once—wash over me. Love. Sorrow. Anguish. And then fear, reminding me we do not have much time. Any minute now, Community Protection will come for him and force him to leave or... Worse.

Shoot him on sight.

"We have to go." I cup his cheeks, fingertips nestled in his neat blonde beard. "I don't know what Robert will—"

"You said his name." Lagos frowns. "I was here in this room, and you said his name. I remember. Who the fuck is Robert?"

A sad smile forms on my lips at his protective leer, and I stroke my hands up through his hair. "The doctor."

Dark energy pulses from him. "Did he taste you?"

"No," I cough out.

A pause separates time. While inside his eyes, I almost see

memories clawing back. "What happened in this room, little flower? I've been here before."

"We can talk about it later. We have to leave." I try to hold his lost gaze. "They will never let you stay."

His expression changes as he studies my face, brows drawn in tighter and eyes sliding from my teary gaze to my wobbling lower lip. "Why… Where is your awe, little flower?"

A sob bursts from me, my nose and throat burning as I try to stifle more emotions. "My awe, brute?"

"I can't…" He exhales roughly.

"We don't have time for this." My hands drop from his face, my mind made up that I need to get Spero, and we need to leave. I can feel the darkness all around Lagos, my skin prickling with his volatility, and I am terrified that at any moment, he is going to explode.

And they will fight back.

I have to get him out of here.

Lagos catches my elbow. "No. You should stay—"

"We don't have time!"

"I did that," he states, staring at my face, his gaze lost and out of focus. This huge man, inhumanly powerful, so crippled with torment.

I force a smile, trying to push it the length of my lips, but they only tremble against the effort. "We don't have time for this, Lagos. Everything will be alright now we are together."

He shakes his head slowly. "I can't dull your awe. It's too… Too remarkable, powerful, big."

He uses the words I did when gazing dreamily at all The Cradle has to offer, the glowworms, the windmills…

I won't let him do this. My swollen throat thickens, and my vision blurs behind tears. "Don't you want to provide for me, Lagos?"

My words make him nod. "*Yes.* But I would rather be dead than the monster who tarnished the way you see this shiny world."

"It won't be shiny without you." He stops and studies me again. Studies the desperation in my eyes. The tear that escapes. Studies my neck— I cover the swollen column, hiding the red finger marks and tender flesh I feel so acutely. His pupils dilate, swallowing pretty steel-coloured rings, leaving only darkness as he forces my hand away to expose the bruising.

"Death," he says, "has always been the best place for a Shadow. It is what we are made of. I have to die. I can't be alive and not be with you, little flower. And I can't be with you."

I panic. "There is no awe without you!" When I cup his cheeks, he closes his eyes, blocking me out. "You remember the farmhouse, right?"

He smiles. He actually smiles with his eyes closed, and the curve of his lips is so perfectly rested and raw. "You loved that house, didn't you, little flower?"

"Yes." I sob, smiling, too. "And remember the shelter underneath? Let's go there. Let's live there. Like we pretended that night."

His eyes open. "Not safe."

"They think we are dead."

"Who?"

"The Trade."

"It's too risky."

"It's been *decades*, brute, and that farm is still untouched. It's ours! Don't you see? We went a different way. We went west. They don't go west. Spero and you and me, and our baby. The farmhouse is ours. I can feel it."

"Our baby…"

I nod, tears rushing down my pink cheeks, leaving a pinching trail. "Yes. They took the coil out, Lagos." My voice trembles with vulnerability. "And Tomar has sent a message to The Trade that we are dead. So, if we leave the last place they saw us, we can just disappear again."

He rises to his full height, a towering seven-foot figure whose mere presence should instil terror in me and yet only draws me closer.

"It's decided then?" A voice states from behind Lagos, slicing through the moment. In an instant, Lagos turns, tucking me behind him with a long, thick arm rippling with muscles designed for destruction.

"It's okay," I say, peering past him to see Robert in the doorway, holding a gun at eye level. "It's Robert."

Lagos is unnervingly rigid, the tendons and veins in his arms taut like steel cables. "This is my little flower! You understand, Common man? *Mine.*"

Robert lowers the pistol to his side and stares blankly at me.

"We are leaving," I say to him, my voice shuddering at the sight of the gun.

Robert nods slowly. "I heard. I have always said you were free to leave. This isn't a prison. It's a sanctuary."

"I know," I breathe. "And it's beautiful, but it's not right for me. I don't fit."

"I cut part of your brain," Robert mutters to Lagos, utter shock and wonder playing across his face. "But here you are, standing and impenetrable. We really don't stand a chance against your kind, do we?"

"Are you waging a war, Common man?" Lagos' voice seems even deeper in contrast to our company.

"No." Robert shakes his head, dwarfed by the massive Xin De Shadow. "Least not yet." They glare at each other. When Robert takes a step forward, Lagos growls and does the same.

"*Easy.*" Robert holds his hands up, one of them clutching the gun. "I just want to give this to her," he says, offering the handle of the gun to me. "It's a taser. Which sends an electrical pulse through the body. For him, Dahlia. Use it on him."

I go to protest. "I don—"

"Good." Lagos snatches the gun and forces it into my hands. "Use it, little flower. This will work better than that little nail file. If I frighten you, use it."

I hold it loosely, my eyes glued to the strange device I've only seen but have never touched. "I don't want it."

"Flower." Lagos' tone drops, deepening with intimacy and throbbing with emotion. I peer up at the formidable man lording over me. "If you take the taser," he says, "I will drive us to the farmhouse."

I don't want the taser, but his dark gaze pools with warm intensity, so powerful and confident that it calms the uncertainty in my heart.

"Okay," I whisper, closing my fingers over the weapon and accepting it. He is a forty-something-year old Xin De Shadow, a trained killer, and I am a pregnant Common girl born for lace. I have to accept that he's dangerous.

I have to keep focus. "Do you have a vehicle? You didn't… walk here. Did you?"

"You can take Tomar's truck." Robert's words throw me, and I blink at him.

"What? What will he take?"

"He's staying here."

My mouth drops open. "What happened to no Xin De in the community?"

He lifts his chin, his expression steadfast. "I stand by that. That rule has kept us safe for decades. So… he is staying in the gorge at our Community Protection base. He has skills and connections we could use. We spoke about it when— When he thought he was going to settle down with… Well, with you and the babies."

I gasp. "He had it all planned."

Lagos' black gaze somehow burns. He strides to Spero's cot and, with one hand, scoops the infant to rest along his forearm, his muscular torso rippling with a loud claim—mine.

This is mine.

He stares down at Spero, the moment binding, the assertion and connection pulsing through the air like tangible matter.

"Get your property, little flower," Lagos warns without looking up from our tiny assassin, "before I decide to hunt Tomar down."

I want to move, but my feet are stuck to the floor, my utter shock is like solid lead in my soles.

He is holding Spero.

He is cradling Spero in one arm, making the six-month-old look tinier than usual.

"Now." Lagos growls. "Now, little flower."

Right. I rush around the house and collect my possessions; my *beibao* with the stockings from Sweets and the silly trinkets from Tide, clattering around inside; a large duffle bag with all my new clothes and Spero's fluffy toys.

As we fill the truck, tucking Spero into a blanket nest on the back seat, the Community Protection officers stand with rifles at the ready. It's a formidable situation, the air stirring with wariness and concern.

I was welcome.

We are not.

Robert waits patiently by the vehicle, overseeing. "Lagos." He calls over as my brute opens my car door for me. "She will need a doctor to deliver that baby."

Lagos frowns at him, mistrust pulsing between them as I climb into the seat.

"You should consider bringing her back here in three months," he states, dangling the offer, letting the dominant Xin De decide for himself. "We may not welcome your kind, but she is Common. I will induce her early and safely deliver the infant. I don't want her to become a statistic of Xin De Maternal Death. Your kind is to blame for this... She deserves better."

To my surprise, Lagos bares his teeth, agitation tight in his jaw, but nods.

And I know we will never really fit in anywhere. He is a rogue, and I am his. He is a loner who doesn't want to live without me.

Even if he wanted to stay and do the same as Tomar, they would never allow him. Tomar, with his gentle, sophisticated words and cooperative nature, yes, but not Lagos. He is everything they want to keep out. The very essence of a dangerous Xin De.

As we drive off, I look out at the greenhouse, happy to know my nail file found a home and sad that I didn't give Lucy a real chance at friendship.

Goodbye, Common Community.

One little death.

Goodbye, Lucy.

One little death.

Then, Lagos feeds his fingers through mine, resting them on his lap as he drives, and I look down at the way his hand encompasses mine. How we fit.

How mine fits.

His consumes.

Chapter Forty-Five

Lagos

I fist the steering wheel with one hand and grip hers with the other.

She inhales deeply, her chest rising, holding, before falling with a heavy exhale. Dahlia sleeps against my naked side, her body swaying with the movement of the truck, her lashes fan over freckle-laced cheeks.

Focus on the road.

My mind prowls restlessly inside my skull. I am at war. Lost. Confused. My possessive and protective core has morphed into something darker.

Unforgiving.

And savage.

At first, the orders were simple. Obedience and submission were carved into my flesh over the past five months.

Kill her, kill Tomar, and retrieve the stolen Shadow baby for The Trade.

But in the compound—

I was too reactive.

When they held her knickers in front of my face and sliced fillets from me, I only inhaled harder.

Too in love.

Too human.

For her...

Too hard to control even with the coil, so at three months, they changed their methods. Made me crazed. Used my humanity. Stroked my cock when I killed for them. Allowed me her scent when I obeyed.

A beast with a bone.

They distorted my memories, infiltrating my recall, planting doubt about Tomar and her, Robert and her. Men she is with, fucking, loving.

Too possessive.

I know now... They didn't edge me to kill her—they edged me to obsess further. Obsess to the point of destruction.

Too volatile.

They made me a bomb. Used my possessiveness. Jealousy. Obsession. Sent me out to find the baby, knowing I would implode emotionally when I saw her.

And I did.

When my cock thrust into her wet, warm pussy, and a voice in my head hissed she likes it rough, *Six...*

She wants to fuck Six.

Not Lagos. Six.

She is not yours anymore.

She has fucked Tomar.

She has fucked the doctor.

She. Is. Not. Yours.

I snarl at the road ahead, the Redwind flogging the metal sides of the vehicle, lashing sounds that remind me of the pits of hell and the past five months.

Releasing her hand, I wrap my arm around her shoulder, pulling her exhausted little body closer.

Her scent thickens my cock.

Blood. Kill. Is she still mine?

The coil may have been removed, but a dark void remains, and inside that bloodied grey matter, paranoia festers.

I cannot trust my muscles, mind, or memories. Betrayed by my body when it obeys The Trade's conditioned response to her, my cock leaks, throbbing with the need to be milked, just from the subtle notes of her hair.

Kill.

Fuck.

She needs to keep that taser.

Last time I came out of this haze, I only had myself to consider. That first year, I only cared to sleep, fuck, and try not to kill too many people in the process.

This time, I have her.

And the babies.

I am physically surged with the need to protect her from the darkness I know is out here, from the depravities and evil I know is inside me.

You're mine until you're safe.

Words I swore to her, words I meant. Little did I know that there is no such place, that no part of The Cradle is completely safe.

So, she is mine.

We drive all day, and by the time we get to the farmhouse, last-light bleeds into The Crust, succumbing to the dense darkness.

I survey the property, the old brick and wooden structure standing defiantly against the weather and somehow… hidden and untouched. Invisible.

But we saw it.

Found it.

'It's ours, Lagos.'

Then, using my body to shield the Redwind, I carry her sleeping form into the house. She trusts me completely, even after… The marks on her neck growl the truth from a missing memory—

I navigate through the dark interior, details and vision snatched by the hour. The air is thick with dust and promises.

Down in the bunker, a hidden cavity beneath the farmhouse, where the walls are cool, and the latch locks from the inside, I feel a sense of calm… This is right. She can be safe here with the babies, and she can lock me out.

Her guard monster.

At the doorstep.

This is right.

This is good.

I lay her gently on one of the beds, the fabric unused but dusty. Leaving her there, I head back up.

Now for the Shadow baby.

I stand in the open door of the car, muscles tense, staring at *him.* His wide eyes, ancient and knowing, gaze back at me, filled with as much suspicion as invitation. It's an electric sense—repulsion and attraction—a silent communication that bubbles in my iron-blood.

When I held him at the Common Community, a primal instinct churned, like hairs on skin rising to duty, an army of impulses at the ready.

"I know you feel it," I say to the infant, my voice a rough whisper, as I scoop him up. "You helped me find her, not once but three times. I hope you don't regret that one day. You might want to kill me when you become a man. If you're smart, you will. Protect your mother against all. Even me. You hear me?"

He babbles.

My chest aches—so vulnerable and simple. *Was I like this once? Who held me?*

I know the answers.

I feel the chains that once tied me to a bed in the compound tighten around my lungs, suffocating all reason.

He is mine.

She is mine.

The unborn child is mine.

I take him into the farmhouse under a cloak of near darkness and carry him down into the bunker. I set him on the bed beside her, prop a pillow to wedge him safely against her, and I leave.

I fucking leave them there.

I will not allow myself to go in. We can share the farmhouse, but that is hers and theirs.

My cock pulses like a heartbeat when I slide down to the floor on the inside of the front door. I will not sleep.

I will not move.

Tomorrow, I need to secure the property, fix the wiring, and add latches, chains—measures to keep them all safe.

I stare into the house. Dark void. Shadows that stretch, though nothing moves, and there is no light. My mind tricks me, trips me, fucks with me.

Time rolls by…

Green eyes.

Pain.

Tight pussy.

Pain.

Freckles.

Pain.

A second heartbeat.

I should have left her at the farming community to be with her kind, free and easy. There, where she is safe, but is she? If they are ever attacked, if a man ever wants her, who will risk it all, who will bring entire towns to the ground, step over children, to get to her. Only her… Only me.

That is my darkness.

Her words stir through the steady resonance of wind. *"Then why can't we do that now! Find a place. Stay together, and we can have new, great experiences. We can kiss, and I will protect you, and you can protect me, and we will be together."*

I will protect her.

Every small noise is like an itch inside my ears, too deep to scratch. I remember coming out of the torture of Noise Conditioning when I was sixteen.

Every time I hear the faintest of sounds, my muscles awaken with the need to protect. To protect my flower and my children.

Even as a rational part of me hears the wind whistling through the windows, rocking them against the frames.

Knock. Knock.

I know it's the wind.

A visceral and primal need wins. I climb to my feet, head outside to challenge the Redwind and stalk the perimeter of the farmhouse. I will protect her—them—from the world, from the depravities and evil that I know lurks within my own flesh.

And blood.

Chapter Forty-Six

Dahlia

I don't remember the final half of the journey, or bringing my bags inside, or hanging my clothes, or going to sleep, but I wake up lighter than I've been in months in the quiet isolation of the shelter beneath the farmhouse.

The weight of our unspoken words and fractured closure is no longer heavy in my lower belly.

I inhale deeply. My chest fills with optimism, awe, and the steady beat from a well-rested heart.

I leave Spero sleeping on the mattress and go to the solid metal doors.

The bunker seems to breathe as I open it. I step up to the ground floor. The first-light haze filters through the farmhouse, highlighting dust and fragments in the air.

This is my new home.

My forever home…

Our forever home.

I pass down the corridor—admiring the floorboards and

trimmings on the walls for the first time—then navigate my way toward the front door that Lagos carried me through months ago.

He *carried* me over the threshold, which is such a lovely story to tell our children one day.

The house is still but for the wind outside. I don't know what the walls are made of, some kind of brick, but it does mute the weather, the only echoes of the Redwind coming from the windows.

I am approaching the front of the house when I see something on the ground. I freeze. Lagos is slumped on the floor, long legs stretched out in front of him, a barricade in front of the door.

No one in.

No one out.

Thick arms rest over his chest, and his third eyelid is closed, the first-light haze shimmering along the pearl-like surface. Not awake, but not asleep either—in a predatory state that is both stunning and terrifying.

I study him, my gaze following a path down his torso and catching on the new scar tissue. My heart twists.

I kneel beside him.

Hesitantly, I reach out my hand and touch the smooth surface, inhaling when I feel the heat from his body. What did they do to you? Were you there the entire time? All five months?

Did they break you, Lagos?

That last thought comes unbidden, and I wish it away because somewhere deep inside me, I know he is… He *is* damaged, but I still want him.

A large, warm hand clamps around my wrist, holding it hostage. "Are you real?"

I gasp, gazing up from his mutilated torso to his blazing black eyes.

"*Yes*," I whisper.

His free hand touches my face, ardently tracing the curves. "This face…"

I cover his hand with mine, being this close to him, being caught in his gaze, possessed by his hands. In love.

"Things I like," he murmurs, soft but deep, "this face."

"You think I'm pretty?" I ask.

His eyes narrow. "Yes." That one-word grunt brings the brightest smile to my face, one I feel everywhere.

"Pretty but plain," I agree.

"Plain?" He stares, his eyes lost for a moment, peaceful, the steel-grey rings returning as his pupils shrink. "Plain doesn't consume. I would happily murder men and women for each one of your freckles, little flower."

I suck a sharp breath in and feel the jagged edges of his gruesome words. "I don't want you to murder anyone for me."

The pause that follows burns like a flame consuming all the air between us.

His expression hardens again. "Do you have your taser?"

I look at my wrist, still banded by his fist. "I'm not carrying that around."

"You will." He unwraps his fingers, freeing me. "Go get it now."

"What happened?" I touch a large wound, the smooth membrane rolling over his strong muscles. "They skinned you. They hurt you. Let me kiss you."

He snarls, and before I can respond, he rises to his feet, dragging me up with him.

"Lagos!"

Please don't be like this.

Manhandling me into the bathroom, he positions me in front of the dusty mirror. His chest meets the back of my head, his body lording behind me.

"Look," he orders.

"I can see," I say, but lift my chin, wanting to gaze up at him.

"Look!" he demands again, grabbing the back of my head and forcing my face straight ahead. "Look at your throat, little flower. Look what I did."

Tears build behind my eyes, but I refuse to blink in case

they cascade down my cheeks and reveal my sorrow. I know what it looks like. I can feel it. The skin on my neck is purple and red, marred by long red bands—clear imprints from fingers.

"It wasn't you," I whisper, voice tight around my nervousness. "It was—"

"Six." The dark word slithers down my spine, conjuring memories of that night. The heat of his breath pressing down on me, my fear and arousal dancing together as I willingly surrendered to him. To be close to him. To comfort him.

I love him so much.

It hurts.

I swallow. "Who is Six?"

"Me," he replies straight away, his matter-of-fact tone is emotionless. "My Shadow number. Zero Zero Six."

A shuddering breath escapes me as I say, "Do you want me to call you Six?"

"If that means you will keep the taser on you, you can call me anything you like."

I try to back away. "I've seen enough."

"No." He holds me in place. "You haven't. One hand. That is all it will take. Creep up on me again while I'm half-asleep, and you might just feel that. I need to know you're prepared."

"If I need to defend myself, I will," I promise weakly. Not even convincing myself because that night I wrapped my arms around him and let him.

"Prove it," he challenges. "Go get it."

The baby in my belly rolls, my stomach churns with nausea, and I swallow over lumps of discomfort. "Okay."

As I walk into the bunker, he waits just outside the open door, not stepping inside, but his sparks of domineering energy trail me down the steps and over to a tall chest of drawers where my *beibao* sags on its side on top.

I retrieve the gun from between the sleeves and return to the open door, stopping in front of him.

"Here"—I twist my wrist, flashing the gun in my fist— "I have it."

"Shoot me with it."

My mouth drops open. "No."

"Do it, little flower. Practice."

I shake my head over and over. "No, no, I don't want to."

"Did you fuck Robert?"

I gasp. "No—"

"Tomar?" He barely lets me finish the word, provoking me, his tone a snarl, a snap of anger. "Did you fuck him? When I came to your room, and you were on the mattress, were you going to fuck him while I was sedated?"

The storm inside me cracks. "No!"

"Did you spread your legs for another man while I was being tortured with your scent? While I was thinking about you, only you, were you fucking other men?"

I sob, shoulders shaking. "No!"

"Shoot the fucking taser!"

My vision blurs behind hot, heavy tears. But I lift the gun and pull the trigger before I can think, or guess, or wonder, the pulse going off in my hand.

The noise is a sharp pang.

I watch as two prongs slice through the air and connect with his chest, almost in slow motion.

There is a pause.

My heart beats in my ears.

Then his third eyelid closes, and his body convulses, heavy, thick muscles jerking around uncontrollably. He falls to his knees but doesn't collapse.

Holds himself swaying.

Regret and grief pummel me.

He growls through the electrified sensation like a beast refusing to be taken down by a mob of tiny, vicious animals. He fists his hands, fighting the wreckage, the take-down of his body.

"I'm sorry. I'm sorry, I'm sorry." I sob, wanting to go to him and hold him, but I can barely see through the salty pinch of my sorrow.

One.

Two.

Three.

Four.

Five.

Five seconds later, he reaches for the prongs and draws them from his chest. As he hauls himself to his full seven-foot-one height, the place between his thighs expands. I swear I hear the bunker gasp to behold such a powerful, erotic being.

"Lagos..."

He heaves, staring at me.

"Lagos?"

"*Good*," he finally states, voice deep and gruff like tyres on a rocky track. "That will slow me down... *Fuck*."

Unable to breathe, I merely watch as Lagos takes a single step forward, but I don't shuffle away from him, only arch my neck to hold his dark gaze.

I inhale the thick air and scent and taste his metallic presence.

Across his torso, his inked skin rolls over dense, chiselled muscles still twitching and contracting with electricity.

Near-black eyes bore into me.

Over me.

Then down on me...

I bite my lower lip when he grabs his dick through his pants and palms the hard bulge, and for a moment, I think he might grab me, kiss me, and drag me into one of the rooms, spread me open and shove inside me, but—

Spero starts to cry.

I exhale in a rush, and finally step backward, needing space and air. "I have to... I have to..."

Check on Spero...

"Go to the infant," he finishes, heated eyes on me, hand on his hard dick. "Go. What I need can wait."

I don't think it can...

Chapter Forty-Seven

Dahlia

First-light comes and goes.

And goes.

And goes.

Three days pass by.

Lagos moves around the farmhouse like a phantom—while he is awake, I can't seem to catch him, and when he sleeps, I'm hesitant to wake him again.

Not after the taser...

He is disconnected and angry. His torment and disassociation cling to him like a second skin.

On the ground floor, I stand by the kitchen window, with Spero on my hip, looking out and seeing a half-built stonewall and the haze of the Redwind.

I set the taser down on the counter. In case he asks me where it is, I usually have it within reach.

My swelling belly stretches my white slip-dress. Admittedly, I wear it to showcase my body, every curve, and the tight, round shape of his unborn child at my hips.

If he is going to avoid me.

I will not make it easy.

As certain as the Redwind, I watch Lagos' huge foreboding figure part the dense crimson haze, loose strands of dark-blonde hair whipping around his face, heavy stones grasped in his arms.

Each stone has a purpose, each one contributing to the protective perimeter around our home.

A stone at a time.

The silence between us sometimes feels like a tear in The Crust, gasping and drawing us in. But there is peace in his solitude, even if mine is filled with angst and yearning.

Don't push him, Dahlia.

To pass the time, I clean and organise the farmhouse. Spero has a playroom now, and we have a nice, clean, organised bedroom in the bunker, though Lagos has been sleeping at the door every night.

I sigh as he drops to his haunches, stacking the stones, hands and forearms bloodied from his toil of madness.

Worry washes over me.

I can see the weight of the Shadow on his shoulders. He carries that part of his personality as though it is a feasting animal, claws in deep, mouth at his jugular.

My stomach clenches and my lungs squeeze, knowing he wrestles with memories that haunt, terrorise him, and confuse him.

Each first-light, each stone, he fights, and I wish I could reach into his beautiful and gruesome mind to pull him out of the darkness, but I know he needs time.

Is he out there because he likes the Redwind? The drone of it?

Is it comforting? So he cannot hear the echoes of his own screaming torture.

Did he scream?

Probably not...

I imagine he snarled and bit back agony in those moments when they cut and tormented him.

When he forced me to shoot him with the taser, he mentioned something about my scent and mind games—I can only imagine what that means…

Don't imagine it.

Oh, how I want to hold him, to remind him that he is safe now, that we are building a future together.

Through the window, he straightens, glaring at the wall he is building, scrutinising each stone as if searching for something beyond its physical form.

Then our eyes meet.

Locking in a moment.

I mouth, "Brute."

And he sighs, mouthing, "Flower."

There's a flicker of something in his gaze—gratitude that makes my heart squeeze. Like he is silently saying thank you for waiting or understanding or maybe it is saying nothing at all. Maybe there is no flicker, only my need for hope.

I smile softly, letting him know that I am here, ready to stand alongside him.

Silent, like he needs.

I wince when his child kicks me, reminding me what we made, what our love made.

He is trying, each day, a small step forward—a stone laid down, another stone added to the growing foundation of our future. This is his way of telling me that we are no longer pretending.

I smile at that.

I stroll through the farmhouse, the floorboards shiny from a recent clean and the walls and trimmings dusted.

Spero drools along my shoulder and chest. His teeth are poking through, so he is grabby and fussy.

Scooping up Spero's fluffy bear, I hand it to him, and he bites down on the ear, gnawing and humming around the fabric.

I sit him down on the floor in our room and walk to the

mirror. Gazing at my reflection, I brush my fingers over the healing bruises on my throat.

Soon, they will be gone.

A tear glides down my cheek.

I swallow. Last time we were here, I created a pretty picture in my mind—a romantic, old-world picture of us, happy and raising our babies—but this… I lift my chin and drop my hand from my neck.

This will change nothing.

Am I afraid of him?

Deep down, I know that I should be, but the beating organ in my chest won't allow me to dwell on it.

I love him.

But it's more than that. When I look at him, my body comes alive, and when he is gone, I feel everything wilting.

And I'm not *just* a Common girl, either. I am—was—a Lace Girl. My Trade is a mental health initiative, one that I once believed in. In many ways, I still do.

While it is far from perfect, it holds an air of fact. Dopamine is released when we have sex and hold another. I know it's true now. Having felt it myself. I am never more settled, hopeful, and weightless than when I am smothered in his thick arms of protection.

Can I offer him the same? To accompany, relieve, and soothe my man in his time of despair.

A real smile slides across my lips.

What would be sweeter than being his Lace Girl? Being what he needs now, while he struggles his way back to reality, claws at the conditioned darkness and peels it back to reveal his own intent.

You can take the girl out of The Trade, but you can't take The Trade out of the girl.

~

"I know what your Ward did while you slept." Gruff words pull me from the dark.

Sleep holds me, but I slowly blink, the bunker ceiling illuminated by dim lighting. Strange; I don't remember seeing it in the dark before.

"Lagos…" I inhale *that* scent. Metallic, sweet, man, and safety—it's him.

He is here…

Realisation throws me into wakefulness. I sit and rub my eyes, gazing across the room to where Lagos is, eyes set on me.

Unwavering.

Intense.

He is in what I like to call his comfort clothing, bare-chested and in only grey pants that do very little to hide his usually hard or half-masted dick. Being in a state of arousal seems to be part of the Shadow DNA, harder, thicker, fiercer blood that is all too eager to pump and fill.

Confused, I frown at him. "What's happening? Is everything okay?"

Without looking away from me, he reaches for the free-standing lamp beside him and switches it on…

He switches it on.

It switches on!

I beam. "How?"

"I fixed it." His voice is that deep, gruff tone capable of rattling bones. "The people who lived here had their own windmill, a small one, hidden just behind the mountain. It's not remarkable or big, little flower, but it's enough for the farmhouse."

My heart races.

"Enough for *us*," I breathe.

"*Yes.*"

Finally.

I place my hand over my chest, feeling the heavy thumping inside. He is here. In the bunker. In the room. In *our* room.

"What did he do?" I ask.

He just stares at me. "Who?"

"My Ward?" I yawn. "Didn't you say you know what he did while I slept?"

"Watched you." Lagos stands, and I arch my neck to hold his gaze. "I have a great experience for you— watching someone you love sleep."

My lower lip wobbles. "So, you love me, brute?"

"Oh, fuck yeah." He sighs. "And I could watch you sleep all night, little flower."

He turns toward the door, and panic rolls up my throat, and desperate words burst out. "Then do it!"

He stops midstride.

"Watch me all night," I add.

Without turning around, his gravelly voice wraps around me as he says, "I want to, little flower. I really do. I fantasise about you all day. You're in every stone I place. Every motivation. Every erection. I fantasise about you in that little lace dress you wear to get my attention, with your hair loose and free and your stomach swollen."

"Stop fantasising about it," I whisper to the dim room. "And *be* with me."

He stands there, breathing heavy considerations that expand his torso with each inhale. "Fine," he agrees, voice rough and deep. Turning around to face me, he says, "I'll watch you all night."

"Here." I pat the spot beside me on the bed. "Right here. Please, Lagos."

"There you go again." As he walks to the bed, he slides his pants down, leaving only his briefs that hug his thighs and waist and form around his engorged dick like a second layer of skin. "Saying my name with that pleading tone…" He almost purrs, prowling onto the bed. "Getting your way."

He lies down beside me, and I feel as though my heart might explode.

We face each other again, close, intimate—it feels like years ago even though it was only months—but this time, my swollen belly brushes his torso.

"Things I like…" He gently brushes a red tendril over my shoulder. "The way you say my name."

"Lagos…"

"Yeah." His lips curve, offering me the smallest of smiles. Not a grin or a smirk. It's the right shape for a real smile. "Like that."

All the things he likes are to do with me. It makes me feel wonderful and sad at the same time. He spent decades with Tomar, a rogue in the waste, and has no beauty to speak of. At the thought of Tomar, my stomach knots.

I can't resist the urge to ask about him. "Lagos…" My tone causes his brows to furrow, reading me easily. "Will you ever see Tomar again?"

He grumbles. "Hm."

"You know nothing happened." I place my hand on his hard chest, fingers fanning out to touch more. "Right?"

"I know…" He chooses his words carefully, using a pause to consider them. "That you didn't fuck him."

"What about the catamaran and the people at The Bite, and Sweets?"

"Tomar will return," he states. "It is his Purpose. Rescuing people from the Half-tower. He'll find his way back there. I'm almost certain of it."

"Wasn't it yours?"

"I was lost. He found me. Showed me how draining my blood can help me move around with less pain. Had a doctor from his faith take the coil out. I had nothing else. Just him. I thought I was fine." He chuckles coldly. "Sixteen and full of myself. I was wrong. I followed him."

"And I followed Maple—"

"And we end up here."

"Wait"—I frown— "What about draining the iron when it gets too high? Are you in agony here? I can't bear that."

"No, little flower. There is no pull here. It's only if I move around and come in contact with beacons. Everything inside me is…" He sighs roughly. "Calmer *here*."

My bottom lip quivers for a moment, so I press it between my teeth and chew.

Lagos moves in and steals my lower lip away, sucking it into his mouth and drawing long moans from my throat. With firm, slow strokes, he slides his tongue in and out of my mouth.

My restraint unravels while his control strains. I flex my fingers on his chest, pulling. His hand grips my hip, palming, needing. *Yearning.*

He breaks our kiss, panting hard already. "No more questions. Sleep."

I sulk but accept.

So, for the following few moments, long ones that roll by like a lazy pet, I gaze at him, and he watches me.

What does he see in me? When I see such virile beauty, dark and thundering energy, and I am just… Dahlia. A little Lace Girl from the Half-tower.

Easily forgotten.

I sigh… Without noticing, exhaustion blankets me. Slumber stings at the edges of my eyes so I slowly bat the vision of him, in and out, slower and slower, until my eyelids win.

And I close my eyes.

But I feel his—I feel him watching me fall asleep in our bed, in our room, in our farmhouse, where we will build stone walls around and raise our children inside.

I fall asleep.

~

The room is quiet when I wake up, and Lagos is asleep opposite me, in the exact position he was when I closed my eyes. It takes me a moment to realise that time has passed and it's probably first-light.

I lift to my backside and check the cot Lagos made the very

first day we arrived here for the second time. Spero is on his back, fists by his head on the blanket, chest rising and falling, deep in sleep.

I sigh, a smile greeting my lips. Lagos stirs and rolls to his back. There is movement in the corner of my eye. When I gaze over, the sight of Lagos' stiff dick tenting his pants snatches my breath. My belly swirls with anticipation, and pressure builds in my core. I squirm and shuffle with the need to quell the restlessness between my thighs.

He is so powerful, so utterly huge. Longer than the bed and thick across the chest and waist, with big arms and huge hands. The thought of them carrying me—holding me down—as he takes me… I moan, unable to stop myself.

Hesitantly, I slide my hand over his thigh, barely touching him, but feel his heat, nevertheless. I should stop. I am practically violating him in his sleep, but… My fingers brush his erection, and I gasp. I thought it would be soft on the outside, have a supple layer, and then a harder one, but—it's not supple.

I look at his face to check to see if he is still asleep and lift to my knees, hovering over him to get a better look. I grip the top of his briefs, pulling them down. The muscles deep inside me clench with excitement when his huge dick springs free, waving in the air like it's saying hi.

"Hi," I giggle.

A deep, gruff voice curls my toes. "Why don't you give my cock a kiss, little flower," he rumbles.

I feel colour rising up my neck, smouldering across my cheeks, warm and glowing embarrassment.

"Please pretend that you're asleep, Lagos," I whisper. "I want to be alone with your body."

"That's going to be—"

"*Shh,*" I hush him.

I lick my lips, looking at *it*, and slide closer until my knees brush his sides. "Just… don't open your eyes yet. Promise?"

"You have my word."

My hands glide over his thigh; the contrast of my pale, freckled skin against his tanned, tattooed flesh makes us appear as opposite as we are—He's a massive Xin De monster, and I'm a Common girl born for lace.

My fingertips feather the long, protruding vein that follows his dick upward to a V-shaped bunch of skin just below the curving head. Instantly, a bead of clear fluid collects on the slit.

He hums.

"Quiet, brute."

A deep sound, like a laugh, rumbles in his chest, and I smile. That is the best sound in The Cradle. My Lagos with no smiles, my big, bad Xin De assassin, my brute, chuckling in the dark with me.

I lean down and lick the bead, overwhelmed with the urge to know what it tastes like.

Salty. Metallic.

His dick jerks. "Careful playing with your new toy while I'm half-asleep. You'll end up stuffed with that toy before you can catch your next breath."

"You're asleep," I scold.

"Then stop answering back."

I beam—is this us?

Can we be… *playful?*

Is this the man he is beneath the Shadow, apart from the Rogue? The one that only rears up when he is alone with me, in the dark, where he can be himself, open and vulnerable.

I'll protect your heart, Lagos.

His fingers slide into my hair, cupping the back of my head and curling around red strands, gentle but dominant.

"Careful, little flower," he warns, stroking my scalp while I lick again and again, my tongue tracing the slit over the bulbous crown. "*Mm.* Fuck. Your silly, little tongue does things to me."

A big hand palms the back of my head, not controlling me but still an authority in the moment.

In every moment.

With my lips and mouth, I explore his smooth skin, the way it stretches around his blood-filled dick, almost like elastic.

Nervously, I flutter my tongue over a throbbing vein. I'm so gentle; I wonder if he can even feel what I'm doing.

"Do you like that?" I breathe.

"Thought I was asleep."

"*Brute*," I complain.

"How could I not like you licking my cock as if you're afraid of it, little flower?"

His fingers continue to circle restlessly in my hair, sending shivers down my spine and lifting hairs across my skin. Sliding over him more, I mouth the warm head, sucking it in and popping it out again.

"Things you like…" I giggle, gaining more confidence from his heavy breathing, and lap all the way, slowly from base to slit, along the lengthy, throbbing underside. When I get to the base again, curiosity draws my tongue down over his heavy balls.

"*Fuck…*" he groans, free hand grabbing the root of his dick as I mouth his balls, tasting skin and salt and something so deeply… male.

Licking, too eager to be methodical, I enjoy him. The way his body responds, tastes, the instinctive contracting of his thighs, and pulsing of his veins.

Jerking his hand up and down, he squeezes, the head flushing as he strokes himself, seeming to draw blood from the root to the crown.

Groaning, he shudders and palms the back of my head. His breaths become heavier. Abdominals crunch together, and thighs tighten.

He is close, hand flying over his dick. More fluid leaks from the tip. His big balls respond to my tongue, the smooth skin bunching and shrinking against my soft, warm attention.

I try not to smile, feeling pride swell in my chest. I make him feel good. Soothe him. *Relieve him.*

The deep weeping place between my legs clenches, and my pelvis lifts, just waiting for him to explode.

Then he does.

Deep, inhuman growls seem to start low in his abdomen, then crawl up his throat, rumbling the entire way until white fluid projects upward, lashing my cheeks, lips, and his thighs.

"Fuck, *yes*. Such a—" He groans. "Such a good little flower."

My eyes roll back, pleasure a hazy blanket over my vision. When he comes apart—body so thick and powerful, bulking and throbbing in such a way—every female muscle inside me squeezes.

No more than a few laboured breaths later, Lagos sits up and takes hold of me, twisting me until my back meets the mattress.

My belly protrudes, and I giggle, nervousness playing in the sound.

"Spread your legs," Lagos' dark demand curls inside me like a coiling snake. He gets on all-fours over me, prowling down, skating his lips across my skin. He lingers over his unborn child, rubbing his face over the warm, swollen mound. "Mine." Then he drops lower. "I'm going to need to eat my little flower out."

Chapter Forty-Eight

Dahlia

Four months later

My legs are caught between his, my body covered entirely, as he brackets me with his arms, thrusting into me from behind.

I squeeze my eyes shut and tense up to stop from yelping at the shock of his body pounding into mine.

I understand his *moods* now.

After four months alone in the farmhouse with a savage Xin De male, a Shadow and assassin, I am becoming accustomed to his insatiable needs.

Still sore from first-light, his relentless friction inside me aches. The mellow pain is agonising and addictive. With each inward thrust, I fist the sheets, but then he draws out, and I moan for him to return.

I let him take me.

His body radiates heat.

Arms and legs tensing.

Just before first-light, after I finished breastfeeding our baby girl and checking in on Spero, Lagos made love to me slowly, teased my nipples until they wept with milk and touched me everywhere.

He can be gentle, soft, tracing fingers, and easy caresses.

But he is also *this*—a brutal lover, obsessive, taking and taking my body, filling me and using me.

I gasp into the pillow as my smaller body jerks on the soft mattress, my breasts filling with milk, tingling from the friction.

He doesn't pull out completely, his huge figure covering me, thighs and forearms walls of muscles boxing me in.

A low groan comes from his chest, rumbling against my sensitive spine. "Such a good girl for your Shadow. You love the way I use you. The way I need you. The way I need to feel your insides."

I whimper as his hips become demanding, motion somehow faster, harder, and I don't have time to adjust or—

I moan long and hard. Heat spreads from my head to my toes, culminating where he enters me.

And I come apart, moaning wildly, clawing at the sheets, but that doesn't slow him down. He merely growls his approval, his hot, dark breath rushing down on me.

Orgasm after orgasm is wrested from me and then absorbed by his thick, unyielding dick.

I run out of air, panting into the pillow. I feel dizzy. "Oh, Lagos… Please."

"I love you." His fingers slide over mine, feeding through the gaps. He squeezes. "You're doing so well. My pure little flower, still trembling for me. Still unsure of what is to come. Or what I am capable of. Tell me you love me."

"I love you so much."

Grunting, he finishes inside me, still thrusting slowly, still so deep. Rough breaths. Deep groans. Long rumbling sigh…

"I want more," he says.

"I need a few hours, brute."

"No." He untangles our hands and slides his between me and the mattress. Cradling my soft lower belly, he says, "Your womb is empty, little flower. I'm going to fill it again."

I nod into the pillow. "Please."

I want more, too. So many more. Our daughter was born at the Common Community at thirty-two weeks of pregnancy. I was induced, and it was a perfect labour, not too long, only a little painful, and Lagos was a guard dog in the room, never leaving my side.

And I have never seen him smile the way he did when he first held his little Wren in his arms.

I was told that thirty-two weeks is early for a Common human, but not a Xin De. They develop faster and easier.

Despite this, she is petite, with big green eyes that match my own. Nothing like her big boofhead of a brother, Spero, and yet, her iron levels are unusually high. A Shadow baby. I don't know what that means for her. Lagos says there are no *known* Shadow females.

My head lolls on the pillow as Lagos stands, briefly disappearing from the room before returning.

He gathers me from the mattress, and I immediately melt into his hard, warm torso. Nuzzling the dirty-blonde hair at his chest and inhaling him, I sigh.

Safety.

Male.

Mine.

As he carries me into the bathroom, perfumed steam dances from the ceramic tub and whirls up my nostrils.

"*Mm.*" I make a low sound of pleasure. "For me? I'm spoilt."

"I was rough," he says, his tone gruff but not cruel, tight with silent concern and loud regret.

Oh, brute.

"You aren't too much for me, Lagos. I'm worried that I'm not enough for you."

He gently lays me into the pool of warm water, and I stifle a sigh of utter ecstasy as the soothing liquid embraces my weak body. This is…

This is perfect.

"Not enough?" He grips my chin, tilting my face up to meet his stern gaze. "Keep your legs together for a while," he orders, "or I'll have to fill you again."

"Yes, brute." I giggle. "If we have another girl, can I name her Maple?"

"Yes," he says.

As I relax into the warm water, I catch sight of his reflection in the mirror, of his tight brows that create a crease in the middle of his steely eyes. He is virile—strong, rugged, and fierce. I only hope that I can hold his interest. Hope the world outside these stone walls won't beckon him one day.

~

I am outside in the enclosed greenhouse Lagos made for me. It is latched onto the roof of the farmhouse and is strong enough to withstand the Redwind and large enough for me and the children to play on the grass and plant seeds. It hasn't been tested in a Redwind Whip storm but if it falls, we will rebuild.

I learnt a thing or two about greenhouses at the Common Community. How to set them up. Where to store seeds.

I may not have been at my best there, but that little place did add a *bit* to Dahlia—like Tide said. And because of my time at the Common Community, we have a healthy baby girl, and I have extra gardening skills.

"I know why the farmhouse is empty." I look up to find Lagos striding toward me, a bulking half-human monster, tearing a path through the Redwind, wearing the crimson mist like a cloak. He is dressed in dark jeans and his black jacket. Tattoos visible, rushing down each finger, and licking up his throat, noosing his neck.

But then I notice the blood splatters on his cheeks. A scarlet gash on his upper lip. And on his left shoulder, he wears the dead carcases of two large animals like they are weightless drapes.

"Oh, my," I gasp. "What happened?"

"Aquilla cats. Close your eyes, little flower. I don't want you to see."

I cover my eyes but peek through my fingers, not as fragile as he believes. Then I see the river of blood pouring from jowls full of busted teeth and turn my back to him, speaking over my shoulder.

"Are they dangerous?"

"Yes." I hear him grunt, then the unmistakable thud of the lifeless bodies hitting the ground. "They'll maul a raider to pieces within a minute."

I swallow, my eyes darting to the door to check it is closed. The children are safe inside. Two under one means lots of intermittent sleeping. "Then why are you happy about the killer animals in the mountains?"

I hear his amused huff and can't help smiling despite the conversation.

"Because I can use them. I can push them back further into a position. Feed them to keep them in place, station them, condition them. They'll have pups. We'll have fresh meat forever."

Pups? Right. Right...

I don't want to know. "*But* you're bleeding," I say, jabbing my finger in his direction. "Did they hurt you?"

"Wasn't prepared. Won't happen again." He sounds deliciously unaffected by the blood and wounds, his tone guttural and hoarse from overuse. Has he been in a fight? Snarling and growling? I often forget he is not a raider, not a Common, barely human—a monster in his own way. I wonder what the Aquilla cats think of him, when they sniff him out. Do they think prey or... No, they know. There is no mistaking that Lagos is a predator.

"Think of them as security," he adds, moving around behind me, rustling and hauling the animals. "No one can come from the west, north, or south without encountering their burrows. I only have to watch the east."

"And the kids? Are we safe."

"I've built you strong walls, little flower. They can't jump over them." He pauses, and I find my gaze wandering up the ancient brickwork of the farmhouse. The weathered stone is entwined with delicate vines, like pretty green ribbons.

"So..." I chew my lip, listening to the subtle movements behind me. I know what he is doing, putting the animals into the crate we keep in the corner. It is full of salt—and other minerals I don't know—and when I go to sleep, he will preserve the meat. "This is a good thing?"

"Yes." I hear him shuffling, grunting some more and then he says, "You can turn around now, little flower. It's safe for your precious gaze."

I turn to face him, my eyes curiously scanning around him, from the solid door to the clusters of pots, to the crates, and back to him. "I like my walls. They are big and powerful walls, and everything is more remarkable when it's big and powerful."

He hums. "Hm. Good."

"I can stay here forever, Lagos, but what about you? You're a rogue."

"No." He strides over to me, his potent energy cracks through the air. "I'm a Xin De man obsessed with a Common girl." Stopping in front of me, his intense stare cuts through his lashes, his expression deadly serious, with blood still splattered across his striking features. "And I want some quiet with her."

I gaze up at the monster that I love, my heart humming in my chest. "The kids might want to leave one day?" I whisper, fully aware of this sad truth. They will need to explore and meet people and visit places to find their *bits*.

"Anything could happen in two decades, little flower." A warm hand slides between my hair and the nape of my neck, cradling my head with gentle dominance. "Let's not get ahead of ourselves."

Two decades?

But he is Lagos the Rogue. Travelled The Cradle, a fisherman, a vigilante, a saviour, a Shadow, an assassin, met thousands of people, probably slept with hundreds—

A niggling entity inside my belly warns me; he will get bored of me, of this life. "What will you do next?" I ask, willing my voice to mask my anxieties.

He cocks a brow. "Next?"

"Yes. What is your next task?"

"Fix the windows," he states, a small grin tugging at his lips, suspicious of my questioning. "Stop them from scaring my girls at night."

"How long will that take?"

"Few weeks," he grunts.

I give him big, pleading eyes.

"And then what?"

"A dam."

"How long will that—"

"A year."

"And then?"

"Repairs on the truck."

"And then?"

"A climbing fram—"

"I don't want you to get bored!" I finally blurt out and huff petulantly, because he didn't end my insufferable questioning like a normal person by asking what is wrong.

A smooth smile glides across his masculine face, easy and genuine, but somehow still bears heat and darkness, still silently warns. "How could I?"

"One day," I shrug, "it'll just be me. No Spero and no Wren, or the other unnamed babies..."

"Just you?" He shakes his head, displeasure weaving across his brows. "*You,* with your too-many freckles. If all I had to do was look at all those pink and cream dots, I still wouldn't be bored."

I smile-sulk. "You're not taking me seriously."

"I take every fucking word out of your mouth seriously, little flower. I don't want to go anywhere, not without you. Everywhere is disappointing until you see it with your big green eyes full of awe. Awe over silly things like a waterfall or a fish or a fucking wall." A steel-coloured gaze drowns me. He sighs—soft for me. "I wanted so fucking badly to find you annoying, but instead, I lost focus, and you became my mood."

"Your mood?"

His jaw pulses. "Listen to me," he demands. "You make everything better, little flower. For me." He drops to his knees and grips my hips, huge hands fully circling me. The look in his eyes... *Oh*, I melt. I cover my heart, or else its eager thumping will crack another rib.

"My sweet little flower." He stares straight at me. "I want to grow old in that mood. I want to *die* in that mood. Do you understand what I'm fucking saying? You gave me awe, joy, hope."

Hope.

Spero.

His words fill my lungs, making it hard to breathe around my emotions.

I wasn't even meant to meet you... It was meant to be Maple. "Hope," I say to him without context.

He nods. "It won't always be easy. *I* won't always be easy. Inside me is darkness and rage, and without you and the kids, that is all I am."

My lower lip wobbles, so I suck it between my teeth and chew on it.

"I will provide for you and my children, little flower, and I will protect you until my impenetrable flesh dissolves. I will *die* in that mood, if you'll let me. If things get—" He pauses, and a rare fragility lowers his tone. "Don't give up on me, little flower. You're all I have. When things get tough, if I'm dark or lost, use the taser, but don't—" He bites back the vulnerable word, chewing it in his tight jaw.

Don't abandon me. He means to say don't abandon me.

A conversation we had at The Bite bounces between my ears.

'You're young, fragile, Common, and you will abandon that Xin De infant when you realise the danger that follows him.'

'I won't abandon him. I promise.'

He was talking about himself or relating, perhaps. He thinks I might leave him one day. After the kids leave, of course, I could go to the Common Community, but Lagos will never be accepted. He doesn't play well with others. He won't obey commands or rules.

A Shadow is designed to be a loner, too feared and dangerous to join raiders or Common, and used and abused by the ones that designed him.

He has no place.

He is rogue.

This farmhouse, isolation, and simplicity… This is right.

I sigh, my heart full. His Shadow can retire here, and the Rogue in him can isolate, and my brute can be vulnerable in my arms, living life's great experiences.

He will always be Lagos and Six, and my brute, and they will war inside him forever. Baby Lagos had no smiles or joy, but my brute has a stunning smile. I won't abandon him.

No matter the danger.

I cup the sides of his thick neck, feeling the cords beneath, and press my forehead to his, our breath mingling, the air buzzing with electricity. With magnetism. "I won't abandon you, brute."

He sighs roughly and stands, a wall of muscle lifting in front of me moments before I am in his arms with my legs circling his waist and my body supported by strong, warm hands.

"Kids asleep?" he asks, and I feel his smile move across my lips as he speaks.

"For now," I answer. "But it's not like you can be quick." I laugh.

So does he.

THE END

Born For Silk - Snippet

ASTER

Buzzing fills the air, the electric notes twisting my spine tight.

This is a big day.

The *biggest*, actually.

Through the cracked window to the tower promenade, men and women brave the red gale to watch. Their grasping eyes move from girl to girl, keen to witness the ceremonial moment take place.

"I'm so proud of all my girls," the Silk Wardeness says, circling us slowly. "You have studied hard and shown true dedication. This mark will seal your Trade. Meaningful Purpose"—she smiles— "is in your future."

The girls squeal once.

I drop my gaze to my worn hide boots and the seam of my mauve dress, avoiding the sight of Iris's arm laying perfectly still for the tattoo gun.

I don't hear her respond to the needles' penetration, but I know they are in her flesh as the buzzing tones deepen.

Behind me, the other girls shuffle in line, anticipation crawling inside their feet. They hide excited chatter in their breath. I, on the other hand, am wary of the pain.

The wind outside the parlour suddenly howls. A moment later, Iris lifts her slim arm to display the brand. She smiles with pride.

"It's official," she breathes in awe. Her green eyes land on me, cruel in an instant. "But not even a brand will make you any more than Fur Born," she says with a snarl.

I clench my teeth and hold her sharp gaze as she saunters to join the line with the other marked girls.

"Next," the tattoo man calls, and a girl behind me bumps me forward.

Time slows.

The gap between me and the buzzing is empty, ready to be filled. The gun is suddenly louder. The man's patience wanes as he stares at me. The girls' shuffling is riotous in my ears, though I am quite certain they are not moving at all.

I am the one moving.

Carelessly, my heels slide backward, recoiling from the tattoo gun when a monstrous form eclipses me, and two huge hands grip my shoulders.

Someone holds me in line.

Someone enormous.

A gasp, a pin drops. Now there is no noise at all, and I wonder where all the breathing has gone... It's too still.

The man with the tattoo gun is staring above my head at the towering figure behind me. His startled expression snaps to submission, and he bows his chin.

It can't be...

As a statue held captive in big hands, I twist my chin and peer up. Up. Up.

To his face.

His face.

Even with his cloak pulled up and shadows dancing the outline of his strong brow, I recognise him. I'd know his face through the dense Redwind.

He is stunning.

His face is a masterpiece. Chiselled yet smooth. Square jawline. Scars that only enhance his virile features. Blue eyes that glow as he stares intensely down on me, penetrating my soul. The colour blue should be peaceful, *calm*, but his eyes are anything but.

They whisper of cruelty.

They demand obedience.

My king.

I turn in his grip.

Everyone in the parlour drops to their knees, but I remain standing, unable to bow with his massive hands wrapped so powerfully around my upper arms.

"My king," I offer, lowering my gaze.

"Why do you hesitate?" he asks, his voice a deep timbre that presses on my chest, making my lungs and heart strain to work.

"I—" I stammer and force my eyes to hold the ground respectfully. *Hesitate? To get the tattoo? To bow? To speak? What?*

I cannot answer.

"Don't you want my mark?"

I blink my confusion, blood draining from my cheeks. *Of course, I want his mark.*

And finally, I look up at him.

This cannot be real.

I've seen him on the big screen in the Silk Aviary—the one for Trade Updates. At least once a month, they show moving pictures of him on campaigns in The Cradle, visiting Trade men at the windmill farms, or shaking hands with lords from Trade towers.

This is *so* much better.

Seeing him in the flesh. Smelling him.

Stunned, I nod my head. "Yes, of course."

His gaze holds me arrested. "Then"—he stretches the word with no mirth— "why hesitate, little creature?"

I swallow the lump in my throat. "It'll hurt."

"Have you not been given any Opi?"

It is like the others in the room have faded away, leaving only him and me. Captured in a time apart from all others.

"The others have applied it topically, but— But I'm allergic," I say softly.

His brows draw in as though he is recalling a painful moment or reliving a feeling, then— "I see," he states, calm resurfacing. "Hereditary, I imagine. From your mother's side?"

"I'm sorry."

"Your name?"

I look at his hands, still warming my arms. *Why are they still there? I like it. But why?*

"Aster." I breathe. "Like a flower." I look up at him again. "We are all just flowers, not like you, my king. You're a city from the old-world. Everyone important is named after a city from the old-world."

I don't know why I said that.

He doesn't need a history lesson.

My head feels as if I inhaled a cloud and now my thoughts are surrounded by white and confusion.

"Just a little flower?" He frowns, the question so curt it stirs the energy around us.

I simply nod, enraptured. "Yes."

His palms slide down the length of my arms, leaving one to circle the column of my wrist. He could squeeze it to dust, his grip so encompassing.

"Would you like me to hold your hand, little Silk Girl?"

I think I nod.

The next few moments I meander through in a dream state. He presses my wrist to the tattoo table, and I anchor myself to his gaze—almost feline. Lots of Xin De have glowing irises.

Unbinding my wrist from his grip, he moves his hand to blanket mine, pinning me to the counter.

"Gentle with my property or you'll discover the true meaning of pain," he orders the man, though his eyes haven't wavered from me.

He holds my hand.

I hold my breath.

Heat from his palm radiates into my skin.

The buzzing starts, his eyes anchor me, pain from the needle fires, dark intent rolls through his gaze, and I practically moan against my conflicting senses. Warm discomfort pools in my bellybutton. Blue eyes pierce through me to my bones deeper than any needle.

Everything is hot.

Painful and pleasant.

And his eyes.

Oh my, his eyes.

"It's all over now," he states smoothly, releasing my hand, a cool absence sweeping across the grieving flesh.

I blink up at him, the loud fantasy of him and me and whatever strange painful, pleasure that was slips away.

Heat flares through my wrist, so I look down to see the tattoo's burning presence. It is pretty. A purple womb created from flowers and stems. The same smile I saw on Iris's face slides across my lips.

I am officially a Silk Girl.

Too soon, he is striding away. I am flooded with desperation that I'll never see him again, that he'll forget about me, that Iris and the girls are right about me being Fur Born, so I reach for him before I can think.

Gasps expel.

Eyes widen.

My fingers clutch at a piece of his velvety shroud.

"Take me with you, my king." The words tumbling from my lips like apples from a barrel.

Shit.

He turns, a creature more predator than man, but his expression becomes one of amusement. I'm not sure I like it. It's playful in the way an eagle might play with a mouse.

Looking down at my small hand, clinging to the fibres of his jacket, he says, "Not today."

"I'm ready," I blurt out, ignoring the girls who gape and the Silk Wardeness who shakes her head, scolding me silently. She doesn't dare speak in his presence. It's a vow. *Speak only when spoken to. Never touch the king without permission…*

Yet here I am…

He studies me, dark eyes drilling through my confidence. "How many years have you bled?"

I swallow. "Five. I can live Meaningful Purpose, my king. I'm stronger than I look."

"You're small."

"I'll eat more," I counter.

"What was stopping you before?" His lips twitch with a smile when I have no answer for him. "You have an answer for everything? But not this."

"I know what I want, my king."

"And that is?"

To prove them wrong.

"Meaningful Purpose."

A pause thickens the air.

He steps toward me again, his gait graceful, contradictory to such a large, menacing man.

He cups my face in both big hands, his fingers cradling the back of my head. He could crush my skull. Pop it.

Gone.

I wonder whether he has. I'm sure he has crushed bones within these warm hands, turned them to powder.

Looking down at me, he drinks in the sight, the intensity in which he maps each feature, in which his gaze slices across my cheeks, eyes of violet, my parted mouth, peels me back to bone and breath.

"You're pretty." The words are licks of warmth, and my knees buckle with each letter. "I bet the other girls *despise* you."

Shit.

I glance quickly at the girls, at Iris and Lavender. "We have no jealousy, my king," I lie. It's one of our vows: no jealousy between Silk Girls.

Meaningful Purpose is what matters.

"*Lies*," he purrs, and all the hairs on my neck rise. "Do you know what I do to people who despise me?" He lifts my chin with his thumb, a silent demand to answer him.

I shake my head. "No."

"I give them more reasons to."

Then his hands drop from my face, and disappointment hits my stomach as he strides away.

The press in my chest gives way when he disappears into the streets, closely tracked by two men who might well be his shadows. But I know they are his Guards. *The Guard.* One of them is *Kong*. His Guardian.

I have studied him. That is surely him. He is large, tanned-skin, and has long dark hair that he pulls away from his face and into a knot at the back of his head.

The quiet stretches to a low, frantic musing between the girls and the Silk Wardeness. "Did he come to see us?" "Perhaps, Ivy." "To check on his property?" "Why would he be in the Lower-tower?" "Visiting Lord Bled, perhaps." "I don't know, girls. Quieten down."

The questioning continues, and the tattoo man calls, "Next," but I'm still staring at the door to the parlour.

Outside, the Redwind now swallows any sight or sound, but for the unmistakable screech from above, piercing and fierce, parting the atmosphere to warn us *he* is here.

His great eagle—Odio.

How I wish to see him. His wingspan must be larger than my outstretched arms to coast the deadly gale.

I exhale hard, finding plenty of room in my chest now that he isn't close. He's an enigma like his eagle, present but too high to ever reach.

Keep reading about the Xin De king and his breeding girl, Aster...

Have you read Born For Silk?

A spicy dark dystopian fantasy romance from hugely popular dark romance author Nicci Harris, where young Aster is sworn to be a servant to the ruthless half-human King Rome, but when the king becomes obsessed with this ordinary girl, it could lead to war.

Young Aster is no different. If selected, she will be the King's Silk Girl. A common human bred to adore and pleasure him, and to provide The Cradle with healthy babies for The Trade.

Adore. Pleasure. Provide. That is her meaningful purpose.

But King Rome is more monster than man. As the heir of the genetically enhanced breed, he was designed to survive and rule this harsh new world. Through fear. Through intimidation. Rome has a heart as black as his giant pet eagle's wings and a singular obsession—to reign.

That stands until one day Aster puts her tiny human hand in his...

Now she occupies his mind...

But The Trade upholds that love is not a virtue, and instead, a weakness. Nothing could be more dangerous to the regime than having its merciless king obsessed with a common girl born for Silk.

Get it now.

Meet other fans on Facebook.
Join Harris's Harem of Dark Romance Lovers
Stalk us.

Don't like Facebook?
Join my newsletter

A Trade Fisher's Shanty

Good first-light, to you, my Collective and friend. We head to the ocean, it's days there we spend.

Though the Redwind is howlin' with a fist full of sand. We prefer it's hard slapin' to The Trade Master's hand.

For our Purpose was certain, so on the waves we do meet. Yet we sing with the crashin' as it's freedom we greet.

Cradled Common Next Up!

2025 the Cradle Common Releases

Born For Marble

A love-sick Xin De Guardian name Kong The Unbreakable, and a broken Queen named Tuscany Of The Strait.

"I want to whisper, 'I'll wait forever, little queen'. While waiting implies progress, movement, her heart beating for mine just beyond the horizon, it's not her heart I'm waiting for. It's for the world to change. *I'll wait forever*." - Kong, Born For Marble.

DON'T MISS AN UPDATE... BONUS SCENES, EXTRA STORIES...FAN ART...
FOLLOW ME:

Meet other fans on Facebook.
Join Harris's Harem of Dark Romance Lovers
Stalk us.

Don't like Facebook?
Join my newsletter

An Urban Legend From The Cradle

Endigos like to tell stories around the fire...

Here one goes:

As no one living has ever seen the Missing Moon or the stars, many do not believe that there is a giant rock in the sky surrounded by twinkling lights.

Legend has it, that the moon is actually the face of an evil spirit that watches all. And if you ever see the face, even for a second while the Redwind parts, it will see you, too, and enter your body.

It will use your body to kill children and scoop out their eyes. As children's eyes glow and sparkle. The Missing Moon will then take the eyes back to the sky. But soon, the sparkle in the children's eyes will go out and so the Moon will watch again, until someone looks back, so it can collect more eyes.

Don't look for the Missing Moon.

Acknowledgements & Extras

The Cradled Common is a **ROMANCE series**, first and foremost. It is spicy, romantic, and wild.

But...

Here are some thanks and extras and ramblings on The Cradle.

Firstly, I want to thank my husband, **Ed Napoleao**, for spending hours and hours... and hours researching past empires, historical events, and genetic engineering, to help create this dystopian world with me.

And for offering his own personal experiences...

My husband is the first generation born from refugees escaping a war with decades of genocide and guerilla warfare that went nearly undocumented.

They are still picking up the pieces.

You have probably never even heard of his country.

<u>This happened in our lifetime.</u>

His perspective on creating and building The Cradle is invaluable. And we have so much more to unravel the further we enter The Cradle with each book.

It is rooted in science, and explores technologies, most of which exists today in rudimentary forms, but are not legal.

It also plays with mythology. The Cradle holds on to real world physics—mostly—and delves into our need as a species for a spiritual connection.

For…

Purpose.

Religion.

Love.

Power.

It is not meant to confirm or deny any spiritual or religious ideologies.

The Cradled Common series is mankind at the end and the beginning of humanity.

It is **completely fictional** but draws inspiration from past empires, world wars, guerilla warfare, and civil unrests.

The things I learnt… **WOW.**

Mankind has a very corrupt history.

I want to thank **Margot Swan** for putting up with all my crazy. I could not have done this without you!

I really mean that.

And **Nat Dune**, you wave a Nicci flag high for all to see. You are always available, and one of the only people I trust with my unpolished manuscript.

A special thank you to Hope and Tara who proofread the raw version of Born For Lace and always support me and make me smile.

Thank you, all.

Nicci Who?

Nicci is an Amazon number 1 best-selling author in Women's Crime Fiction, Organised Crime, Romantic Er0tica, and Romantic Suspense.

Nicci is from Perth, Western Australia. She has lived many lives. Vet Nurse. Journalist. Barista. Corporate Sales Consultant. Mother.

Now she is a fulltime author, and she lives even more lives. Mafia Don. Ballerina. Doctor. Biker. CEO. Concert Pianist, to name a few.

She considers herself an independent woman... BUT all that womanly power goes out the window when her red flag-waving, morally grey heroes appear on page...

She writes about men who kill, who control, who take their women like it's their last breath, pinning them down and whispering "good girl" and "mine" and "you belong to me" and all the red flag utterances that would have most independent women rolling their eyes so hard they see their brains.

So... if you don't like that... if you don't like reading about controlling, over the top possessive men... then don't read her books. You won't like them. But Nicci wants both. She wants her cake and to have a six-foot-five, tattooed, alphamale to eat it with her.

facebook.com/authornicciharris
amazon.com/author/nicciharris
bookbub.com/authors/nicci-harris
goodreads.com/nicciharris
instagram.com/author.nicciharris

Stalk Me…

Stalk me.

Meet other fans on Facebook.
Join Harris's Harem of Dark Romance Lovers
Stalk us.

Don't like Facebook?
Join my newsletter

facebook.com/authornicciharris
amazon.com/author/nicciharris
bookbub.com/authors/nicci-harris
goodreads.com/nicciharris
instagram.com/author.nicciharris

Printed in Dunstable, United Kingdom

78192626R00251